EVASION AND DEFIANCE

VIRTUAL WARS

BOOK 1

ANDREW SWEET

Andrew Sweet
andrewsweet.net
author of
Deliciously Dark Dystopian Fiction
for the discriminating palette

This message was **not approved** for circulation by the Ministry of Truth. By being in possession of this material, unless Level Three cleared, you are in violation of legal code Section 3, Subparagraph 5. Possession and Distribution of this material is punishable by no less than a $2,000,000 fine, 50 years in virtual prison, or, in extreme cases, the Death Penalty.

If you see something, say something!

CHAPTER 1

THE LOFTING CHAMPION

LARKEN MARCHE TIGHTENED her grip on her lofting crosse, twisting her hands around Martian eik wood worn smooth from overuse. The aqua ball flew toward her through the sticky heat. She swung hard for the catch—too hard. She felt the crack as soon as it happened. A glance told her that her crosse survived, but barely. Larken could tell by the weight of it that a hairline fracture hid somewhere in the soft wood. Her favorite crosse had just sacrificed itself to her obsession...and it might cost her the game if it didn't hold.

Larken spun, cupping the tennis-ball-sized rubber orb in her net and trying to choose one of seven goals made of wire mesh netting along the far fronton wall, equally spaced from one side of the fifty-yard-wide field to the other. Three of these were guarded by heavyset defensive players called guards, and the opposing team's faster offensive players, repurposed to supplement their guards, closed in on two of the others. The final member of the opposing team, the forward, hovered between the last two. She couldn't guard both, but she probably didn't have to as the goals were toward the farthest corner, a longshot by any stretch should Larken try for either. Larken's teammates had been caught unprepared again and had all ended up clustered behind the opposing team's offense, sprinting to provide support for Larken. They were too slow. Much too slow.

Larken swung her crosse. The top lagged behind the bottom as the crack grew in the shaft. It was too late to stop. The head of the stick came off and tumbled through the air before it gave up the ball. Both sailed toward the wrong goals. The guarding forward swung and connected with fragments of the crosse, sending a shower of splinters raining back at Larken. Larken ducked away too soon to see what happened next. She heard something connect with the mesh wires, but she couldn't be sure what it was until the crowd cheered.

Wiping dust and shards of wood from her face, Larken looked out over the crowd for the first time since the game began. She whipped her head around toward the chatter of interlopers swarming the field in blues, whites, and grays. Sweat stung her eyes. Larken motioned furiously to the swell of fans rushing the field. Back! Back before they cost her the game. Nobody stopped.

Hands seized her waist and lifted her into the air in one violent thrust. Rapturous screams echoed across the sports field, bounced over the heads of high-school students, and confirmed the game was over and Brighton Bison had won.

The other Bison forward rushed in from the bench and pushed her hands under Larken's thighs, hoisting her even higher. More girls in Brighton-blue jerseys flocked to the trio. Larken rode atop too many shoulders to count. Across the field, Larken made out her coach's angular features gleaming with pride.

· · ·

Steaming shower water swept away well-earned sweat. Larken's skin shrieked under the near-scalding heat. The steady beat of the droplets cleared her mind to that moment when the ball left her crosse and hurled its way into the net.

Endorphins pushed against other thoughts that too frequently crowded her mind. After the cheering and the celebration that Molly no doubt had in store, Larken would be herself again, and her old problems would return. But for now, she left the clutter of unsigned notes under her bed in the bottom of her makeup case and focused only on the sweet sensation of victory.

She closed her eyes and let the water trickle through her hair. Yes, later, she would deal with her mysterious benefactor. Much, much later.

Larken toweled off and donned sandals with a throwback bright yellow sundress. The synthetic fibers scratched against her freshly scrubbed skin, causing her to shimmy her shoulders in search of comfort she couldn't find.

"I can't believe how your brother turned out," Molly Kostic whispered. She wore a grin Larken sometimes saw when they talked about their love for the local shop called Voodoo Doughnuts and the unique pastries they created. Molly's eyes were locked on something in the distance beyond the locker room door that she had propped open with her left foot. Larken ignored the comment as she pushed through the opening.

"I mean...damn," Molly said, following closely behind. "He shot up, didn't he?"

True enough. Larken's brother stood half a head over a group of boys in an overgrown courtyard. He'd grown as quickly as the weeds that had dominated their lonely square for each of the ten summers they'd spent at Brighton Academy. Year eleven wasn't looking good either as clover fanned away from the lonely gazebo at the bottom of the hill.

"Are you sure you're twins?" Molly persisted, asking the same question for the billionth time.

"Fraternal," Larken said. Again.

"That curly hair of his," Molly said, egging Larken on. "I could just run my hands through that and—"

"Ugh," Larken said. "Someday, you'll learn that not everyone wants to know everything about you. How'd you get that way having a mom like yours?"

Larken ran her hands through her hair. It was the same color as Oliver's, yet not kinky unless the humidity was over eighty percent. Molly leered as though Oliver had become a chocolate eclair.

"Two moms," Molly reminded her. "Only one is an uptight lawyer. And all I'm saying is maybe I'll break off a piece of..."

"Just stop, Molly."

Larken shuddered and faked gagging. She examined her brother from afar, following the gaze of Molly's brown-black eyes. The same deep blue eyes in which others lost themselves were just Oliver to her.

"What would you think if I date him?" Molly continued.

Larken shook her head. Molly was many things including a great ally, but her relationships all seemed to fail tragically.

"Why Oliver? You can literally get any boy you want."

"Why not Oliver? He's smart, funny, and everyone likes him even if he is a bit bookish," Molly said. "Besides, I'd be good for him."

"Oh, in that case..."

Larken shoved her way past Molly. She knew Molly too

well. It grated on her that Molly was asking her for permission to date Oliver because in reality once Molly put her mind on someone, very little stopped her. Larken stared at Molly without words, trying to divine from her eager eyes if Oliver was just another of Molly's passing fancies, like when she absolutely had to have a keyboard synthesizer and yet never bothered learning to play once she had one. Molly chewed on her bottom lip, looking more innocent than she had ever actually been.

"No thanks," Larken said as she gave Molly a stern look. An untimely lock of hair fell into her face. She blew at it furiously, but the stubborn thing fell again into her eyes, diffusing her glare. Molly skipped to the next item on her list.

"Celebration then," she said as though nothing had happened. "Replicated doughnuts and cider."

"How can I resist?"

The doughnuts were jelly-filled glory. Larken licked the raspberry syrup on her lips as the pair left Molly's jelly-emptied donut carcasses for the automated robot MiniMaid to collect later. The hallway walls arched high over their heads as they walked side by side. Larken examined the figures on the walls of children in different uniforms while Molly did her best-friend duty and gushed about Larken's earlier performance in the match.

"Every uniform the school adopted since its founding," said a woman's voice. "That was in the grand old days of the twenty-twenties."

Larken looked up to see a mousy-looking woman with green eyes and greener hair staring down over a pair of what Larken already knew were augmentation specs.

"That makes Brighton Academy a hundred and eighty years old."

Larken stifled a giggle as she caught Molly mouthing along to the words.

"Good evening, Ms. Carrish," Larken said.

"Well done tonight, Larken. You've earned the right to wear that uniform. Do you remember what the colors stand for? Blue, white, and gray. Loyalty, honor, and determination."

"And determination," trailed Molly a little too slowly. Ms. Carrish didn't seem to notice.

"You showed all three on the court today. Well done."

Larken beamed from the compliment while Ms. Carrish pulled herself away from her and clipped down the hallway in her low heels. The very last uniform of the hallway was the modern-day suit jacket with a priest collar over a traditional pleated skirt of blue and white plaid.

"You showed all three today," Molly said, speaking through her nose and shoving imaginary glasses over the bridge. She burst out laughing, and Larken joined in.

"Jocelyn's going to be pissed that we didn't bring her any doughnuts," Larken commented.

"If she wants doughnuts, she can join the lofting team and earn them like you did," Molly suggested with a wide smile.

"Riiiight," Larken said. "You know how sensitive she can be sometimes. Want to swing by the cafeteria and see if we can replicate her some?"

"You can," Molly replied. "I've got to go see Oliver."

Larken glared.

"I'm joking. Just going back to the room," Molly said.

They parted ways in the hallway, Larken heading toward

the modest cafeteria on the first floor and Molly heading toward the stairs that granted access to the second floor and the girls' dormitory wing.

Larken decided after four failed attempts, one of which produced a doughnut that was solid and black like a hockey puck, that it was time to give up on the doughnuts. Her skills lay entirely in the lofting domain and definitely not in food replication. No amount of wishing or well-meaning was going to make her a better cook.

Neither Molly nor Jocelyn moved when Larken entered their shared dormitory room empty-handed. Jocelyn sat in her usual position, propped atop her pink dragon-adorned blanket, one leg tucked under the other. There wasn't a hiccup in her rapid-fire hand movements. Beside her, an intensely focused Molly sat with her back to the Larken, bobbing along with her head in rhythm to Jocelyn's motions. The only sign that either had noticed her enter was their voices dying down to whispers until Molly stopped mid-whisper and turned, wearing a thin, secretive smile.

"Kansas City is playing tonight," Jocelyn reminded the group as though there hadn't just been voracious whispering moments earlier. Jocelyn reached for a fist-sized rubber figurine on the window ledge near the head.

Larken couldn't help but follow Jocelyn's hands but caught her eyes drifting up to look through the window beyond. The two wings of the school splayed out like spokes that joined together in a small courtyard. Clouds blotted out the sun, and rain clouds gathered in the distance. Darkness lay over everything, turning the bright greens of the flower-packed landscape drab and empty. She exhaled slowly. A lofting game could help settle her unease at Molly's earlier disclosure.

"Who are they playing?"

"Angels versus the Passion," Jocelyn replied, shrugging as though the Mobile Passion weren't her favorite team. Larken's head snapped downward to meet Jocelyn's eyes.

"Mobile Passion? I bet they have the game on in the lobby," Larken replied.

"Not Mobile. The Newark Passion," Molly smirked.

Larken laughed.

"That would be a bloodbath," she said. "Could you imagine? Even if Newark were a major league team, they would be slaughtered in minutes."

"Maybe," said Jocelyn. "But remember the Olympics tournament last year? Some of those minor league players are good."

"There were like three minor league players on the Nigerian team," Larken replied. "And none anywhere else in the league. But that's Nigeria. Newark doesn't remotely compare. They don't take their lofting seriously enough."

"Nobody takes their lofting seriously enough for you, do they? Just because not everyone can make a thirty-yard goal at crunch time and win a game doesn't mean they're not serious," Molly said with a smile. "Want to watch in the lobby?"

Larken suspected Molly wasn't remotely interested in the match, and she could tell by the look on Jocelyn's face that Jocelyn didn't believe that to be the case either.

"You just want to see if Oliver is down there," teased Jocelyn. Larken's teeth clenched together as she tried to pull her lips into a smile and laugh it off.

"There's a bigger holovid," Molly said.

Larken committed herself mentally not to get involved

but to focus on the match. If she ignored Molly's obsession, perhaps she could navigate the turbulent relationship waters unscathed. Besides, what was the likelihood that book-smart Oliver would find Molly to be romance material?

"If we go down now, we might get lucky. Seeing the players' faces for a change would be nice." Larken caught Jocelyn's blush. "No offense, Jocelyn. Your holovid is nice too. Really."

Barely a square foot and fourteen inches high, Jocelyn's portable holovid made it challenging to make out the lofting ball.

"We can watch it in 2D in the library," Jocelyn offered.

"Lobby, girls. Lobby," Molly insisted.

"Do you think the meta-lab has it on their approved list?" Jocelyn added as though she hadn't heard.

Larken shivered a little at the idea of the cold rubberized haptic suit against her skin. She and Molly had suffered through those suits for the bi-annual International Lofting Championships. Once Larken had gotten past the itching and figured out how to tamp down the impulse to continually pull at the material when it wedged into unwelcome places, the experience hadn't been that horrible. Adding the approval process and waitlist, the experience was too mediocre in the school's sub-par haptic gear for the effort involved. "By the time we get in, the match will be half over."

"Okay, lobby then," Jocelyn finally agreed, running her thin fingers over the statuette she'd retrieved. Larken's eyes fell from the courtyard of the figure Jocelyn held just under five inches tall. A sallow face peeked out between Jocelyn's fingers as she stroked a head with her thumb. Pointed ears adorned the sides, and the entire body was covered in thin fur. Claws extended from beneath Jocelyn's palm.

"What is that ugly one?"

"Gulmen. She's the demon goddess who birthed Europa and Ganymede," Jocelyn replied, turning the hairy creature over to expose its distended belly. "Then she tried to eat them."

"What's with gods always trying to eat other gods?" Larken asked, thinking about her western civilization history lessons.

Jocelyn eyed her figurine, and Larken as she heaved her body upward, rolling forward to a sitting position again.

"No idea," she said. "I thought she looked neat."

"Neat isn't what I'd call her," Molly said, her face scrunched up into a look of repulsion. "That one's almost as bad as...what was that other one you had? Vrenofed?"

"Yep, Vrenofed," Jocelyn laughed, pulling to her feet. "Yeah, that one's pretty disgusting. She ate her children, then vomited them out into Saturn's sky, making the entire satellite belt."

She stood and jammed the demon goddess into her pocket. Jocelyn smiled impishly at Larken. "Gulmen is also the goddess of good luck. For the Passion."

Gulmen may have been helping someone, but it wasn't Larken. The holovid might have been showing the game when they emerged into the expansive common room from the hallway. It might also not have been. Larken had no way of knowing through the stragglers of schoolchildren who had already gathered around it.

Peeking over the head of a shorter boy, she saw that it was the game. In the lower right, she read the score: Angels were up by two already, an almost impossible score to overcome in a balanced match. Molly took less than half a second to examine the situation and turn to head back to the room.

"I'm not watching here," she said. Jocelyn turned to follow. Larken didn't. She scanned the room for her brother. He wasn't there.

"You two go ahead," she said. It was either watch in the common area or try to make out tiny figurines dancing atop Jocelyn's holovid.

"Suit yourself," Molly said. Larken let the offense roll off and walked to the other side of the holovid. Oliver hadn't been concealed by the players either. She scanned the room again but still didn't see him.

A rumble of thunder tumbled through the walls, causing the sensitive and almost obsolete holovid to flicker a thin flash of static in three dimensions. A storm approached outside. Giving up on the holovid and about to head back to her room, Larken glanced through the window at the clouds gathering above. It would be a raucous one. Movement trapped her mid-glance and held her. She squinted through the far window, then stepped around three students to get close to it. She made out three figures gathered under the gazebo in the far distance. She recognized Oliver from his stance with one hand resting on his hip.

A few minutes later, Larken emerged in the courtyard. Another roll of thunder shook the air. Cold had invaded and replaced earlier warm summer heat with a night's chill. Shivering, she folded her arms and stepped into the darkness, carefully keeping the people in the pavilion in sight.

"Oliver," she called when she got close, and one of the faces turned. A grin appeared, followed by a wave and a long arm motioning her to come.

"Larken," he said. When she was close enough that she

didn't have to yell, he said in a low voice—almost a secretive whisper, "Meet Elijah."

From her vantagepoint, she only saw the back of Elijah's head. When the boy turned to face her, she sucked in her breath. Eye color and gender aside, the boy looked exactly like the face she saw in the morning mirror.

"Elijah just transferred here from Our Lady Guadalupe in Dallas."

Larken's new twin stuck a hand out.

"Nice to meet you," he said, his voice cracking as Oliver's did sometimes.

"Larken," she announced, shaking Elijah's hand. Then she noticed a slight girl standing in the shadows beyond. The girl shared Molly's splotchy oversized freckles.

"Via," the girl said. "I'm Via. Like the way. Or the road. I prefer the way. Sometimes I say it's like the journey, but that's not exactly correct."

Then she shut her mouth and stared through Larken toward the main house.

"What the hell is going on?" Larken asked, eyes stabbing at Elijah. "Where did you come from?"

"I ran into him after you left earlier," Oliver said.

"I'm not from Our Lady Guadalupe," Via offered, though nobody asked. "I'm from the TX-9001 group home in California."

A monotone rode in her voice as if only facts existed behind those reddish-brown eyes. Larken thought she'd finished and was about to speak again when Via continued.

"I've always wanted a sister," Via said and glanced at Larken with a half-smile while her eyes never settled for longer than a half-second. Larken's teeth ground as she processed the creepy stare.

"There you are!" A voice called out from the direction of the main building. Larken turned toward the voice though she already knew to whom it belonged.

"There you are," echoed Jocelyn. "Whoa."

The pair stopped their advance as their faces turned to each in turn. Molly was the first to break the silence as her eyes fell firmly upon Oliver.

"Now this is interesting," she said, licking her lips even though the sheen revealed that they were already well-saturated with gloss. She glanced back from Larken to Elijah. "There are two of you, Larken. You do make a handsome boy."

CHAPTER 2
STOLEN KISSES

MOLLY COULDN'T HIDE her smile when she ran into Oliver in the wide hallway before her first class the next day. Falling into step beside him, she gave him a quick hip bump and then giggled as his head jerked around.

"She's not here," Molly whispered. "Not yet anyway. It's fine if you want to kiss me."

Molly knew he wasn't about to kiss her. Not in the hallway where there were spies who eavesdropped on every action. Of course, that was all in Oliver's head, which in Molly's opinion Oliver spent too much time listening to. And he seemed fixated on the irritating idea that Larken wouldn't approve of Molly and Oliver dating (which Larken had all but confirmed the day before). Molly tried to snake her fingers into Oliver's but he pulled away. Oliver turned toward her, his eyes gentle and unblinking as they stared into hers.

"I love you, Molly, but I wish you wouldn't do that," Oliver told her, focused on navigating through the other students. "If we just started making out in the hallways, she's going to know that we've been hiding from her."

"And whose idea was that anyway?"

Three months. Three long and torturous months of clandestine hand-holding and stolen kisses. And the absolute worst part was that it had also been three long months of lying to not only Larken but also to Jocelyn. Well, until yesterday anyway. One down, one to go.

Oliver gave a weak smile and responded the same way he always did.

"Soon," he said, following up with a wink.

"Sooner than you think, lover boy," Molly said, winking back. Jocelyn couldn't keep secrets. Now that Molly had hinted at her and Oliver as a thing, Jocelyn would let it out. The question was how would Larken react?

A girl in an Angels T-shirt passed her by and gave them a suspicious glance.

"Keep your voice down," Oliver whispered harshly. The girl turned as she passed and stared even harder at her than before. Oliver was many things, but he was not skilled at keeping secrets. His face went bright red the longer the girl stared. Molly glared back and gave the girl a quick lift of her eyebrows and nod farther down the hall. The girl ducked her head and sped away. Molly tried for Oliver's hand one last time as they approached their Advanced Biology classroom. He yanked his hand back away from hers.

"Larken's in your next class," he said. "Not so fast, okay? I really want her to be okay with us."

"No promises," she told him as he continued down the hallway without her. Oliver didn't look back, but Molly saw a distinct shrug as he walked, letting her know that he heard her. Just in time too. A second later, Larken rounded a corner nearby and flashed Oliver a smile before her eyes fell on Molly.

"Hey," she said as she approached. "Ready for Advanced Biology?"

"Prepared, yes," Molly replied. "Ready to deal with more of the same bullshit from Anthony Lee and Human Pride Movement Lite? No, I'd say never ready for any of Anthony's bullshit. And you know he likes to get under Ms. Carrish's skin, right?"

"He does have guts," Larken said. "That's at least something I guess."

"I wouldn't have dated him if he had no redeeming qualities," Molly attested. "But his end at courage."

"Maybe," Larken replied. "Not sure that you've *always* been so picky. And even when you were going out with him, Anthony was a bit of a problem."

"Not like he is now," Molly said. "And he didn't have the entourage then either. Something changed in him after we broke up. It's like he turned mean."

"Meaner. Or maybe he was faking being nice," Larken said.

"Yeah, or that. Ready to go in?"

With that, they took their usual seats near the front of the classroom.

Molly watched a year of abstinence disappear as Larken shoved her scarred gray stylus between her teeth. Larken had gotten better about it, really. Something was causing this resurgence, and Molly had a suspicion that her possible relationship with Oliver hovered near the front of Larken's mind.

"Great game," someone commented in a loud whisper. Molly nodded in response. The question was probably directed at Larken since she was the star of the previous evening's match. Molly found lofting a welcome pastime, but she didn't take it nearly as seriously as Larken did with her nightly practices.

A cracking sound drew Molly's attention to the stylus that Larken gnawed on like a dog bone. Larken stopped for a second when she saw Molly. Only for a second. Larken pounced on the stylus again. Ms. Carrish's throat-clearing warning stopped Larken this time. Larken pulled the stick from between her teeth and placed the dripping thing on the corner of her desk.

Yes, something was definitely wrong.

Molly tapped her fingers against the edge of her desk to get Larken's attention. Larken didn't seem to notice. Molly tapped harder while Ms. Carrish explained once again how the cloning process operated. It was stuff Larken and Molly had already learned, and Molly never focused intently on Ms. Carrish's instruction anyway, but still, Molly got no response. Finally, Larken turned her head, ponytail flipping around behind.

"What?" she whispered loudly enough that Ms. Carrish shot them both a glare, and Larken turned her gaze downward. And at that moment, Molly saw the sandy-brown hair and Larken-doppelganger face of Elijah peering through the window. She scrunched up her eyes.

"*Why aren't you in class?*" she mouthed.

Elijah's eyes were focused on the wider room and the other students within. Even if not, reading Larken's lips through the thick glass was tricky, assuming Elijah even knew how to read lips. Molly tried to shoo him away as Ms. Carrish continued her lecture. Her subtle motions had no apparent effect. Elijah seemed engrossed in whatever was happening inside the classroom from his vantage point in the yard.

"The test will cover the cloning and modeling process, industries, and key players like Dr. Alexander Toussaint, going in-depth into his revolutionary lab in League City, Texas," Ms. Carrish said. "Gallatin Hamilton and Beckett-Madeline Enterprises will also be covered..."

Elijah wouldn't leave. His face was pressed into the window, and Molly clearly heard a group of students behind her chittering excitedly. She motioned once again and then turned to Larken, who finally paid attention. Molly motioned toward Elijah with her eyes darting back and forth between Larken and the tiny window that overlooked the courtyard. When Larken finally looked and saw Elijah just beyond, peeking through the glass, Ms. Carrish seemed to notice too and turned at the same time. Elijah ducked from view just in time.

Ms. Carrish swiveled back, but Elijah was faster. A giggle worked through the crowd when Ms. Carrish's eyebrows knitted together for a second, staring at the empty space Elijah's face once occupied. She shrugged and continued her lecture without breaking stride.

The classroom holocube was a several generations-old holovision that had probably been around before the Larken could walk. At Ms. Carrish's direction, it displayed a medium-height man with kinky black hair spread out in a halo. Deep azure eyes—almost as blue as Oliver's—peered out of warm, tanned cheeks.

Anthony Lee raised his infernal hand.

"Anthony?"

"What happened to the clones? You said thirty hatched and proved his experiment. What happened to the rest?"

Ms. Carrish pulled her glasses down from her face and wiped them on the corner of her shirt, exposing her rotund belly, eliciting another round of giggles from the first row. Ms. Carrish replaced the glasses on the bridge of her nose, none the wiser.

"*Nobody* knows that, Anthony. With all that had happened, Dr. Toussaint lost a lot of paperwork. After publishing what's now considered a foundational paper in cloning, he abandoned his work. He hasn't been seen in public since."

"My dad says it serves him right that his woman left him," Anthony *fucking* Lee continued, unprompted. "He says anybody bringing more shills into this world *should* suffer."

Students, even Anthony, rarely used the word "shill," *especially* not in front of teachers. Ms. Carrish let out something that might have been a sneeze, which knocked her glasses halfway down her nose. Using the index finger of her left hand, she shoved the glasses back up.

"Anthony," she corrected, "I let you all use exactly one swear word in this classroom. Do you remember which one it is?"

"Fuck?" someone guessed wrongly.

"Shit?"

More giggles.

"Damn. It's damn," someone else swore.

Molly knew the word was "bloody." The class went through the same exercise almost once a week, trying out every curse word they could think of. Ms. Carrish raised her hand, and the deluge of swearing diminished to a slow roar and then into silence.

"It most certainly is *not* 'shill,'" she corrected. "Try again, Anthony."

"My dad says that anyone who helps create more clones—"

"Models, Anthony. Just say 'models.' That's what they are. Do you know *why* they're models and not clones? It's on the final."

Jocelyn's hand shot up in the back of the classroom.

"Jocelyn," Ms. Carrish called. "Can you tell Anthony the difference?"

"Clones are direct copies of real, living humans without modifications. *Models* are bioengineered. They start with cloning human DNA, but then add things like strength modifiers and tune intelligence levels to prepare them for the industry they'll be working in."

"Correct. Anthony, care to try one more time?"

Anthony did not want to try again. Their brief "dating" experience had taught Molly all the signs. His beet-red face and habitual gnawing on his upper lip were definite signs of an impending explosion.

"*Models* and *model sympathizers* should all be shot," he retorted and slammed back into his seat. Three loud voices of indeterminate sources shouted in agreement.

"Shills will not replace us," came another, softer voice from the crowd. The voice was Anthony's second, Susan Priest. No surprise there. The stern look on Ms. Carrish's face told Molly that Ms. Carrish knew exactly who it was.

"Anthony, Susan, Isaac, and Sun," Ms. Carrish said, rounding up the usual suspects and pointing to each in turn. "To the office. Now. Detention."

Three of the four left the room. Anthony stopped short and turned his full head of black hair so that he could scowl.

When he did, Elijah's head bobbed into view. Anthony's eyes darted toward Molly and back to Elijah in the half-second before Elijah disappeared again. Then Anthony's eyebrows furrowed. The corner of his lips curled up into a smile.

"My dad's right," he blurted out. "The education system is corrupt."

As Molly watched, Anthony sucked in air, filling his chest to prepare for another tirade of words, but he was cut off.

"Leave, Anthony. Now," Ms. Carrish said, staring and drilling holes through everyone she flagged until she landed her gaze on Anthony, who took the cue to straighten up and let his breath out as a single long sigh. Then, he followed the others from the room. Ms. Carrish glanced at the projected time on the wall above the door.

"Class, we're late for lab, thanks to that interruption. Gather your things, and we'll head over. Today, we're going to try out the Southern Blot. Then, if we have time, the Northern."

"Ms. Carrish," a voice called out. "Simulation lab or wet lab?"

"I don't think we have time for the wet lab setup today. Simulation only. Everyone, flip your goggles into augmented mode when you get them. I'll be there in just a moment."

Larken gathered her things. She glanced at Molly, who was too preoccupied loading her bag to notice. A side-glance toward Jocelyn told Molly that Jocelyn had also seen Elijah's face in the window. The girl tried to emulate Larken's single-minded focus, but her telltale blush gave her away—that and the fact that she couldn't keep her eyes from sliding in Larken's direction.

"Larken, Molly," Ms. Carrish said. "Come up here, please."

Larken shoved her pinamu tablet into her bag. Had she known that they were watching a display on the desktop classroom holovid in the front of the room, she might not have pulled the clipboard-sized device out in the first place. The class-specific pinamu held her book and class notes in it, in the rare occasion that she bothered with notes. Larken reached in after it and pulled what was left of her stylus back toward her teeth Ms. Carrish stared directly at her as she tilted it toward her mouth while Molly cringed. Larken clamped her mouth shut before biting and shoved the stylus into her waiting pocket. Then she shouldered her bag and took the long walk from the middle of her room up to the teacher's desk with Larken right behind her.

"Girls," Ms. Carrish said, her glasses back on her face. Even though she said "girls," her focus was entirely on Laken. "Tell your brother that if he wants to get your attention during my class, he should have a legitimate reason. I'd accept family emergencies or bringing your pinamu to class if you forgot it. Something like that. And *if* that's the case, he should have no problem getting an actual *permission slip*. Am I clear?"

"That's not my brother, Ms. Carrish," Larken said.

The thinly veiled accusation Molly had witnessed in Anthony's eyes only echoed what she'd been wondering. How could Elijah look so much like Larken and *not* be related? Playing Elijah off as her brother would have at least kept the teacher's lounge from collectively wondering the same thing. Molly watched Ms. Carrish's face as the woman processed the information. An accommodating smile followed confusion as one eyebrow went up.

"All the more reason not to have whoever it is interrupting my class," Ms. Carrish said. Then, almost as an afterthought, she said, "It's uncanny how much that boy looks like you. Are you sure that wasn't Oliver?"

"Ms. Carrish, Larken's twin is *fraternal*. He doesn't look like her *at all*," Molly interjected.

"Good use of your genetics vocabulary, Molly. I see. How interesting."

"I think my glasses are broken," a meek voice chimed in. It was the same girl who had asked about simulation versus wet lab.

"Let me see," Ms. Carrish said, which Molly took as a dismissal to begin their lab work. She turned away at the same time as Larken, and they made their way toward the door that connected the small classroom to the uncomfortable stools and hideous goggles.

"That's going to be trouble," Larken whispered. "Did you see how Anthony ogled Elijah?"

"Like he wanted to date him," Jocelyn said, causing Molly to jump. She hadn't expected Jocelyn to be with them yet. Molly then let out a nervous laugh.

"More like he wanted to kill him. Or *Larken*. That's bad," Molly said. She shot Jocelyn a disapproving look to reprimand her for what Molly considered a bad joke.

"It'll be worse if he catches Elijah and Larken together. I saw it on his face. He thinks Elijah's a clone, and seeing them side-by-side would prove it to him."

"Via seems like what would happen if you and Oliver had kids, down to the unfortunate personality defect," said Jocelyn and then immediately grit her teeth and squirmed where she stood.

"Shut up, Jocelyn. That doesn't help," Molly said. She had to admit to herself that it was true.

"I'm telling you, Anthony's going to be a problem. He and Human-Pride Movement Lite over there. He's telling them right now that you're a shill."

"And he's usually so friendly," Molly mocked. "I'm *not* a model, so it doesn't matter."

"Identical," Jocelyn tactlessly reminded her. "I mean, did you see the shape of his eyes? Elijah looks *just like you.* Exactly. Not sort of. Not kind of. *Exactly.*"

"Well, not exactly," Larken interrupted, grinning. "I'll bet he has a penis, and last time I checked, none of us do."

Larken chuckled, and Jocelyn breathed out a thin sigh. It was a joke. And models weren't identical—just sort of the same anyway. So it didn't really mean anything to say, but it diffused some of the tension anyway. She took it a little further.

"Besides," Molly said, "you have a pasty-white, round face, and he has an oval one."

"What?"

"His face. You have the same nose, eyebrows, and hair color. But his face is thinner, and he has an Adam's apple. He looks a lot like you, but if brainless Anthony bothers to think about it, there are some obvious differences."

Not all of that was true, and none of it changed things for anyone who knew that models didn't look like each other. It was good to hear the words even if they didn't still Larken's growing fears. She fished her stylus back out of her pocket and shoved it between her teeth.

"Seriously, Larken, you need to stop. That thing will die, and then you won't have a stylus. Or teeth."

Larken ignored the advice and bit down firmly. The existing cracks now extended the length of the tube.

"There's a protest downtown today," Molly said.

"And?"

"Jocelyn wants to sneak out," Molly whispered.

"I can't go. I'm busy," Larken replied.

"Doing what?"

Larken feigned hurt and didn't answer as they entered the lab. Molly's eyes fell to Anthony, already back and diligently starting his assignment. Whatever penalty they'd received, he'd been cowed into not making eye contact with anyone. Sun Selinsky sat with him, and the two nudged at something invisible.

"Serves them right," Molly said, nodding toward the pair. "What do you think happened at the office?"

"I hope they got a week's worth of detention," Larken answered. "Poor HPM Lite. No more harassing students in the hallways. For now."

Molly stared at Anthony. She could tell he knew she was looking, but he didn't look up once.

Molly and Larken worked their way through the other students toward the back of the laboratory room, far to the opposite side from Anthony and Sun. No point in taking chances, as bitter as they were. Molly eased onto a stool just high enough that her feet couldn't touch the ground (and just low enough that her feet couldn't sit on the attached footrest). Whoever designed laboratory stools seemed determined to use reverse ergonomics to keep the occupant awake.

"Turn on your goggles and select the *Southern* Blot lab," said Ms. Carrish. "Then you can go through the steps as outlined. We're working with DNA first."

Molly stalled Larken from putting on her goggles while

everyone else did. Then they both watched the other lab students waving their hands around in front of their faces. Larken smirked and shook her head.

"It's like a tortured dance routine."

Larken giggled, and Molly couldn't help smiling at the relaxed response.

"I guess we better get started," Larken said. The pair donned their goggles at the same time. A shallow tray with sixteen wells appeared before her on the counter. At the bottom of each well was sample DNA for testing. Two droppers accompanied as well as a Southern Blot tray. Molly looked past the projected visuals to see Susan in her direct line of sight.

"Look over there," Molly said. "Susan is by herself."

Larken held a dropper over one of the sample slots, and thick scrunched eyebrows told Molly that her focus remained on the classwork.

A tall man in a business suit stumbled through the lab doorway.

"You're interrupting my class," Ms. Carrish said, staring at him over her goggles.

Students took notice and dropped their imaginary pipettes. The entire classroom followed Ms. Carrish's gaze— including Larken, though she resisted longer than most.

"Ms. Carrish, a word," the man said.

Ms. Carrish nodded sharply.

"Mr. Beverly. What can I do for you?"

"In private, please."

The two walked out into the hall. Anthony grinned (he always looked creepy when he did) and rose from his stool. Then it was as though he couldn't decide what to do next, so he stood like a sadistic lost puppy.

The door slowly swung shut behind the teachers and the class—mostly. Since the door had been broken for half the year, an inch gap remained. Students looked around nervously, unsure whether to return to their lab work and pretend not to be able to hear or focus on squeezing out every tantalizing detail.

"...governor signed a state law. It's about viewpoint diversity, Carol."

"Anthony spoke about shills and spewed Human Pride Movement talking points *in my class*. He was being disruptive."

"The law says that we have to entertain *all* different perspectives."

"He said, 'Anybody bringing more shills into this world should suffer.' He said they should be *shot*. And you want me to let Anthony Lee say things like that in my classroom?"

"He didn't say that. His *father* said that, and he only told you what his father said."

"No. And what about the chanting, Dick. That's hate speech. The law doesn't allow that, and neither will I."

"*You* don't get to choose, Carol. Your job is to teach. Period. Children can say what they want if they aren't being disruptive."

Molly could imagine Ms. Carrish furiously shoving her glasses up her nose.

"What about the other students? You want me to let those kids turn my classroom into an HPM rally?"

"You're overreacting, Carol. They were out of line, yes. But they didn't need to come to the office. And they certainly didn't deserve detention."

"*You* gave them detention, Richard."

Molly snickered.

"On *your* recommendation. We can't afford the governor to come down here and cut our funding." His voice fell to a sharp whisper—useless given the width of the door gap. "What do you think Anthony's father will do? His best friend is on the governor's staff."

"If you expect me to play that bullshit game, you'll have to fire me. I'm not teaching in a class like that."

The door swung open hard enough to slam the knob into the wall, echoing down the hall.

"Anthony Lee, pack your bags. Get out of my class."

Molly gasped and saw Larken doing the same. Anthony's grin disappeared as he collected up his belongings in slow motion.

"Anthony Teregard Lee, don't stall. And you can tell your father to call me if he wants to discuss your behavior."

Molly caught a glimpse of Principal Beverly fleeing in the background. Larken's stylus returned to her mouth and cracked in two between her teeth.

"Told you," Molly reminded her.

"I know." Larken held the pockmarked pieces before her.

Molly hated that she was still on the campus where people like Anthony were far too familiar. Her eyes floated over to Jocelyn, who stared at Larken impatiently, probably wondering what Larken's response would be to the prospect of sneaking out later. Molly's attention turned to Larken as well, who finally seemed to sense Larken's gaze. With an aggravated half-smile, Larken nodded, and Molly exhaled. Some time off-campus might be precisely the thing Larken needed to clear her mind and maybe lighten up a bit.

And it would give Molly time to see Oliver unchaperoned.

CHAPTER 3

SECRETS REVEALED

LARKEN'S NEXT three classes passed in a blur. The three o'clock bell announced her last class of the day. She flowed with a wave of students through the saturated hallway toward Literary Arts, where Larken was certain at least one student would die from boredom at the monotone of Mr. Bernhild's lecture.

"How's Oliver?" one boy who had fallen into step with her asked.

"Okay, I guess," she replied, raising her eyebrows at the question. He seemed sincere when she examined him, so she thought for a second about how to respond without being rude. Then she noticed it wasn't just him. A student group of almost eight students all seemed to be watching her at once. Larken towered over the boy, who had to be a freshman. The boy stepped back and lowered his voice, no longer meeting Larken's gaze.

"Is he ready for Fouriedon entrance exams?" the boy whispered. "They're hard. Nancy took them last year. I'm not taking them until next year."

He motioned to a taller girl beside him, presumably Nancy, who still only came up to Larken's ears.

"She didn't know," said Nancy, who had bright red locks and matching lipstick. The girl reminded Larken of Molly's mother except for the snarl curled into her bottom lip.

"How do you know?" Larken challenged, failing to keep the irritation from her voice.

"Jamie told us," Nancy bragged, nodding toward a different boy at the back of the pack. "He sits next to Oliver in Classical Studies. I'm *so* sorry. We wouldn't have mentioned it if we thought you didn't know."

Larken's face heated as she tried to push ahead through the group. Hallway traffic stalled outside the classroom and student density kept her pinned in place. There was no exiting the mass, so she ducked her face and tried to ignore the whispers that flared around her until she could slide through the doorway.

She sidled through into her Literary Arts class. The room was far too small for the forty students who were supposed to occupy it. Desk space was a premium and some students already stood near the back. Universally recognized as the lofting queen, Larken didn't usually have a problem getting a desk. But when her gaze fell to her usual seat, Molly had beaten her to it. It was the only class Larken had with Oliver, and she sat by him every day. She chewed her lip thinking about what to say.

Larken's newfound "entourage" took over the seats behind Oliver and Molly while Larken was lost in thought. Nancy flashed a sad face at Larken just before taking the last seat that was anywhere close to Oliver. Larken wanted to punch Nancy in the teeth but instead searched for a different place to sit.

The aroma of popcorn and old cigars suddenly wafted over the room, a sure sign that Mr. Bernhild had entered. Larken hadn't yet figured out if he actually ate popcorn and smoked cigars just before class, but his presence was a certain indication that her seat-searching time was up. The last seat in the back of the room was the only one available. Larken even let her eyes roam the room to search for another, but only saw a small group of students standing against a far wall, notably *not* sitting at the last available desk.

"Everyone, we have a lot to cover today. With only a couple of weeks left, I thought we'd try to get through some of what will be on the final."

Mr. Bernhild stared at her with his arms on his hips, and the elbow patches on his smoking jacket jutted out like harpoon points.

"Ms. Marche?"

"I...I," was all she could muster. Her face had pushed past warm and now burned furiously. She was sure she'd turned bright red. There still were no better options for sitting. Larken's head pounded with every heartbeat as she looked again toward Oliver who stared right back. Larken narrowed her eyes at him as she backed up down the aisle toward where the lone empty desk remained in wait. A half of a wad of either gum or tar lay in the middle of the seat. Larken slid into the seat and then up to the edge. She had to press her belly against the desktop to fit.

"Thank you, Ms. Marche," Mr. Bernhild said, then turned to the board and scribbled his hand across it, leaving it as clean as when he'd started. Larken hadn't donned her augmentation goggles yet. The other students were already jotting down whatever the instructor wrote on their pinamus instead of staring at her, offering her a bit of relief.

Larken pulled her glasses from her taupe, gold-trimmed messenger bag and placed them on the bridge of her nose, bringing to life the words that Mr. Bernhild had written. The names of long dead works of fiction appeared beneath his stylus. She jotted them down carefully, and the focus gave her time for the heat in her face to dissipate.

A light flashed on the corner of her pinamu tablet. With a hesitant breath, Larken pulled the edge up with the tip of her half-stylus. It was a note from Molly.

"Are you okay?"

Larken raised her head and gazed across the other students' bent bodies as they scribbled desperately to keep up with Mr. Bernhild's uncompromising dictation speed. Her eyes met Molly's. Larken donned her best smile and mouthed, *"I'm fine."* She caught Oliver staring in her peripheral vision and shot him a stony glare. Molly seemed to catch on that something was amiss between them. Then Molly nodded once before returning to her studies. Larken might be able to make it through class if she only pretended that Oliver wasn't there.

Half an hour later, Mr. Bernhild completed their lesson with foot-high letters spelling out *"the end."* As Larken slid her pinamu into her bag, the group that had "escorted" her into the room gathered around her desk. The crowd split apart seconds later to allow Oliver through, followed by Molly, who sent glares to everyone around until they all skittered off.

"What's the matter, Larken? You're obviously not okay," Molly said after the room had emptied of all but the three of them. Larken ignored her and circled on Oliver.

"When were you going to tell me?"

"Tell you what?"

"About Fouriedon?"

He clenched his teeth shut and closed his eyes. Oliver's chest rose and fell before he spoke again.

"About trying to go to college *halfway across the country* in Missoula, Montana, without letting your only sister know. When were you planning on telling me? When you *left*? Was *Molly* supposed to tell me?"

"It's not a sure thing," he told her. "I didn't think it was worth talking about until I knew for certain. The exam is around the same time as finals, and I thought that—"

"That you would tell Jamie Heicht and not me?"

"He sits beside me in class. It just came up. I'm not trying to keep a secret. I just didn't want to hurt your feelings."

Molly's eyes latched onto Oliver and her eyebrows furrowed.

"You didn't think to tell me that you are *leaving* me?" Molly asked. A confused Larken turned her head from Oliver to Molly. She stared daggers into Molly as Oliver turned for making the conversation about *her* and not Larken.

"Why would he tell you? You're barely friends. Stay out of it."

She felt sorry, but there was no fixing it and it was the truth as Larken knew it. Molly's face melted under the accusations, and she backed down the aisle, face frozen in a grimace. Oliver bounced back and forth between them until his eyes landed on Molly, who had turned to flee by then.

"Wait, Molly. She didn't mean that."

That sent the fire back up Larken's spine as she blurted out more unintentional words. "I sure as hell did."

This time, Oliver glared at Larken and ran after Molly. He overcame Molly before they walked through the door.

When he grabbed her elbow, she stopped. Hostility filled his eyes as he turned to Larken.

"You don't own me, Larken. We're twins, brother and sister, but you don't own me. If I want to go to Fouriedon, I'll go."

Larken realized then that he'd completely misinterpreted what she'd been saying. He thought she didn't want him to go when she only wanted to be the first to know as she'd always been before. She shook her head and began to respond, but he'd already started talking again.

"And there's no reason for you to attack Molly. She has a right to feel however she wants."

Oliver paused and his stern gaze softened. "I thought you'd be happy for me. It's not like I'm going to *disappear*. You'll always be my sister, Larken."

Except that was exactly what it would be like, Larken thought. *He just didn't know it yet because he hasn't thought it through.* All he'd thought about was *his* future.

Oliver turned to leave the classroom, and Molly darted after him, not sparing a glance back for Larken. The augmented reality glasses slipped down Larken's nose. She caught them in her left hand, staring blankly at the undecorated walls around her.

A minute passed, and Larken stood. With nothing left to say and nobody with whom to speak, she worked her way through the beige door and out into the corridor beyond. Absent students, the classroom hallways possessed far too many open doors through which anything might lurk. Larken wasn't as familiar with the maze-like hallways in this part of the building. Almost ten minutes had gone by before she found the guard desk at the center of the boys' and girls' wings. The night guard—a woman with bright green hair and a face that looked like someone had tried to squash a jack-o-lantern flat—greeted Larken with a smile and an enthusiastic wave. Larken walked past with her head down, not acknowledging the guard's feigned interest.

When she made it up the stairs to her room, she burst through the door and collapsed on her bunk. A deep sob emanated from her throat before she remembered to choke it back and make sure she was alone first. Looking through blurring eyes, she saw Jocelyn standing in ballooned yellow slacks and a thin T-shirt by her wardrobe against the far wall from the bunks.

Larken quickly wiped her hands over her eyes as she searched the room for Molly. Molly wasn't there. Good.

"Get ready, girl," Jocelyn exclaimed over her shoulder as she removed the T-shirt and replaced it with an orange crop-top halter. Frills adorned with tiny green beads hung down from the bottom of the shirt and ended just above her waistline. When Larken didn't respond, Jocelyn turned her entire body, causing the beads to flail before settling again. "We're going out, remember?"

Larken's stomach sank. She had completely forgotten they were going out that evening to engage in the marathon event that was Jocelyn's social life. Accosted by the wall of figurines that decorated Jocelyn's bed, it was easy to forget that the girl had friends beyond just her and Molly. Larken settled her eyes on Jocelyn's.

"Oh, no. What happened?"

As desperate as she'd been for a friend, Larken couldn't share her humiliation with Jocelyn. Rumors had already started flying, and she couldn't bear Jocelyn being a confirming source. Instead, she forced a smile and finished wiping her eyes.

"Just something in my eye, that's all," Larken said, then considered what to wear. "Why so early?"

Jocelyn's face lit up as she exclaimed, "Boys. And not Brighton boys either."

Larken searched through her things and produced her T-shirt with elaborate print across the front. Jocelyn shot her a frown.

"Do you *see* what I'm wearing? Dress like you're going out to a club or something."

Larken ignored her correction. She wasn't going to have fun, and she knew it, despite the smile that she kept firmly in place. She could at least be comfortable. Besides, if her memory was correct, they were going to a protest of some sort. There was nothing sexy about screaming in a mob.

"Suit yourself," Jocelyn said.

"What do you mean not from Brighton?"

"You remember the Underlander tournament a few weeks ago?" Jocelyn asked. As usual, every time she mentioned the tournament, her eyes slid toward her headboard where her second-place trophy sat cloaked behind a batlike creature with a dog's head. "I met a Jason Keller there. He was in first place, but I didn't know he was from Portland. He goes to Protégé and says he's got a friend...Greg, I think."

Larken paused mid-tug on leggings that she should have discarded ages ago.

"College boys?"

Jocelyn looked shocked in that exaggerated way she sometimes did when Molly or Larken inevitably knocked over a figurine. Half of it was fake.

"Well, of course," she said, her smile glowing more as she

talked. "But, how great would that be if you and Greg hit it off?"

Larken doubted hitting it off with anyone in her current state was possible. But she said nothing further, pulled the leggings up to her waist, and stepped into the platform "going out" shoes that she'd never worn beyond the confines of the room.

"Here," Jocelyn said as she tossed something small and cylindrical toward Larken, who grabbed the object from the air like a lofting ball and turned it over in her hand.

"What's this?"

"A protest onboarding kit."

Larken took another long look at Jocelyn's crop top.

"And you're wearing that?"

"Jason's going to be there, so yes."

"And what if it turns violent, like the one downtown last week?"

"Different protest, Larken. This time we're protesting *against* android usage in factory jobs. The time before last was a protest *for* modeling rights. The Human Pride Movement will not show up and start beating people at this one."

"And what is it, exactly, that you dislike about androids in factory jobs?"

Jocelyn smiled, and her cheeks turned a pinkish-brown color. "I'm not exactly sure," she said.

Larken turned the object over in her hand and noticed a button on the side. She pushed it once and projected it into the air before her were the words: "Androids aren't human. Humans are." The sign flickered for a moment, then transitioned into new words: "Stop Prop 5 and Save Human Jobs."

"Jobs. That's it," Jocelyn said. "They're stealing our jobs."

Larken thought for a moment.

"Isn't that the *same thing* people have been saying about models?"

"But models *are* human. Androids are machines," Jocelyn replied.

"I guess," Larken said, shrugging her shoulders. "You don't care about the protest, do you?"

"No," Jocelyn admitted. "But like I said..."

"Jason's going to be there," they said in unison, and Larken and Jocelyn burst out laughing after. Larken clicked the sign off again. She grabbed her green and purple hip bag from her wardrobe and dropped the sign handle into it.

"Shall we?"

"Go on our protest double-date?"

Jocelyn grinned.

"It's not a set-up."

"Sure."

As they left the room, Larken couldn't help her eyes floating back to Molly's jumbled bunk. She noticed a jumble of discarded clothing options strewn over the foot of the bed. She cocked her head and examined the pile. Three halters and two crop-top sweaters.

"Jocelyn," she said, standing in the doorway before passing through. "Where's Molly?"

"Molly? I don't know. She said she had a study date or something," she said, then laughed loudly. A little too loudly. Larken noticed that she didn't make eye contact.

"With whom?"

Jocelyn's flushed cheeks told her that Jocelyn knew, but the girl didn't answer. Instead, she shook her head.

"I'm going with you on your protest date, Jocelyn," Larken reminded her. "You can tell me."

"Molly said that you wouldn't understand."

"Wouldn't understand?"

It took a second for her brain to process, then it clicked. Of course. Molly would need comforting, and Oliver, her knightly brother, would *have* to help do that. Molly's earlier faux-wounded act made more sense even as Larken's smile evaporated from her face, irritated that Molly's obsession with Larken's brother *irritated her so much*.

"Oliver," she said.

"You're still coming, right?" Jocelyn asked, eyes pleading. Larken ground her teeth and took in several shallow breaths through her nose. It didn't make her feel better. She took one more deep breath this time and blew it out slowly. The rage in her mind subsided enough to be under her control, at least. The hostility she felt shouldn't be directed at Jocelyn, whose only crime was to be a confidant to the ever-scheming Molly.

"I'm still coming," she confirmed flatly.

CHAPTER 4
GALLATIN'S GIFT

ALEXANDER "TORRENT" Toussaint stared through the south hotel window overlooking Seattle below. Canopy walkways interconnected like spider webs, trapping the bulk of the city beneath their weight. Ice clinked against his glass as he paced.

The latest experiment would work. It had to.

His boss, Gallatin, considered himself a patient man, as he was fond of telling anyone who knew him. With the life of Gallatin's granddaughter, Christine, hanging in the balance, Torrent knew the man's patience was wearing thin. After twenty years, the man had a right to expect results. Every day, the odds that Christine would rise from her coma diminished further.

Torrent wished for another patient, a *test* patient, on whom the experiment might fail again without anyone taking notice. They had tried many times before and consequently sent many models to Bremerton for reclamation. This subsequent trial wouldn't be a quiet death he could sweep away like the other quiet deaths from the parade of failures. This time it had to be Christine. Gallatin was clear on that point. He'd latched onto the idea that Torrent wasn't trying hard enough. Gallatin thought that the man needed more motivation. Gallatin's granddaughter would be the next experiment.

Torrent had installed the animus module already. Christine Hamilton, sixteen going on forty because of a tragic coma-inducing accident, had to have the device installed surgically. It wasn't what Torrent would have preferred because the method was far riskier than pill ingestion. Torrent's doubts about whether the pill would work on the unconscious girl made him choose surgery. Also there was the question of how to get her to ingest such a thing.

He took another deep sip from his highball and let a sigh drift across his lips. Turning his attention beyond the thick silicone-composite glass he held, Torrent looked out over the city. It brought him peace sometimes, but tonight roving thoughts struck him. Memories from the past seeped into his mind. He saw his deceased lab partner's face for a moment, stuck outside the window, somehow suspended in the night sky. A blink and her brown eyes faded away with only the shine off of her pupils visible as stars connected to Orion. He took another shaky draught from his highball, then turned away.

The hard part was done already. He told himself that the module, transported from Christine's frail, dying form into a new vibrant host, had adequately captured all of Christine's personality. That was a gamble itself, as there was no way to be sure before the transplant. Cognitive tests didn't work on the comatose. It would be hours before he knew whether or not the operation had been a success. Only then would Torrent know whether Christine Hamilton would open her eyes for the first time in twenty years, and how exactly she would react finding herself in a new body.

Torrent's communicator chimed. He nearly spilled his drink as he frantically searched for the device, keeping his left hand elevated and scrambling around with his right. When he found the cylinder wedged between couch cushions, the caller's name sucked his voice away.

Harper Rawls.

He placed the drink on the floor in less than a second and flipped on the projection button. When Harper's face came into view, Torrent's clouded mind searched for the right words to say. She wouldn't want to talk to him. No matter how hard he tried, she barely more than greeted him during their calls. As she said, the calls weren't to try to save or rekindle anything between them. The calls were for their son Bodhi so that he would know what his father was like. Harper insisted that father and son have a relationship, even if she wanted none.

Her lack of stoicism raised alarms in his mind when her long black hair and hazel eyes projected into the space before him.

"He fell," she told him, clearly having been crying. "I don't think that he can talk to you today. Can we do this tomorrow?"

A thousand questions came into Torrent's mind. What was Bodhi's red blood cell count? Had he been eating well? Was the erythropoietin pump no longer keeping Bodhi's body working? He asked none, having long since learned that Harper equated such questions to accusations. Instead, he settled on a simpler one.

"What happened?"

"He'd gone off into the woods this time. The car went with him—so no, I didn't send him alone."

"I didn't—"

"And he *forgot* to eat again. The car came and got us when he fell. Torrent...we almost didn't make it in time. It's as though he's *trying* to get himself killed."

"I'm sure he's not doing that."

Bodhi had a fatal, chronic disease that sucked his energy away. Even in virtual reality, from the brief sessions Torrent had shared with him, the condition seemed to sap him of will and ability to do anything. Of course, he'd be depressed and suffer from all sorts of related mental ailments. But he was also a teenager. That meant that rebellion and pushing limits were par for the course. Probably the walk had been nothing more than a test to see whether Bodhi could do it or not.

Torrent recalled speaking to Bodhi's doctors—all six of them since Aiden Periam, Harper's confusing not-quite-significant, other—could afford six different specialists at once. One after the other, they admitted that they had no clue what was going on. The boy's red blood cells didn't seem to carry enough oxygen. They'd managed to get his body to overproduce blood cells with the erythropoietin pump, but that spike didn't last long. Supplementing with high-iron foods seemed to help. They all swore the disease looked like anemia, but the standard anemia treatments didn't halt its advance. Bodhi would die before he turned twenty. He was already sixteen.

"He might be, Torrent. It's possible, isn't it? Next time you talk to him, can you ask him? He only tells me that everything's great. But I can see it in his eyes. He's suffering, but he won't talk about it. Aiden..."

She stopped, and Torrent knew why. Aiden was the one

who'd found her in the desert. Aiden Periam—a reclusive something-aire—had spotted a pregnant woman clawing across the baked earth, as he just so happened to be flying by. As the love of Torrent's life was dying in the heat, she seemed by all examinations to have been fleeing *Torrent*. She never talked about why, but when he looked back, Torrent knew. She faced a court trial for grand theft *model*, as she'd stolen Ordell Bentley from Emergent Biotechnology. At least, that was the accusation. It was flight or prison, and as usual, Torrent's focus had only been on himself.

"Sorry. I know you don't like to talk about him."

The idea that Torrent didn't want to talk about Bodhi was Harper's invention. Torrent would talk about anything to keep her on the line, and he cared for Bodhi more than Harper ever seemed to recognize.

"It's okay," he assured her. Three knocks penetrated their conversation, and he knew that he would answer. She did too.

"I'll call back," she said, tears still yet to dry. He looked at her longingly, wishing that he was someone else. But he wasn't, and the person at the door carried the results of Christine's operation with them. She was either awake, and he and Gallatin had just created the world's first immortal, or she'd gone brain dead, and he was certain Gallatin, in all of his decency and "business is business" talk, would never speak to him again.

"I'll call," he said. "Just need to answer this."

"I know."

He kicked himself as he disconnected and wondered briefly if he would ever learn.

"Come in," he called, but the door burst open as soon as he said the words. Gallatin strode through with a fresh bottle of scotch in one hand and two highball glasses in another. It looked like a celebration, but Gallatin was strange, and what looked celebratory could have been a parting ceremony.

"News?" Torrent asked. Gallatin's eyes swung to the glass on the floor. Suddenly self-conscious, Torrent leaned his creaking back over to pick it up.

"The best kind of news," Gallatin shared. "But first, a drink. For me, I guess. It looks like you've already started."

Torrent shrugged.

"Haven't stopped since yesterday. What news, Gallatin?"

Gallatin didn't answer. Instead, the vibrant older gentleman, who always seemed to have more energy in every step than Torrent had for a full day, popped open the bottle and sploshed two fingers into the crystal highball he carried.

"Top off?" he asked Torrent, who extended his glass. Gallatin had had the good sense to bring Torrent's brand. Once the one finger became two again, Gallatin stopped and raised his glass.

"To you, Torrent. Damnit, I believed in you but didn't *believe in you*. Most of that was talking to keep you motivated."

Torrent had never been naïve enough to believe differently.

"She's okay?" he asked.

"Like you ever doubted."

"You have no idea."

Torrent's mind shifted back to the call that he'd had with Harper. Success for Christine meant that the operation was safe. Well, safer than it was before. Bodhi was on borrowed time. The idea germinated in his subconscious and tickled the back of his mind: now he had a way to save Bodhi. Maybe.

"We need to scale, Torrent," Gallatin said. "And we need a couple more successes, don't we?"

"More like a hundred more, maybe a thousand, if we want to market."

"No, not that many. Just one more would do it. Repeatable. Then people will beat a path to our door."

Gallatin Hamilton didn't need anyone beating a path to his door. Like Aiden Periam, he was one of those people who had so much money that he could, for example, sink billions into pulling his only granddaughter out of an otherwise irreversible coma.

"How does she like the new body?"

"She's not awake yet, but stable," Gallatin said, a smile plastered across his face. "Brain wave activity is normal, and not that weird repeating spike while she was in the coma. She'll be awake soon, and I want you to see her and give her a once over."

"Doctors have already done that."

"But you're *you*, Torrent. I won't believe it until you say everything's good."

Torrent nodded. It wasn't a request anyway. He thought again about Bodhi in that crippled body of his and how he'd nearly died again. Then he looked at Gallatin, and the man cocked his head slightly and ran those too-perceptive gray-blue eyes over Torrent's features.

"What happened to you? I thought you'd be happy."

"Bodhi nearly died today."

"I thought Aiden had it managed."

"The doctors don't even know where to start. They're afraid to tell Aiden that."

The growing idea shoved aside his thoughts and his remorse. He focused on it, developing it for a second, and once convinced, he opened his mouth to speak again.

"Gallatin, I have an idea," he said as he sipped.

"And?"

"What if we bring Bodhi in for our second? He might have a chance in a new body—like Christine. And if I can get him down here, it could help Christine have someone making the same adjustments she is."

Gallatin swished his glass around. Ice clinked against the sides for five seconds, then he grinned, exposing his long thin teeth.

"Why not? Dying boy saved by eccentric trillionaire? I love the news headlines already. Almost as good as 'Eccentric trillionaire spends billions on a quest to save granddaughter.' Those together would be terrific public relations."

And save Bodhi.

Of course, Gallatin wouldn't care about that part of it, but Harper would. And maybe that would be enough to get her to speak to him again. Perhaps that would change him from an obligation to a friend.

"Good, then," Torrent said, allowing himself only a casual remark and nothing more.

A beeping interrupted them.

"She's awake," said Gallatin, after checking his communicator.

"Do you want me to come to check her out?"

Gallatin thought for a moment and didn't answer at first. He swished his drink around and swallowed down the remainder.

"Yes. But not yet," he said, lowering his voice. "I'm sorry about Bodhi. Take some time. But not too much."

Torrent thought he saw the glistening of tears hidden under Gallatin's eyes. Gallatin carefully placed the rest of the whiskey down on the mantle, having not made it past the living area in Torrent's tiny apartment.

"For you," he said through a toothy grin. "You've earned it and more. And I want to make you a vice president, Torrent. Don't say no. Think about it. You could shape the direction of the company for years to come. Maybe even *centuries*."

Before Torrent had a chance to complain, Gallatin spun and made his exit, leaving Torrent holding his remaining finger of scotch and staring at the closing door, thinking about what had just happened. He'd found a way to save Bodhi maybe. Of course, with Harper's feelings about models and treating them as humans, what would she say about taking a life to save their son? The operation would require the sacrifice of one model's life. There was no way to transplant someone's consciousness except into another body. Torrent couldn't imagine Harper allowing him to do that. Still, he felt he had to try—before he finished Gallatin's gift.

"Call Harper," he said to his communicator.

CHAPTER 5

ANGEL OF KNOWLEDGE

A FULLY DRESSED Larken clicked her teeth as she waited for Jocelyn to pick an outfit. Several failed alternatives flew atop the clothing pile on Jocelyn's bed, making it look a more garish version of Molly's rack. Irritated at the amount of waiting required of her to go somewhere she didn't want to go, Larken diverted her attention through the single window above the beds.

Her gaze took her down a long drive through patchwork grass and abandoned pavement. Like much of the school grounds, the drive was as overgrown as the courtyard. Plants like ivy that once might have been proud imports encroached over the roadway. The road ended at a loop, in the center of which loomed a giant statue. Large enough to be seen from every single room in the school—at least on the southern side —the one-time white statue of the angel Jophiel reached toward the sky as though it might lift into the air.

It was the Christian Angel of Knowledge, installed the year the school was built. It codified the lofty aspirations of the school's founders to be an institute that furthered the community by spreading knowledge "like seeds to blossom therein." Larken wasn't sure how well that worked given the seeds were blossoming, considering that Ms. Carrish seemed to feel the need to remind the students every year with the same speech. Beyond the angel was the solitary bus stop occasionally dropping students off at their new homes. Across from that was the bus that went into town, in full view of a hundred or so pairs of eyes.

"Do you want to try for the angel?" Larken asked.

"I was thinking about Eighth and Rose instead. The alarm is broken again, and we won't have to try to hide in bushes or anything," Jocelyn said, swapping out her yellow tank with a green top. "The lock on the second floor is broken too. It should be pretty easy."

"How do you know that?"

Jocelyn shook her head as she straightened her green sweater.

"Molly," she replied. "Molly always knows what the sneaking-out options are."

After a few minutes more, they were on their way. Silence followed them out of necessity. Being invisible wasn't the same as being inaudible. Larken's wandering mind considered adjustments she might make to her training technique to improve her lofting game—a self-imposed focus that kept her from mulling over Molly and Oliver. She wrapped herself so firmly with her thoughts that she didn't see the growing gap between her and Jocelyn.

"Can you keep up?" an impatient Jocelyn warned Larken—which did nothing to move Larken's feet any faster. The shoes dictated the pace. Besides, keeping her commitment took so much focus that faking excitement couldn't be accomplished. The nudging scold reminded Larken of the platforms, then of Molly, and once again of Molly and Oliver. She would still have the problem to deal with when she returned, and now it stalked her thoughts.

"I'm moving as fast as I can," she replied. The leggings chafed, and those damned shoe straps rubbed against her ankles, making walking painful. When the two passed Sixth Street and Larken got an eyeful of a flock of prostitutes—one also wearing platforms like hers—the experience jarred her into the realization that she must also look like a woman of the night. Even her tights were the subject of mimicry among the chattering women.

Larken sighed as the bus descended from the skyway less than a minute after they'd reached the stop. The bus looked like the elongated cigar box on the corner of Mr. Beverly's office desk, blown up a hundred times. The illusion was so complete that the door remained invisible on the smooth cardboard side until a hidden door slid open and a thin ramp extended down to where the pair stood. The bus driver cast a look toward them with one raised eyebrow.

"You're not Brighton students, are you?" he asked.

"Protégé," Jocelyn replied without hesitation. "Freshmen this year."

A whoop was elicited from somewhere near the back of the bus. Larken flipped her head up at the sound. In the back, she saw a group of students in the university's purple and green colors seated together near the back. She flashed a quick smile before she followed Jocelyn to a seat four rows from the driver.

"Where you heading?" the bus driver said, looking toward them in his oversized rear mirror.

"Downtown. FLT Plaza, by the Central Bank," Jocelyn said.

"We drop off at Strata 3 on Campden. You'll have to cross over to Burgess and take the pedestrian bridge across."

Jocelyn replied, "Thanks. We'll watch for the exit." She lowered herself into the seat while the driver droned on.

"Be careful down there," he said. "Protest today. Last one was pretty ugly. Damn models causing all that mess."

"Damn models," Jocelyn repeated as her bottom hit the faux-leather material. Larken sat beside her, relieved when the throbbing in her feet faded to an almost imperceptible tingle.

"It's not the models doing the protesting. They can't legally organize like that," Larken remarked.

"That's why the cops went in, Larken. Keep up."

Larken shut her mouth. To continue meant to rehash an old argument again. Jocelyn would disagree with her anyway, no matter how long they fought about the cause of the military lockdown and men in uniforms carrying proton rifles at the ready. Neither had been alive then anyway.

"You met Jason at a tournament?"

Jocelyn's eyes brightened. She nodded, glanced out the window quickly, and then turned back to Larken.

"I beat him at the tournament," she said. "In the first round, anyway. Then he played the loser's bracket well enough to pick up the wildcard and beat me in the last round. It was romantic!"

Romantic. Larken shook her head while a whimsical grin worked its way onto her mouth. Jocelyn's world, as busy as she always seemed, remained simple at the same time. Jocelyn liked what she liked and had her own definitions of romance, kindness, friendship, and *secrets worth keeping*. Jocelyn had the self-confidence of someone who had defined her place in the world by the time she was three.

"How did he ask you out?"

Jocelyn shifted uncomfortably, and her demeanor changed from floating on clouds to looking like she now wanted to hide behind the seat.

"Technically," she said, "he didn't. He just said that he would be at the protest for Humans Over Androids."

"Ah," Larken said, nodding her head. "I see. So we're stalking him."

"Kind of," Jocelyn giggled. "But not just him. His friend will be there too."

"Great. We're stalking the pair. Is his friend another gamer?"

Jocelyn grinned. "He wasn't playing. He's like you—just along for support. And he's *so* handsome."

"I thought Jason was your man."

"But if Jason weren't there, Greg would be a close second."

Jocelyn laughed loudly. Larken didn't. A second later, Jocelyn's hand shot into her pocket, and she pulled out a grotesque-looking twisted snake figurine.

"That has to be the ugliest thing I've ever seen," Larken said.

"That's only because you don't know what it is. This is one of the gods of the models, Coru, the Lever of Justice."

"And you brought Coru because?"

"They're rare. You can't buy them anymore. Not politically correct and all that." She shrugged as she put it back into her pocket. "I brought it as a back-up. Just in case it's a little weird just showing up, and we have nothing to talk about."

Since Jocelyn never stopped talking, Larken didn't think a conversational gap would be a problem. But when the bus deposited them on Campden into a small crowd of others heading in the same direction, Jocelyn went so silent that Larken glanced over to see if she'd somehow left Jocelyn behind. Jocelyn kept pace still, walking with that almost waddle she had left from when she'd been a heavier child.

"Do you think he'd be coming from the same direction as us?" Larken asked, looking for anyone in the crowd who looked like a college student, including all of them. Half seemed male; there was a mixed bag of hairstyles and skin tones. "What'd he look like?"

"Just a bit taller than Mr. Beverly," Jocelyn said. "He had blue hair at the tournament, but I'm not sure what color it will be now. Thin face, like he couldn't ever eat enough food."

The size description made him about five foot nine inches by Larken's guess. That cut down the search significantly, but the blue hair cut it down to zero. Larken wasn't sure how to search for "skinny face" in the crowd, and she'd left her AR goggles back in their room. Technically, they weren't supposed to bring the school-issued lenses off-campus anyway, but they had a facial recognition feature that could have sped the process along.

"I don't think he's here yet," said Larken. "Do you want to continue to the protest and see if we can find him there?"

"But what if there are too many to see? What if I can't find him?"

Jocelyn's eyes bounced erratically across the small crowd.

"Don't worry," Larken sighed. "We've got all night to find your man."

She'd hoped that Jason would remain a mystery forever. Larken entertained herself by soaking in all the different outfits and body types. Three girls clustered in front of them wore jerseys from two different lofting teams: the Palo Alto Lions and the Tacoma Wildcats.

"There," Jocelyn said, pointing into the crowd. Larken's head jolted away from the girls, and she discovered what a "thin" face was compared to Jocelyn's round one. Larken had to stop herself from laughing. Jason's face was severely ovaloid, and he held his lips as though protecting braces when he smiled. But he looked *nice*. Larken stored that away for something kind to say when Jocelyn inevitably asked what she thought.

The boy's friend looked unremarkably normal. Greg fell short of Larken's height, though most boys did. She realized she'd hoped he would be taller. And female. Jocelyn seemed to always forget that Larken wasn't as into boys as much as she was. Sure, Larken went on the occasional date with a boy, and Larken supposed if a guy was perfect enough, maybe she'd give him a chance. But mostly boys weren't her thing. It didn't help that Greg slouched when he walked and his girth made him look like a miniaturized linebacker with no neck.

Jason's eyes lit up when he saw Jocelyn. *He's been thinking about her*, Larken thought. She suspected more had happened at the tournament than she'd been told when Jocelyn embraced Jason and planted a kiss firmly on his lips.

"Oh, I'm sorry," Jocelyn said when the two broke apart. She made introductions around the group, and Larken flashed an uncomfortable smile at Greg. By the looks of his one-sided grin and the apprehension in his eyes, Greg shared her burden of being moral support. Larken stepped away from the embracing couple and toward Greg, whose hand had fallen back to his side after a quick, nervous, and sweaty shake.

"Do you know what this protest is about?" she asked, lowering her voice.

"Androids," he said. "I think." He shrugged his shoulders and looked around them. The crowd had thinned considerably. "More of Jason's thing. But we'd probably better get started if we want to protest anything. People are already starting to leave."

"I don't think the protest the priority for these two," Larken told him. Greg's smile showed that he agreed. Jocelyn and Jason, as if prompted, moved toward the escalators that would deliver them to Strata 1, the level on which the protest was being held. Greg stepped after them, but Larken deliberately waited back. When Greg noticed Larken's immobility, he stood with her instead.

"Giving them a bit of space," she explained. She began walking again, ten feet behind Jason and Jocelyn. She took a deep breath and resigned herself to starting small talk. "What are you studying at Protégé?"

She felt the heat emanating from his body and caught the vague whiff of salty perspiration hiding behind his excessive cologne.

"Pre-law," Greg replied with confident pride. She looked at him and could easily imagine him in one of those cut-black Nehru suits that lawyers wore.

"Pre-law? What does one study in pre-law?" she asked, trying to seem as college student-like as she could. His face took on a serious edge that vaguely reminded her of Oliver.

"Pre-law is the answer I give my parents. I'm studying philosophy," he confessed. "Which technically is a pre-law major, but I haven't applied for the program. Don't think I'm going to."

She smiled at his desire to be honest with her—this girl

he'd just met—and wondered what it must be like to have parents to deceive.

"A philosopher, huh? I thought there aren't a lot of philosophy jobs out there," she joked.

He laughed. "None. And that's why I tell my parents pre-law. What's your major?"

"Lofting," she said without hesitation.

"Are you on the team?"

Her face heated up as she realized her mistake. She closed her eyes and opened them quickly, trying to reset her face from panicked to hopefully embarrassed about her major.

"Not good enough," she said, though she'd seen Protégé matches, and she was better than at least half of the team. "I'll probably end up a philosophy major too. Undecided so far."

He grinned widely. "Look at us. I'd guess most likely to end up working in menial labor jobs and pursuing our passions on the side."

Larken imagined herself in the minor leagues, zigzagging across the country in a beaten-up volantrae to pick up games. She could see in her head the vehicle sputtering its ancient internal combustion engine and lifting, wobbling, into the air. Unbidden, her imagination worked on Gregory, pontificating on points nobody cared about to keep her entertained during frequent road trips. She let out a low giggle at his squat body and legs which, in her imagination, could barely reach the pedals.

"Yeah," she agreed. "Pretty sad. At least *they* have it figured out." She motioned to the pair walking before them.

"I don't know about that," he said. "Not sure about Jocelyn, but I think Jason's still looking for a way to make a major out of Underworlder."

Jocelyn and Jason abruptly stopped just after the escalator disappeared beneath the pavement.

"We're here," Jason said as he turned to face Greg. Larken couldn't tell where "here" was supposed to be. She stepped over the escalator lip on the right side, splitting from Greg to go around the two.

"There's nobody here," Larken said. The crowd they'd been following, which she'd implicitly expected to be heading toward the protest, had scattered at the bottom of the strata. She scanned from right to left, looking at the store windows and limited-motion robots peddling goods. A group clustered around the sign that displayed the strata number. It was the correct strata. And on what appeared to be a strip-mall building before them was a floating sign that read "Office of Android Affairs"—significantly less intimidating than she'd expected.

"Where is everyone?" Larken asked, mirroring the confused look in Jocelyn's eyes. Jason, avoiding eye contact with either of them, scanned right past her, and his eyes landed on the group of three that Larken had already discounted as non-protestors.

"There," he said, pointing to them and stepping in their direction.

"They don't have signs," she told him. "Nobody is yelling. I would have expected maybe a police presence or remote droids."

"Not for this," Jason said. "It's more of a flash thing. Don't worry."

The closer he got to the cluster of people, the more they

seemed to notice and cast wary glances at him. Larken moved to walk abreast of Jocelyn, and Greg walked behind.

"What do you think?" Larken whispered.

"We haven't stopped talking this entire time," Jocelyn whispered back. "He's so much like me it hurts. He already invited me for drinks after the protest."

Larken looked at her closely, waiting for the implication of what Jocelyn had just said to become clear to her. After ten seconds of waiting, she pushed the issue.

"And *where* are you planning on going for drinks, Ms. Reed?"

"What do you mean?"

"Last I checked, the drinking age was still eighteen."

Jocelyn's eyes shot wide before she immediately furrowed her eyebrows.

"That is a problem," she replied. "Maybe we'll go to his place."

"That seems like a mistake," Larken stated the obvious, then looked ahead to see that Jason was still preoccupied before turning back to Jocelyn. "Look at this protest. There's *nobody* here. He made it up just to get you to come out. Maybe *he's* stalking *you*."

Jocelyn shook her head, swinging her shoulder-length blonde hair around to settle back in a perfect upside-down u-shape.

"Well, maybe. But this seems like a lot of trouble to go through."

A girl about Jason's age with splotchy makeup and a too-easy smile trotted toward them.

"Are you here for the protest?" the girl asked.

"Thank Coru. I thought we got the date wrong."

"You're a dork," volunteered Larken.

"No, you're in the right place. The *Portland Inquisitor* labeled our protest as hate-based. This is all we got," said the girl.

Greg whispered from behind Larken—much *closer* than she'd thought he was.

"Liberal rag," he said. "They claim that androids and artificial intelligence qualify as sentient."

"How do they think that? Don't companies *make* those things?" asked Jocelyn.

"It comes back to lifting the Madison Rule, they said. What's a 'Madison Rule'?"

"The law that keeps models in their place," recalled Larken. "I don't get this protest. What's the difference between engineered models and machines? How can one be considered sentient and the other not?"

"My replicator should have rights too? It talks back to me," said the girl. "It says 'your food is ready.'"

Larken closed her mouth and wrapped her fingers around her elbows, shrugging herself away from Gregory. The girl seemed to notice her discomfort and extended a hand, morphing her sardonic smile into a deep, welcoming one.

"My name is Jessica," she said as Larken reciprocated her handshake. "I know there's a difference between a toaster and an android. But there are already prototypes of volantrae flying around with onboard AI. How much different can that be from android AI? And where does it stop? It's a slippery slope, and one that we're better off not sliding down."

No families Larken knew could afford an actual android. Not even Brighton Academy had one, as flush with money as the institution was from high-profile alums. She'd never *seen* an android outside of ads and guessed that nobody in the protest group had either. For all Larken knew, androids could have been a scam to give people something to fight over. Jason seemed convinced otherwise, though. He nodded vehemently along with Jessica.

"Exactly. Do they get to vote next? It's the same as the models. Everybody wants rights that they didn't earn," Jason said. A flash caught Larken's eye and Jason's simultaneously as they both spun their heads to the left. "That news leak might be exactly what we need. Look over there."

He pointed to one of the nearby shops where a news anchor worked hard to be interested in anything other than their group. Larken turned away immediately. News crew meant cameras, and that meant identification as Brighton students. Jocelyn could kiss her beau goodbye when that happened, not to mention whatever trouble they got into for sneaking out.

"Jocelyn, we can't be on camera," she whispered. "They'll kick us out of school."

Greg overheard and leaned in. "No, they won't. Even as liberal as Protégé is, they won't kick you out for this. A slap on the wrist at most. It's not a hate thing. We don't hate androids. They have a place, and so do we."

Larken grabbed Jocelyn by the hand. Jocelyn resisted, pulling back to stay with the group. Larken tugged harder and finally got Jocelyn to move but not until after Jocelyn offered an apologetic smile to Jason. Larken mentally kicked herself for not thinking that the protest, of course, would draw some media attention.

"We need to go," she commanded as Jocelyn shuffled after her.

"Bye, guys," Jocelyn grumbled through clenched teeth. She all but stomped after Larken as the two of them left the crowd. Larken glanced back at the group, who mostly seemed to fall into a confused silence as a fourth of their number disappeared. The boys' feet slapped the pavement behind her a moment later. First, one set of shoes, then another, and she squeezed Jocelyn's hand.

"See," she whispered. "It's not a problem. Jason's coming too."

This seemed to brighten Jocelyn's fallen features. Jason scooted up beside Jocelyn, and Greg did the same on Larken's side.

"It's just a protest," Jason said. "It won't get you in trouble."

"We're not going to a hate protest," Larken said, irritated that he either didn't hear her or didn't care.

"That's fine," Greg said, holding his hands up and slowing his gait. "We're not trying to convince you to."

Larken looked at Jason, but he'd already moved on to chatting up Jocelyn, who beamed as though the sun revolved around her.

"Where are you going, then? Can we come?" Greg asked, and Larken realized that Jocelyn had stopped walking beside her and had fallen a few steps behind with Jason attached to her side. Larken had somehow become the leader. She couldn't take the group back to Brighton Academy. Her mind scrambled as she thought of the different places she liked to go, dismissing each as she realized how typically Brighton she was. The Coffee Hut on First Street was a standard Brighton student hangout, as was the Prosser National Library on Fifth—which they were dressed entirely wrong for anyway.

"Let's go to Banneker Books," Greg suggested only to Larken. "They host games on Wednesdays. That'll give these two a chance to geek out together. And Banneker has coffee, which honestly I could use right now."

"And booze," Jason interrupted.

Greg seemed slightly annoyed at this and ignored Jason. The power dynamic between them seemed different than it had before. At first, Larken had thought Jason was the more dominant of the duo. But it seemed now that Jason was more the fringe friend, like Jocelyn, who lived partly in the "real world" and spent much of his time in his head instead. They seemed a perfect match, and Larken decided then that if it took being bored for hours while Jocelyn and Jason bonded over gaming to make that relationship work, she would do it. She gave Greg a silent nod, and he grinned in response.

"Besides," he said, stepping closer toward her. "That will give us time to know each other. So far, all I know is your name."

"How do you get to Banneker from here?"

"Seriously? You can't miss it. It's halfway down First Street on this same strata level. We're only a few blocks away."

"I've never been."

He eyed her with suspicion.

"Everyone from Protégé goes to Banneker Books. You've missed out." He grinned. "Allow me to be your guide."

They only had to turn a single corner before a monstrosity of a building blotted out the sky. Spanning four strata, the south entrance of Banneker Books hid multiple escalators that Larken saw only after entering, each one going to a different level and extending into the sky. Aisles of thin pinamu tablet spines filled the shelves before her like a confused, never-ending rainbow. One sign, projected above the longest escalator, read "Paperback Section" and seemed barely larger than Larken's dormitory room. She could see the thicker, varying spines of paperback books she knew she would never have the money to buy.

Larken focused on keeping her mouth from falling open as she followed Greg. The group split in two as Jason and Jocelyn descended toward Strata 0, where an Underworlder game was underway in the dregs. Greg and Larken went up, instead, toward Strata 2, where they settled into a tiny café that overlooked a central courtyard. Once seated and with coffees in hand, Larken finally felt her nerves settle after the failed protest.

"Did you always live in Portland?" Greg asked. She gave a slight nod as she carefully sipped on her mocha. "I thought so. I'm a transfer. Typical, I guess. I was going to school up in Bellingham. My first time away from home. It didn't work out there."

"Where was home?"

"Vancouver," he said, nodding to the north. Larken knew where Vancouver was conceptually, but she'd never been there, even though it was only a five-minute volantrae ride.

Greg didn't ask anything else for a full ten seconds. They both sipped their drinks and dodged each other's eyes. Larken's newfound sense of comfort evaporated under the weight of avoiding scrutiny. She wished she could leave, but not enough to force Jocelyn to give up her evening. Larken almost choked on her coffee as her eyes fell on Elijah, scanning some tablets just beyond the coffee area. Greg picked up on her look and followed it before she could correct herself.

"Who's that?" he asked, motioning toward them. "People you know?"

"No," she said, not convincingly at all. Trying to back out, she said, "Just someone I thought I knew."

She was sure it was him. Via was with him. As Larken made to turn away, Elijah grinned wide and waved, destroying any chance of Larken convincing Greg of her ignorance. The pair closed the distance between them and Larken and Greg.

"They seem to know you," Greg whispered as they approached.

"I was wrong. I think I do know them." Her mind raced as she thought through possible explanations to offer Greg as to why she knew these two Brighton Academy students. Elijah and Via stopped at their table, and Elijah was the first to speak.

"Larken, right?" he said. Via stared at Greg as though he were made of chocolate. Larken nodded, struggling with a way of signaling the pair to avoid mentioning Brighton.

"We're leaving Brighton," Via said. "Tonight only. Want to see the town."

Well, that didn't work.

A deep burning sensation spread across Larken's face as her gaze turned to Greg, who pushed back from the table.

"What?"

"Our school," Elijah explained as Larken's hands and face met, suspending her hair around her head in a vain attempt to conceal her embarrassment. Greg twisted his head around from Via toward Larken.

"You're a Brighton student? But you don't look...I mean..."

He stuttered and stood, then took a step backward,

running into his chair. Larken clamped her mouth shut. Anything she said would damage Jocelyn's rapidly evaporating chance at happiness with someone so clearly her soulmate.

On the positive side, Greg didn't seem to see the likeness between Elijah and Larken. Or if he did, that wasn't his priority. Elijah seemed to pick up on the anxiety in the air while Via's eyes roamed the room free of obligation.

Elijah interjected, "Larken graduates this summer."

Larken played along.

"I'm taking classes at Protégé, remember?"

The confused look passed from Gregory's face, followed by a look of relief.

"Well, then," he said, grinning. He stuck his hand out for Elijah. "Gregory, but friends call me Greg. Are you taking classes too?"

"Greg, hi," Elijah replied. "Advanced course. It's a pleasure to meet you." Then as an afterthought, he said, "This is Via, and I'm Elijah." Elijah turned a direct stare at Via and seemed to focus his willpower on her reaction. "We're all in the same programs at Brighton, right, Via?"

Via wasn't paying attention. Her eyes followed a girl tapping her feet while riding up the escalator. A lime-green dress flowed around the girl's ankles.

"What's up with her?" Larken asked, eager to move the subject along.

Elijah shrugged. "She does that sometimes."

The conversation flowed on after that, though Greg peeled himself away from Larken during their talk. He no longer hung on every word she said. Whatever interest he had had before seemed to have disappeared with the knowledge that she attended Brighton. That made her life easier, as she didn't have to work to keep him at bay or deflect prying questions any longer. But part of her missed the way he had obsessed over her. Now he seemed to distribute his attention among all three of them carefully.

That wasn't her primary concern. She had to tell Jocelyn somehow that their story had changed. Or did she? Just because she and Jocelyn hung out together didn't mean Jocelyn was also a Brighton student. They could play that off with a bit of work. Jocelyn could have graduated Brighton the year before, and they were still friends, Larken being a *senior* now.

Larken glanced upward toward Strata 3 above, and she saw the outlines of a dance club in bright neon pinks and greens, coupled with a landing platform for a bus. Squinting her eyes, she made out the number nineteen. Seeing that brought her mind back into Brighton as she longed for the warmth of her bedroom. Only now, she equally longed for the opportunity to catch Molly. The idea of them going to sleep angry with each other set her heart racing and her mind scrambling.

"Greg," she said, careful with her annunciation of his name to say it the way he had. "Should we go get Jason and Jocelyn? I think it's time for me to head back."

He seemed far too enthusiastic as he replied. "Sure, Larken. Love too." He bolted down the far escalator without looking back.

Larken pulled another draught from the room-tempera-ture remainder of her Arabica beans, cacao, and synthetic milk foam. The lighting. That had to be why Greg over-looked her doppelgänger. The lighting was speakeasy dim. She looked at Elijah and smiled.

"Thanks."

"Don't mention it. I think he bought it. Is everything okay?"

Via grunted at something and scratched her cheek. Larken nodded.

"Not my problem anyway. This is Jocelyn's thing, and I'm just trying not to blow it for her."

She shook her head. No reason to say more. Larken glanced after Greg to make sure he wasn't coming back immediately.

"Why do you look so much like me?" she asked Elijah, who only shook his head.

"It's weird having a chick that looks like me running around campus. Sometimes people look the same, I guess. It happens."

Larken shook her head.

"Not like this. It's like you're my twin. I already have one of those." Larken pondered what to say next. The feeling that spun around in her chest pinched at her insides. It was familiar, but she couldn't quite name it.

"There's a ninety-eight percent chance that Elijah is related to you."

Larken's jaw dropped open. Elijah gave a half-smile that didn't reach his eyes.

Via continued unperturbed. "You were born on the same day."

"Was it a Monday?" Larken tried to joke. She and Oliver had looked up their birthday many times. January 31, 2185 was a Monday. They'd often joked about being "fair of face," but it was true about Oliver. Once she started wearing makeup, Larken felt she could also say that about herself on good makeup days.

"Fair of face," Elijah laughed at first, then stopped as recognition spread across his face. "How did you guess?"

"January 31, 2185," Via stated. "Monday."

The blood drained from Larken's face.

"That's impossible."

"What's impossible?" the voice behind her chimed in. She turned to see that Greg had made it back without them noticing. Larken turned back to Elijah, imploring him for help, too rattled by the discovery. Elijah didn't disappoint.

"Lofting match earlier," he said. "It was an upset. The Angels lost two to one."

Greg grinned and seemed to relax, embracing the new conversation turn.

"That was ridiculous. It was a good game, though. Did you see when Turner cast the ball past Wiley and scored? *That* was epic."

"Yeah. Wiley got her back the next round...setting for Moreno like that."

The conversation continued, and Larken contributed nothing to it, though she knew lofting better than either participant. Instead, she processed that Elijah had been born on the same date that she had. She turned to Via to whisper the obvious next question while she let Elijah and Greg pine away about lofting teams.

"How did you know my birthday?"

Via smiled that creepy grin. Her eyes focused somewhere in the background. "January 31, 2185. A Monday. An auspicious day for us all."

"W...what?" Larken asked. "I guess so. It's better to be born than not born, I suppose."

"Not born," Via said. "All of us."

"Why are you..."

She wanted to say "so strange" but couldn't think of a way to ask it politely. Via's eyes floated, never seeming to focus on anything for longer than half a second. For the first time, Larken noticed their color and their shape. Via didn't look a thing like her or Elijah. But Larken knew those eyes. Those eyes belonged to Oliver.

"You too? January 31, 2185?"

Via nodded. Her eyes shifted again, moving on to a man with hair pulled back into braids with the sides of his head shaved. The man gave Via a wary glance and then focused on the escalator steps before him. A second later, Via seemed to remember she was in a conversation again.

"Sorry. I don't talk well."

"I think you communicate just fine," Larken lied, but it was a worthwhile lie. Via continued staring after the man, but her lips curled up into a thin smile.

"No, I don't," she said, pulling her eyes back toward Larken in a movement that seemed to take some effort. "I get distracted."

As if to emphasize, her glance shifted past Larken again, focusing on something behind her.

"Jocelyn," Via said. Larken turned to see Jason and Jocelyn approaching. Jason's arms were wrapped around Jocelyn's shoulders. In Jocelyn's hands was another trophy, larger than the one in her room. Jason had a matching one in his arm opposite her.

"Congratulations?" Larken called out, breaking Elijah and Greg from their lofting-induced sidebar.

"Congrats," Greg said. "Again. You two are unstoppable. I see you won the random match tourney."

"We did," Jocelyn said. "We were spectacular. You

should have seen us, Larken. It was like music. We dodged, parried, struck—all in concert together."

"I heard you want to head back to Brighton," Jason said, grinning in the afterglow of the victory. Larken spared a glance for Jocelyn, who seemed unfazed that he knew.

"We have to," Larken said. "Early days there and then college...makes for a long day."

Jocelyn's look didn't waiver. She must have figured out the deception and been playing along.

"If you're on campus tomorrow, come by the quad," Greg told her. "We hang out there most days. That's the easiest place to study."

"We'll think about it," Jocelyn said with a flirty smile, aiming her words at Jason.

"Well, don't think too hard," he said. "I will think of you the entire time we're apart."

The two kissed, and Larken wondered just how long it would be before Jocelyn told Jason her actual age. That was a break-up she didn't want to be anywhere near. She grabbed Jocelyn's hand and pulled her away.

"Let's go," she said, flashing a smile at Gregory. "Thank you for an entertaining evening."

"Of course," he said warmly, responding with a thin grin. "See ya, Brighton."

She forced down a blush while pulling Jocelyn after her. As she walked away, she heard Elijah making his goodbye and Via saying something about how volantrae used to be called "flying cars" until the discovery of distributed ion engines made it possible to build them in almost any shape... blah, blah, blah. Greg and Jason were courteous enough to laugh in response politely. Larken heard Elijah and Via start after her and Jocelyn as they made their way up to the number nineteen that would ultimately deliver them back to the Angel of Knowledge.

Back in their room, Jocelyn fell asleep almost as soon as she put her head on her pillow without even bothering to clear the mess from her bunk. No sign of Molly, but Larken didn't care. She had a new problem to puzzle over. As Jocelyn snored, Larken turned over the coincidence of four same-day births in her mind. She asked herself the same questions repeatedly but got no answers, at least none she was willing to accept.

CHAPTER 6
PLANNING A WEEKEND
GETAWAY

LARKEN AWOKE to blackness and thunder. The wind scraped branches against their dorm room window as the remnants of a dream still echoed in her mind. The sound of driving rain and darkness chased away the buzz of fluorescent overhead lights of her dreamscape. Vague recollections of analgesic odors and clanking instruments followed. Otherwise, Larken could remember nothing except the sense of terror clamping down onto her chest as tightly as she clung to the bedsheets.

Larken escaped the bed and drove her feet into her slippers covered in various treatments of the number "86"—the number of the starting forward for the Angels. She slogged her way toward the door across the hardwood. The morning alarm would sound in twenty-two minutes by the projected wall clock. Molly's bed was still unoccupied, exacerbating Larken's unnamed fear. Mild pain flared just beneath her belly, reminding her of her destination.

In the abandoned bathroom, rows of stalls all proved to

be available. Everyone else still slept. Larken helped herself to one, slid the door shut, and locked it.

Molly had been gone the entire night. Larken clenched her teeth as the idea took hold of her mind as to where Molly might be. In between boys and with her sights on Oliver, Larken had a guess as to where Molly was, and her opinion of her brother would plummet significantly if she was right.

Part of her hoped that Molly would get caught. Although for the life of her, Larken couldn't remember if there was a punishment for sneaking into the boys' dormitory. Probably just a lecture. Brighton Academy was big on talking things out. They didn't live in prison, after all.

When she left the bathroom, Larken still had a handful of minutes before the morning bell. She took the hall toward the guard's station on autopilot. The common area seemed unnaturally silent when she crossed and entered the labyrinthian hallways of the boys' wing. Whispers stopped her from simply pushing the door open when she arrived at number 206, Oliver's room. She longed to enter raging with righteous indignation. She stalled outside the door, seduced by the ebb and flow of secrets shared between confidants. One of those voices was Molly, muttering something unintelligible to Larken. Oliver's deep tenor passed through clearly.

"She'll find out," Oliver said.

"Who cares? She needs to know, and this isn't working, Oliver."

The note of agitation brought Larken closer to the door after a quick check for hallway traffic. The sound of her drumming heart nearly overpowered her hearing. Molly's voice cut through as Larken pressed her ear against the door.

"No, and that's the end of it, Molly. She won't understand."

"You tell her or I will."

"An ultimatum?"

Larken couldn't tell if the lump in her chest was due to rage at the confirmation of what she'd suspected or guilt because her brother didn't trust her to let him make his own decisions. If she was honest, though, spending a night with Molly on a campus that didn't hold its secrets well didn't exactly strike her as good judgment.

"Don't you want her to know?"

"Sure. But you *know* Larken, at least as well as I do. If it could impact her lofting future, she won't do it."

She missed something in her self-indulgent rumination. The pair had switched topics and she hadn't heard the end of the last conversation. But it didn't matter. Larken's throat seized up. Whatever Oliver and Molly were talking about, it wasn't fair of either of them to exclude her based on what Larken *might* do. Her eyes welled up at the notion that they had drifted apart so entirely that Oliver didn't even think he could *talk* to her about whatever it was. Larken forced a swallow.

"Larken and Elijah are identical. Do you think he's related to you two?"

"I don't know what to think, Mol," Oliver said.

Mol? After two days, he had a cutesy nickname for her. Larken rolled her eyes.

"He's from Our Lady Guadalupe, right? We could ask them for records. It doesn't have to be a big deal."

"How far is it to Our Lady Guadalupe, do you remember?"

"Texas. I was thinking we could just call them."

"Sure, you could do that," Molly suggested. "Or we could..."

Molly trailed off. Larken couldn't hear what it was she'd suggested. But she told herself that she'd found Molly and that Molly was fine. More than fine. Molly was living her dream and shacking up or doing whatever she was doing with Oliver. Whether Molly felt guilty about it or not, Larken felt betrayed by Molly's presence in Oliver's room, especially after she'd expressly told Molly that she didn't approve.

Larken felt her chest tighten, and the sharp points of her fingernails digging into her palms. She forced herself to relax her clenched fists. She compelled herself to breathe through the pain. Larken tried rationalizing her problems away.

Molly and Oliver had spent the night together. It didn't mean much. No big deal. It was none of her business. Sure, it set off alarm bells how quickly Molly had moved, but it wasn't Larken's right to say anything about it. Except that it was her brother. Larken forced herself to turn away from the door if only for the fact that if she got caught there, nobody would care about Molly and Oliver anywhere near as much as her eavesdropping.

Larken tiptoed her way back to her room, ignoring the sounds of waking that seemed to follow her down the hallway. Back inside, Jocelyn still snored beneath the new trophy she'd just added to her collection. Larken willed herself to reset the day. She shoved under her blankets and tried to sleep until the sun broke through her bedroom window. Less than three minutes later, an annoying buzzing told her it was time to rise so she admitted defeat.

But Larken wasn't ready to get up. She retrieved an orange box from beneath her bed and leafed through her collection of letters. They were all the same, and none of them held the secrets of her origin. Flustered, she tossed the one in her hand at the box and watched it glide to the floor when it missed.

"What are you doing?" Jocelyn's sleepy voice asked.

"Looking for a postmark," Larken suggested absently, picking the letter back up and examining a few more closely.

"Didn't you do that already?"

Larken nodded and shrugged and looked anyway. "You never know." She laid the envelopes back into the box and turned her attention to Jocelyn's problems—much less anxiety-producing than her own.

"So you and dreamy Jason," Larken said. "Did you get his ansible number?"

"What do *you* think?" Jocelyn said, her sleep-filled eyes opening wider. "And we're going out this weekend."

"Does he know how young you are?"

Jocelyn only smiled...until her gaze fell on the empty bed that Molly usually occupied.

"I guess it's just the two of us for breakfast," she said, too casually. Larken tried to read how much Jocelyn knew from her body language. Whatever secret she was keeping, Jocelyn seemed intent to hold onto it.

"I hope she makes it to class on time," was Larken's only response. Larken broke her dark eyes away from Jocelyn's blue ones and shifted her weight. She rolled out of bed for the second time that morning and back into her fuzzy slippers while Jocelyn rubbed more sleep out of her eyes. Twenty minutes and two laser showers later, both girls shuffled down the hallway together, dressed and carrying bags but otherwise zombies.

They found Molly in the common area, still wearing her clothes from the evening before and presenting nothing resembling embarrassment. Larken didn't think Molly was capable of that particular emotion. Molly waved them over and away from the line for the replicator.

"You're up! Good. We're meeting the group for breakfast in the cafeteria. Want to join?"

Larken took a deep breath.

"We'll come," she said, then glanced to Jocelyn, whose mouth hung open. The sleep seemed to have left her eyes. Jocelyn gave a thin eek and cut across the café to throw her arms around Molly, nearly knocking her over. Larken followed behind and did not eek. She craved the comfort of her blankets.

"Where were you?" Jocelyn asked in a harsh whisper. "Did you even come back to the room?"

"Eat with us. We ran into Elijah this morning, and there's a lot to talk about."

"Who is 'us'?"

Molly didn't answer.

"Elijah's there?"

"Yes. And Via too, I think, mostly. But it's so hard to tell with her."

"Won't people talk when they see me and Elijah side-by-side?"

"Larken, people are *already* talking. There's no use in hiding from it. Besides, as I said, there's a lot to discuss."

Like Our Lady Guadalupe, Larken thought.

Elijah and Via's plates were empty by the time the four of them arrived at the table. Oliver nodded once in Larken's direction and shifted over to make room beside him for her to sit. The cold metal bench chilled enough to penetrate Larken's rubberized leggings.

"I'm sorry," he said before she could get a word out. "I should have told you about Fouriedon. I should have let you know. You're my only sister."

His eyes drifted toward Molly, and Larken's eyes followed. Molly's tented up and glistened as she looked on, yet she said nothing. Instead, Molly took the seat on Oliver's far side, so close that she almost landed in his lap. Jocelyn took the last space farther down so that the four sat on one side of the table while Via and Elijah sat on the other.

"What do you all want to eat?" Elijah asked and took orders for everyone. It was only the cafeteria and made no sense. Still, Larken thought it polite and passed on that she wanted eggs with toast. Via went to fetch the food after, which concerned Larken as it introduced an element of uncertainty in whatever Via might bring back.

"Are we having a secret meeting?" whispered Jocelyn.

"You don't need to whisper," Larken told her. She couldn't help smiling that Jocelyn once again pointed out exactly what the clandestine atmosphere felt like. "Nobody's listening."

Occasionally a student did a double-take when passing, and Larken knew they were comparing her to Elijah, who for some reason it didn't seem to bother. Maybe he didn't know that some of those individuals also concocted theories about *why* the two of them looked so much alike. It was inevitable that the rumor that they were all clones would start. And probably Anthony Lee would be the one to create it.

"Eighty thousand dollars," Oliver said, addressing Larken in an aside, in a low whisper. "That's our spending money this time."

"Why so much?"

Usually, the trust freed a few thousand a year for

spending money, though it had gone up the year before by double. Oliver shrugged. It was possible that as they got older, they simply got more money.

The whisper must have carried since Elijah perked up at the mention of so much money, but he seemed to catch himself gawking, and his eyes widened and then narrowed again.

"Our Lady Guadalupe," Oliver said, cutting to the point. "Molly and I have been talking—"

"*Talking* is what we're calling it now?" Jocelyn asked. Molly glared at her, and Larken glared at Molly. Molly didn't even look at Larken to try to deny it.

Oliver continued, "We've been *talking*, and this is too much to be a coincidence. Molly thinks we may have been switched at birth or something."

"Or maybe we're *models*," Via said loud enough to garner looks from the other students nearby. Larken raised her hand in the universal sign to quiet down. Via only repeated the last word, this time in a whisper but otherwise just as loud as before. "Models."

"No," Molly said, shaking her head. "Models are engineered for things like beauty, build, and intellect. You don't look like any models I've ever seen, and my mother represents models all the time at Walsh and Moody." She turned to Larken and offered what seemed like a failed effort at an apology, "Not that you're not beautiful, Larken. You're just not *Caldwell* beautiful, but neither am I. Nobody, I mean..."

"It's okay, Molly," Larken snapped. "It's fine. I have bushy eyebrows and a big nose. Nobody will confuse me with a glorified sex doll."

"But...," Molly continued with a slight smile, "you are the queen of all lofting. Maybe you could be a Briggs?"

Larken didn't respond.

"Nah," Jocelyn said, chewing thoughtfully on the end of a sausage. She swallowed. "Larken's good, but not *impossibly* good. Not a fighter either. And remember that *drama club* adventure in junior high? Larken, *I* think you're pretty enough to be a Caldwell."

Larken smiled to let Jocelyn know that she wasn't angry with *her*.

"Briggs models are vicious competitors. You're too *nice*, Larken. Caldwells are made to *love* though," Jocelyn said, matter-of-factly, then chewed thoughtfully on her lower lip. "No. I don't think either describes you. Maybe if a Briggs and a Caldwell had an illegitimate child though?"

Elijah slammed down a plate with two cinnamon rolls and an egg in front of Larken.

"I think you look like a Caldwell," he said with a mischievous grin. She met his eyes, looking into her reflection. "We're two sexy bitches."

"I bet you do," she said, admiring how much better her eyebrows worked for him instead of how they worked against her. Even her furious plucking couldn't fully tame her threatening unibrow.

"I heard you love cinnamon rolls," Elijah said, shoving the plate closer to her. The smell of cinnamon and icing drifted into her nostrils and made her salivate. Whoever Elijah had been talking to had been right about Larken's fixation on cinnamon rolls, but she had questions and needed answers. Eating would have to wait. She turned back to Molly, leaving the delicious aromas and light, flaky dough to rapidly cool in the chill of the sanitary cafeteria air.

"Are you planning to *go* to Our Lady Guadalupe? Seems like a lot of work to satisfy curiosity."

Molly said, "A flight out of PDX flies into Dallas direct."

"And you want to use our school money to do it," Larken asked, rubbing her forehead.

"*My* school money," Oliver said. "But only some of it. Just Molly and I should run only about two thousand for one round-trip ticket."

Larken's mouth dropped open. Oliver seemed poised and waiting for her to respond. One day. One day and they were planning trips together. She squeezed her eyes shut and shook her head.

"It's only a weekend. That shouldn't be too bad," she replied, mostly to herself.

"I'll come too," said Elijah. "And I think Via probably will want to."

Via said nothing, engrossed in the other tables of chatting and laughing students. Something about her seemed serene at that moment, without the jerky mannerisms and incomplete thoughts that she tended to utter. She appeared as content as a goldfish as her unblinking gaze soaked up the scenery. Larken followed that gaze to its conclusion where Anthony Lee leaned against a table near the empty guard's desk.

When Anthony met Larken's gaze, he winked. Then his eyes slowly moved from her to Elijah, a subtle movement of focus that she only picked up on when he did it a second time. Larken glared.

"Don't worry about him," Molly said. "He's just bluster."

Susan, Isaac, and Sun also stared. Molly's attempts at consolation seemed to Larken remarkably close to denial. A fair number of students at nearby tables were also staring. As Larken had suspected, the resemblance drew a lot more attention when they were together.

"Remember what happened last year," Larken said.

"That wasn't *Anthony*."

"It was the Human Pride Movement, and who's to say it wasn't him? Nobody admitted to it, and nobody was caught. The teachers all sort of wished it away."

"It wasn't him, Larken," Molly repeated, firmed her voice, and fixated on Larken. Under that gaze, Larken thought back through reasons why Molly could be so sure and only remembered then who it was that Molly had been dating at the time: Anthony Lee.

"Oh," she said, careful not to mention anything else about it in front of Oliver. "But it could have been Susan or any of the rest."

"Let it go, Larken. Just because they're assholes doesn't mean they'd *do* anything. Most people talk more than they act. It's bluster, and he's just being a dick for attention."

Larken once again shut her mouth, keeping her fears to herself. She seemed to be the only one who detected the stares and the hushed voices nearby. At least, she believed that until Jocelyn's hand landed on her shoulder with a gentle squeeze.

"I think you're right," Jocelyn whispered as the rest of the group moved on to planning their adventure. "Anthony is a problem, and have you seen how people look at us? Look at you?"

Grateful to have an ally, Larken nodded. "I *know*. It's like nobody else notices."

"I don't think they *want* to. Sometimes people only see what they want to see."

Larken turned her face up to Jocelyn's.

"This trip is dangerous too," she said. "What if something happens on the way? What if Anthony tries something while they're gone, like breaks into Oliver's room and trashes it or something?"

Jocelyn shook her head.

"I think the trip would be a good thing," Jocelyn said, her allegiance having met its end. "Out of sight is out of mind, and it *is* Friday. If you all weren't here this weekend, then it might give things time to cool off."

"You all? I'm not going."

"Maybe you should."

"Assume I did," Larken suggested. "It would give them time to plan with impunity. We could come back walking right into a mess."

Jocelyn shrugged.

"You're giving Anthony and his crew too much credit," Jocelyn said. "They'd never be able to do anything too terrible. Oliver's popular here, and his roommate will still be here batting for him. I'm here too. We can keep things under control until you all get back."

"You still seem to think I'm going."

Jocelyn's confidence is ill-founded, Larken thought. The two of them never "kept things under control." Molly was the one who solved the social problems the group came across. Jocelyn was like a well-meaning yet socially obtuse confidant, but what choice did she have?

If Larken thought more deeply about the matter, as her churning mind insisted, she knew there was more to her discomfort than Anthony. The insidious talons of jealousy clawed at her heart, however much she loved Molly and Oliver both. Unbidden images accosted her of Oliver and Molly's "investigation" in a hotel room half a country away. She took one deep breath, then another, swallowed, and squeezed Jocelyn's fingers on her shoulder. None. Of. Her.

Business. And definitely not something she wanted to experience firsthand.

Among the flood of images her mind insisted she see, she caught a glimpse of fluorescent lights again, flashing row after row as she zipped past. Bits of her dream came back, forcing themselves through. Pain in her chest, immobile and strapped down to something flat, she watched lights go by and struggled for breath.

Then it was gone. She sucked in the air and realized that she'd clutched Jocelyn's fingers to the point of turning them bright red before letting go. Tears had collected in her eyes, and Oliver had turned his attention to her as he spoke, addressing a question that Elijah had posed. His face turned inquisitive. Larken blinked the tears back and forced a smile, accented by a quick nod. Oliver nodded and turned his full attention to the impromptu planning session, waving his arms through the air as he described how the plan would work with Elijah's most recent modifications.

CHAPTER 7

TEXAS OR BUST

IN A DAY AND A HALF, Molly and Oliver had become as inseparable as a twenty-second-century pop duo, and Larken was sick of it. Seeing her brother moon-eyed over Molly as they continued to hint at and develop their weekend getaway/family research trip turned her stomach.

And Larken kind of thought it was sweet.

And it turned her stomach.

By the final day before the trip, part of her was glad they were leaving without her. At the very least, she could get off the emotional rollercoaster her life had become and pretend to be normal. No Oliver and Molly, no Elijah and Via. Larken was looking forward to a few days of nothing but lofting practice.

The day of departure was pleasantly uneventful. Larken went through the motions of attending classes, studying in her room, and eavesdropping on the trip planning. She occasionally tried to convince the group that the trip was a waste of time and they could only submit a digitally-signed authorization (via ansible) request. The excitement of being unsupervised for an entire weekend seemed to make the trip worth it to them. It had morphed from an idea into an adventure.

"We'll pay a premium for the seats," Oliver said, standing dangerously close to something that resembled poison ivy while leaning against the pavilion after school let out.

"It wouldn't have made any difference if we'd bought them on Wednesday. We'd still have had to pay full price," Molly reminded him. Elijah leaned against the inside of the gazebo entrance, just licked by the setting sun. Larken took up the only bench, entirely in the shade.

"Student discount?" she offered.

Molly shook her head. "Not enough to matter. For Brighton, anyway. *Protégé* students do."

"We can afford it," Oliver said, addressing Larken by the direction of his eyes. "Just budget a bit more afterward, that's all."

"Maybe we can get a rental volantrae instead."

Elijah shook his head. "Nobody would rent to us. High risk or something. We could rent a *car*," he said, "but not a volantrae. And a car would take all weekend to get there."

The Angels played the next night, and not having Molly and Oliver around while watching lofting suddenly seemed the way to go.

"I don't understand. Why couldn't you call or email?"

"Because it would be less fun," Via said without a smile.

"Of course," Larken replied, looking at Via, amazed that Via understood what was happening around her behind those wandering eyes.

"Can we focus?" Oliver asked. "If we want to fly, the plane leaves in two hours. I'll buy the tickets. Meet at the bus stop on Eighth."

. . .

An hour and a half later, Larken lay supine on her bed. She tossed a lofting ball and caught it over and over again. Jocelyn tried to start up a conversation. Larken responded to her prods and nudges with terse single-word replies. She was too intent on wondering where Molly was and how she expected to leave in less than thirty minutes without packing. And then Larken reminded herself to butt out of other people's affairs.

Molly burst through the door. Her body shook, and she opened her mouth to speak, but no words came forth. Tiny beads of sweat pocked her forehead, and she scanned the room twice just after she entered. Molly's eyes furrowed together in a tent above downturned lips. Larken's heart pounded in response as she felt her legs tense up. She caught the ball and held it.

"What happened? Did Anthony do something?" Although Larken pitched Anthony's name, she had no idea why the boy loomed so large in her mind. Molly was right. He was mostly talk. Jocelyn yanked her head out of a gaming manual.

"They took your brother, Larken," Molly said. "Two officers burst right into his room and grabbed him. They left his roommate and me and took him."

"What...why?"

Molly shook her head furiously, sending her straight hair into arcs around her face.

"They said he had the right to remain silent."

"They *arrested* him? For what?"

"Our trip? Do you think they found out?"

Larken could have laughed had her brother not just been

taken. Molly didn't seem to be thinking clearly—another strange thing for her roommate, but sometimes she reverted to almost childlike innocence. It was a defense mechanism, Larken guessed, and she'd seen it before.

"Skipping out of Brighton is a disciplinary problem that doesn't require cops, Molly."

Their door flung open for a second time, and a portly, matronly woman in a bright-red pantsuit stood in the doorway.

"Ms. Marche," was all she said.

"Ms. Carrish?"

"Duty tonight," Ms. Carrish said, answering the unasked question of why she was there. The severely-dressed woman tilted her feather-capped head upward to ensure that she could look down her nose at Larken. Ms. Carrish then glanced at Molly before settling back on Larken again.

"You're probably aware of your brother's...situation?"

Larken nodded mutely. Molly side-stepped toward the door.

"You may as well stay, Molly, so I only have to say this once. No doubt you'll hear about it soon enough."

Molly stopped.

"What was he arrested for?"

The woman didn't say at first. She lowered her gaze to meet Larken's.

"A grave crime that I can't disclose to students. Do you know anything about what he might have been doing last weekend?"

"He hasn't done *anything*. Study for finals maybe— or entrance exams—or whatever."

The woman cast one look at the packed bag on Larken's bunk.

"Right," she replied, notably not commenting on the luggage. "We've informed the police and will do everything in our power to ensure his safe return."

"Do they have proof that he did whatever it was?" Larken asked.

"I don't know. It was a very short conversation. I think DNA or fingerprints or something." She paused, exhaled slowly, and said, "I'm sure it's a mix-up, though, Larken. Your benefactor has been informed. He's authorized us to pull funds from your trust for defense purposes. We'll get to the bottom of this."

Her words dripped out of her mouth like the drip of a leaky faucet. Five minutes before, the worst thing that Larken had to worry about was pissing her brother off. She felt herself sway as she stood and gathered her willpower to stay aloft, despite the growing weakness in her knees. Larken stumbled once and caught herself.

"Larken, please speak with our counselor. She'll be by to set an appointment," Ms. Carrish said, this time not hiding her look at the luggage, "I would consider not going to wherever it was you *think* you're going. It would not help his case if you suddenly disappeared."

Larken could only nod. The large woman turned, floated out of the room, and closed the door with a click behind her.

"What do we do?" Molly almost jumped as soon as the click sounded.

"There's nothing *to* do," Jocelyn said. "She said the counselor will be by, so we must wait. No trip. Someone should tell Elijah and Via."

"They know," Molly assured her. "I messaged them already."

"That stupid trip was a bad idea anyway," Jocelyn chimed.

"So you say now. You were all in helping to plan it, weren't you?"

"Just because I think it's a bad idea doesn't mean I want you to screw it up," Jocelyn said, with a dominance that made Larken step backward.

"I'll screw it up?" Molly replied.

"That's not what she meant," Larken said. "Can we focus on the fact that Oliver has been stolen away by the police?"

Molly stood like a lofting defensive end, like she would tackle Larken any second. She blamed Larken for Oliver's arrest. Larken could see it in her eyes even if Larken didn't understand why. Larken's eyes clouded as her pulse raced. She sought the words to bring Molly down, but she was horrible at these parlays. Larken slammed her eyelids shut and struggled to think through the building rage.

For Oliver.

She blew out through pursed lips and opened her eyes again. Molly now glared. There wasn't anything Larken could do, or that any of them could do for that matter. Molly's glare morphed suddenly into a deep look of concern as her eyes misted over.

"I'm sorry," she said, another unusual thing for Molly to do—apologize. Larken nodded.

"I know," she replied.

They sat in silence for five minutes before Jocelyn cleared her throat.

"You should take a trip," she said.

"Now? We can't possibly."

"Yes, you can. Not *that* trip. A different trip. Find your benefactor. He would have all the answers you would look for at Our Lady Guadalupe, wouldn't he? And are you sure he was told?"

Larken trusted the school faculty. As far as she knew, they'd never lied to her before. She shrugged.

"They already notified our benefactor," Larken said. "If he wanted to talk to me, he would. He doesn't."

"He needs to know the truth about the situation and not whatever watered-down version the school gave. They probably told him they had everything under control. You know, public relations."

"As Ms. Carrish said, they already told him," Larken said. "How do you sugarcoat your ward being arrested?"

"Exactly. That's what Ms. Carrish *said*," Molly said, as her eyes bounced with excitement. "But we don't know for sure."

"We don't know where he lives," Larken said. "No postmarks on anything he's sent to me anyway. Nothing."

"My guess? Seattle," Jocelyn says. "That stationery is all Mt. Rainier, anyway."

She motioned to the box where Larken kept her letters.

"I mean," she continued. "How many pictures of one mountain do you need?"

Larken managed a weak smile as she pulled out one of the cards. Sure enough, what she'd thought were abstract lines on the front formed something that looked like a stylized version of the mountain Jocelyn talked about. Larken hadn't put that together before, and she was slightly irritated that Jocelyn had only found *now* to be the right time to tell her.

"My mother was from League City," Larken protested. She knew at least that much.

"Maybe, but look at the summit. That's Mount Rainier,"

Jocelyn said. "And who has stationery around with someone else's mountain?"

"So you want us to go to Seattle?"

The idea was dumber than going to Our Lady Guadalupe. But on the scale of staring at the wall while slowly going insane and wasting time and money traveling to Seattle, Larken preferred the latter.

Jocelyn shook her head.

"No. That's just a guess. But you know who would know? The people who are taking your benefactor's money."

Molly's face scrunched as she thought.

"You mean to break into the file room."

"I was thinking labyrinth," Jocelyn said. "I mean, we could go downstairs and try our luck finding the file room door. That might be faster."

Deep in the basement of the girl's wing, there existed a room that held backup copies of all records about every student who had ever attended Brighton Academy—allegedly. And in those files somewhere must have been some tidbit of information that could tell them, if Seattle, *where* in Seattle to go on this substitute mission. Larken had misgivings, but also nursed a feeling that finding her benefactor would be much more helpful than talking about her feelings to the prison-guard counselor. Larken had already had too many of those types of talks.

"Okay then," she said. "Let's do it."

When Jocelyn grabbed her bag from the bed and stood, she dropped it to its wheels on the floor and looked at Molly.

"Where's your stuff?"

"Still in Oliver's room," she said.

"Uh, Larken?"

Larken turned to see Jocelyn poking at her pinamu tablet on her bunk.

"I think we need to figure this out soon. Things are going to get worse."

Jocelyn flashed the pinamu screen at Molly and Larken. There, on the news feed, a picture of Oliver's face filled the area. Across the bottom: Fugitive Apprehended in Bizarre Double-Homicide.

CHAPTER 8

CLANDESTINE CINNAMON ROLLS

"DOUBLE HOMICIDE? OLIVER?"

It made no sense. The headlines forced the reality of the situation, but Larken couldn't wrap her head around the idea. For the past at least six months, all Oliver had done was study. He didn't have much of a social life at all. The idea that he would even have left campus, aside from possibly visiting Protégé or some other university, seemed ludicrous.

"Coming?" Jocelyn asked, standing in the doorway.

The brightness of a skylight made Larken jump. Twilight loomed beyond the sparse windows, yet the sky was an unnatural yellow as it sometimes became after a thunderstorm.

Molly stepped briskly past Jocelyn to lead their scavenger hunt.

"This way," she said, steering them past the girls' mini-café. The smell of cinnamon rolls diverted Larken's gaze to a pile sitting inside of an opened replicator. Her stomach rumbled, and she guiltily thought whether another thirty seconds would change anything about Oliver's situation.

"We didn't eat dinner," Jocelyn said. "Maybe just one?"

"I wouldn't...," Molly started. Larken turned to look at Molly but stopped when she saw Jocelyn with sticky fingers and a smile on her face.

"Jocelyn?"

"I was hungry."

"Now you're going to leave sticky fingerprints all over everything. And besides, those weren't even yours," Molly said, piling on.

"What do you want, Molly? I'm hungry, and we're not going to stop for food soon. Cinnamon rolls are quick and easy."

Molly stared at Jocelyn without further comment. She turned through the door beyond the replicator and held it open, revealing the darkened staircase beyond. Larken gulped.

"After you," Molly said.

Larken summoned her courage and passed through first, then Jocelyn—once she'd finished licking her fingers. Molly pulled the door behind them until it latched and only the glow of exit signs lit the landings above and below them.

"The files are going to be locked up," Larken said. "And we don't have a key for the room. There's so much wrong with this plan."

"And we don't know where the room is," added Jocelyn.

"Maybe," Molly said. "I guess we should just go back to our room and talk to the counselor then?"

"You don't have to be a jerk about it."

"You're saying we should give up," Molly said, her face taking on a pinkish tone. "You're saying you don't want to do this, and we should give up and let Oliver fester in prison."

"They're not taking him to prison. Jail first. And Ms. Carrish said…"

Larken stopped as she realized that even *she* didn't believe anything she was saying.

"I'm upset too, Molly," Larken continued instead. "He's *my* brother, remember? I have a right to be nervous about the plan."

"You're busy trying to get us to give up. And, Jocelyn, coming along as though this is some grand adventure."

"Trying to be *supportive*," Jocelyn complained. "But I can see *that's* not appreciated."

In a huff, Jocelyn turned and pushed back past Larken toward the café. Larken longed to follow. They could find another way. When Molly got into this state, there wasn't much to be done about it.

"Jocelyn, come back. *I* appreciate you."

Jocelyn turned to her and smiled with sticky icing across her lips.

"I figured you did," she said. "I wasn't going to leave. It just seemed like a good opportunity for another cinnamon roll. Want one?"

She held up her hands. In one was a cinnamon roll about the size of her fist with a bite missing, and in the other a backup, Larken supposed. She shook her head.

"Can we go? I feel the sooner we get this over with, the better."

"Hey," Susan Priest's scratchy husky-for-her-age voice penetrated the air. "Stop that. Those are mine."

Larken extended a hand and took the backup cinnamon roll from Jocelyn. She took a slow and deliberate bite, feeling the richness of the icing coating her tongue. Susan's nostrils flared as she crossed the room and clenched her teeth hard enough for Larken to hear the grinding sound. Larken turned and ducked back into the stairwell, giggling, Jocelyn following close behind. The sweet icing took her mind off Oliver for half a second. Then, her eyes landed on Susan Priest standing in the cracked doorway, and the sweetness turned sour.

"Do you see that look? Glaring with those squinty little eyes of hers. I *hate* her."

"Who?" Molly demanded.

"Susan Priest," Larken said, descending past Molly on the stairs, intent on finishing the pointless trip to the filing room, given the alternative of dealing with Susan Priest. She clunked down the steps, and Jocelyn followed her lead rather than Molly's pouting stance. As Jocelyn passed, Molly took up the rear.

"What if she follows us?" Larken asked over her shoulder without looking. The landing was only five steps away, and it wasn't as though they could hide in the stairwell and not be seen.

"She won't," Jocelyn said between bites of a cinnamon roll. "She's too busy protecting her rolls from unscrupulous grazers."

Larken caught Jocelyn's smile as she turned to grin at her. Jocelyn's mouth burst into a wide, toothy grin with icing-covered teeth.

"Gross," Larken said, noticing that when Jocelyn turned to show Molly, even Molly's face lit up a little.

"I'm sorry, guys," Molly said as she stepped down. "I don't mean to be so agitated. It's...the police. They burst through the door and shoved me onto the bed. They wouldn't listen or even talk to me. Then Oliver was gone. I couldn't... didn't...do anything about it. I didn't even try."

Larken paused. She turned, instantly sober, and made her way past Jocelyn to where Molly had stopped on the stairs.

"There wasn't anything you could do against them," she said.

"Except punch them in the balls," Jocelyn said, then laughed at her joke. Larken rolled her eyes.

"Except get arrested yourself. Oliver didn't *do* anything. You know it. *I* know it. They will apologize to all of us at the end of this."

"Your mother will sue them," Jocelyn added, making Molly smile.

"She will too," Molly said. "And make our cookies for the trial."

Molly's communicator chimed loudly, amplified by the stairwell's emptiness. Larken looked to Jocelyn, who met her eyes and nodded. They both knew that Molly's mother, as supportive as she was, wouldn't likely support them sneaking around in the off-limits stairwell. Molly fished her communicator out of her pocket and put it to her ear in voice-only mode.

"I can't talk now," Molly said in a harsh whisper. Then she stopped and nodded along. "I told you they barged right in and put their *hands* on me, Mom."

More listening.

"I'm not doing that. You can't call the police on the police, Mom. It doesn't work that way."

More listening.

"I'm not coming home."

More listening. More nodding.

"What am I going to do? I'm going to go get his stuff out of his room, so nobody messes with it."

Nod. Shake. Nod.

"Okay. Yeah, I love you too."

Larken made her way back to the front of the line. As she left Molly's side, Larken wondered what had tied Molly and Oliver together so fast. The concern Molly expressed was touching but so overly dramatic and atypical, especially only after a couple of days. Something was suspicious about Molly's behavior, and she tried to tell herself that it had little to do with the utterly irrational jealousy which gripped her insides.

The stairs ended at a landing flanked by only one room. A tarnished brass sign reading "File Room" hung on the door from a tack to make it even easier. And it was unlocked, which should have been Larken's first clue that she was about to be disappointed. Sure enough, as they passed through, they found only open space, dust, and the occasional skittering of an insect from one dimly lit corner to another.

"Too easy," Jocelyn said, wiping excess frosting onto her pants. "I knew it was too easy to get here."

"This isn't a file room," Molly replied. "It's...I don't know...a utility room?"

"There's nothing here," said Larken. Her flats left footprints in the dust. "Nobody's been in here for ages. Look over there."

A cluster of cobwebs clung ardently to one of three six-foot windows, swaying under the influence of the occasional vent breeze. Despite her earlier words and Jocelyn's cynical warnings, Larken *had* hoped to find rows of filing cabinets containing data coins, documents, and perhaps some sign of her benefactor. An old computer terminal where they could try out their nonexistent hacking skills would have been something. But her stomach sank as she surveyed the room, sliding her gaze from the windows and along the empty walls. Empty rectangles testified to there once having been paintings as tall as she was hanging.

"What *was* in here?" Jocelyn asked, following Larken's slow walk around the interior.

"A teacher's lounge," came a voice behind Molly. All three turned at once to see Ms. Carrish standing behind them. "Used to be. I thought I asked you to wait for your counselor."

"How..."

"Ms. Priest was kind enough to inform me," Ms. Carrish told them, staring daggers through each of them. "And you will do nothing to her for the courtesy. Am I understood?"

Larken nodded. Molly and Jocelyn did the same.

"Now, do you care to explain what you're doing here?"

"We thought it was the file room," Larken gambled on the truth. "We need to know who my benefactor is to help Oliver."

Ms. Carrish's left eyebrow jumped slightly within her otherwise unchanged stare of death.

"How do you expect him to do anything about the fact that Oliver is in *police* custody *here* when he lives in *Seattle*? Do you think he'll stop his work and fly to Portland?"

All Larken heard was that their benefactor was a man who lived in Seattle, which confirmed what Jocelyn had assumed. But there were over two million people in the Emerald City. The futility of their task began to sink in.

"Not exactly, Ms. Carrish," Larken said, as the hopelessness made her eyes water. "We just want to know.

Maybe he'll help, maybe he won't, but is it too much to ask to try?"

That seemed to soften Ms. Carrish. Her eyebrows fell at the same time as her shoulders.

"And I suppose these are your friends," Ms. Carrish said. "Come with me. All of you."

With that, Ms. Carrish spun and made her way back through the door into the hallway so quickly that Larken had to run to catch up and then fast-walk to keep pace. She heard Jocelyn and Molly tramping along behind her. They traveled back the way they had come, passing Susan in the process, who followed them with her eyes in a look of ecstatic bliss. Larken took a second to snarl at her quietly while Ms. Carrish wasn't paying attention.

A few turns and an elevator ride later, the group found themselves in Ms. Carrish's office. The room was a testament to good order, with every single item in its proper place, from what Larken could tell. The desktop was devoid of anything save a tiny data coin.

"Sit," Ms. Carrish said as she circled the desk. "One of you will have to stand."

Larken chose to stand, feeling the moment's anxiety manifest as excess energy. Jocelyn and Molly took the chairs one by one, and Ms. Carrish slid her hand across the top of her desk, projecting the back of a monitor up from the unmarked surface. With additional hand motions, Larken guessed, she worked through the navigation menus. Finally, with a triumphant sigh, Ms. Carrish slid her hand back across the other direction. In place of the monitor back that had been there previously, the image of a smiling woman with sandy-brown hair and dark brown eyes peered out at them.

"I can't share the benefactor's information with you, Larken. There's a confidentiality agreement in place for a reason, and it's better for all of us that you aren't aware. But it occurs to me that you're old enough now to at least know something about your mother."

In the woman before them, Larken saw her own eyes staring back. Oliver got the nose. Larken's hand went up to grasp the end of her sandy-blond locks. The woman's eyes seemed sharp, as though she were looking through time into Larken's soul. She shivered at the thought but continued to examine the woman. Their mother had had a Roman nose, a sloped forehead that was almost imperceptibly too big, and a smile that looked precisely like Oliver's. The truth of their relationship was right there in the woman's face.

"What was her name?" Larken asked softly.

"Railynn Marche," Ms. Carrish replied, matching Larken's tenor. "When she died, she left your care to your benefactor. I believe you were two at the time, maybe three. You must understand that the benefactor, as far as I know, is *not* your blood relative. He was a well-trusted friend, and he's done an amazing job providing for you. You have never wanted for anything here, have you?"

Aside from countless nights spent lying awake and wondering why their parents had abandoned them, Larken hadn't.

"She loved you both," Ms. Carrish said. "But not like we do, child. You have to understand that you were the only twins we've ever had dropped off together. You must have noticed how the staff treat you. You belong here as much as anywhere, Larken. We all want you both to succeed—in life and love."

As she said the last bit, her eyes darted in Molly's direction. Larken wondered for the first time exactly how closely the teachers and staff at Brighton monitored their students.

"Was she nice?"

"I've never met her. Not once. But I know some things about her. She worked in a modeling laboratory in Texas. League City, I think. It's not there anymore. As I understand, she didn't have any other relatives besides you."

"Thank you, Ms. Carrish," Larken said.

"You still have detention in the morning," Ms. Carrish replied, her voice still soft. "There must be consequences when children go where they're not supposed to. Staff areas are off limits for a reason."

Larken nodded and then felt Molly's hand on her back.

"Off to your rooms, children," Ms. Carrish said. "That's all I can share. I trust you will stay in your rooms now that you know there's no point in continuing your search."

The girls left in a muted convoy with Larken again leading. It was as though Molly had given up her mantle of leadership, and, voluntary or not, Larken had taken it up instead. Being the first through the door, Larken took in the space. Jocelyn's bags remained packed and on her bed undisturbed.

Larken's mind punched through the last couple of hours. When it slid to a slow stop, it landed on Elijah and Via.

"They told him, right? That's what she said. They informed our benefactor about Oliver's problem?"

"Ms. Carrish said that she *thinks* that's what happened," Jocelyn agreed, interrupting her yawn. Molly nodded.

"Do you believe her?"

Molly shot one eyebrow up and examined her beneath it. "What do you mean?"

The way Ms. Carrish had so skillfully deflated their ambitions seemed calculated. Distrust made little sense given the image of Larken's mother, Railynn Marche. There was no doubt in Larken's mind whether that part of the conversation had been in earnest or not. And if Ms. Carrish had wanted them to stop seeking him out, she could have simply placed a guard by their rooms. Susan Priest, for starters, would love that duty.

"I think maybe they *intend* to tell him," Larken decided. "I don't know if they will tell him until Monday. Maybe they feel like they have it under control with the trust money."

Molly's eyebrow fell back down. She seemed to have made a decision.

"You're looking for excuses why he's not here yet. My mother would already be here if I didn't force her to stay away."

Jocelyn kicked her paisley bag over the edge of the bed. It collided with the ground in a thunk.

"But he's not going to do anything," Molly continued, thinking out loud. "He can't care that much. Remember when Oliver broke his arm? He didn't show up then, and he's not going to show now."

Had Larken ever told Molly that story? She stretched her mind back, looking for the moment but couldn't find it. Jocelyn pulled out her pinamu tablet and poked at the screen. Molly seemed to have lost some of her steam, and her eyes seemed puffy and red, jarring against her pale skin and freckles.

"Listen," Larken said. "Our benefactor has never seen us. I think we still need to take that trip."

Jocelyn let out a low whistle. "Larken, I know who your

benefactor is. I don't think Ms. Carrish was telling us *not* to go. I think she was telling us *where* to go. Look."

Jocelyn flipped the screen, and Railynn Marche's face peered back out, smiling in a bright orange dress. Beside her stood a man with penetrating blue eyes, his arm wrapped around another woman with hazel eyes and straight black hair.

"Recognize him? No wonder your benefactor is so mysterious. Listen."

Jocelyn began reading the caption below the image.

"Pictured from left to right: Railynn Marche and Alexander Toussaint, lab directors. Harper Rawls, lab administrator, and litigant in the Rawls v. Emergent Biotechnology. Shown here celebrating a revolutionary advancement in human cloning—a celebration overshadowed by pending criminal and civil court cases involving grand theft of the model Ordell Bentley (not shown)."

Molly stared at the picture, as fixated as Larken was.

"Those eyes," Jocelyn continued, turning her gaze to Larken. "Those are Oliver's eyes. I bet Dr. Alexander is more than just a benefactor. I bet he's your *father*, so he's stayed away. Imagine the scandal if his girlfriend or wife or whatever found out."

The idea made Larken's head swim. There was no denying those eyes. Deep and impossible, like the evening sky over the mountains just before dusk, when the light had been sucked out, the entire world had been distilled down to the essence of blue.

That was the difficulty of it.

"I have to go," she said, standing. She turned toward Jocelyn. "Do you have a spare bag?"

"Tournament bag," Jocelyn said. "One sec, I'll empty it."

"Emptying it" turned out to be dumping everything on the floor in the closet. Larken packed some of her clothes while Molly looked on, dumbfounded into silence.

A single tap sounded against the door, reminding Larken that the counselor was due. She thought the woman would have been down and gone by now. Larken glanced at Jocelyn and Molly, then grabbed Jocelyn's tournament bag and threw it under her bed.

"Come in," Molly called as soon as they were all packed away again. The door swung open.

"Elijah," Molly said, eyes following him across the room. He wore a light-yellow bomber jacket over jeans. Behind him came Via in a tank and leggings with something that resembled ballet shoes on her feet.

"Are we still going?" Elijah asked. "We heard about Oliver. Should we stay?"

"*We're* going," Larken announced. "Just not to Texas. Seattle. Looking for my benefactor to help Oliver."

"We're in," Elijah said. Via's eyes floated away as she followed an invisible butterfly.

CHAPTER 9
A LUKEWARM RECEPTION

ON SUNDAY, Torrent went to see Christine Hamilton, the child he'd begun to think he had saved. She learned about her new body more each day. Walking challenged her more than head, neck, and arm movements, but she would get there. She could stand for almost five minutes without tiring as long as she didn't have to move much.

Torrent popped a lemon drop into his mouth—a taste sensation that brought back images of Harper and her streaming black hair in the wavy distortion of Texas heat. Only for a second, he allowed himself to relish in her memory. Then he heard three knocks on the door marked "Patient 1".

"Come in."

The room looked very much like the patients' quarters it was. A bank of machines stood against a wall, some of which Torrent knew how to use and others which Gallatin had brought in on the advice of "specialists." Those had never even been turned on. On the edge of a bed just high enough to make it impossible for anyone's toes to touch the ground sat Christine Hamilton, blondish-brown curls framing tired-looking blue eyes.

The lemon drop had dissolved to almost nothing.

"No more questions," she pleaded when she saw him.

"No questions, I promise. I need a favor."

"Favor?"

"Yes." Torrent crunched the remains of the candy to nothing with his teeth before continuing. He took a deep breath. "My son is dying."

The news didn't faze her. Christine had been in a coma until two days prior, so Torrent forgave the lack of response.

Now she was in a new body; Christine looked utterly different. The mousy brown-haired girl whose limbs had atrophied to nearly nothing had been replaced by a vibrant, alert specimen of (eventual) fitness. She was breathing with her own body and no longer on life support—all courtesy of her grandfather's company and the expertise of one Dr. Alexander Toussaint.

"What's the favor?"

"Talk to my son's mother, and let her know you're okay. I can *tell* her that, but it'll be better if she can talk to you instead of me."

"Your son's mother? Wife? Partner?"

"Neither. It's a long story."

"And you want your son to be like me?"

Christine scrutinized him with her eyes. Eventually, she must have decided that he was being honest because she nodded slightly. Torrent took his win and excused himself long enough to step into the hall and retrieve a hover chair he'd brought with him just in case she agreed. It wouldn't do for Harper to see Christine on the bed, surrounded by all the machines.

Torrent pulled the chair beside the bed and helped Christine down into it, gauging as he did how much weight she put on him versus how much control she kept to herself. She slipped only once on the way down, and he caught her quickly. Then he pushed her away from the medical ensemble of tools and machines and toward the far wall before he called Harper.

When Harper answered, he made sure he was the only one in the visual sensor range.

"I'll get Bodhi," Harper said before her projection had fully materialized.

"I need to talk to you first, Harper," he said. "I want to introduce you to someone."

Torrent shot a glance at Christine to see if she was ready. She pulled her hair back over her shoulders, straightened her back—muscle movements that showed further rapid adjustment to the new body—and formed a smile. Torrent swiveled the communicator's sensor toward her.

"Ms. Rawls, hello."

"Who is this?" Torrent could tell that Harper had addressed the question to him by the pivot of her head, even though he'd carefully moved out of the com's line of sight. He ignored the question and let Christine speak for herself. She had her grandfather's gift for direct speech and a convincing tone.

"Christine Hamilton."

"Tell her how old you are," Torrent said, barely concealing the giddy feeling that grew in his rib cage. Harper *had* to say yes. How else could Bodhi be saved?

"Fourteen."

"Your real age."

"Oh. Thirty-nine?"

He swiveled the camera back until he again took up the entire image.

"Remember that treatment I told you about? We figured it out! Look at this."

Torrent reached toward the communicator and flicked a button to project another image of Christine's original body. Harper's mouth dropped open.

"You did it?"

"We did. Christine was in a coma until a day ago. Do you remember Gallatin? This is his granddaughter. And because of the treatment, Christine is up and moving around. The Hamilton line continues."

It was an exaggeration and unnecessary, but he couldn't help himself. This much progress with only one day of recovery seemed much more impressive than the four it had taken, and Torrent was trying to negotiate for his son's life. He'd found a way to save him, and he would do whatever he had to do to make that happen. He panned the camera back over to Christine again and caught her unguarded, her smile now missing. He cleared his throat to get her attention.

"Christine, how do you feel?" Harper asked.

"Aside from tired, fine. I can't describe what it feels like to be back in the real world. You wouldn't believe me if I told you what a coma is like."

Endless nightmares, from what Torrent had already learned from the girl. He held his breath, hoping that Harper wouldn't ask and Christine wouldn't volunteer any negative information. To his relief, Harper seemed more interested in the physical than psychological complexities of consciousness transfer.

"You don't feel any side effects? I mean, the chair. Is that permanent?"

"No. Torrent said I'd been in a coma too long. I have to relearn how to walk."

Harper nodded.

"Bodhi won't have that problem. That's not all," Torrent interrupted and reached for the communicator again. This time an image flashed of a boy, around the same age as Christine, with a fit body and a wide smile. The way he stood with his arms in the classic Superman pose, he revealed the tattoo on his left wrist.

The door swung open behind Torrent, and a burly nurse entered unannounced. Torrent flashed a guilty look at her. She had undoubtedly had come for Christine. He then grinned wide and did his best to ignore the woman.

"This one's for Bodhi," Torrent told Harper. "Isn't he great? Thanks, Christine. Nurse, can you take her?"

After Christine was out of projection sensor range, Torrent continued, ignoring the nurse's stares and calling her to silence with an extended index finger as he continued his pitch.

"I've already prepped everything. All you have to do is bring Bodhi to Seattle. The H Hotel is where we'll do the procedure. It's a one-stop-shop."

"I need to talk to him about it. He's old enough that he should understand."

Torrent clenched his teeth before forcing his jaw to relax.

"I guess you're right. Tell him *soon*. Gallatin's doing me a favor, and it won't be available forever."

She sighed.

"I will, Torrent. Let me get Bodhi, so you two can have your normal father-son time. Not a word about this. I'll tell him."

He smiled at Christine and the nurse and headed back

into the hall while holding the communicator aloft. He thought—guessed really—that Harper had taken the bait. After all, the doctors told them the boy hadn't long to live. Even Harper's support of models and their cause couldn't sway the woman from wanting to save their son—or so he hoped.

The conversation with Bodhi was brief and amounted to a breakdown of the progression of the disease. After running through the latest doctors' statements, identical to before, Bodhi was tired and excused himself. Torrent recognized the reality of the exhaustion the condition created but still couldn't help the rising disappointment when the call came to a premature end.

Then he considered his past mistakes.

Every single time.

It wasn't long ago that every time he called the boy, Bodhi begged him relentlessly to come to Canada and visit. One time when he'd disagreed with his mother's boyfriend, Bodhi had called him in tears pleading for Torrent to take him to the United States. He didn't understand that the police still searched for Bodhi's mother *nationwide* and that if Bodhi came to Seattle, Harper wouldn't be far behind and might end up in jail or prison. The twelve-year-old had difficulty understanding no, regardless of the reason.

Torrent continued down the hallway, deep in thought about how close Harper and her new man, Aiden, really were or if she was only using the man for his admittedly staggering wealth. Grudgingly he shook his head at the idea. Harper was a lot of things, but "gold-digger" wasn't one of them.

When he turned the corner, he came to a dead stop. Five children, approximately the same age as Bodhi, he would guess, slouched in the hallway outside his door. Alarms went off in his head as he considered what these children could want. They didn't seem to notice him at first, and he took that opportunity to duck back into hiding and peeking around a corner to see what they were doing.

One girl leaned against his door. Her almost iron-flat black hair hung down around her bored-looking face. Dark brown freckles dotted her cheeks and surrounded her eyes— eyes that seemed focused on something far away. To her left were three other girls, chattering amongst themselves. One of them looked familiar, like his ward Larken, but it couldn't be her. Larken lived in Portland and went to Brighton Academy, far enough away so that nobody would ever suspect the two had any connection. One of the girls besides the Larken look-alike was blonde and smiled too much. She seemed the type of person who didn't take life seriously enough and was headed for a cruel future. Beside her, the last girl stood as stiffly as a flagpole and, by the darting movements of her eyes, seemed to take in everything at once, including him.

That was the one who said something that he couldn't hear to the other two girls, and suddenly all three turned toward him.

The boy turned.

He looked almost exactly like the Larken-ish girl.

Torrent's heart raced as he realized he'd been spotted. He gulped and then presented himself, trying to show that he'd only been coming around the corner and not hiding from them.

"That's him," said the girl who leaned against the door. "I told you this is the place."

The girl who looked like Larken was the first to approach him.

"Dr. Alexander Toussaint?"

He nodded while absently shoving his glasses back up onto his nose.

"Y...yes. Who are you?"

"Larken Marche," she introduced herself. "I think that you knew my mother?"

The time had arrived.

Each year, Torrent intended to introduce himself to Railynn's children. After sixteen years, he felt that sharp stab of guilt every time he saw an image of them. Like now, he saw Railynn in those eyes and, to a lesser extent, the way Larken zeroed in unflinchingly into his face—unintimidated. Or if she was, she did not show it.

"I knew your mother," he admitted, then looked to the right and the left to see if anyone was coming. Quickly he crossed the hallway toward his door. As he approached, the bored-looking girl moved to give him access to the biometric sensor. The door slid open, and he passed through, nearly tripping on a small black bag he hadn't noticed. That wasn't the only item of luggage clogging the hallway, but it was the one that had been strategically placed just outside of his door to trip him.

"Come in," he mumbled. "Before somebody sees you."

The entire group followed at once. He made his way across the room in a beeline for the bar at the back. Two blocks of ice and a healthy half-highball of scotch later, he found the courage to address the expectant faces behind him. He spun slowly, bringing the glass down from his lips.

"And this must be Oliver?" he asked, looking at the boy. "You've changed. I don't remember you looking that much like your sister."

"Elijah," the boy said, jutting his hand out, which

Torrent ignored. The boy slowly lowered his hand to his side. Torrent examined him. If this wasn't Oliver, it had to be another of his Firsts. But they weren't supposed to be able to find each other. Railynn, his former lab partner, made sure that they were geographically distributed when she found them homes.

"I told you he didn't know," said the flighty blonde girl.

"Interesting," Torrent replied, ignoring her as well. "Where is Oliver, then?"

"He's been arrested," Larken said. "The school said they told you?"

"Nobody's told me. Why would they? What's he doing getting arrested?"

"We don't know," said the bored-looking girl, who suddenly didn't look so bored and seemed a little on edge.

"And you are...?"

"Molly," Larken chimed. "And that's Jocelyn over there. Via is here beside me, and you've met Elijah."

"Pleasure," he said, taking another swig before he continued. "And you're here because you expect me to do something about this?"

He could do something. Hire lawyers for one, but that would compromise the futures of all involved. People would ask *why* Alexander Toussaint hired a lawyer for some child in Texas. He paid the school an obscene amount of money to ensure that problems like this went away *without* him being the wiser.

"That depends," Larken said, eyeing him suspiciously as though she were trying to tease out the core of who he was. Torrent took another quick drab of whiskey and felt the burn trickle down his throat. She squinted. "Are you our benefactor? Oliver and me? Is it you who pays the bills?"

He scanned the group, searching for the right words in his mind to lie with. To simplify the situation enough to call him the benefactor—that was not entirely accurate. Torrent, alone, didn't have anywhere near the amount of money that Brighton required by himself. Without Ordell Bentley and the laundering services of the quasi-terrorist Siblings of the Natural Order, those payments would have stopped long ago.

Both Oliver and Larken would have been ejected out of the expensive boarding school and into an experience that Torrent loathed considering. His childhood was spent in Our Lady of Guadalupe, alone and fending for himself in a school that siphoned off government funds but provided little more than a warm bed. That was something that both Torrent and Ordell had agreed would never happen to Railynn's children —not after she'd saved Harper's life.

"It's not me," he said, accurate yet not true simultaneously. Being a model, Ordell had few rights to pay for anything, even if he was technically one of the nation's wealthiest men after Harper's successful lawsuit against Emergent Biotechnology. Torrent had signed for the trust that now paid for the costly school experience. "I mean it is, but not entirely."

"He's our father," Via said. Strange name, but she was a peculiar girl too. Torrent hadn't been prepared for her comment and nearly spewed scotch out of his nose. The way Larken looked then, hopeful and reticent at the same time, turned his stomach.

"Are you?" she asked, and he could tell from her expression that this one was the most genuine out of all of the questions until now.

"N...no. Well, yes. Maybe. It's not so simple. You don't..."

He looked again at Via, and there it was. Not in direct physical features but in the sardonic look that Railynn had often given Torrent when they'd been lab partners. It was hard to see because Via's eyes darted around the room, but Railynn was in them. Something had gone wrong with this one, so distracted and detached. Torrent wondered how many of the thirty had come out damaged like her. What he wouldn't give to figure out what had happened during the replication process to cause it.

"Try us," Molly said, interrupting his thoughts. She straightened her slouched posture until her eyes were roughly level with his Adam's apple. That one wasn't a First. Neither was the silent and aloof girl (Jocelyn) with the devil-may-care life approach. Something about that one just bugged him.

He took in the rest. His eyes went from Elijah to Larken. Revealing the truth to five students, he'd only just met seemed unwise. But Elijah looked so much like Larken that denying it seemed ridiculous, especially since they'd made it to Torrent's doorstep. There was only one explanation, and nobody was going to like it. They probably had already guessed but didn't want to accept. Still, he was indebted to Larken—not the rest.

"Do you trust them?" he asked, directing his question at Larken and motioning to the group with his scotch.

"What? Yes. Or they wouldn't be here."

"Good. What I'm going to tell you can't leave this room," he said and took a sip from his glass. "I knew it would come to this someday, but I'd always hoped I could delay it until you were older."

"I'm sixteen," she said. "Plenty old."

"Almost the same age as my son," he mentioned in automatic response. Then, catching her downcast glance, he tried to backpedal. "I mean, my natural son. No, I mean…you have to understand that you're not *really* my children."

"What does that mean?"

Torrent bit his lip and clanked ice around in his glass while considering whether to validate their suspicions a bit longer. It would feel good to let the secret out, despite the army of NDAs he and the receiving parties had signed when he'd parted most of thirty children sixteen years earlier. He took a quick draught, debating whether the truth was worth the pain it would bring within that brief few seconds. After he swallowed, he met Larken's eyes —Railynn's—and the thought of lying to her evaporated as quickly as it had materialized.

"We made you," he said. "Your mother and I made you, but she wasn't supposed to keep any of you."

He looked to Elijah and Via.

"You two went into the Orphanage Program directly. Railynn had to work out where to put you. Which school?"

"Our Lady of Guadalupe," Elijah said in a subdued voice. Torrent cringed slightly to hear it.

"I'm sorry," he said. "Railynn had many children to place quickly under a lot of scrutiny. She did the best she could."

And maybe whoever had given Torrent up had done the same: the best they could. He'd never discovered the identities of his parents.

"NDAs are in place everywhere, so it's not surprising that you don't know."

Via was the first to catch on.

"We're clones."

"Not clones, exactly. You're more aligned with models. But Larken," he said, ignoring the others. "You and Oliver.

Your mother loved you. And you have to understand that she chose you after we'd placed the rest. You both were special to her." He sighed and took another sip of his drink. The alcohol started working, and he couldn't help commenting on his past failures. "I'm just a foolish old man who never really understood what love meant."

Three of the four, Via, Molly, and Elijah, found seats on his couch. He downed the rest of his whiskey, waiting for the barrage of questions that must surely follow. For a moment, he thought he'd avoided them as the entire group stared in stunned silence. Then it occurred to him that in his work to take care of Larken and keep her past secret, she likely hadn't seen many pictures of the earlier days of her relationship with Railynn. He crossed the room, ignoring the silence, and shuffled toward the kitchen. When he returned thirty seconds later, he carried a small metallic box. This he opened as he crossed toward the group, who had found some seats on the couch. As he approached, the boy moved to leave him space near Larken, who still stood only now with crossed arms.

Torrent slid the lid off the box and pulled out a data coin. He felt his eyes well up as he caressed the worn thing between his finger and thumb. He plopped it down onto the table, which erupted into a holographic display. Railynn's face was adorned with a weak smile in the space before him. He felt a lump form in his throat at the sight of the bank of machines that worked so hard to keep her alive. The holograph was the start of a recorded video segment—one that he should have shown Larken years earlier. He'd seen it enough to repeat it word for word.

"They're perfect," Railynn said as the visual frame expanded to reveal the two infants at the end of the hospital bed. Tears gathered in her eyes despite the smile. Torrent knew why they were there. Her love had changed from research to these children, only she'd just gotten the news about the brain tumor that wouldn't let her see them grow up.

There'd been no Immortality Program then.

"They are," he heard his voice agreeing, mouthing along.

"Look at those eyes," she said. "Have you ever seen anything so beautiful?"

"Nothing," he'd said. He recalled not feeling any of what she described. They were still lab experiments for him then. Standing before him, he couldn't find a paternalistic impulse toward Larken. Yet he revealed everything he'd kept hidden for nearly sixteen years because he felt compelled to be honest with her, so perhaps that was something.

"She made me promise to take care of you," Torrent told Larken. "Made me swear. And I've been doing it. Have you ever wanted for anything?"

"No," he heard Larken say, but her arms closed before her, locked as her lips formed a straight line. "No, we've never needed anything."

"You're pretty dumb for a scientist," Jocelyn blurted out. Her gaze shifted to Larken from him. "I've been with you almost as long as Molly. How many nights did we stay up while you tried to figure out who your parents were? How many times did you cry yourself to sleep?"

"When I was younger," Larken corrected her. "When I was *much* younger. It-it's okay, Jocelyn."

"It's not okay at all. He owes you an explanation," Jocelyn retorted. "Why did you never call? Never visit?"

To keep Larken and Oliver safe.

That was the canned response that he'd given himself for

sixteen years. Now, looking at Larken and seeing the frustration that mounted behind her eyes, Torrent understood that his decision had been more about himself than her. Who needed the disruption while he was picking apart the universe's secrets? He swallowed down a lump in his throat.

There was no reclaiming the past. But perhaps, it occurred to him the future was still being written. Maybe he could make up for a little.

"And now," he continued, "we have to figure out what to do about Oliver."

Shaking his empty glass, he dropped it to the coffee table surface with images of Railynn still spinning in the air. Extending a drawer from beneath, he retrieved a fresh tin of lemon drops. Raising his eyebrows, he offered them around, and when no one accepted, popped a fresh one between his teeth and remembered Harper, sunshine, and ocean waves.

Then it was time to get to work.

CHAPTER 10

HOMEWARD BOUND

A GATE AGENT gave Larken and Elijah a double-take as they unloaded in Portland. When Torrent stumbled along behind them, his black and white hair splaying out around his head and his bright-yellow suit made the same agent's eyes widen even more. The agent's attention locked in, and Torrent was nearly strip-searched. Torrent was saved only by his extensive and stern lecture about not being a jerk. Larken found herself vaguely impressed.

The last leg into Brighton Academy departed from the Portland airport via rental. A volantrae large enough for six to occupy wasn't cheap, but Torrent didn't seem bothered about financing it. He handed over cash coins to the man behind the rental counter, and the man gave him keys in return. Then Torrent looked over both shoulders before he pocketed the keys.

"Why do you do that?" Larken asked, taking the passenger's seat beside him moments later. The volantrae took the form of a traditional recreational van, so she and Torrent were, for most purposes, walled off from the rest of the group.

"There's a reason I left Texas," Torrent told her, not looking directly at her. "My lab was broken into and then sabotaged by a police officer. They vandalized my apartment and sent death threats to Ordell. Organizations like that have long memories."

"Nobody in Portland is connected to them." Then she thought about Anthony and HPM Lite and bit her lip.

"What about this group?" he asked, motioning to the back.

"Via is a bit strange," she suggested. "But harmless."

"Not her," the man said, turning his shaggy head, so their gazes finally met, making Larken self-conscious. "She's a model, just like you and Elijah. The other two."

"Molly and Jocelyn?"

He nodded and stole a glance in their direction. "I suppose it's too late now," he said, lifting his glasses and wiping his other hand across his eyes. "I shouldn't have said all I said in front of them."

"You can trust them," she said, leaving off the word "mostly" that flitted into her brain after. Molly would keep a secret—if she wanted to. She would also threaten anyone who challenged her version of a story. Her lies had a staying power that few others could manage. Jocelyn, however, would really, really want to be a great friend and confidant. It just wasn't in her. And when they got back, she'd be good for a while, but by late Monday afternoon, it was anyone's guess who she'd have told. Larken nodded at Torrent.

"The secret isn't all that much of a secret, is it? Elijah and I look exactly alike. There are already rumors. *This* secret isn't long for the world; whatever else happens."

He shot her a sharp look.

"Not if. You're just a kid, so you don't understand. We

must keep it, especially since the modeling industry has become controversial. With the Madison Rule on the back foot, can you imagine how furious people will be? There's rumor of civil war and too many people clamoring to fight in it."

Larken knew all of the rumors. She tried to avoid them, but the school buzzed with them. That was another thing that she'd hoped would stay a rumor. It made no sense to her why someone would want to kill someone else just to ensure that models would remain non-citizens. The thought that came next frightened her. She was a model. The last twenty-four hours had proven that she was one of what Torrent had called the "Firsts." She, Oliver, Elijah, and Via were all in the same experiment.

"Oliver," Molly chimed in. "That's what we're doing, rescuing Oliver. The rest of this doesn't matter."

Torrent turned his head to examine Molly before speaking again. He seemed to Larken as if he'd only just remembered that Molly was even there, even though he'd just been talking about her.

"If he's in jail, then he's not at Brighton. I'll get a room in the hotel downtown and head over to the courthouse on Monday to figure out the situation. Give me your a.p. address, Larken, and I'll let you know when I've got him."

"We're coming," Elijah shouted from the back. Larken turned to look at him and wondered how he had heard what they were talking about from the back.

"Not you," Torrent said as he pushed his glasses up again. "You aren't listening. Nobody can know that you're models. *Nobody.*"

He turned to Larken.

"Can you get into Oliver's room?"

The volantrae jolted, and Larken felt momentarily airborne as it began its descent more quickly than she'd expected. Shifting her gaze back through the window, she saw the Brighton campus splayed out before her like a giant obtuse "v." She nodded.

"Good. I'll let you know once I know what's happening. You search in there just to be sure there's nothing that connects him."

"You think he did this?"

"Maybe," Torrent cast a wary look at Via. "I don't know. I don't know what Oliver is really like. Maybe he *did* do whatever it was. Either way, him landing in jail won't be good for any of the Firsts."

"You mean it won't be good for you?"

He didn't answer her. The wheels turned in her mind, and, like tumblers in a lock, she felt them slide into place. To be back at school meant to be ridiculed, harassed, and forcibly counseled. And it would mean every day having her doppelgänger walking the halls, piquing the interests of a nosy student body or Anthony Lee.

"I'm not going back," she decided, setting her jaw as she said it. The volantrae slowed outside the school gates, next to the angel of knowledge. "I'm going to get Oliver, and we're leaving Portland."

Molly let out a gust of breath, tinged with a nasal whine. Larken looked at her.

"You know we have HPM Lite on campus. There's no way that we can hide from them in our classes. It's only a matter of time, Molly."

"You have to go," Torrent said. "Otherwise, they'll come looking for you."

"Not if *you* formally withdraw me. They just let the

police walk out with your child. A *real* parent would be furious about not being notified. A *real* parent would care enough to pull their other child out and protect them."

"It's not that simple," he said, looking somewhat abashed as the volantrae stopped moving. The door popped open at the bottom of the brief steps while the vehicle settled. Elijah was the first, passing nervous glances toward Torrent and Larken, who continued their fight. "You have to get an education, and Brighton is one of the best schools in the nation. I promised Railynn that I would..."

"That you would take care of us. I know. The thing is, all I want you to do is get Oliver out of jail. I can handle the rest."

Whether that was true or not remained to be seen. Torrent was annoying her with his indecision and what she considered intentionally myopic focus on Brighton. He didn't seem to realize there was more involved in caring for someone than planting them in a distant institution and forgetting about them. Brighton had been the end of his plans for them, and that sort of attitude would never get Oliver out of jail.

Via flashed with a quick, knowing smile and descended with her head bobbing and twisting as she took in everything around her. Larken refocused on Torrent, feeling the stone of obstinance seated firmly in her gut.

"There's no way, Torrent. All this time and you haven't visited us once. I don't think you get a say in it. We can just leave if it comes down to it. At sixteen in Texas, we could sue for emancipation. Just help me get Oliver, and we can go."

"Where?"

"I don't know. Back to Seattle with you? Canada?"

Molly chimed in then. "I can't go," she whispered. "Mom won't just let me run off to Seattle."

Larken turned her attention to Molly, suddenly aware of how much she was hurting her lifelong friend. She no longer doubted that Molly's intentions toward her brother were serious enough to make Molly stop being Molly for two full days. Larken could tell from a side-glance that Jocelyn already knew what Molly hadn't figured out—that Molly wasn't getting an invitation to join them. Not from Larken. Larken swallowed.

"You can't come, Molly," she said, knocking Molly back down into her seat with the words.

"Nobody's *coming* anywhere," Torrent interrupted. "I'm going to check on Oliver and pay bail if necessary. Then *you both* are going back to Brighton. And that's final."

Larken could tell from the way he now kept his fingers permanently on the bridge of his nose that he wasn't as sure as he sounded. Larken reached for Molly's hand, only to watch Molly yank it away.

"I'm disposable? You want to leave without me?"

"No," Larken told her, reaching quickly to catch her hand before Molly could pull it back farther. "I want to bring you with me. And you." She turned her head toward Jocelyn. "But now that we know what we know, and thanks to him," she swiveled her eyes out after Elijah, who neared the court-yard with Via, "we're not going to be able to keep the secret. You two aren't models, and you don't need to be wrapped up in this."

The sound of Madeline Lindholm's raspy voice echoed through the car. The Neo-Punk singer rattled off a short verse about fighting authority, startling Larken until Torrent's hands suddenly patted down his pockets. He pulled a communicator from the breast pocket of his suit coat and clicked the button. One eyebrow lifted as he examined the girls again, still staring at him expectantly. Making contact with Larken, he mouthed the word "fine."

That was enough for her. She leaned back in her seat and closed her eyes while she thought through what must happen next. The communicator buzzed to life, apparently still on speaker.

"Mr. Toussaint, this is Mr. Gomez's office confirming your appointment tomorrow at nine AM."

"N...nine?" Torrent replied. "Are you sure? I'm a little indisposed."

"Yes, Dr. Toussaint. Would you prefer to reschedule?"

"Can we move it to Wednesday?"

"I need some things," said Molly with a severe look focused on Larken. "I've got to go inside, to my room, and get some things. But I want to come with you."

"No," Torrent said.

"I'm sorry, Dr. Toussaint. You don't wish to reschedule?"

"One second," he said into the communicator and then clicked another button that Larken assumed was to mute the call.

"I still can't bring a bunch of schoolgirls with me. I have a reason to be with you, Larken, since I guess I'm your guardian technically. Molly and Jocelyn will have to stay at Brighton. Period."

He clicked the button again and returned to his call.

"Can we do Wednesday instead? Same time."

"Sure, Dr. Toussaint, no problem. Confirmed for Wednesday at nine."

"Good. Thank you."

"Thank you, Dr. Toussaint. Please know that Mr.

Gomez is extremely busy, and we may be unable to accommodate another reschedule."

Larken watched as Torrent's Adam's apple slid up and down.

"Understood," he said. "Thanks."

"Who's Mr. Gomez?" Jocelyn perked up immediately as Molly made her way down the aisle, eyes downcast, steps a slow shuffle.

"Not that it's your business," Torrent said more curtly than Larken would have expected given his mild demeanor, "but Saul Gomez is a good friend I'm working on a project with."

"Saul Gomez? Emergent Biotechnology's Saul Gomez? He's co-sponsor on four of our gaming tournaments."

"He does work at Emergent Biotechnology, yes," Torrent admitted.

Jocelyn's eyes lit up. Once she seemed to catch on that nobody else shared in her glee, Jocelyn followed Molly down the aisle, hand extended toward Torrent, who took it and shook it quickly.

"Pleased to meet you, Mr. Toussaint," she said.

"Doctor."

"Sorry. Dr. Toussaint. Please introduce me to Saul Gomez sometime."

"Have a good evening, Jocelyn," Larken said, shooting a warning glare at her.

"I'm leaving," Jocelyn said. "Call me soon. Remember, we're here to help if you need us."

Molly looked lost as she stood outside of the vehicle, staring at the school against the background of the bright red setting sun gleaming into an otherwise overcast sky.

"And you both steer clear of HPM Lite," Larken said. "I love you."

With that, Jocelyn flashed a smile, and even Molly gave a thin-lipped grin before the pair single-filed around the bus stop and took the worn path toward the school.

"Well," Larken said. "What next?"

"Get some sleep," Torrent said. "Which means find a hotel that won't think it's suspicious for a man my age to check into with a girl your age."

"Just lie and tell them you're my father," Larken said. "It'll be fine. I meant what to do next about Oliver."

"Oh. Are you going to tell me what he did?"

"No." Torrent seemed so skittish that she feared he would bolt at the truth before getting to the courthouse. "They wouldn't tell us. Something bad, I guess."

"Bad like *stole a pen* or like *murdered someone?*"

She shook her head. Torrent plugged some numbers into the control panel, and the door slid shut. The volantrae then lifted into the air slowly as Larken nestled down into her seat, enveloped by a plaid beige-brown cushion.

"You're going to have to find out," she said. "They'll tell you since you're an adult and his guardian."

"We'll need a lawyer," Torrent continued. "I mean, hopefully, it's nothing too bad, but we'll need one just in case."

He seemed weary as he said it, as though the thought of litigating Oliver's freedom was too much for him to bear. His eyes looked far away, like he was staring back into history, remembering. She almost asked about the pause, but he was back in the present before she could.

"A good one," he suggested. "Someone licensed in Texas."

"Molly's mother is a lawyer. She's a partner at Walsh and Moody. Brigid Kostic."

The mention of the name drew the blood from Torrent's face, making him fifty shades lighter. He bit his lip, and she watched as he swallowed again. One of his hands went to his eyebrows and squeezed as the other gripped the overhead handle to keep him stationary while the volantrae went into a sharp turn.

"You *know* her," Larken said. "How do you know Molly's mother?"

"It was a long time ago," Torrent replied. "And I don't know her. Didn't know her. Harper did. I'm glad she's okay, and from what it sounds like, doing well for herself."

"She can afford to send Molly to Brighton Academy," Larken reflected. "No tuition assistance or Orphanage Program help."

"Good," he said, but she wasn't sure if he meant it. "Good. Tonight, we sleep. Tomorrow morning, I'll call the school and tell them you're with me. Then we'll work on the courthouse."

CHAPTER 11

OLIVER NEEDS US

THE LAST ROOM in apparently the only hotel in the entirety of Portland good enough for *the* Torrent Toussaint had only a queen bed, one which Torrent claimed the because of his "old bones." Larken would have slept better on the bus than on the hard couch with slippery pillows. Tossing and turning all night was complemented by the sun smacking her in the face at six in the morning. A groggy and scowling Larken slid off cushions that were only too glad to be rid of her.

Larken pulled a change of clothes from Jocelyn's tiny tournament bag loaner and realized she'd given up her tooth-brush to make room for a travel makeup kit during her packing frenzy. After a quick shower, she found some hotel-provided mouthwash and scrubbed her teeth and gums with it until she could no longer make out the stale taste of condensed saliva. Larken then changed into thigh-length beige shorts with tan boots and a flowery blue blouse that buttoned down to just above her belly button.

She checked her communicator for messages.

None.

Not that she'd expected any. The evening before, they'd all been exhausted, and she expected everyone else was as asleep as Torrent, whose snores crawled through the halls from the single bedroom and into her ears like evil little spice worms.

When she wound her way, hair dripping, across the hallway and past the kitchen, she saw Torrent had left something resembling a chubby stylus on the counter. She shoved her old, dirty clothes into the tournament bag and craned her head toward it. Torrent sniffled but didn't wake. Larken wove her way around the couch, discovering as she got closer that the device was his communicator sitting on a stand to aid projection mode. He must have talked to someone during one of her more restive periods of the night.

A shiver went up her spine as the reality of her situation dawned on her. She had spurned the relative safety of Brighton and isolated herself in a hotel room with a man she'd never met before. This same man had been sneaking calls within feet of her while she slept. Her breath quickened as she reached for the device, carefully measuring Torrent's snores from the other room.

What if he wasn't their benefactor but some creepy older man who'd decided to humor her to get her alone? Of course, he would send away Jocelyn and Molly. She tried hard to remember if he'd volunteered any information she could verify, but she'd done most of the talking. Nothing he'd told her was anything she could prove against what she'd known before.

She remembered the pictures he'd shown her of her and her mother—or the woman he claimed was her mother. But the video of them had to have been real, hadn't it?

Larken's heart pounded against her ribs as she reached for the button to see what exactly he'd been doing while she slept. As she pressed the button, her worst fears were realized. In all of her three-dimensional glory, there was an exact replica of Larken sleeping on the couch.

He'd taken her picture while she was asleep.

She staggered backward as she fumbled to push the button again and hide the holograph before Torrent awoke. Her fingers found the switch, but her hand moved too quickly and sent the device clanging to the floor. She bit her lip and listened. The snoring had stopped. Larken raced back to the couch to grab her bag and scooped it up to her chest. Three seconds later, she reached for the door handle to open the door to the hallway.

"Your brother has my eyes."

Her hand stopped, suspended above the latch. Larken turned her head. Torrent stood in his pajamas—off-white and red striped—looking like a demented candy cane with hair. His eyes were clearer and bluer than they had been the day before. She lifted her hand from the door handle and turned to face him.

"Go if you like," he continued. "It was your idea to come along, remember? You'll probably want a ride back to Brighton. I can check on Oliver without you and let you know."

Her fears melted away at his mannerisms, and she realized how foolish she'd been. Torrent wasn't some kidnapper. He was trying to help. She grinned and rubbed her eyes with her free hand. Larken's cheeks heated up, but she did her best to ignore them as she too casually dropped the bag onto the ground.

"Why does he *sort of* look like you? Why do I look *sort of* like Railynn?"

"We're all genetically similar," he said. "You both were the mixture of my DNA and Railynn's. As scientists, we have to use what we have available, and, well, we were available."

"So we *are* your children?"

He shook his shaggy mane and cut the corner into the kitchen, where he tapped some buttons on the replicator.

"No," he said, rubbing his eyes. Closer, she could make out the fine red streaks in them. "You're not our children. You were our *experiment*."

Torrent bent to scoop up the communicator from the floor, placed it back on the table, and then pushed the button again. He glanced toward Larken at the same time the replicator beeped. From within, he produced a steaming mug of coffee.

"Do you want some?" He offered the mug to her, but she shook her head no. She liked to have coffee when cramming for exams, but that was the only time.

"That makes sense," she confirmed, nodding her head slowly. Her eyebrows scrunched together. Heat rose from the back of her neck, which she rubbed and squeezed. "We're just an experiment, something to be thrown out."

"Of course not," he said. "That's not what I meant."

"Did she even love us?"

"Railynn? So much. You don't even know how much she went on about the two of you before you hatched."

The word rolled off his tongue like butter, like breathing. He strung together several other words that Larken didn't hear. "Hatched" bounced around in her head, knocking away all other thoughts. Like an insect. Hatched and unleashed onto the world. Vermin.

"I...I don't want to talk about this right now," she said. "Can you call about Oliver?"

For a second, he seemed lost in thought. Then his eyes sparked and darkened under his tented eyebrows.

"It's only six-thirty. They're not open yet." He rubbed his eyes again. "Larken, you're important and special. You changed your mother's life and brought her joy. It's not your fault that I'm *me*. I'm not the type of person who *connects*."

"Stop," she said. "I get it. I understand. Just...can we talk about something else?"

Larken's stomach grumbled loudly, and Torrent's head yanked in her direction.

"Food?" he asked. She hadn't thought she was hungry. Even with her stomach protesting, Larken didn't feel inclined to eat. But eating seemed better than listening to Torrent continue his conversation about how she wasn't human. She nodded.

"Okay, hold on," he told her. With movements too spry for someone who looked as old as he did, Torrent sped to the replicator and punched some numbers into the control panel. Then he stood hovering near the door as the replicator spun up, issuing popping and rattling noises as it prepared whatever he'd entered.

A few seconds and a lot of banging later, he produced a plated waffle with syrup. He retrieved a fork and knife from a nearby drawer, all of which he shoved toward her awkwardly. She approached the kitchen counter slowly and took a seat, examining the food as her mouth watered. She pushed a forkful of waffle into her mouth. Her tongue danced across the syrup-covered squares. She gulped down the first mouthful, then stopped for a second. Torrent would want to talk, since he seemed incapable of not talking. Larken took the opportunity of his brief silence to steer the conversation away from her humanity.

"Tell me about your girlfriend...the one you were talking about earlier. What was her name?"

He took a seat in a chair opposite her. For a brief second, his eyes darted toward the refrigerator and back. Her eyes followed his and landed on a complimentary bottle of whiskey. She looked back at him and saw that he had that watery, tired look in his eyes again. Then his gaze shifted to meet hers, and he swallowed before talking.

"I thought you knew," he began. "I'm not sure how you could have figured out about Railynn without knowing about Harper."

"I know who she is, Torrent. But can you tell me about her? What happened with you two?"

Larken bent over to edge apart another piece of waffle, then lifted a forkful into her mouth. Her mouth watered as she chewed, letting the sugary syrup slide over her tongue. Her eyes bolted open.

"This is good."

"My favorite compensation for being trapped in the H Hotel for many years was becoming an expert at the replicator." He grinned. "Harper. What can I say about her?"

While he talked, Larken formed a mental image to go along with it. According to him, Harper was an old soul with a face that rarely saw a smile. Perhaps it had been because of her parents' deaths, which happened the same year he'd said he met her, but he didn't seem to have bought into the idea even when it fell across his lips. He spent a good two minutes just describing Harper's hazel eyes and how the irises floated in that sea of white. He described her tan complexion and the straight, black hair that fell down her back. Larken didn't have to say much to keep him talking. Clearly, the man was still entirely in love with the woman. Only when he finally paused to collect further thoughts could Larken ask a question.

"Did she leave because of the police?"

To her, a man who seemed as in love as Torrent must have been hard to leave. And after he'd been with Harper through the entire fight with Emergent Biotechnology, which he'd laid out in bits and pieces around his adulations, she wondered what would have driven Harper away.

"No, not really," he admitted. "I mean, yes. She was wanted by them...for stealing Ordell. But she could have gotten past that, I think. And I've had a long time to think."

His eyes once again drifted over to the bottle on the counter. It grated on her nerves to see him do that.

"Then why?" she said, more sharply than she'd intended, and his eyes swiveled back toward her, downcast with her too obvious rebuke.

"Me," he said, pulling from his coffee instead. "It was me. I was there for all of it—the trial, the escape, her hospital stay. But I wasn't invested. I was more interested in getting the science to work than helping her through a crisis. Once Railynn died..."

He stopped for a moment, looked to Larken, cleared his throat, and spoke more softly.

"Once your mother died, there was nothing to keep Harper here. I'm sure she thought she'd lost me, and she had. It took me five years to realize how selfish I'd been and another four to admit it to anyone besides myself. *I'm* the reason she left."

His communicator buzzed, and his eyes darted toward it.

"Excuse me," he said and picked it up again. He was about to push the button until his finger stopped, hovering above it. He looked toward Larken and then back.

"I'll be right back," he muttered and made his way into the main bedroom.

A thousand ideas popped into Larken's mind as to who could be calling. It could be the school seeking her whereabouts and requesting her return. It could be the jail calling to talk about Oliver. Or, this tantalized her the most; it could be Harper, the mystery woman who disappeared so many years ago. After another quick gulp of waffle, she tiptoed to the door and pressed her ear against it.

"Yes," she heard, then a pause. "Yes. That's right. He can come to meet her and then decide for himself. I'm sure Christine will be through most of the rehabilitation by then."

Another pause.

"It's not written in stone, Harper."

She stifled a gleeful squeal. He *was* still in contact with Harper. She listened harder.

"Gallatin said it's fine. Just bring him, and we'll get everything ready."

Still another pause, then Torrent's tone took on a somber edge.

"Oh. Yes, I guess Aiden can come. There's room. You're right, his private jet makes sense to keep you out of the corporate registers, but I don't think Emergent cares about that anymore."

A beat.

"But there's a statute of limitations on grand theft. I checked. It's five years, Harper. You should be in the clear by now."

He took a deep breath.

"Okay, you're right. Human Pride Movement are still active, but not as much on the West Coast. There's minimal risk. It'll be fine."

Larken could almost make out Harper's harsh whisper but couldn't distinguish words.

"No. Since we set up the trust, I haven't been in touch with Ordell. Honestly, I haven't wanted to, but I have *heard* about him. He's in SNO now, promoted to captain or lieutenant."

Larken clenched her mouth shut and drew her lips into a thin line. The Siblings of the Natural Order were a group of models and model sympathizers who believed that nonviolence would never gain equality. Some said the group didn't even want equality but domination. She wasn't sure how true that was. Still, she'd heard that the name meant models were the Natural Order of evolution and would one day replace polli, people who had the disadvantage of not being genetically engineered. And Ordell, who she now knew was her *other* benefactor, was a member. The more she learned about her situation, the more apparent it became why Torrent had maintained such a distance.

She heard the telltale click of the communicator being deactivated, followed by footsteps heading her way. Quickly, she padded her way back to the counter and hastily shoved half of the remaining waffle through her teeth. She looked up to see him exit the bedroom and smiled a syrupy smile before chewing and swallowing, gritting her teeth through the pain of a lump forcing its way down her throat.

"Who was it?" she asked.

"Nobody."

He didn't say another word.

After breakfast and Torrent's morning routine, which took at least forty-five minutes by Larken's count, eight o'clock had finally arrived. Larken felt empty as the call was made. She'd spent an entire weekend apart from her brother, possibly the longest she'd ever gone without *seeing* him, even if they didn't spend as much time talking as they used to. Every prison holovid she'd ever seen rolled through one after the other through her mind. *The Fighter*, a vid about a man who'd been framed only to end up in jail and then in the hospital, shanked on his first day, recurred the most, seconded by *Freedom is for Other People*. That one was a documentary about late twentieth-century punishments like solitary confinement and meal deprivation, along with work gangs.

The buzzing of an outgoing call on Torrent's communicator broke through her thoughts. Torrent paced before it within the device's projection sensor range. When a woman's voice crackled over the connection, he stopped.

"Dallas County Courthouse," came the nasal twang of a woman's North Texas accent. "Can I help you?"

Larken nudged Torrent with her eyes when he looked at her. She wondered how it was possible that this man, in his limited capacity to navigate the world, had ever been considered a revolutionary scientist. He seemed to take the hint and cleared his throat.

"Dr. Alexander Toussaint speaking. My ward was picked up on Friday, Oliver Marche. Can I speak with him?"

The woman seemed to clang something around on her desk, but in voice-only mode, Larken could only imagine that she might have picked up a pinamu to check some records or something, then placed it back down again.

"Oliver Marche," the woman's voice repeated. "Marche... Marche...ah, yes. Oh."

"What?"

"Uh...Mr. Toussaint—" she began, only to be interrupted by Torrent.

"Doctor."

"What?"

"Doctor Toussaint. But what?"

"I see." She took an exaggerated breath on the other end, then emphasized her correction. "*Doctor* Toussaint, I show that he's still in processing, so he'd likely be at the police station on Fifth. Picked up at Brighton Academy, right?"

"Ask her why he was picked up," Larken whispered, trying to avoid being detected by the communicator.

"Who is that?"

"His sister, Larken. Can you tell me why he was collected?"

Larken rolled her eyes at his manner. Collected, like Oliver was a fossil or one of Jocelyn's figurines.

The woman replied. "Yes, let me see. Code is..." She sucked in her breath loud enough for Larken to make out a low whistle through her teeth. "Oh."

Torrent shoved his glasses absently back up his nose. Larken waited for the inevitable reveal of what she already knew.

"Well?" both Larken and Torrent said at the same time.

"Okay then. It looks like murder." A pause. "Hello? Are you still there?"

"I...yes. That's not possible. Oliver couldn't have killed anyone." Even as Torrent said the words, Larken could see the doubt in his eyes.

"I see it right here," the woman said. "Traffic cam picked

him up at the scene—rather *fleeing* the scene. There's a picture and everything."

"But...," Larken said.

"You're not the first person to discover that their loved one may be a murderer, hun," the woman's nasal voice continued. "I can't do anything about that. You can probably find out more there if you want to go down to the precinct."

"But—" Larken started again. Torrent interrupted.

"Thank you," he said. After a second pause, the communicator clicked off.

"There's no way that Oliver killed anyone," she protested, fighting against his nonverbal cues.

"I didn't say anything."

"You're thinking it," she said. "You think he's a clone, and something could have gone wrong with the process. You're thinking about Via and how messed up she is and wondering if Oliver could have something wrong with him too. You're wondering if you even know your brother."

She clamped her hand over her mouth as she finished, realizing late what she'd just admitted and that the doubt she'd thought she picked up in Torrent's face was only a projection of what was in her heart. The lump was back in her throat again, blocking her as she tried to swallow. Her eyes grew heavy with tears, and suddenly it took more effort than she'd needed in her life to stay on her feet. She bit her lower lip and blinked to keep the tears at bay. The room before her blurred as she battled her insecurities. A second passed in silence, and then suddenly, she felt something pressing her close, blocking the light. Tears forced their way from her eyes as she buried her head into Torrent's blood-red shirt and wrapped her arms tightly around him.

He smelled like Oliver, and she soaked it in, letting her

mind believe for a second that she'd had her brother back. She let the tears flow and felt the arms tightening around her back, securing her sobbing, shaking body in place.

"It's not fair," she muttered. "I know him. He's my brother. I *know* him. He couldn't have done this."

"No," Torrent agreed. "No, he couldn't have. You would know. Trust yourself."

Suddenly, he wasn't the bumbling idiot of a scientist any longer. Even when he cleared his throat, and she heard the rumbling of mucus rattling through his chest cavity, she squeezed tighter and let the tears fall where they might. After more seconds had passed, she pulled back against his arms, and he let her go. Then he wiped his own eyes, lifting his glasses with one hand and giving the other one quickly over both. They stared at each other.

"I'm sorry," he said, and it could have been for anything. She thought she knew what the apology was for, but let him say it. He cleared his throat again. "I'm sorry I haven't been there for you two. I thought I was doing the right thing. I thought it would be dangerous for you if I were close, especially given the national spotlight. I thought..."

"I understand," she said, nodding her head. "It's okay."

"It's not," he said. "And after we're through this, I'll do better. I swear I'll do better for both of you."

Larken backed away from him. As the crippling anxiety and sadness left, the awkwardness worked its way back in. She flashed a thin smile and turned away, feigning looking for her bag though she knew exactly where she'd left it.

Torrent made one more call before they departed—to Molly's mother, Brigid, who made them swear to stay put until she could collect them to take them to a nice brunch.

"No," Larken protested as the time to reconnoiter with

her brother threatened to be pushed back one more time. "Brunch? You have to be joking."

"Larken," Torrent admonished, as though he had a right to do so. She glared at him.

"We're not going down there without a plan," Brigid said. "And I haven't eaten yet this morning. Brunch. Plan. Precinct."

CHAPTER 12

THE LEGAL MOM

"I TALKED TO THE STATION," Brigid told them as a man in a black suit jacket deposited them at a square table. The texture of the tabletop reminded Larken of the flooring in the gazebo at Brighton—mostly smooth and undeniably harder than the human skull—as many a student could attest. Brigid's hand rubbed a spot on her left temple. "We have a problem."

"Already?" Larken asked.

Brigid took a deep breath that expanded her chest and shoulders. Her face seemed to swell enough that Larken thought her overapplied makeup might crack.

"This won't be easy," Brigid said. Then she didn't say anything for about three seconds as her eyes darted up and down what little of Larken's torso was visible over the edge of the table. The waiter poured water for all three of them and left before Brigid Kostic continued.

"They're saying he *killed* someone. Some poor guy was at a traffic light when a bunch of thugs pull up. One of them gets out of the car in full view of the traffic camera—Oliver. Then he beats—excuse me—the *shit* out of the driver."

Larken's heart pounded in her chest, and her teeth ground together. Her eyes blurred as she sat in silence. Then, she let out a terse one-line response when the emotions were almost uncontainable.

"Not a chance."

"I don't think so either. Here's the problem, though. They have already run a DNA test. The woman wouldn't give me the exact results, but she says they're conclusive. That usually means at least seventy-five-percent similarity—higher than with a sibling."

The woman's eyes, green like Molly's, had until then been focused on Larken as though she was the only one to whom the story might matter. When she reached the end of that last sentence, her eyes drifted toward Torrent.

"I know Oliver's been in school at Brighton that whole time. I *know* he's old enough to take day or weekend trips with guardian permission. And it's not like the place is a prison." Her eyes darted back to Larken, whose presence here instead of in her classroom proved the point. Then she looked back at Torrent one more time.

"Can *you* think of any reason Oliver's DNA would match someone who bludgeoned a person to death in the middle of the night?"

"Which night?" Larken interrupted. "Which night was it? He's been studying for college entrance exams. His roommate should be able to vouch for him."

"There are no cameras in the bedrooms, Larken. Even if his roommate does testify, it'll be his word against what the jury sees with their eyes and against DNA evidence. We need a better reason for the match."

Brigid's eyes moved back to Torrent and parked there. His blue orbs somehow managed to hold Brigid's gaze, though it was clear he didn't want to.

"There's a reason," he said, despite the warning glance that Larken stabbed at him through the space between them. She could already see Brigid's reaction when she had firm evidence that Oliver was a model. The idea even made Larken shiver, and she'd had two days to come to terms with it. She could only imagine how Brigid, Molly's mother, who had for so many years been a mother to her also, would react to learning that her daughter's affection had been stolen by someone less than human.

Less than human.

The idea had leached into Larken's mind without her permission, but it was there, and she felt her chest seize at its effortless possession of her faculties. She thought of Oliver and the last time they'd been together. Larken pondered over his mannerisms. Which of his quirks gave him away? And then, inevitably, her mind circled back to herself. Which of *her* quirks betrayed her model history? Did being a model explain her worst impulses?

Could Oliver have done it?

Torrent shoved his glasses up against his eyebrows, and his lips met in a solid line, parting again to let him speak.

"He's one of the Firsts, Brigid," Torrent said. The words lit up Brigid's eyes, widening them until a sea of white surrounded the green irises.

"And you kept them a secret for this long?"

"Yes. Oliver, Larken both. And as of about a week before, they aren't the only two at Brighton Academy. I don't know how it happened, but there are four of them there now."

Larken nodded. "Elijah looks almost exactly like me. But Via...well, she looks like Via."

Torrent frowned.

"I'd never expected that they would look so much alike."

Larken studied Brigid's face—easy to do without detection because, since the revelation, the woman seemed to avoid looking at Larken. The woman's features had a tired look, as though she was already exhausted at the work that loomed before her. Her lips were forced into a plastic smile that didn't even try to mirror in her eyes.

"This is a problem. Your success overshadowed the question of what became of the Firsts, Torrent. I'm guessing we all—I know I did—thought they'd been reclaimed," Brigid said, directing her eyes to Larken. "It's a serious problem. To claim Oliver's innocence is to admit that he's a model and reveal that other Firsts are out there. His freedom might be forfeit anyway if we do that. And once we admit that he's a model, in the minds of some, that would only cement his guilt."

She closed her mouth as the waiter approached and dropped something that looked like fried onion rings on a white dish before them.

"Have you decided?" he asked, stepping back to wait for her response.

"We need a few more minutes," Brigid said, continuing as soon as he was gone. "Torrent, you remember what it was like. You *know* what we're up against here. The minute they discover he's a model, then *you* go on trial. You broke the Madison Rule as a model producer. Where are the barcodes? How are you tracking them to ensure they don't cause problems like this? You could end up in jail without guaranteeing that Oliver will be freed."

Brigid took another breath and turned her toward Larken. She didn't have to say what they were probably both thinking: no college for Oliver and no lofting for Larken.

"The law is clear, Torrent. Models don't have rights. Not yet," she said, apologizing to Larken with her eyes as she said this. "He's guilty if he's not a model because of DNA and cameras. If he is a model, he's still guilty. I'm being as honest as I can here."

Brigid's hand went up to her temple again, tapped once, and then came down. Larken stared at the spot long enough that Brigid's gaze found hers, and she stopped a halfway-raised hand from hitting the site again. The makeup seemed thicker there, and a little had flaked off to reveal what Larken thought might be the edges of a scar. Brigid pretended not to notice Larken's stare.

"I don't know that there's a way to win this," Brigid said, then motioned with one hand to keep the overeager waiter at bay in the distance. "I don't. The public isn't there yet."

The hand went up again, then tapped and fell quickly.

"Even if they were, it would be too close. No. This cannot ever come up in any conversation we have going forward. I'm only going to say this once. *If Oliver were to disappear, there couldn't be a trial.*"

Larken's mouth dropped open. Brigid reached across and tapped her chin to shut it, shaking her head. Then Brigid continued.

"A non-model could be released on bail, especially someone his age. The judge is *looking* for an excuse to keep him out. Suppose he was not to make court and never, ever surface again. And suppose, then, that someone who looked exactly like Oliver suddenly appeared and had the same DNA. The court would then have to conclude that it was not Oliver and try that person instead. Is this making sense?"

Torrent nodded, but Larken wasn't sure what she was hearing.

"Are you saying that we should run away with Oliver?"

"I'm not saying that. As his lawyer, I could never recommend that. I'm only laying out a hypothetical. If you and he were to run away, and then if the true culprit was found out, I don't think any police would have a reason to continue looking for you."

Larken looked toward Torrent. His eyes focused on Brigid for three seconds before they dipped toward Larken. She could see the same idea that churned her stomach pressed on him. Larken hadn't considered that anti-modeling bias would work against her brother, mainly because she'd never considered that she might be a model before a couple of days ago. She'd had no reason to think about the fate of models as anything but a thought experiment. She'd never even met a model before in person.

Larken's communicator buzzed loudly in her pocket. All eyes, from their table to the kitchen, turned disapproving looks her way. In a flush, she fished it out, carefully setting it on private mode before answering.

"Is that the only way?" she heard Torrent asking as she answered her call. Brigid said something, but Larken had already invested in the call and didn't make it out exactly.

"There's trouble here," Larken heard Jocelyn's voice on the other end of the call. "HPM Lite are harassing Elijah."

"Why? What happened?"

A deep breath on the other end. The waiter put a dish in front of her that looked like porridge and smelled like sour cabbage. Larken closed her mouth and blew out through her nose to avoid the foul odor.

"Oliver's roommate couldn't keep his mouth shut. He's been talking nonstop about the police barging in and taking Oliver in the middle of the night. Then Elijah showed up in class this morning, and Isaac said something about how much he looked like you. Now HPM Lite is telling everyone that you're a model, and *Oliver's* a model, and that's why the police got you both."

Molly's voice floated over the receiver, a plea mixed with a scream.

"Stop it! Oliver's not a clone, and Elijah just *looks* like Larken. It's a coincidence."

"You're a model lover. I always knew it," came Anthony's voice.

"But don't worry," Jocelyn said. "Molly and I can handle it. That's not why I'm calling."

"In the middle of class, and *that's* not the reason?"

"The school is looking for you, Larken. Whatever you two did, nobody told the school. Ms. Carrish is in the hall talking with Mr. Beverley right now. I overheard a bit, and they think you ran off to look for Oliver."

It wasn't too far off, though their lives would be much less problematic if the school didn't think she'd run away. Larken thanked Jocelyn, disconnected, and turned to Torrent. His eyes had that lost look she'd seen when she'd first found him in his home in Seattle.

"...there's a road north from there. Then we cut across. If we can make it to..."

Both heads turned at once toward Larken, and Torrent's mouth slammed shut simultaneously.

"Well?" his eyes read.

"There's trouble at school. Did you call to tell them?"

His eyes went wider, which she hadn't thought was possible. Larken watched Brigid's hand float over Torrent's, her fingers stroking his knuckles.

"It's okay. Just call and tell them, that's all. Not a big deal."

"I don't want to do this," he said. "My son...I have other things to deal with right now."

Larken hadn't expected the pain to rise in her chest. *My son.* He'd said the words, and from the look on his face, Torrent had no idea the damage his words had done to her. *She* wasn't his daughter. *Oliver* wasn't his son. They were inconveniences and interruptions to his otherwise perfect life with his *real* son.

Because he doesn't consider me a daughter.

Larken felt like less than an afterthought, and the little effort he'd been putting in was about to run out because his *real* son needed him for something. She imagined it was probably a school project or some dumb household responsibility. His *real* son wasn't about to be locked away for the rest of his life, Larken guessed. His *natural* son wouldn't have to hide from law enforcement.

She turned her eyes downward to focus on the unappetizing dish before her.

"Try it," Brigid said. "It tastes much better than it smells."

Larken tapped the spoon emerging from the mushy bowl and watched it settle into the soup. She didn't try to raise it to her mouth, trying to keep her eyes from filling with tears and afraid to lose control. The words bounced around in her mind, knocking emotions loose that she'd shelved long ago. Fear of abandonment and that nobody loved her. The lone isolation of someone who had no real place in the world. She now realized she'd only saved these fears to find a person to relieve her of them, and some of her thought Torrent was that person. That part of her was wrong.

"I want to see Oliver," she said. "Now."

"I'll take you," Torrent said, rising. "We need to get over there and check on his bail."

"No," Larken said, her voice quivering. "No, we don't need your help, Torrent. It was a mistake bringing you into it. This isn't your problem."

"He's my responsibility," Torrent said. "And you are too."

"No, we're not," Larken told him. "You've done enough. Just give us whatever is due from the trust to cover the bail. Go back to your *son*."

Torrent seemed oblivious to the inflection in her tone, but Brigid focused her green eyes sharply on Larken. Larken tried to ignore the look and continued her tirade.

"You have other problems. We're old enough to be emancipated, and we'll do that. You won't have to be inconvenienced again."

"You're not an inconvenience...," Torrent said before he stopped himself. He seemed then to catch on and lowered his voice.

"I didn't mean it that way," he said, his hair shaking like a tree in a strong wind.

"Yes, you did," Larken said. "You didn't know what you were saying, but you meant it. Why shouldn't you? We've been nothing but a burden to you. I don't even know who you are, not really. And for all you know, Oliver and I worked together to kill that person."

"Don't ever say that out loud," Brigid whispered. "You

never know who might be listening. You're innocent, always, any time you talk about it. Understand?"

"You don't know who we are," Larken continued, ignoring Brigid. "And it's not fair of us to ask for your help. Just please call the school, and get them to stop looking for me. And when you get the emancipation documents to sign, don't fight it."

Torrent looked lost for a moment, still standing and yet not moving. His eyes lowered slightly as he mulled over the decision she'd put before him. She wanted him to stay and to insist that she was wrong. She wanted it so much that her eyes burned. As his back straightened, he looked to Brigid for guidance, Larken thought. Brigid conveyed nothing. She probably made an excellent lawyer. Just as Larken thought he might sit back down and insist on being there and helping them—just when she thought he might protest that he was her *father* and needed to be part of her life—he turned and walked a slow, staggering pace away from them.

"I can stop him," Brigid said loudly enough for only Larken to hear. "If that's what you want. I can go after him and convince him to stay."

Larken swallowed, and a tear trailed down from her left eye. She angrily swiped at it with her palm and missed the first try. On the second attempt, she lifted too hard and felt the throbbing pain of accidentally punching herself in the eye. The waiter approached, apparently thinking she'd waved to him.

"We need a minute," Brigid said, dismissing the confused man.

"Of course," the man said and returned to his state of perpetual waiting against a far wall.

"I don't need him," Larken said. "And he doesn't need

me. It was just a big misunderstanding bringing him in the first place. His son needs him."

Larken felt the tips of Brigid's fingers sliding over the back of her hand to console her. All of her emotions assaulted her, and she found herself flinging her arms around Brigid's neck, as she had many times as a young child, and seeking comfort in the warmth of her embrace. She subdued her sobs into quiet, tame, grumbling noises and held on while the wave slowly passed. Once finished, she scooted herself back into her seat, placed her napkin across her lap, and spooned a bit of the disgusting-smelling soup into her mouth. It tasted of bacon and cheese, despite its unfortunate aroma, and had she not eaten waffles and syrup, she might have eaten more.

"Shall we go?" Larken asked and tossed the napkin over her meal.

LARKEN MOVED QUICKLY between the tables, followed by Brigid, who kept up with Larken's near-sprint in heels. They breached the door leading back out to the lower-canopy levels of walkways, and both of them abruptly stopped.

Torrent hadn't left. Larken didn't know whether to be relieved or annoyed that he stood beyond the doorway, staring absently toward the sky. He squinted his eyes at something. Larken followed his gaze to where a volantrae that looked like a flattened basketball descended toward him. He just hadn't left *yet*, she realized. Panic swelled inside her as the vehicle lowered itself to land before him. One of the arc-bounded panels swung upward for admittance.

"Torrent," she blurted out. He turned his head to look, seeming confused at first about who would be calling him and why. She saw at that moment a timid and concerned older gentleman who was so far out of his element that he wasn't even able to properly hail a cab. A pang of guilt pushed her forward when she thought about what it must have taken to give her and Oliver the safety they'd enjoyed most of their lives. It wasn't Torrent's fault that Elijah and Via had shown up at Brighton Academy and screwed it up. Nor was it his fault that someone had been killed. Like Larken, he had been tossed into the turbulence of this new life without anyone's consideration.

"Larken?"

"I didn't mean it," she said, running now, leaving Brigid by the entrance. "I didn't. You've done a lot for us."

He cracked a smile.

"I didn't think you did," he said. "We've been running since we met, and there's so much we haven't talked about."

He shook his head, white hair flying left and right.

"Get in," he said. "This ride is for all of us."

He hopped in and slid over until he was on the basketball's far side, pressed against the translucent wall. Larken followed and made room for Brigid after her. Once all three were seated, the driver's voice sounded from around them.

"Where to?"

"Police precinct," Brigid said. "Dallas, Texas."

"I can get you to Vancouver. My license is only in the state. A bus depot there can get you the rest of the way."

"We'll take it."

The precinct reminded Larken of the bees moving around in artificial beehives that her class had visited on field trips. People clambered about, bumping into each other and all but climbing over one another. Had there been the persistent slick sheen of royal jelly on everything, it would have been a perfect analogy. The buzz of chatter ebbed and flowed in undulating waves. Larken filtered through the voices, seeking out the one she knew in her heart she wouldn't find among the crowd.

"Can I help you?" A man dressed in a dark green top with brown trim against a pair of clashing green pants slid in front of her, blocking her forward progress.

"Yes. I need…," she started, then realized quickly that the man wasn't paying attention to *her*. Instead, he looked past her and Torrent and focused all of his energy on Brigid. The man posed, leaning against a desk with a leery smile as he licked his lips. Larken wondered if the man knew how lecherous his behavior was. This man had no interest in helping anyone but himself, and he'd be disappointed if he thought of pursuing Brigid, who'd been happily married since she and her wife had adopted Molly. The man slicked back a lost strand of graying brown hair, tucking it into the rest of his greased mop. Brigid seemed utterly unfazed.

"Only if you know where I can find Oliver Marche," she said. "I'm his lawyer, and these are his relatives." She motioned to Torrent and Larken.

"He didn't say he had relatives," the man replied, his smile fading with Brigid's apparent lack of interest. "Holding cell nine. I'll get the chief."

The man disappeared into the mass of bodies, only to re-emerge a minute later with a woman behind him who Larken assumed to be the chief of police. The chief was shorter than Larken and wore close-cropped black hair. A thick black belt stretched across her waist, tucked under what seemed like an extended cardigan that reached her knees. Blue and green swirls covered sleeves that ended toward the end of mostly manicured fingernails—except a broken one on the index finger of her right hand. Larken noticed this because the woman's other fingers seemed to flick at it as though teasing it. As she watched, the other fingers ran from it, and the hand lowered itself and outstretched toward her. Instinctually, Larken shook.

"I'm the chief of police," the woman said. "Carrol Shmueli, at your service. You're interested in Oliver Marche?"

She directed the question at Larken as she shook the hands of Torrent and Brigid in turn.

"Yes," Larken said, surprised at the softness of her voice in the woman's intimidating presence. "Can we see him?"

The woman flashed a quick smile to Larken.

"Of course," she said, though she didn't make any move to lead them anywhere. Instead, she turned her attention back to Brigid. "And you're the lawyer, right?"

"That's right. My client..."

"Your client doesn't seem to know you're his lawyer. He hasn't asked for one."

"The family has hired me," Brigid explained, motioning toward Larken and Torrent.

"He mentioned a sister," the woman parried. "But who's the man?"

With that last sentence, her gaze switched over to Torrent. Larken could see in her unwavering stare that the woman was looking for a reaction. He did what Torrent always did—stared nervously back.

"Are you taking us to him or not?" Brigid asked, her voice taking on just a hint of annoyance. The woman broke her gaze from Torrent and started walking quickly between clusters of people and furniture.

"This way," she said, without looking back.

The woman's brisk pace through the minefield of scattered desks and discarded rubbish kept Larken's eyes focused on where her feet would land next. From that vantagepoint, she saw the corners of desks and occasionally the impossibly shiny black of corfam shoes. Her focus was so siloed that when the train of people finally stopped, she collided softly with Brigid.

"Through there," the woman said, pointing to a door ahead of them. For half a second, Larken thought it was a trap and that if they went through the doorway—which the woman had no intention of going through herself—they would never leave again. She exhaled a slow, steady breath and followed Brigid, with Torrent close behind. Her breath immediately sucked back in when she saw Oliver's face, puffy from crying, she guessed, but it was him. She ran to him, elbowing past Brigid, and threw her arms around his head. Her tears, a wall of which she felt that she'd been holding in for three days, erupted into his neck as she sobbed mercilessly.

When Larken didn't feel his arms around her, she stopped her quaking body and backed up. He wore hand-cuffs that were also fastened to the table. She bit her lip and tried wiping away her tears, but the effort was useless as they only smeared on her cheeks beneath the palm of her hand. There were too many to wipe away.

"Larken," he said as his eyes cleared. "I didn't do it. They keep asking me about someone named Armondo Mills. They showed me *pictures*. That poor guy, just minding his business at a traffic light."

He seemed to notice Brigid then, who surveyed the room.

"Ms. Kostic?"

"I'm representing you, Oliver. Molly told me about the trouble, and your sister asked me to help. We'll have you out of here in no time. Listen carefully. We can talk all about why you're here later. For right now, I need you not to say another word. Can you do that for me?"

He nodded, and Brigid motioned to Larken to take the sole seat across from him.

"Just wait a minute, everyone. Someone will be in shortly," she told them, and sure enough, as soon as the words left her lips, the door behind Torrent slid open again, causing him to shudder and twist his head to see that the chief finally entered.

"You can let him go now," Brigid said. "He's a minor. Holding him in here without a parent?"

Brigid shook her head slowly from side to side, her fine, dark red hair swaying.

"It's murder," Shmueli told her. "We're treating him like an adult because that was a very adult crime he did. Right, Oliver?"

Oliver began to retort, but Brigid shot a look at him that sealed his lips together.

"Alleged. He didn't do it, and when it comes out that he didn't, there will be questions about how you've been treating this innocent young boy. I heard that you were showing him pictures of dead bodies. I'm sure the press would love to hear about that."

Shmueli crossed around the table and worked on his handcuffs. Larken didn't see any other indication that Brigid's words had had an effect. As Oliver slowly stood, she turned to address all three of them at once.

"He was only here for questioning. Time's up, but don't go far."

She turned to Brigid and shot her a grin.

"And we have DNA," she said. "Don't go anywhere. We'll be in touch."

"You can't use that DNA," Brigid said. "Taken from a minor without parental representation or a lawyer present? You should know better."

"He's sixteen and gave it voluntarily. Don't lecture me about the law. I enforce it daily."

Larken let the two of them fight and left her seat to see her brother again. She made her way to his side and gave him a smile, which he returned in a thin, stressed grin. She wondered exactly what they'd been doing to him this entire time. His eyes refused to settle on Shmueli as they kept drifting toward the door.

"Let's go," he said, making his way around the table. Larken followed, and Brigid swayed so that her body was between Shmueli and the pair.

"We'll be in touch," Shmueli said, staring after them. Larken felt her gaze through Brigid's tense body.

"Oh, do," Brigid said. "I can't wait to hear from you."

"Can I borrow your communicator?" Oliver asked Larken as they left the room and re-entered the beehive buzz of the open office space.

"Sure," she said, grabbing his hand and squeezing, then not letting go while they walked. "As soon as we get out of here."

A pocket of silence enveloped them as they walked. Groups of people suddenly stopped talking and stared as they traversed the floor. As soon as they passed, the chatter began again, livelier than before. Larken couldn't determine what the people were saying to each other, but it wasn't hard to imagine that everyone in the precinct was confused by his leaving—even if he wasn't under arrest.

"That was easier than I thought," Brigid said as they passed through the entrance. "It's good to know the DNA was a bluff. That could make things easier."

"It was?" Larken asked.

"Of course. We wouldn't have been able to walk out with him if they'd had matching results. They either haven't processed the sample, or the sample didn't match, and they need more evidence."

"The DNA will match," Torrent said, breaking his longest stretch of silence since Larken had met him, not counting sleep.

"It may not," Brigid said. "Possibly, it's just a case of mistaken identity."

"I saw that video. One of the other officers had it playing on their holovid. That young man looked almost identical to Oliver."

"I'm sorry. Who are you?"

Torrent stopped and turned his far-off gaze into Oliver's general direction.

"I guess you could say I'm your father."

Larken's jaw dropped at his rapid admission, and Oliver had a similar reaction. Torrent took in both of their looks and then began to retract.

"Not...like your *father*, father. But I've been charged with your care for the last..."

Before he could finish, his communicator chimed. His eyes darted over them both, and then his hand jetted into his pocket to retrieve it. Switching it to private mode on the way up, he placed it next to his ear and turned away from them, putting a finger up. Larken felt her teeth clenching together and felt a tug on her shoulder. She turned to look into Brigid's eyes.

"I think you're expecting too much," Brigid said. "Torrent is...very self-involved. If you're waiting for him to come around and be an actual father, I don't think that will happen. It's not *intentional* cruelty. His mind doesn't work the same way as everyone else's. Terrific scientist and pioneer, but from what I've seen, often not a very present person."

Larken shook her head and forced her jaw to relax.

"I'm fine," she said, eyes sliding toward Oliver. "Are you okay?"

"What does he mean?" Oliver asked. The tiredness loomed in his eyes.

"Nothing," Brigid interrupted before Larken could answer. "That's not important right now. Oliver, did they take your DNA?"

"They said it would help to prove my innocence."

"So they just haven't processed it yet," she surmised. "When they do, they'll be even more interested in finding you—and it won't be just because of a murder."

"...Wednesday? I'm kind of in the middle of something," Torrent's voice suddenly rose over theirs. Brigid paused for a second and then continued.

"Listen to me very carefully. Torrent is going back to Seattle. He's not going to want to miss his work for much longer if I remember anything about him. When he does go, you need to go with him."

"Won't that get us in trouble? They said I couldn't leave. I didn't do anything, Ms. Kostic; you have to believe me. My books...*Molly*."

Brigid's green eyes suddenly glossed over with shine as she shook her head.

"Oliver, you *can't* go back to Brighton Academy. You are

a *model* in the eyes of the law, whether you want to be or not. That means you don't have any rights. This case is not going to prove your innocence, however it plays out. You'll end up in jail."

Oliver's eyes squinted closed as he seemed to try to make sense of her words. It was probably his first time learning that he was a model, and Larken still felt the shock from when she heard it. Listening to the word out loud made it real. Larken had felt her rights ripped away with the force of it. She knew what he would say next.

"That's not true," he said. "Whoever spreads those rumors must stop before it gets out of hand. People get hurt for things like that."

It was as though he'd completely missed that the speaker was Brigid, an adult and the mother of his—girlfriend?— who'd leveled the accusation.

"It is true, Oliver," Torrent confirmed, sliding his communicator into his pocket. "You both are models. You're one of the Firsts. Sixteen years ago, you helped revolutionize the modeling industry. I...I tried to keep you safe, but..."

He trailed off into silence, then cleared his throat with an annoying hacking sound. Larken cringed.

"Follow me to my car," Brigid said, casting glances around them. "More privacy and we can talk about an actual plan."

"I can't, Brigid. I have to leave," Torrent said. Brigid's eyes slid toward Larken, and she raised an eyebrow.

"Why? Is it your *son*?" Larken didn't mean the words to come out as angry-sounding as they did.

"He's *dying*, Larken. A blood disorder. I've invented a treatment that will cure him, but I'm the only one who can administer it, and he's coming to the H-Hotel on Wednesday. I *have* to be there. It's life or death."

Larken grabbed Oliver's hand and squeezed, feeling his energy course through her.

"I'll come back," Torrent said. "The operation doesn't take long. I can come back next weekend, and we can plan for the next steps."

"Not good enough," Oliver said. His words came out flat and cold. "That's not good enough at all. They will arrest me again before then."

"You have to take us with you," Larken said.

"I can't do that, Larken. If I do, they'll come looking for me too, and I can't risk not being there for Bodhi."

"They won't know it was you, Torrent," Brigid suggested. "Here's what we'll do."

Her plan was workable, thorough, and impressive for having come up with it during the short departure from the police precinct. Larken and Oliver would make their way to Seattle. The bus was still a relatively anonymous way of traveling and would take them for a few thousand dollars. Torrent could take his flight, a short hop, and then pick up the twins from the bus station after he landed. There would be no record of either of them leaving the state, and both Brigid and Torrent could claim plausibly that they had no idea anything untoward had happened.

It was a mostly good plan. All that remained was actually doing it.

CHAPTER 14

THE FEARFUL LEADER

"YOU MAY AS WELL COME with us," Elijah said His dark brown eyes were echoes of Larken's. Elijah seemed to think he was the de-facto leader of a group that consisted of him, Via, Molly, and Jocelyn. He wasn't. Molly was. But the most irritating thing about the entire situation was that she let him do it by going along.

What else was she supposed to do?

Molly found herself bereft of ideas and lacking the willpower to develop new ones. Nobody understood what she had with Oliver. He'd never thought of her as Larken's friend any more than she'd thought of him as Larken's brother. They'd circled each other in Larken's orbit, afraid to hurt the person they both loved. That hadn't stopped them from seeing each other, even before Larken gave her blessing. Being with Oliver was natural like she'd waited for him since she was born. It was as though something had clicked into place in the universe. And then he'd been taken away. There hadn't been enough time for all the conversations they had yet to have.

"Peach?" Via asked, drawing Molly back into reality. Molly took a seat beside Via and accepted the peach. She noticed a carefully stacked pyramid of them before Via on the table as she took it.

"You're going to get in trouble if the student monitors catch you," she said. "Peaches aren't synthesized, and the monitors are cautious about rationing the real food."

Via beamed at her and took a bite out of the one in her hand. Juice dribbled down her chin. She wiped a stream away casually. Her wide eyes darted to where the student monitors stood huddled together in the corner of the cafeteria, casting wary glances.

"They don't seem to want to talk to me about anything. So, more peaches!"

Her face glowed with excitement, sinking Molly's stomach. To Via, she guessed, Oliver being locked up was a fair trade for an endless supply. He was little more than a name to her and Elijah both. Molly's eyes strafed over Elijah. The empty seat beside her, where Jocelyn usually sat, emphasized the hollow feeling in her chest. Her eyes darted involuntarily to where Jocelyn now resided, chatting eagerly with gaming club members.

Jocelyn seemed to sense her gaze and met her stare, then furrowed her eyebrows into a quick tent. As she began to raise herself from her seat, undoubtedly to console Molly, Molly shook her head no. It was okay for Via to enjoy the peaches, and it was okay for Jocelyn to be with her other friends. Molly had no say in it and didn't think she should, a sentiment she realized wasn't her usual center-of-attention position. Jocelyn sat back down and rejoined the conversation.

Across the room, Molly's eyes landed on Anthony Lee,

who she had been staring at the entire time with his unflinching eyes. Surrounding him were the usual crew. Molly nudged Elijah with an elbow and motioned with her eyes.

"Shit," he said.

HPM Lite had traversed the room directly toward the table where they sat. Molly got up, feeling exhaustion drain any desire for confrontation. Via touched her arm for assurance, but Molly lifted her shoulder to shrug the touch away.

"I'll be in my room," she said and stormed away from the table. As she did, she noticed HPM Lite change direction and circle back toward where they'd been sitting. Any doubt about whether they'd been coming for her evaporated with the glare Anthony passed at her as she exited.

Three minutes later, she found herself outside Oliver's room instead of her own. She ran her fingers along the composite door frame and then, surprising herself, twisted the doorknob. The door sprang open with its motorized assist, exposing the entrails of the room to her.

It looked the same as when she'd last been there. Clutter oozed out from Oliver's roommate's side, though it seemed to die off at about halfway between his bunk and Oliver's. There, the bed lay empty; blanket tucked meticulously beneath the twin-sized mattress and headboard cluttered with tablets and data coins.

Roommate absent, Molly strode to Oliver's bedside and deposited herself on his blanket. She lay back and let the scent of him fill her nostrils. The muscles in her clenched stomach loosened, and she felt herself drifting off into sleep. Her mother's face surfaced in her mind, stern yet forgiving. She knew the expression and the incident that had forged it.

"It's too hard," a five-year-old Molly had complained.

She'd sat for half the day on her bed, refusing any work. Her mother, busy with clients, hadn't had time to ensure that Molly did her cleaning, so it never got done. Instead, Molly leveraged her mother's hectic schedule against her by stalling with "it's too hard" repeatedly. That memory was one of a handful she still had from that time in her life, and her mother's reaction had built itself into the foundation of her character.

"Nothing is too hard," she heard her mother's voice. "Nothing is too hard. You pick one small thing and do that. Then you do the next. Eventually, you find that your room has cleaned itself."

Molly smiled at the memory. She took another whiff of the pillow, drenched in Oliver's aroma. She thought through what small thing she could do to help the situation. Stuck here, in Brighton, a place in which Molly knew she'd risen to be both feared and worshiped, yet all of her power here was useless in the world beyond the walls. And even here, with HPM Lite stalking her, there were limits to her influence. In a perfect world, she would have Oliver back. She would...

Molly paused as she considered. The closet was closed before her, but she saw an opportunity. If they managed to get Oliver out, she knew they wouldn't be coming back to Brighton. Her mother had hinted at what her guidance had been when they'd talked the night before. Molly crossed to the closet and slid it open, pulling out Oliver's suitcase. She tossed it on the bed and rummaged through his dresser, gathering clothes he might need.

"What are you doing?"

Molly turned toward the voice, cringing at the same time. In the doorway stood her ex-boyfriend Anthony, flanked by

Susan and Isaac. Behind, she could make out Sun's too-cute round face. She gritted her teeth.

"None of your business," she said.

"Shill-lover," Anthony said flatly.

Molly's first instinct was to deny and say that Oliver wasn't a shill or that she didn't love him. As she thought about it, she realized that love was the right word for what she and Oliver shared. And Oliver was definitely a model. Crudeness aside, Anthony was right, but she would never let him be.

"You don't know what you're talking about, Anthony," she said, spitting the words through teeth that only ground harder into each other.

"Oh, we know," Anthony said. "There's no use in denying."

"Oliver's a shill," Sun said, her voice tinny. "And you love him. So, shill lover's about right."

"Shut up, Sun," Molly said. She took a deep breath and stood upright. "Why are you in Oliver's room?"

"Why are *you*?" asked Anthony. "We have as much right to be in here as you do. Let's see what you've got there."

He walked toward the bed where the suitcase lay partially filled with clothes.

"Are you going somewhere?"

Molly said nothing. Her mind raced as she searched for ways to change the direction of the conversation. She needed a new strategy.

"It takes one to know one, isn't that right, Sun?"

The diversion worked. Anthony's eyes slid from the bag toward Sun, whose face became a scowl.

"You're full of it."

"Really? How would *you* know if Oliver's a model?"

"Elijah looks like a boy Larken. You can't deny that."

"And I look like Mina Stone. Maybe *she's* a model?"

Molly didn't look anything like the world-famous actress but was too busy making a point to correct herself.

"Coincidence."

"I don't think it is. I think maybe I'm Mina's clone."

"What's the bag for, Molly?" Susan's persistent voice cut through the questions.

"None of your business."

"*I* heard that your man *murdered* somebody. *I* think you're trying to help him."

Susan had always been too perceptive.

"Oliver didn't murder anyone."

Anthony laughed. "You know how shills are. They'll kill you as sure as look at you. Doesn't matter to them. Life has no value."

"If only," Molly said, as anger took root in her chest. "Then we wouldn't have to deal with your kind anymore."

"She admitted it," whispered Sun as she narrowed her gaze and twisted her lip into a smirk. "There you have it. Shill-lover, just like I said."

"Did I?" asked Molly as she felt the tension between her eyebrows. "Or did I admit to *myself* being a model?"

She shot out her hand, latched onto Anthony's wrist, and then yanked it back from the bag.

"*That* doesn't belong to you," she said. "And like you said. What if we're killers? Give it back *now*."

Molly swung her face toward the door. If Oliver and Larken could be models in the minds of HPM Lite, then so could she. Molly reached her hand again toward Anthony's wrist, her teeth still clenched together.

"Be careful," Molly said, widening her eyes into a mad

look and darting them at the group. "If you get too close, you could catch Influenza X. You wouldn't want that, would you?"

It was a dumb gamble. She hoped that the mystique of models and the superstitions the group had worked themselves into had the power that would sway them against whatever plan had brought them to Oliver's room. Surprisingly, it seemed to work—even on Anthony.

Anthony yanked his hand back, and Susan went mute, suddenly deep in thought and probably tracing her steps for the last several weeks to see if she'd come into physical contact with Molly.

"Idiots," Molly muttered, slamming the suitcase shut. They stared at her as she yanked the bag off the bed. She steered it toward the door. Susan took an obvious step in the opposite direction from Molly's advance, while Sun tried to be more subtle and went sideways. Molly could taste the fear. She knew how to sell a lie, but that one had taken no skill. They were already so drenched in terror that a nudge was all it took.

"I don't believe you," Anthony growled as she passed.

"*They* do," she whispered, careful to keep her voice down so those behind her couldn't hear. "And you're not that impressive." She glanced down at his crotch, lingered there long enough for him to get the double entendre, and then elbowed him out of the way. Her bony joint dug into the soft flesh beneath his rib cage, causing him to double over in pain and offering her a brief satisfaction.

"Bitch," he gasped out.

"You should know by now," Molly said. She glared at him over her shoulder. He swallowed and sealed his mouth.

HPM Lite had seen her sadness and mistakenly interpreted it as weakness. A little reminder of what it meant to be on her bad side should help keep them at bay.

"Go crawl back under a rock," she said and bolted out the door. Somewhere, Oliver needed her, and she'd spent the time moping and feeling sorry for herself. She *had* to do better. She exhaled and slowed her pace to less of a flight and more of a casual stroll.

The first thing she had to do was excise the fear that kept a stranglehold on her chest and throat. She swallowed and then stepped into the elevator. She worked her way down the hallway and across the common area back on the main level. The students parted for her, aware she was at least superficially back to her old self. She hoped her insides would catch up to the façade. Tilting her head back and keeping her chin up, she bounded toward the exit.

TORRENT RUBBED his nose with his left hand, vaguely aware of the touchdown on the tarmac. He shoved a handful of trash down into the back of the seat in front of him, lost in thought as he planned his arrival. It would be a whirlwind. He barely had enough time to meet Saul Gomez before retrieving the children from the bus station. Gomez first, since his approval dictated whether or not Bodhi's operation could proceed. Oliver and Larken would be fine if they had to wait a few extra minutes at a bus stop—if it came to that.

Fifteen minutes later, a taxi dropped Torrent at the H Hotel lobby, and he made his way up to the fourteenth floor. He raised his hand to knock when the door, adorned with a brass plate reading "Dr. Saul Gomez, Executive Director of Engineering," swung open and slammed into the wall. A woman as tall as Torrent emerged from within. He recognized her as Saul's wife, and they'd been discussing something serious from the rapid dissolution of her polite smile. The woman gave him a quick nod and whisked past him. Then it was Torrent's turn.

Torrent passed through the entryway. Saul Gomez interacted with a holo display over his desk, a holo display that flashed the words "Overton Institute" in a three-dimensional font. His eyes were red from lack of sleep, and his usually pressed sherwani suit looked crumpled and worn. Torrent saw a distinct tic above his heavy brown eyes as Saul lifted them from the display. He caught sight of Torrent and fumbled with something to make the words disappear.

"Is everything okay, Saul?"

Saul brought his lips up into a weak grin.

"Fine, Torrent. Just fine," he said in barely more than a whisper.

Good enough. If Saul was keeping up pretenses that Torrent hadn't seen the name of the world leader among infectious disease institutes over his desk, Torrent didn't have to waste time talking about it.

Saul continued, "You're here about Bodhi?"

"I need the procedure authorization form. You…I haven't seen it in my messages yet. Did I miss it?"

"No. No, you didn't," Saul said as he rubbed his forehead with the four fingers of his left hand. "I keep forgetting to send it. Kind of have a lot happening right now."

"Do you need a copy? I brought one on a data coin," Torrent offered, trying his hardest to steer around the potential minefield of Saul's relationship with his wife. Get the form, and get out. That's all Torrent had time to do.

"I'm sorry, Torrent. Of course, I will." Saul extended his hand into which Torrent dropped a small flattened disc. Saul placed it on the desk, and the form popped up, opening to where the signature would be required. Torrent gnawed at the inside of his cheek and shoved his glasses back up his nose. He accidentally bit down too hard and winced as his teeth grabbed more of his cheek than he'd intended. Saul's hand paused before the single button within the three-dimensional display that required his pressing.

"It's my wife, Kal," he said. "You saw the Overton Institute stuff, didn't you? That's for her."

"And you let her in here?"

"I *just* found out a second ago. Besides, we have the Harrison Brander filtration system and microbe detection nanites. It's not like she will infect anyone in *this* building."

Saul didn't have to say *what* it was that afflicted her. The only thing that it would likely be that started Saul down this maudlin path was Influenza X, although Torrent hadn't considered Saul's wife to be an anti-vaxxer. The vaccine didn't work for some people, and he couldn't assume the worst about Kal because she was infected with something so contagious. Until Saul opened his mouth.

"She'd already had the first dose of the vaccine anyway," Saul continued his monologue as if reading Torrent's thoughts. "The second was coming soon. It took so *long* to convince her, you know. Once Ramsey's talking points took root in her head, it's been such a struggle, Torrent. She tried to get me to quit my research, did you know? Came back from one of those rallies claiming models were the devil. That was a month of couple's therapy."

The meek woman had always at least tried to fake a smile when they'd met in the hallways. The idea of her being a rabid anti-vaxxer and an anti-modeler and supporting that lunatic who had been a welt on American society since he lost his bid for the presidency nearly fifteen years before seemed incongruous. Saul must know though—it was his wife after all.

"It wasn't her fault, Torrent."

"I'm just here for the form," Torrent reminded Saul, motioning with his fingers to the button with which Saul had yet to interact.

"You need to do better at hiding your repulsion from your face. I don't like it either, but she's coming around. And you remember, I was gone all the time. She didn't have anything else to spend her time on but those stupid rallies."

Saul trailed off. He slid his finger over the button, which glowed green upon activation.

"There you go. Good job bringing Christine out of her coma. We should be celebrating right now, not talking about my situation. Drinks later?"

Torrent nodded as he reached for the data coin.

"Sure," he lied, not wanting any additional details about Saul's Ramsey-loving wife but also recognizing that Saul was the one person who could change his mind about Bodhi's operation if Torrent misspoke. "Happy hour sounds good."

He pocketed the data coin quickly and turned to leave.

"And Torrent," Saul continued, "please don't tell anyone."

"Not my business," he commented, more gruffly than he'd intended. "But you need to stop bringing her in here. We may need to immuno-suppress people to get the animus module to take some time. The last thing we need is an outbreak of Influenza X here in the H."

It amazed Torrent that businessman Saul was not thinking well enough to understand what a death blow it would be to the program if one of their successful cases succumbed to the virus. Or worse, what if someone succumbed while *waiting* for their chance at immortality? The fact that Saul also seemed to believe that a fancy filtration system would protect others from getting the disease would have been laughable in a holovid sketch comedy. There was plenty yet unknown about the airborne pathogen.

Torrent imagined the minuscule droplets of death floating across the room toward him so vividly that he backed away from Saul's desk. His communicator buzzed, a timer telling him he was already picking up the kids late. One more stop down to medical to check on the preparations. Aiden and Harper would be in today, Harper's first time back in the United States since she'd fled the country. Bodhi would be with them, a thought that comforted and terrified him at the same time. What if they had nothing to say to one another in person? He'd almost forgotten Saul.

"Torrent," Saul said. Torrent twisted his neck so that he faced Saul's desk again.

"Yes?" he said, fingering the data coin in his pocket.

"I hope it works. For your boy, I mean."

Saul's eyes seemed misty and dark, like he was staring out of a cave. The whites had gone gray around the brown irises. His mouth closed, and he swallowed as he finished saying the words. Suddenly, Saul's degrees and business acumen seemed less imposing, and for a brief second, Torrent saw a person beneath the overachieving veneer. Then it was gone. "If this works, the program can begin in earnest. We've been sitting on buckets of money, waiting for enough successes in a row to begin advertising. Can I show you something?"

Torrent wanted to say no. Larken and Oliver might be on there by now, and *someone* had to pick them up from the bus terminal on Strata 6 nearly five blocks away. He searched the room for a clock, realizing that he'd never actually cared to look at the time in this office before because his visits with Saul had intentionally always been brief. He found two hands floating against the wall to his left, near the door and breathed a short sigh of relief that there was still enough time if he left soon.

"Sure. What?"

Saul smiled, and his eyes brightened as he ran his hand over the desk. With a few flicks, an older man's face materialized in the mist, looking as tired as Torrent felt. The man spoke.

"I've worked hard for what I've got. A lifetime of achievements, only to die? I want better. I *deserve* better."

The shot zoomed out until the man was lying on a beach with a drink and a pinamu tablet in his lap. He addressed the audience again, staring toward Torrent with fire in his eyes.

"This isn't what I wanted. I have so much left to *do*."

A younger man walked by, full of energy, blocking the shot momentarily. The older man's eyes trailed after as a young woman in a swimsuit joined the man, grabbing the young man's arm and smiling a wide grin full of brightness and laughter. The older man turned back to the camera.

"You deserve more too."

Then his face morphed away until he looked twenty years younger, then thirty, and finally, he seemed as capable and young as the other man who'd passed.

"Immortality Program," he said. "Who says you only live once?"

The cube area went black over the desk, and then the holovid faded, leaving only an empty desktop.

"What do you think?" asked Saul, a grin spreading to both ears.

"We haven't even had two successes yet."

"We will, and it's close enough. Officially 'Immortality Program' now. We were *heading* in that direction, but now it's official. 'Immortality Program' is the name. 'Serial Living' didn't test well with the focus groups. Add the word immortality, and suddenly people pay attention. What do you think people will pay?"

Torrent bit his lip. His mind slipped to Bodhi and Harper and the desperation Torrent had felt for so many years. The first thing he'd learned about his only son was that the boy was born dying. He'd have given every single thing he owned for the boy to survive. And even now, if Gallatin had asked him to pay for the operation that he planned to convince Bodhi to accept, he'd still easily cash out his life insurance policy and life's savings to do it. Ordell would probably loan him the money anyway, but Torrent would go destitute if that's what it took. And Torrent, being the chief scientist on the program, knew the risks. Plenty of attempts had failed.

"Everything," he confessed and watched as Saul's eyes lit up. "Absolutely everything."

"It won't cost that. We're selling them like houses. You get a thirty-year lease, only two million per operation."

Torrent's jaw dropped.

"Don't worry, don't worry. Yours is gratis as part of the experiment, and we're working on a company discount. Nothing builds loyalty like offering immortality for you or your loved ones. Eventually, the price will come down."

Torrent's fingers slipped around the data coin, clutching it tightly.

"Saul, I've got to get this down to the lab," he said. "Bodhi's coming in today."

"Sure, yeah. Go do that. Just wanted to let you know what your good work is going toward. By the time we're done, Beckett-Madeline Enterprises will be the largest corporation the world has ever seen. We've got the supply chain on lockdown with Emergent Biotechnology in the fold."

"Good to know," Torrent muttered, finally finishing his turn. He made his way once again toward the door. As he passed through the door, he felt his communicator buzz again and retrieved it from his pocket opposite the data coin. He clicked the voice-only connection.

"Torrent? Can you pick me up from the bus station? A strange man is staring at me like he wants to hurt me."

"Molly?"

"Yeah, it's me. Can you come?"

He sucked in his breath and rubbed the arches over his eyes.

"How did you get my number? What are you doing here? Does your mother know you're here?"

"He's coming this way," she whispered. "I've got to move. Reception isn't good...lose...call."

"Molly? Molly?"

The communicator chimed that the call had been disconnected. Torrent's head hurt behind his eyes. It was already going to be a busy day, and now it had turned into an impossible one. Whatever Molly's situation, he had to get the signed contract to the lab first, so they knew they had the authorization to prepare the lab for another operation. Who knew how long it would take him to remember to send it if he didn't do it right away?

Checking into the lab and dropping off the data coin took only a few minutes, even with friendly chatter. There was one frustrating moment when the machine refused to read the signature. Otherwise, transferring the approval went as smoothly as he could have hoped. That part of his mission complete, he headed out toward the valet's desk to pick up a cab to the bus station.

"Where to?" asked a grubby-looking man in green shorts and a pale blue and yellow shirt from the other side of a transparent glass-looking boundary separating the driver from the passenger. It was a North Cross cab—the least expensive, most available...and most questionable. The guy's demeanor was consistent with Torrent's expectation of the cab ride, nonchalant and with minimal expectations being met.

"Where to, buddy?"

"Bus station. And that's *doctor*, not buddy."

"Oh?" The man turned his head to examine Torrent in his bright-green suit with a matching hat in a mop of graying hair. "Well. Excuse me."

The man's smirking grin left little to be interpreted and spoke more clearly than his words. He turned back to the front and pressed forward on the throttle fast enough to force Torrent back into his seat.

"The one on Third or Strata 6 near the stadium?"

Two. Torrent had only ever passed the one on Strata 6, and there being two hadn't occurred to him.

"Which one has inbound from Portland?"

"Buddy...er, Doctor...both of them. Portland has like twenty inbound buses a day."

"Which one has a bus from Portland arriving within the next hour?"

"I don't know. But how about I take you to one, and if that's not it, we try the next?"

Torrent mentally tallied the cash coins he carried in his pocket. He probably didn't have enough in direct cash.

"Take Biopsi?"

The man sighed heavily.

"Yeah, I guess. Didn't you read the sign?"

Torrent looked for whatever sign the man was talking about and finally found it just above the door handle on a little yellow sticker affixed to the wall. "Cash coins only."

"I don't have enough in cash coins."

"There'll be an extra charge. The biometric withdrawal network charges an arm and a leg."

The man began to chuckle. Torrent caught expectant eyes staring back at him and gave an uncomfortable smile at the bad joke. The biometric withdrawal network used physical recognition and biomarkers to authorize financial transactions. The man was trying to tie together the fact that one could use their body biosignature—ostensibly including arms and legs—to transfer money, if they could afford the several hundred dollars a month for the service. Torrent understood the joke. It simply wasn't funny.

"Funny," he muttered.

"Because of...arm and leg...and biometric?"

The man began to guffaw loudly and slapped his knee, a movement Torrent had never seen in person for the entirety of his life. He'd thought it was an expression left to novelty plays.

"Hold on," the man said, pivoting his gaze back forward in the direction of motion. Torrent was still pinned to his seat in the constant pressure of acceleration. The vehicle slowed and swayed to the right, sliding Torrent over the bench seat and into the far door. His hat tumbled down, and instinct drove him to chase after it only to realize the turn wasn't finished yet, and pitching forward threw him off balance. He rolled toward the wall, his head colliding with the seat.

"Can you drive a little less erratically, please?" he asked

once he managed to right himself.

"I can," the man said. "But if I do, you're not getting there until tomorrow. Traffic is bad this time of day, and I'm guessing you need to get there in a hurry."

Torrent bit his lip and focused his energy on watching the scenery go by outside his window and convincing himself that he wasn't going to die before finding Molly. Every rapid drop in altitude caused his fingernails to cut into the armrest, and by the condition of the armrest, Torrent was sure he wasn't the only one who'd feared for their lives in this man's custody.

To his relief, five minutes later, the volantrae shot up three strata, leveled off, then slowed to a park.

"I'll keep her running," the man said.

Torrent debated whether it was worth it to get back into the volantrae again and decided that having a vehicle waiting was more important than his fear of certain death, especially if Molly wasn't at this terminal. Then he'd need to make it to the other terminal *fast*. Now he had three lost children in the city to worry about. Torrent felt his day wasn't going to get any better.

The door opened automatically, lifting up and inward to latch itself to the ceiling. This motion drew Torrent's eye upward where flying buttresses kept the high roof suspended above his head. People crossed his path to the left and right, none making eye contact, and most staring at their pinamus while walking using their peripheral vision. The massive open-room floor and its possibilities for airflow did nothing to subdue the overwhelming odor of sweaty armpits. Torrent took a tentative step forward before acknowledging that he knew nothing about how bus terminals worked. He flagged down a passing woman in a green sari.

"Excuse me," he said. She came to a quick stop and smiled at him, focusing every inch of her attention on him—or so he felt.

"I'm looking for the inbound from Portland."

"You're in luck, hun," she said, licking her lips in a manner that Torrent thought should probably offend him. "Just came from there. Got family?"

He nodded, feeling the little beads of sweat across his forehead for the first time that day.

"Kind of," he answered. "Is this where you got off?"

"I came all the way from San Diego if you can believe it. Coming up to visit family myself. Up in Bellingham, and this is a transfer stop for me. I have some time, though, and really must find *something* to do for the next hour."

She winked at him.

"Where did you get off the bus?"

She batted her eyelashes, and her face seemed to struggle to restore her smile.

"Back there," she said, raising a finger toward the right of where Torrent stood. "Terminal two."

Without saying anything else, Torrent turned and pushed his way through the waxing sea of people, searching for terminal signs. They had been hidden in plain sight. The terminal numbers were highly artistic. Once he understood that the two lily plants intertwined in what looked like stained glass were an eleven, he could see the rest.

Then he saw Molly. She was pinned against the wall with wide eyes staring across the terminal. She didn't seem to recognize him at first. At her feet was a suitcase that looked as though it had been opened and not entirely shut all the way. One shiny trail traced down her left cheek. When she saw him, she left the bag and peeled herself away from the wall. In a quick, teetering walk, she closed the space between them and threw her arms around his neck.

She buried her face in his chest, and sobs echoed out, filling the cavern and turning everyone's attention to them. Torrent noticed that even though heads shifted toward them, they didn't go all the way. People were watching, yes, but only out of the corners of their eyes.

"Are you okay?" Torrent asked her, careful to squeeze her gently. He told himself not to pull away too soon, even though the tight grip made him uncomfortable.

"Yes. No. I don't know," she said, sniffling into him. "That guy...he came over and..."

She stopped talking. He felt her muscles seize up and her back straighten. Torrent tried to adjust so he could see her face, feeling something more needed to be said, but she didn't let him, tightening her grip as he struggled to move.

"We have to go," he whispered.

"Oh." Molly released her grip slowly, then wiped her face with the palms of her hands. With each wipe, he saw the edgy anxiety disappear.

"Okay," she finally said. Curiosity egged him on, and even though he didn't want to know, he had to ask.

"What happened?"

She shook her head.

"It doesn't matter," she replied. "It doesn't matter...do you have Oliver?"

Most of her body had stopped trembling by then, but he could see in her eyes that fear still hid there. Torrent wondered if the fear was because of whatever had happened to her or if the worry was for Oliver. He reached down to grab her bag, and she didn't object. Torrent fastened the clasps down and lifted the bag to its wheels.

"Come on."

Back at the cab, the driver had waited patiently. Torrent felt the man's eyes soaking them up: the dark-skinned man with a taste for eccentric clothes and the teenage girl he escorted with him. He felt his pulse spike sharply. He couldn't meet the man's eyes. Torrent felt the judgment and assumptions about what this man, who wasn't related to the girl he escorted, was doing with someone that young.

Perhaps it was Torrent's imagination, but when the man let out a "Where to, *Doctor?*", he felt judgment in the tone.

"The H hotel," he replied, not helping his case in the trial of the man's judgment. Pick up young girl and take her back to the hotel—skeevy check. "What time is it?"

"Three," the man said. "About."

Torrent turned toward Molly, who stared silently away from him out the window.

"Did you see Larken and Oliver here anywhere?"

At the sound of Oliver's name, Molly spun her head around.

"Why would I have?"

"I thought maybe you saw them in the terminal. They should be arriving soon."

Her eyes shimmered.

"No," she said in a low whisper. "I thought they were with you already. The next bus here isn't until five."

Torrent turned to the driver.

"There's an extra hundred in it if you can get us to the other bus terminal first in less than five minutes," Torrent said, and as soon as the words left this mouth, the judgmental staring cleared from the man's face, and Torrent was pressed back into the seat again, eyes glued to the back of the driver's head.

CHAPTER 16

URINE AND POPCORN

THE AIRBORNE BUS had a distinct aroma of urine and popcorn, two things that should never be experienced simultaneously. Larken's seat next to the window allowed her to see the tops of trees flitting by as she wished desperately that they could open the window and bring that fresh air in to clean out whatever it was she smelled. Oliver had taken the aisle seat beside her and had donned a stocking cap as a "disguise" to conceal him from the police. It wasn't worth the bother. They hadn't seen anyone wearing the telltale black and white uniform of a police officer on the bus or at the departing station. Larken didn't expect any to be waiting in Seattle, where they weren't criminals yet.

Criminals.

Larken's tongue felt rubbery and seemed to take up the entire inside of her mouth. There was no room to swallow. She chewed her teeth together, feeling the tension of ligaments pulling on the joint in the hinge connecting her lower jaw to the rest of her face. Stretching her mouth open as far as it could go, she tried to pop it or pull her jaw muscles enough for the stiffness to yield. Nothing worked because the tension wasn't physical.

They were criminals now.

Oliver was no more guilty than she was. Everything they now faced was done *to* them and not *by* them. Oliver was falsely accused of a crime. Their very births, or faux births, had been stamped from the start with DNA that would flag them as being models if anyone looked closely enough. They'd been stripped of their rights and futures by little more than existing. The lofting career trajectory she'd set herself on since early childhood had evaporated over a few days. The worst part was that she wasn't sure she even cared right now. Her desire had been stolen from her as well. All she longed for was her bedroom and for Molly to be telling another one of her lies. Jocelyn with her snarky clap-backs and aggressive spirit. Larken even missed some of the teachers who had been less than supportive. Her fourth-grade teacher had twice told her that she'd never amount to anything if she didn't apply herself to something besides lofting. Larken had been sketching lofting plays during tests instead of finishing her prescribed examinations. Larken couldn't help feeling empty when the woman's frown surfaced in her memory.

"Do you think we'll see Brighton again?" she asked, redirecting her gaze from the passing trees to Oliver.

"Shhh," he said, eyes darting around. "We shouldn't talk about that."

"Nobody's listening. Tell me about what happened in jail. What happened when the police came to your room?"

"Not here."

"What *can* we talk about, Oliver?" she asked, feeling heat rush to her face. "We passed Vancouver already. We're in

Washington State now. On a bus somewhere in the wilderness, and I'm *bored* counting trees. *Talk* to me."

He stared at her with that corrective look he often used when she did something he thought was wrong. She returned the same. They locked in a staring battle until the fury passed and she noticed how silly he looked with his eyes furrowed into angry trenches. A giggle worked its way out to her lips. As soon as it did, his eyebrows relaxed, and his eyes lit up. A smile emerged on his face.

"Okay," he said. "Maybe I am being a little overbearing here. What do you want to talk about? Just leave the police out of it, okay?"

"Deal," she replied. "Tell me about Molly. What's up with you two?"

His smile widened. "She's nice," he said.

"Nice? That's the best you can do? Suddenly you're spending every waking moment together until...you know, she spends the night." She lowered her voice to a whisper. "People think that you're having sex."

"And you think I want to talk about that with you?"

"Well, are you?"

He looked at her through narrow slits. "I'm not telling you."

"Nice, though? You have to give me more than nice."

"More than nice. She's amazing. She's kind and fun and looks out for people around her. I like her a lot, Larken. A lot, a lot. And I miss her."

She licked her lips and turned her face toward the window again.

"Yeah, I do, too," she said. "She is *nice*."

Sometimes.

"Told you."

Larken felt his fingers on her hand working their way between hers. She gripped the tips of her fingers to her palm and turned back to him again. He wasn't going to tell her why he and Molly seemed so close, so suddenly. But if she wasn't going to insist that they break up, then she needed to wave the acceptance flag.

"You could do worse, I guess. You could be dating my *other* roommate."

"Jocelyn? Then I'd have to get into that gaming thing she does. What's it called?"

She scrunched her nose. "Underworlder? Yeah, that's kind of weird. And those creatures..."

The conversations for the last few days were centered around Oliver and jail, Human Pride Movement, or their shared past. She and Oliver were talking for the first time in a long time—even before the police arrested him. To be gossiping instead of planning was a welcome change and reminded Larken of when they were younger and shared *everything*.

"Oh, she has a *boyfriend* now," she continued.

His eyebrows shot up.

"Really?"

"Not officially. One of the boys she met at a tournament. He goes to *Protégé*."

"Does he know she's a local?"

"Kind of. But she hasn't told him *everything* yet."

"Like how young she is?"

She nodded. He shook his head, and the way his hair moved reminded her for a moment of Torrent.

"That's going to be a problem," he said. "When he finds out, he's going to flip."

"She told him she goes to Brighton and takes classes at

Protégé for a head start or something. He thinks she's a senior."

"Except for that last part, not all a lie. Not bad. Didn't she take a class there last year?"

She nodded. Then she looked at the back of his knuckles and noticed again that they seemed a little swollen. "What happened to you?"

"I'll tell you. I promise I will, just not here. There's no telling how many of these people are listening in right now or who they'll tell. It's just not safe."

She complied and changed the subject, this time without complaining. It had something to do with the police. Check.

"Tell me this then. What do you think about Torrent?"

"Our *father*?" He shrugged his shoulders. "No, not our father. Benefactor, I guess. Seems distracted to me, like he's got something else going on that's more important than help-ing. He seems actually like a slightly more stable version of Via."

"*Right?* He mentioned something about a dying son too." She shrugged. "I don't know how to read him."

"At least he's helping."

"Some, I guess."

Larken felt her stomach tug forward as the bus slowed. She glanced out the window and down to the treetops and endless wilderness.

"Why are we stopping?" she whispered to her brother, who stared past a couple and a baby in the seat between them and the window beyond. The baby stared back.

"I don't know," he said. "We're not in Seattle yet."

"Model patrol," said an older woman in the seat in front of them.

If she'd heard *those* whispers, then she'd been listening to their entire conversation, Larken realized. Oliver was right not to want to talk about some things. Larken tried to remember if they'd said anything too revealing and came up with nothing.

"Is this normal?"

"Canada's a free country, and this bus continues through Bellingham to BC. There will be a few stops like this. All routine. Nothing to worry about."

Her consolation didn't stop Larken from casting a worried glance at Oliver. He smiled at her and squeezed her hand gently, but she couldn't see the smile in his eyes. The older woman started speaking again.

"It's okay," she said. "I promise. Happens all the time. Whatever you're running from, this isn't related."

A harsh male voice came from the front of the bus.

"Looking for twins Oliver and Larken Marche. They're about sixteen or seventeen and wanted for questioning about a crime in Oregon."

Larken bit her lip and kept her gaze out the window, focusing on one tree and then the next, to feign disinterest. Oliver pulled his hand back.

"*Lacey*," he reminded her. "I'm *Junior*. Don't forget."

The bus held steady, still high up above the trees. Larken searched for the police vehicle but couldn't see it past the front of the bus. She couldn't see over the heads of the people in the seats before them and didn't want to draw attention by standing as others did. Larken listened to the slow thud-thud of boots and shuffling for identification as the police approached. She swallowed and looked to Oliver for assurance. His smile had abandoned him, and he only looked at her with the same inquisitive stare. Oliver's hands shook.

"It'll be okay," she assured him, taking on the role that

he'd generally assume. She forced a smile when all she wanted to do was scream. The boots came to a stop beside their row, finally.

"Identification, please."

The man was so tall he had to stoop in the aisle as he waited on them to produce their IDs. His face was sunken around the eyes as though he'd not had a decent night's sleep in ten years. Thin lips formed a straight line beneath his prominent nose. Larken's mouth opened, but no sound came out. Oliver visibly sweated as he trembled just slightly enough for her to feel shake in the seat.

"Lacey? Junior?" the older woman's voice came over the seats. "Officer, we don't have their IDs. We aren't going far, just to Seattle to visit relatives. We completely forgot about the checkpoints. They're with me. Here."

She hoisted her identification coin toward the officer, who then scanned it with something that resembled a handgun. His scowl lifted with his eyebrows as he nodded at her.

"Sorry, ma'am. Of course."

He handed her data coin back, and she dropped it into her purse. Larken looked at the woman and gave her a small smile. She was older than Larken had thought initially. The woman had a small nose and eyes from which laugh lines fanned out like tree branches. She had an easy smile and gray irises on the verge of clouding over. The officer moved on as Larken mouthed the words "thank you." The woman only smiled back. A handful of minutes later, the bus was underway once more.

"Thank you," Larken whispered.

"It's quite all right," the woman said. "I don't know why they're looking for you, but I can't imagine that the two of you have done anything so serious that it warrants stopping my bus."

"We didn't do anything," Oliver tried to explain. "It's just tough to convince people of that."

"So you *are* the two they were looking for. I thought so," the woman said, smiling as though she'd just won the lottery. Larken's stomach sank. She'd assumed, and now they'd confirmed. They would have to do better than that if they made it to Seattle.

"Don't worry," the woman continued. "Your secret is safe with me. What *do* they think you did, anyway?"

Larken looked at Oliver, who gave her a warning via a slight shake of his head. She nodded at him, ignored his protest, and swallowed.

"They think my brother killed someone," Larken admitted. "But he couldn't have. He was with his girlfriend."

"Then why run?" The woman asked the question as a friend might. It felt more like an attempt at understanding than an accusation. Larken opened her mouth to speak again, but Oliver interrupted.

"Since our dad left and Mom died, I've gotten in trouble a lot," he said. "We don't have money for a lawyer. This bus ticket was the last of the money we do have. If we can get to our cousin in Seattle, they might help us get an attorney. Otherwise..."

"Otherwise, your record works against you, and nobody believes you. I've been there before. Oh, it must have been twenty years ago. I took an elevator to my office in Reconnaissance Plaza downtown, and this man boarded with me. I didn't think anything of it at first..."

Larken zoned out as the woman recounted some story of some wrong that someone did and how the courts didn't believe her either. Once the conversation moved on, away from Larken and Oliver, the woman was pleasant enough to talk to. She had a son about Oliver's age who had signed up for early military service. He wanted to be a pilot in the Space Force and fly sorties in the upper atmosphere. He was good enough to get accepted early, so that was something.

While the woman continued to chatter on, Larken imagined what it would be like flying in the blackness of space. She imagined accelerating past the moon and even on toward Mars if the mission called for it, protecting travelers making trade between the Earth and Mars. She dismissed the idea as quickly as it arrived. It wasn't for her. In part, it was because of military service. Always being screamed at and told what to do didn't strike her as fun. Although, her lofting coach was known to scream and didn't mince words in her overbearing instruction. It felt different doing something she loved.

The woman continued. As she explained, United Africa had the most ships and took on the bulk of the job securing interplanetary transports to Mars and beyond. If anybody wanted to get those jobs, they'd best move to Africa or ace the entrance examinations like her son had. Then sorties in space translated directly into high-paying jobs protecting trade routes or running them. Eventually, someone could become a station commander.

"You must be proud," Oliver said to the woman, who beamed back at him.

"Oh, I am. He's going to be wonderful at it, I just know. What about you? What do you two want to do once you get, well, more stable, I suppose?"

Larken's life had been about lofting. That game should have spilled off her tongue as a reflex. But models weren't allowed to play professional sports alongside polli, and there wasn't a lofting league for models that anybody except models watched.

These thoughts pounded against her skull as Oliver, seemingly oblivious to the repercussions of their new lack of humanity, rattled on about his entrance exams for universities he would never attend.

Larken felt a bulge growing in her throat and didn't feel like talking any longer. She turned her gaze out the window and lay her head back against the seat, staring as the trees continued to clip past. Her turn to speak came and went, and she swallowed at the thought of what her future probably had become. Running would never stop. The police in Portland had already figured out that the pair had fled and were looking for them. What's to prevent them from being deported from Washington back to Oregon? Nothing. The only thing they could do was make it to Canada. All the while, they would be hiding, running, and hiding some more. A tear slid down her cheek. She was thankful that Oliver didn't seem to see it as she wiped it away.

Half an hour after, they said goodbye to the older woman. It was an awkward sort of goodbye, as Larken didn't know if a hug was appropriate, while a simple wave or handshake seemed somehow less than deserving for a woman who had saved their lives. She settled on a half-handshake, half-hug, only to be squeezed into a full hug by the woman's frail-looking but powerful arms.

"You children be safe," she told them. "Remember not to lose hope. It's so easy to lose that. My great-uncle fled from London to New Zealand when the Akston Society took over. He had to go over underneath a false floor in the bottom of a ship. The one thing that kept him alive was hope. If you have hope, you can overcome anything."

Larken nodded, though the woman's words did nothing to ease her angst at being in a new city and almost broke.

"Thank you," Oliver told the woman as he gave her a genuine-looking smile. The older woman turned and walked away from them in a slow shuffle. Oliver turned to Larken and asked, "Why do you think she helped us?"

As she walked away, Larken caught a glimpse of the woman's left wrist. There above the meat of the woman's withered palm was a mark that looked like someone had cut straight across with a razor blade. The woman nonchalantly waved the same hand back over her shoulder and Larken didn't think she was mistaken to see dots in a straight line tandem to the incision.

"I think she had her reasons," Larken said and cut her gaze short in case anyone was watching her too closely. *That woman probably had a lot more stories in her than what she'd shared,* Larken thought as she followed Oliver from the bus port into the terminal proper.

The one thing that Larken could appreciate about the bus terminal was that it didn't smell like a mixture of popcorn and urine. The bad thing was that the urine had won the competition and was nearly stifling and omnipresent. She scanned the crowd with her eyes, examining every face for Torrent. Oliver nudged her arm.

"Over there," he said. She followed his gaze to see a giant mop of graying curls jutting out above the crowd. She was about to say something when her brother pointed to someone else. Larken's eyes slid to the right, and she saw what he was pointing to. Multiple men in uniforms stood around the exit. Two had eyes focused directly on Torrent, and the others looked out over the crowd. Larken ducked her head down.

"What now?" Oliver asked.

For once, she wished that he was the one who came up with ideas instead of her. She thought for a minute, then looked behind them toward where the bus had dropped them on the landing pad. The bus that had dropped them slowly lifted from its port.

"Pretend to be waiting for the next bus," she said. "For now. We can figure it out later but not if we're caught."

Oliver followed as she led the way, working against the traffic flow. She wondered if it was too evident they were going in the wrong direction, away from the guards. She wondered if that would draw suspicion. The urine smell lightened as they approached the entrance, where a steady stream of air from outside blew across the port. The smells of roasting food rode on the breeze and made her mouth water from the hunger she guessed would be a permanent part of their lives. Gritting her teeth, she made her way toward a waiting bench and took her seat there. Settled in, she ensured her back was to the guards before speaking.

"I don't think we can stay with Torrent," she said flatly. "They know he's our benefactor, and they're following him."

"We're out of money, Larken," Oliver complained. "It's not as though we can even feed ourselves. We *need* somebody to help us."

"We're not *completely* out of money, just low. We're going to have to figure it out ourselves."

CHAPTER 17

WAITING FOR OLIVER

THE TAXI DRIVER'S eyes fixated on Molly as she awaited Torrent's return from the bus station entrance. The volantrae that Torrent had selected was small. Too small. It was round like a doughnut without a hole in the center. The driver pretended to fiddle with various controls as though keeping the volantrae parked at the platform's edge required his total concentration. His wandering eyes and how he eagerly licked his lips when they happened upon her sent shivers down her spine.

"Where you from?" he asked unprompted. "Traveling long?"

Molly's throat seized from a fear pounding against her ears with each heartbeat. Her silence was a message he might misinterpret, so she tried to overcome it. Her eyes teared up, and she found that she couldn't even make words.

"Hey, are you okay?" the man asked, his eyes firmly planted on her through the too-thin glass pane that separated them. She wrapped her arms around her chest and stared after Torrent, willing him to appear. Molly nodded to keep this man appeased with some sort of response but gave him no more than that.

"That man. Is he keeping you against your will?"

She almost laughed at that question and couldn't prevent a weak smile.

"Ah...pretty when you smile," he said to her.

The words turned the corners of her mouth back down. The man at the last bus stop had worn spring water after-shave like a baptismal bath and said over and over again how pretty she looked. Molly gingerly slid her fingers across the bruised shoulder that hid beneath the sleeve of her dress. That was her gift from the last man who had called her pretty and asked her to smile. Even now she loathed that she *had* smiled, even if only to get rid of him. It hadn't worked. He'd licked his lips and grabbed her shoulder. Molly had pulled away from the man's grasping hands by herself since suddenly everyone else in the lobby found something more interesting to do. The taxi driver took one more leering glance then scrunched his eyes, snarled, and turned his attention out the front window. Molly's arms started shaking

She'd almost convinced herself to flee when she made out Torrent's poofy white hair hovering above his green suit on the sidewalk, looking lost as usual but heading in the general direction of the taxi. The pounding in her heart slowed until she saw the taxi driver resume his staring. Molly immediately popped the hatch and stood on the seat, waving at Torrent.

He seemed puzzled and disoriented as he approached. His eyes loomed large behind his glasses as he got closer, making them look like large blue and white marbles. He shoved his glasses on his nose, cleared his throat, and worked his way up the auto-extending steps and into the seat beside her. A side-glance told her the driver's gaze had shifted back toward his panel of whatever it was he faked obsession with to pretend to ignore her.

"Where are they?"

Torrent shook his head.

"Not here," he replied, turning simultaneously toward the driver. "This is the only other station that brings people in from Portland?"

The man looked over his shoulder at them. As he answered, his eyes never left Molly, and she shivered with the cold touch of his gaze.

"Only one, sir," he said in a deferent tone. "This one and the other you've already been to. Nothing else unless your friends took an airplane or private ride."

"What do you think?" Torrent asked Molly. "Private ride?"

Her hand slipped over Oliver's bag in the seat beside her as she considered the question. Her fear had subsided some now that she had Torrent back, but the fog of anxiety had only begun to clear. She looked at the man and then back at Torrent.

"I...I don't know," she said. "I guess. I hope not. We'll never find them."

She clamped her mouth shut at the end of her sentence. Hearing her words relay the hopelessness of the situation turned her already churning stomach into a small knot. Torrent bumped her bruised shoulder as he climbed in beside her, and she bit her lip to prevent calling out in pain.

"They were supposed to be on a bus," he muttered. "I don't think they would have changed plans."

"Look, sir," the driver said. "I can hang out with you all day. Good fare. But sometimes—take it from a man who originally wanted to be a chef—plans change. Anywhere else you want me to take you?"

Torrent cast a glance at Molly and then looked back at the driver. He didn't say anything, only stared with his giant eyes.

"H Hotel, I guess," he finally said. Torrent looked back at Molly as the man flipped the volantrae on. Molly couldn't help noticing that it only took a single button and not one on the panel of switches the man had been playing with in Torrent's absence. "We need to get you safe. We'll call your mother when we get there and figure out what to do next."

Floating away from the stand, Molly felt a tug in her chest. She looked out the window, watching the building get smaller and smaller as they floated up to join the swirling traffic above.

The ride back to the hotel took seven long minutes. Despite some wayward glances from the crowd toward them—at the tallish man in the dark green suit and glasses and the teenage girl dragging a tan and black suitcase behind her—they made it through the lobby without incident. Molly felt the forced anonymity of the city working for her now, whereas in the bus station, as she'd stood there fending off the spring water man's hands and screaming out, she'd been buried and stifled by it. She bit her lip and her eyebrows furrowed. She closed her eyes mid-stride for half a second, inhaled and exhaled, then opened them. The elevator doors slid apart and deposited them in a hotel hallway that smelled of antiseptic and disease, jarring her attention. Seconds later, they were back in the "safety" of his room, and he had his communicator in his hand, ready to call her mother.

At that moment, she felt the powerlessness of her situation gather around her like a swelling tide and pull her into it. Once her mother discovered that she'd fled to Seattle chasing a boy, a model no less, she'd get a permanent guard assigned to her, she was sure. Though technically offered as a Brighton Academy service, she'd never actually seen any student followed around by a private guard. After this, Molly would be the first. Then she would be stuck back at the school, going through the motions and pretending that everything was fine while being slowly chiseled at by HPM Lite. Her strength had disappeared, replaced by an ever-present fear that she couldn't shake since the incident. She wanted—longed—to curl up in a bed. Even the disparaging thought of returning to Brighton Academy wasn't entirely unwelcome. The routine and safety of her school tugged at her need for security.

But she would never see Oliver again if she went back. She rifled through Oliver's side bag while Torrent seemed to catch a glimpse of her out of his eye as he crossed toward his bedroom, likely for privacy. It didn't make any sense to her since he was supposedly calling her mother, but maybe there was some secret that he wanted to share. It is evident from how they talked that their shared history was much more complicated than it was presented to her. They could keep their secrets, and she would try like hell to save hers.

"I'll be right back," he said.

"Wait," she said. "There are two of us. You could wait at one, and I could…"

Molly couldn't finish the sentence. Terror grabbed her when her mind went back to the cool water man. Torrent looked at her and nodded, but in a way that didn't give her comfort.

"Absolutely not. We checked both stations, and they weren't at either. So you have to see it my way. I'm an older gentleman running around with a high-school aged girl who has run away from home. *You* are going home, and *I* am going to keep looking."

He turned and was gone through the bedroom door before she could say anything else.

She closed her hands around her handbag and clutched it to her chest, pondering what to do next. If they weren't at either bus stop, then maybe they were already in the city. Any second now, Torrent would step back through the door and tell her that her mother was on her way, or worse, her mother demanded her on the next flight, bus, or hired car down to Portland *immediately*.

Molly bit her lip and stood, slowly and deliberately. Finding Oliver would take work, and she was willing to put it in. They were soulmates, whether Larken saw it or not. But she couldn't take Oliver's bag with her. It was too heavy and would slow her down. With only her handbag, she tried the doorknob leading into the hallway as soon as she overheard Torrent's throat clear, indicating that her mother had connected the call and the conversation was about to start.

Trembling with fear, Molly stepped out. The click of the door into place behind her caused her breathing to go shallow, but she walked toward the elevator, taking more and more rapid breaths to compensate. She'd never been as afraid as she was at that moment, nearing the elevator. Molly willed herself not to run from the opening doors. She forced her way inside, then pushed the button for the lobby. Mentally counting her money, she came to about a thousand dollars in cash coins and whatever she had in the bank if her mother didn't cut her off when she discovered that Molly had once again fled.

The elevator ejected her onto the first floor to the wide and staring eyes of a large family waiting to ride up. She gave a weak smile as she exited and pushed through them. Quickening her pace, she made her way toward the door.

"Excuse you," came a voice after she jostled someone in the lobby. Molly turned to see another girl, a little older, with long blonde hair staring after her with a fixed hatred in her eyes. She raised her eyebrows in an apology but said nothing. Something about how the girl pivoted and walked away seemed artificial—as though the girl didn't know how to do it correctly. Every step seemed forced. Molly pulled her thoughts away from the girl and back toward the exit, spinning just in time to avoid colliding with a bell cart hovering toward her unattended.

The city's force bore down on her when she breached the exit. The volantrae taxi had shielded her from it before, but now the people, the sounds, and the chaos crowded around her. She worked her way into the foot traffic. Molly lurched away from the people who jostled into her. Stomach churning with revulsion at every contact, she bounced like a pinball through the crowd only to emerge at the collision of two buildings into what would have been an alley several strata lower. The cement bridge was cluttered with discarded cans, bottles, and the unwanted sons and daughters of the city. An overpowering odor of feet and caked dirt brought her to a complete stop at the entrance. It was either take the alley and get out of sight or remain on the main throughfare, where Torrent would think to search. She gulped once and stepped into the space between buildings onto a walkway that seemed too high for the darkness to have invaded so completely. Stepping around cans and past tents, she chided herself for having left in the first place.

But she told herself that she hadn't had a choice. If she'd stayed, she'd have been made to get on the next bus back to Brighton and Oliver would still be here in Seattle...somewhere. She peeked over the side of the walkway through a crack and could barely make out the tiny body of a person below. Her foot stubbed against something that heavy but soft.

"Hey, girl, watch out," a gruff voice called from the pile of blankets Molly had stumbled into.

"S...sorry," she stammered and stepped around the formerly sleeping man, who grumbled something and pulled the blanket tightly around him. Only then did Molly realize how truly late it had gotten. The dim sunlight that made it into the alleyway faded by the minute, and Molly had no place to sleep and nothing to eat. She missed her mother and her friends, and a voice inside kept telling her to give up, followed by another voice saying that she was a moving target out here and that spring water man would get her.

Like the bogeyman, the spring water man had wedged his way into her mind and lurked around every corner. She shivered as the first icy chill of the night breeze worked its way under her clothes. She ignored the buzzing in her purse that told her Torrent had finished his conversation with her mother, and both of them were probably ready for her to return. The tents that had seemed shoddy a moment before now seemed warm and protective against an unending night.

But they weren't for her. She didn't know what she was doing, but it wasn't spending the night on a sidewalk. Molly did have some money, and she could afford a hotel if she could find one where they didn't ask too many questions about what a girl would be doing alone in the city. Emerging from the alley just beyond the buildings, she found a dead street. No traffic flowed, and no people walked along the sidewalk. A dog park took up one corner of a lot flanked by the sides of large apartment complexes. She continued until she saw hideaway malls and novelty shops, all locked up for the night, lined each side of the sky walkway. Another time of day, or closer to the weekend, the area might have been busy with tourists. As it was, the place was a ghost town—save one small café that looked about the size of her third of the campus bedroom. A young man worked at the window. She fished in her handbag for a cash coin and stepped up to the window. On either side was a sizeable handwritten menu of the coffees for the day.

"Café mocha," she said, plopping one of the several coins she found onto the counter without looking too closely at it.

"Just about to close up," the man said with a genial smile. "Don't have the system going anymore."

She felt her stomach clench and her shoulders tighten. Something else must have changed in her face because the man's expression grew softer as the curves of his smile softened.

"Wait there. I'll see what I can do," he told her in a calming voice full of baritone. She stood at the entrance, and he disappeared into the back for a moment. The sound of a steam wand filled the air, and a few moments later, he re-emerged to the window, holding a steaming cup of hot mocha.

"On the house," he explained, grinning blithely.

"Well, thanks," she said and tucked her coin back into her handbag before securing it under her arm. Then she accepted the coffee mug with two hands and let the warmth flow into her arms before taking a sip. She relished the soothing heat that flowed down the length of her body with the fluid.

"You're not from here," the man observed.

"Portland," she said, licking the foam from her upper lip as she focused on the coffee's warmth in a vain effort to pretend nothing else existed. Just her and warm chocolate. "Just for a few days."

"Can I tell you something, Portland?" he asked, eying her up and down. "You're pretty, you know that? And you're alone out here. Not a good move. Want me to call you a taxi or something? It might be safer than walking around. Nice enough during the day, but even up this high, there can be trouble sometimes."

Pretty. Spring water man had thought she was pretty too. Her hand shook so hard that hot coffee sloshed over the sides, leaving red streaks on the back of her hand where it touched her. She winced while switching the cup to another hand. The driver raised his eyebrow at her as Molly did her best attempt to casually flick the scalding drippings from her hand.

"I'm fine," she said without making eye contact. She turned slowly, her mind still locked up in terror that she knew wasn't helpful. This wasn't spring water man. Her logical, rational mind kept bringing that fact up, as though the vise-clamp tightening around her chest would heed reason and good sense. Molly forced a few short breaths and stepped away from the stand. One foot in front of the other, into...nowhere. Her eyes watered as her feet locked into place and refused to carry her without a destination.

"You okay, Portland?"

Molly's hands trembled. She wrapped both of them

around the coffee cup and tried to take a sip without spilling down her dress. She regretted the dress now. It was picked specifically for Oliver, for when she found him and he saw her and she would be the most beautiful thing. But what if that's what had caught spring water man's attention. Was it the way she walked? Molly couldn't remember if she'd said anything to the man before...

She shook her head and tried to remind herself that she was here for a reason. Somewhere out there Oliver and Larken hid, probably in the process of fleeing the country. It had to matter. Molly couldn't keep the her eyes from watering because it didn't matter. No matter how much she forced that longing for Oliver and her fear for her best friend's safety, all she could think of was how dirty she felt. And that emptiness was the worst thing she could imagine. Molly swallowed and made a decision. It didn't matter how she felt. She'd come to do something, and she would do it. She turned slowly back to the man, who was also the only living, breathing human anywhere nearby. He was offering support, and she would take it.

"I'm trying to find my way to the bus station," she said. "Got to pick my boyfriend up, and I got a little lost."

"Then you *need* a taxi. Or," he said, waiting and staring at her for long enough to make her nervous before he seemed to realize he had done it and looked away. "Never mind. Taxi to where?"

"I don't *want* a taxi," she said. "Can you just give me directions to the bus depot?"

"The closest bus depot is about a block over and several strata down. I think on First. It's down in the dregs. The one over on Fifth has more inbound from Portland, though. Probably ten blocks from here. You don't want to walk that."

"Thanks for the coffee," she said, as warmly as she could manage and even offering a slight yet quivering smile. Then, she turned to head in the direction he'd indicated with his head nod. She only got two steps into the journey when he called out again.

"Portland," he said. "Hold on."

Molly's hands turned white-knuckled against the coffee she held. She turned slowly back to see that he'd emerged from the booth through a door she hadn't noticed. Her heart pounded, and she took an involuntary step backward as he pulled a metal sliding door down over the front of the booth. The man slid a lock onto the bottom, where it connected with the ground below.

"Molly," she said as she faced him, heat rushing to her cheeks. She tried to straighten her dress, but nothing she did made it pretty again.

"I'm Stephen," he said, fastening the lock. Then he raised his hand to point behind her. "Come on. I'll give you a ride. It's not far by bike."

"Bike?"

"Yeah," he said, looking past her. She forced a deep breath in, then turned and saw a black tarp-covered object that looked just a little larger than her mother's faux-oak desk.

"That?"

He nodded as he walked across the deserted street toward it. She followed, and he yanked off the tarp in one movement. It fluttered through the air like a cloak to reveal something that looked like a statue of a water bike. The bottom was flattened, and handlebars were attached to the base near what she thought must be the front, near the point of an oval. Behind that was an elongated seat—she guessed big enough for two very intimately positioned people.

"Uh...no thanks," she replied and took another step away from him. "I'll just walk."

"It'll be safer on the bike," Stephen said. "Much safer. I'd feel horrible if you walked and something happened to you. Look, I'll stay on the sidewalks and go slow, so if you feel nervous, you can jump off. There aren't seatbelts or anything so it's not like you'll be trapped."

The admission didn't make her feel any safer. What it did do was tell her how poor of a job she did of hiding her discomfort. She wiped her eyes to make sure no tears lingered there still.

What's wrong with me? she wondered. Her customary bravery and fierce attitude had been edged out by fear since she'd learned that Oliver was in jail. Suddenly, every action came with a multitude of dangerous possibilities. Then the spring water man's hands had fondled their way over her body in full view of an entire bus station of people while she had fought, but had she fought hard enough? She gagged at the memory of soaking in the stench of him. Molly had somehow become a victim, and the heat in her mind brought tears into her eyes. Molly had *never* been a victim, and her fury at the notion did nothing to assuage the persistent terror that had taken lodge in her chest.

"Hey, easy. I didn't mean anything," Stephen said. "If you want to walk, walk. Just trying to help."

She gulped and nodded at him but didn't move. Instead, she bit her lip and tried another thin smile to see if it would stick. Weak and straining, she found herself able to maintain it despite her fear. She could be brave again.

"You're right," she said and sucked air in deeply. "I do need a ride."

This man wasn't looking at her the same lecherous way the taxi driver did, nor did he ooze the ferocious immobilizing aggression that spring water man had. He just seemed like someone who might be able to help and who was willing to. She climbed onto the back of what he called his bike.

"Here, take this," he said as he produced a helmet from within a storage compartment between his legs. As she did, she noticed him placing a black domed helmet atop his own head.

"You always carry a spare?" she asked.

"Never know who you might run into, Portland," he said with a smile.

They lifted away from the parking spot.

CHAPTER 18

TIME KEEPS ON SLIPPING

TORRENT'S MORNING disappeared in a flurry of phone calls and pointless wanderings. Molly was gone. He doubted she was returning and had to explain to Brigid how he had lost her daughter.

Torrent sympathized with the girl. He recalled with perfect clarity a similar overpowering need that had pulled him out of his routine and had almost cost him his career. All because of Harper. Another to-do on his list: he still had to get her to convince Bodhi to go under the knife. It was an operation that violated Harper's ethics and lately made Torrent bristle too. But it was the only way, and she needed to see that.

But he still had one more thing to do. He had to ensure that the only survivor of said experiment *stayed* alive. It had been touch-and-go during the surgery. Christine Hamilton pulled through though and now, after round one with Harper, seemed in good enough spirits to verbally assault anyone around her. He'd probably lash out too. The truth was that the girl had always been difficult, per Gallatin's admission. And he was about to walk right back into the line of fire.

Deep breath. Pause and collect. He shoved his glasses back up on his nose and cleared his throat before delivering two knocks against the modified hotel room that passed as patient quarters.

"What?"

There was no mistaking her condescending tone and sharp edge. He shuddered once and shoved the door open before he could change his mind about going in. Plastering on a broad smile, he stepped through. Christine sat on the edge of her bed as though she were about to step off. Torrent bolted to her side to catch her and helped "encourage" her back into the reclining position.

"What are you doing?" he asked as he lay her head back on the pillow. She let out a thin whimper, and her head lolled to the side. As he'd expected, it had taken a lot of her energy just to stand up.

"Didn't seem to bother you the other day," she chastised. "Is your wife on board yet? Nobody tells me anything in here."

Torrent nodded as he scooped her legs under the blanket and pulled it taut.

"That was life or death," he said. "And I appreciate it. But you aren't ready for *unassisted* walking. You could seriously injure yourself. How are you feeling?"

"I can get by if I work at it. Besides, it's boring in here."

"Physical therapy should pick up again soon," Torrent assured her. The device wasn't working as he'd expected because her body had atrophied during her comatose period, and her animus module, through her tossing and turning, had inadvertently learned to use the wasted muscles and weakened arms. That meant something completely unexpected happened when she was "installed" in the new body. Her animus module mind overshot every muscle movement. Movement required coordination of muscles that her mind thought were weak to nonexistent. That made her movements jerky when she didn't concentrate enough. A fading reminder of a bruise on her right cheek was a testament to her incomplete bodily control.

"I hate therapy. That woman can't even speak English."

"She's from Ukraine," he said. "And she speaks English fine. The most advanced rehabilitation techniques were pioneered there, and she's the best in the world. Your grandfather spared no expense."

Christine's mouth closed. Even though the reporting of grievances had stopped, he could see in her watery blue eyes that she held back a lot of emotional pain. Torrent grabbed her pinamu chart from the bed to take a look. Vital signs were all good, as was mental activity. He pulled advanced diagnostics from the animus module. Brain signals were on par with what he'd expect. He scanned some numbers around mental acuity as the nurses had charted out. Seemed aware and sharp. From the notes scribbled into the margins, a little too sharp-witted. She'd made one of the nurses cry.

But she was *alive*. That was the critical thing here. Nearly twenty-five years in a coma, she'd been rescued by the procedure and had become the first immortal. A spark flashed in his chest at that notion. And Bodhi would be the second.

"What happens if I die in *this* body?" she asked, lifting one of her arms too quickly and almost slapping herself.

"We'll find a better one," he said. "But they're not cheap,

so don't do anything to that one, please. Rehab won't be any better in a different body."

"It's not rehab that bothers me," she said. Her voice faded to barely over a whisper. "I don't look like me, you know? This body...it's not me. It looks more like that girl I used to compete with for popularity in the fifth grade. Not exactly, but you know what I mean. The fingers are too perfect, the hair too blonde, the face. It's not me."

"Your grandfather picked it out," he told her. He'd warned Gallatin to get as close as he could to her actual physical appearance, but Gallatin had lost both his granddaughter and his daughter at the same time. The body he'd chosen had looked more like her mother than a mousy black-haired little girl, as though he'd tried to cheat and wanted both back at once.

"I'm not me," she said again, quietly and absent the hostility that he'd come to expect.

"You'll get used to it. Isn't it better than being in a coma still?"

"Everything in this body *feels* wrong. I can't explain it."

"I understand," he assured her even if he couldn't really. Given the opportunity, Torrent would have jumped for joy— or at least wobbled for joy—having woken from a coma that would have likely eventually killed her.

"How can you?" she asked.

"You're not quite settled in yet. Your mind thinks your body is still the one you had in the coma. The rehabilitation will help. I promise. You just need to keep at it."

"You're not even listening. With that *woman*?" Christine asked. He couldn't see her face from the angle she lay in, back to him and face to the undecorated wall. But he could imagine her mid-pout with that bottom lip doing that quivering thing that it did before she screamed or cried. Fifty-fifty odds on which way that would go.

"Yes," he risked. "I told you she's the best in the world. She will get you better if you trust her and follow her instructions."

"I can barely walk to the door and back, Torrent, and it's been over a week. It's not working."

Gone was the confidence and false bravado.

"It *will*," he said, taking the free moment to fish out his communicator and check the timestamp on the side. A mistake, he soon realized, because there was no unknowing that the day had escaped him and that he still hadn't heard back from Brigid, Molly, or Larken and Oliver. It was as though they had all decided life was easier without him—a conclusion at which he should have suspected them to arrive.

"Go," Christine told him, her words lingering and lacking in volume. "I know your boy is here. Go and check on him already. I'm sure my grandfather will be along once he's done with his meetings."

Torrent caught the cynicism in her voice, but he took the opportunity anyway. There were too many things happening to remain trapped in her with this emotionally needy *recovering coma patient*. He gritted his teeth as he thought the words. The girl had been trapped in a coma for years, being fed by machines and kept alive by technology, yet he couldn't spare a conversation to help ease her pain. Sometimes, there were no good answers.

"Your grandfather will be back in time for your next round of rehab tomorrow," Torrent said, taking his leave, as heavy in his heart as it was to do so. He didn't even turn back around when he heard the tiny whimper she often gave as a sign of her disappointment. Bodhi awaited, and then he would have to figure out what happened to Larken and Oliver, with or without Brigid's help. And then there was Molly.

As he stepped from the room, the overhead light spun away from him. The more he tried to focus on it, the faster it moved until the entire room seemed as though it had become trapped inside of a tornado, twirling around him. He stumbled forward, seeking to stabilize his footing, only to discover the floor wasn't there. His foot swayed in the air. The room tilted. And a second later, he found himself careening toward the hard laminate flooring, face-first. He barely had time to turn his head to avoid a full-faced collision with the ground. As the solid surface slammed into his head, the lights around him flickered once and then went out completely.

"Torrent," came the voice of an angel. Harper's face materialized above him, swimming in the air over his head.

"Harper?"

"What's wrong with you, Torrent? You fell."

But it wasn't Harper. At least, he vaguely knew that Harper would have aged as he had. Seventeen years is long, and she should have had some wrinkles. But she didn't even have the laugh lines that were permanently etched in the corners of his own eyes. Her hazel irises had locked into his, and her hands slid gently through his hair.

"I don't know," he said. The words came out funny. "Know" sounded more like "nah." Torrent licked his lips and tried again. "I..."

That came out "ah." He couldn't speak, but she seemed to understand him anyway. His heart lifted as he felt the fingers of her hand interlock between his.

"Don't speak," she said. "Help is on the way. I signaled the nurse, and they usually only take a few minutes."

"Ahn."

"It's okay. I owe you an apology, so listen. I'm sorry. You must be under an enormous amount of stress."

That didn't seem like something Harper would say. Her eyes didn't lie, though. He stared into hers and felt a tear roll down his cheek. She'd always been so beautiful. The shoulder-length black hair was straight yet always in motion. Her gentle breaths landed against his forehead, and he could see how much she loved him in those same eyes. If he could have moved, he would have tried to kiss her. They would have embraced, and he would have soaked up the lavender smell of her expensive but not-too-pretentious perfume.

Only he knew it was all a lie. He'd already met Harper when she'd arrived, and her eyes held nothing for him. The hazel had gone darker, almost brown, and her black hair had begun graying around the temples. This wasn't her, however much he wanted to gaze at her, hold her, and ask for her forgiveness for the time when he'd been so selfish that she'd fled the country to get away from him.

"Harper, I'm sorry," he said. This time the words congealed correctly in his ears. The effect on her was immediate and heartbreaking.

"It's Christine," she said, her eyes misting up. "The nurse will be here soon, Torrent. Just lay there. Don't talk."

She kept biting her lip. That wasn't a Harper thing to do. Harper had too much of her mother in her for that. Her response to something she couldn't control was to set her lips into a straight line and say nothing until she exploded into an outburst. Christine. He *knew* her. He searched his mind for an answer, and then it occurred to him. Gallatin's grandchild. The impetus of all that Torrent had become. In a way, the unknowing jailer who had locked him into his solitary life. And she was...*crying?* He didn't know why. He tried to move and realized that his arms weren't his own. He could feel but couldn't control his body. His breaths were raspy and shallow.

She shouldn't look like Harper. He tried to blink away the image, but it stubbornly persisted.

Then it all came back at once. His son. His...not son, and not daughter. His friend—or the closest thing to a friend he had. *Her* daughter. What had begun as a quick trip to try to help had turned into a nightmare. He gasped for air while a new set of hands clamped down wrench-like on his wrist.

"Heart is racing," a voice said. "Doesn't look like his eyes are focusing either."

"He just fell," Harper's doppelgänger said. No. Christine. It was Christine. He stared at the eyes, filled with tears and turning slowly from hazel to blue.

"Christine?"

The lips parted in a slight grin, and she laughed. The straight black hair changed to blonde before his eyes, morphing along with the eye color.

"What happened?"

"You fell. Got to the door and dropped like *me*."

He felt his breaths coming easier now, one after the other. The room still seemed ephemeral and bit unreal. The other woman was Christine's nurse, he saw.

"Ah," the woman said, pulling on him to get him into a seated position and off of Christine's lap, where he hadn't realized he'd been laying. "I'd say you had a panic attack."

Torrent's heart jumped, and his breath staggered. He gulped at the air until he finally corrected it.

"How long have I been down there?"

"About twenty minutes," Christine told him. The tears were real. He saw the redness of her eyes and the shining tracks down her cheeks.

"I kind of have a lot happening right now." He tried to lift himself to his feet, but the nurse pushed him back into sitting.

"No, you don't," she said. "You go out after that, and you'll end up on the ground somewhere else. You need to stay here, and we'll look you over."

"Nurse, I'm fine. Let me go."

She shook her head.

"No. And I'm *her* nurse, not *your* employee. Don't make me pull medical rank on you, *researcher* Toussaint."

"Doctor," he corrected her.

"Don't doctor me," she said. "You had a panic attack because you're doing too much. You need to slow it down. If I took your blood pressure right now, it'd be off the charts. Stay there while I get the *medical* doctor to look at you."

"He'll just say I'm fine."

"Stop. Nobody's listening to you." She directed her attention to Christine. "How are you?"

"Fine."

"Good. He doesn't move until the *medical* doctor takes a look at him. I've got to get some equipment. Can you keep him here?"

Torrent tried to get up again and was surprised to find that a gentle shove from Christine was all it took to plant him back down on the floor.

"I can," she said and turned to address him. "You're weaker than I am right now. Stay there, and let the doctor fix you."

"All that stuff…"

"About Harper? I think you should tell *her* that. I had no idea how bad you still have it for her. Does she?"

"Back in ten," the nurse said, leaving the two of them talking.

"I don't know. It doesn't matter anyway, does it? She has someone new."

"You never know."

He thought back to Harper of nearly twenty years before and the defeated look she'd given him when she'd asked him to walk away from his research to save their relationship, and he didn't answer. The pain welled all over again inside of him.

"You *do* know."

It had been obvious how Harper looked at Aiden, and no amount of wishing would unmake the mistakes he'd made. He rolled himself over at a turtle's pace, and Christine let him this time. Still panting for breath, he pushed up to his knees.

"Torrent?"

"Yes, Christine?"

"Are you going to be okay?"

He considered the question as he examined the backs of his hands pressed against the floor beneath him. Torrent couldn't make out the veins or the definition of his knuckles. He splayed his fingers and slid them over the floor, seeking his glasses.

"I don't know, Christine," he admitted as his hands finally closed over their hard edges. Straightening them out and placing the back across the bridge of his nose, he saw clearly that she wasn't Harper—not even a little. He cleared his throat and gave her an uncomfortable smile.

"I know I could use coffee or, better yet, a glass of whiskey," he told her.

"You'd better settle for the coffee," came the nurse's voice behind him. "And why are you sitting up? I brought the doctor."

"And me," came Saul's irritating tenor behind him. Torrent rolled his eyes, and Christine stifled a giggle. Two hands went beneath each of his arms and lifted him to his feet, supporting him as he swayed.

"Steady, boy," Saul said. "We've got a lot invested in your brainpower. We don't need you crashing out on us. Doc here will take your vitals to make sure it's not more than a panic attack. Just hold steady for a minute."

The nurse directed the blood pressure monitor at him and tapped the green button that shot a wide-berth laser over his chest. She scanned him for temperature and took the echocardiogram test for fat composition around his abdomen. But when it came time to tell him anything about the readings, she deferred by a glance to the doctor who stood nearby, standing disinterestedly.

"Dr. Toussaint," the woman began, "there's nothing wrong with you that some rest won't cure. Take today, even tomorrow, and go home. Do something light and easy and fun. Forget about the work and invest some time in a hobby—besides whiskey."

"I was joking about the whiskey."

"As you say. *I'm* not."

"Well, then."

Torrent shook off the supporting arms and shoved his glasses back up his nose. Strands of hair fell in his eyes, so he pushed those back too.

"I'll be fine."

"Go be fine," the doctor said. "Somewhere else."

Torrent looked to Saul, who nodded a little too enthusiastically. Then his gaze slid back down to Christine, who he noticed nobody had bothered to help up from the floor where she sat. He bent forward to do so when his head swum again. Instead, he shot the nurse a look, and she seemed to take his meaning. She pulled Christine to her feet and escorted her— one heavy step at a time—back to her bed. As Christine backed away, she mouthed something that Torrent couldn't make out at first. Then she did it again, and he saw her lips.

Bodhi.

If only he hadn't burned twenty minutes, he would have had time to talk to Bodhi. But Torrent knew where Bodhi was, safe and closely watched by the army of medical staff that Gallatin had on hand at all times because of Christine. What Torrent didn't know was where Oliver was or Larken. Railynn would never forgive him for letting them slip through his fingers if she were alive. Brigid, who was still very much alive, would be no more forgiving for him losing Molly in the big city.

Bodhi had to wait.

Torrent had to leave, however much it hurt his heart to tear himself away from the relative peace of the hospital room and the possibility of seeing Harper caring about him again—however fake it was. It was time to accept the chaos in his life and go to face it. If only he had any idea where to start looking.

Shoulders slumped, he let the nurse escort him as far as the door to Christine's room before shaking free again.

"I've got it," he assured the woman.

"So you do," the doctor said behind her. "I hope that's true. Don't come back to work right away. I'm serious. Take some time and relax. Your body is trying to tell you that you have too much stress in your life."

"I'm sure I do," he muttered, stepping into the hallway. "Thanks, Doctor."

Unexpected Adventure

CHAPTER 19
UNEXPECTED ADVENTURE

A LOW GRUMBLING sound in Larken's stomach reminded her that she hadn't eaten for almost an entire day. Oliver glanced back at her.

"We could just call Torrent, and maybe he could send someone," he said. "I'm hungry too."

"If they're watching him, they're probably tapping into his comm."

"That only happens in holovid movies, Larken. It's been a week. There's no way Seattle police care enough about us to tap his comm."

"You saw the men in the bus station?"

She stumbled to a stop at an intersection in the road. To her left, Mt. Rainier rose into the sky, silhouetted in the moonlight. To the right, evergreen trees with trunks as wide as she was tall.

"Which way?" she asked, hoping that giving Oliver some input into making some of the decisions would cool his anger at her insistence on them going it alone.

"Does it matter?" His calm nature had disappeared, and every tone he took with her was sharp and jagged.

"It *could* matter. That's why I'm just asking your opinion," she replied. "This sucks for me too."

"Call Torrent or Brigid. Either one will send us money if we need it. Given all that's happened, Torrent would probably open up our trust fund. Then we wouldn't need *any* money at all."

Larken sighed openly.

"Then the police would find that out. They would watch the transactions and find us. It's better to stay invisible."

"Do you even have a plan?"

"Do you?"

He stared at her with his eyes bulging. He gesticulated his arms up toward the sky and shook his head.

"Well, I do, sort of," she said. "Go north. Stick to the side of the highway, and stay in the brush where we can. Washington State is brimming with trees we can use for shelter."

"We've never even been camping," he complained, swatting a mosquito from his neck. "These bugs are everywhere. We have nowhere to sleep. You plan to *walk* for the entire way?"

She looked away while she thought it through and did the math again in her head just to be sure.

"Yes. That's exactly the plan. We'll be tired and hungry after two days of walking, but we'll make it to Canada. Once we're there, we can claim asylum."

"From what?"

Oliver seemed to have given up thinking things through. Maybe it was the hunger. He never handled being hungry well. Or maybe cracks were showing in his self-denial that his entire plan for the future had been sidelined by events he didn't control.

"What the hell, Oliver? You just spent two nights in *jail* and discovered you're a model. Do you not get that there's no such thing as a fair trial for you? Forget about your college and university tests. Forget about Torrent or Brigid, or *Molly*. Your life is over, *just like mine*. The best thing we can do for us is to get to Canada. When we get there, we'll let Molly know we're okay. I promise."

"Jail or even prison is better than dying in the wilderness. It's cold and getting colder."

"It's *June*, Oliver. This is as cold as it's going to get. If we keep moving, one foot after the other, we'll get to the border in a couple of days. That's all we have to do. One step. Then another. We're not going to *die* out here."

Unless a mountain lion gets hungry and wants them for a snack. Or if a pack of wolves or coyotes decided they were hungry. Or a bear...but none of that would help convince Oliver, and he hadn't come up with those himself yet. For him, it was just the bugs. Oliver swatted another mosquito.

"If we don't get eaten up first," he replied. So he had gotten there after all. But at least she'd steadied him for now. They plodded along in silence. Overhead, volantrae streamed past in overlapping columns as commuters left the city heading for home. Their less-glamorous paved road was flanked by overgrown brush on the sides, which had ceased to be manicured, she guessed, since the skyways went in. Beyond the edge of the bushes, she heard the crash of something large and squeezed up against Oliver to grab his arm. He yanked it away. Still angry, she reasoned.

Larken shivered and put her hands in her pockets to give

them somewhere to go. She leaned her head against his shoulder while they walked; this time, he didn't resist.

"I miss Molly too. I hope she's okay."

"Can I use your communicator to call her?"

Larken's eyes went damp at the blowback she knew she would receive. She could do it. Saying no when they were both aggravated would only inflame their tension. With two days of walking and increasing exhaustion ahead of them, Larken blinked back the tears of her anger at the situation and lifted her head from his shoulder.

"Sure," she said. "Once. Only once, okay? My communicator has to be for emergencies only."

His eyes lit up as she fumbled through her bag for the device. She pulled it out and shoved it toward him, then pushed the button to dial Molly's number as she set it in his hand. At first, he wore a wide grin. Oliver held the communicator to his ear and waited for the connection. Then the corners of his lips sagged, and his eyebrows furrowed up as he stared into space.

"Nothing," he said, handing it back to her. He'd tried, and she'd let him. She didn't know if she could ever say no to him, so she did the only thing she could think of and launched the communicator into the brush. He turned toward her.

"What did you..." He seemed to realize why she'd done it as he talked and only trailed off. "Yeah. Yeah, I guess that makes sense. Sorry I've been such a jerk, Larken."

"It's a bad situation. Let's just keep walking."

An older volantrae still used the internal combustion engine screamed overhead and catapulted volumes of air downward which Larken could feel even from two strata above their heads. Her hair whipped around her face, slapping her in both cheeks before finally settling with several strands hanging down before her eyes. She used her left hand to wipe the hairs aside.

"You're serious about walking?" Oliver asked. "You don't think that maybe we're overreacting? This is a misunderstanding, and it will work itself out."

"For it to work itself out, Torrent would have to have lied to us. Molly's mother *knows* Torrent. And she's a lawyer. If Torrent was lying, she would have picked up on it, even if you or I wouldn't have. And what's the point in lying about something like that anyway?"

He shrugged. She took a short step forward to get them moving again, looking back and up at him. The bushes shook again with something large in them, sending a shudder through her body. He seemed not to notice, lost in thought about the situation. She could tell that, unlike her, he still struggled with that overwhelming desire for normalcy. For Larken, her lofting dream had seemed more distant with every step and now hovered near extinction. He probably still schemed about how to become the captain of industry he'd always seen himself as. That would be a hard dream to kill.

Her stomach grumbled again.

"Did your escape plan involve food?"

"My escape plan only involves one foot in front of the other," she replied. "Food is optional. But yeah, I'm hungry. Let me see."

Without slowing, she reached into her pockets to pull out what she had left of cash coins. She didn't have a scanner to tell the exact denominations, but they were the red ones with white-gold rims, so they couldn't have held more than about five dollars apiece, and she had twelve. Thirteen if she counted the one that linked back to her limited-access bank account, but that one, silver and gold plated, would set off alarms, she thought, if she tried to use it.

"We can eat now," she said, scanning the horizon for anything that looked like a diner or convenience store. There were several options, as close as they were to the city.

"I guess maybe we should stop now. Once we leave the city, we'll run out of places."

"Next exit down?"

The exit wound through the trees and around to the overgrown brush. Near the bottom of the exit ramp, it became clear where state and federal maintenance had stopped. Cracks appeared, and it was overgrown with weeds. Trees loomed over the road, having not been cut back in decades, and created a small canopy through which even the shallow moonlight only illuminated to the level of turning every plant and bush into a dim, silvery shadow. Another crash sounded in the woods, and Larken looked to Oliver to see if he'd noticed this time. His eyes had gone wide.

"What is that?"

"I don't know," was all she could respond with. Her own eyes swiveled back to where the noise had come from. "It's been there a while. I thought I might be imagining it."

He shook his head.

"No. There's something back there. Let's cross over."

She humored him, and they crossed, the residual heat from the day's warmth still keeping the air above the pavement a few degrees warmer than where they'd been walking along the shoulder. She relished the change and, for a few minutes, debated internally whether it would be wrong to just walk down the middle of the abandoned street to stay warmer. As if the universe heard her and responded, a car wound down the exit as they reached the other side, rolling over the place where they had just been standing.

Larken's legs hurt. The realization hit her as the car zoomed by behind her. She was tired. The energy sucked out of her body as though the passing vehicle had stolen it from her and used it to propel itself down the road. She stumbled, and her stomach growled once again.

"Oliver," she said, grabbing his arm for support. Instead of supporting her weight, Oliver went down with her, and the two stumbled to the ground in a tangle of arms and legs.

First, Larken's face felt hot with embarrassment. Moments later, she burst out laughing. Looking at it from the outside, they were a mess. Two borderline adults, wandering down a major highway short of money and prospects. That narration fit any number of houseless people she used to see occasionally on field trips downtown. Depending on which accompanied them, the teacher sometimes would give out a couple of cash coins to help. Larken had a pocket full of cash coins, no idea where they would sleep, and only a vague idea about food. The absolute tragedy of the situation was so extreme that she had to laugh at it, despite the fresh cuts on her elbows from the fall and the pain of irregularly shaped rocks digging into her back. When she laughed, Oliver laughed back, and the two of them seemed to be in the same mental place for the briefest of seconds.

A light emerged from the brush across from them, gathering her attention up in it. The crashing sound had stopped, and in its place, a woman floated out of the bushes. *Floated.*

"Do you see that?" Larken asked, examining the billowing gowns flowing out from behind the woman who looked like royalty in her teal sari and gold diadem woven into hair so dark that Larken could see it only by virtue of it being shades darker than the shadowy night sky.

"See what?"

"Over there," Larken said and tried to point until she realized her hand was still firmly wedged behind her back. She rolled over, pinning Oliver a second as she freed her arm. The woman seemed to wave at her. Larken pulled herself to her feet.

"There's nothing there," Oliver said. Even as his words left his mouth, she saw the woman more clearly. Sad eyes, deep and dark, looked as though they'd never seen sleep, even somehow without the usual telltale sagging bags. Her hair flowed out behind her, tendrils defying gravity and reaching toward space in small groups. Dark eyes pierced into Larken and sent a shiver down her back.

She'd seen this woman before. A sleeping memory came back to the forefront of her mind. Jocelyn had dared her to find a downtown fortune teller, and Larken had gone to on a whim. Must have been two years prior. That woman had morphed from a frail older woman into this person floating before her.

Oliver lifted himself from the ground behind her, and the sound echoed as if he were in a tunnel far away.

"What are you doing?" he asked. The words were tinny and weak. The woman came more into focus.

"Larken," the woman said without her full lips moving. "There's a danger coming. You must be prepared."

"Who are you?" Larken asked, fearing the answer almost as much as the resurfacing of the premonition the clairvoyant-claiming fortune teller had laid upon her. "Empires will crumble before you." That's not something you tell a high-school girl just worried about exams.

It had to be the hunger bringing all of this back.

Now with her tan complexion brightened by the same moon reflected in her cherrywood-brown eyes, this woman had captured her full attention.

"Inconsequential," the woman said. "I can't remember anyway." She paused as though she seemed to think about what exactly that meant, then nodded as though she'd decided but didn't bother telling Larken any of her thoughts on the matter.

"What danger?"

"Oh, Larken," the woman said, her closed lips curling into a smile. "I don't know *that*. I only know that there's danger and a lot."

"We're already *in* danger. That's hardly helpful."

"Was I trying to help?" The woman asked the question with her eyes cast down. She couldn't seem to remember what her reason was for being there. Larken's stomach grumbled again, and the woman snapped her head as she finally seemed to remember. "Yes, I suppose. I forget sometimes. Danger—bigger than what you've been through already. So much bigger, Larken. And it's not just about you. I can sense it. This danger wraps up everything around you and squeezes you until it destroys your essence. You'll be too late if you wait to fight it until you see it."

The woman nodded, seeming to have convinced herself.

"It's a danger that if you fail to fight it destroys not just you but everything you've ever loved. And worse, everything *I've* ever loved."

The admission surprised Larken and drove her curiosity about who this woman was. She asked again.

"*Who* are you?"

"You remember me," the woman said, nodding. "You

remember. I haven't changed at all, and you haven't changed enough."

"Larken, what are you doing?" Oliver's voice kept the tinny quality to it, but he was yelling now somewhere far away.

"I *think* I was...yes, I'm sure of it," the woman continued. "I was Aayushi a long, long time ago. So long."

The woman's face faded—or the world brightened around her. Larken couldn't tell which until she could make out the silhouette of the tree line through the woman's partially transparent face.

"Wait. What danger?"

"What danger?" Oliver asked as the remaining echoes of the woman evaporated into smoke. "We need food."

Larken's stomach grumbled. Not sure that she could explain herself, she only nodded.

"You're right," she admitted. "I must be hungry."

CHAPTER 20

MORNINGS ARE HARD

THEY'D GONE ALL over the city. Stephen dodged in and out of traffic while Molly dug her fingers deeper into his sides, hanging on for her life. She welcomed the adrenaline pushing away her thoughts and the immediate fear of death forcing its way past spring water man. The crisp air slapped across her face whipping the hair that the helmet hadn't secured into a frenzy around her eye-shield.

"One more stop," he declared in as jovial a voice that anyone could have mustered having spent half their night chauffeuring some stranger around. "The Public Market. Everyone who comes to Seattle stops at the Public Market sooner or later."

While taking a hasty turn, Stephen leaned his head to the side, something she realized was her cue to voice an opinion. Since she needed him focused on the road, Molly's only response was "Sure."

The Public Market spanned fourteen strata into the air, each level open like the layers of a parking garage. Parking was relegated to a block away, so they left the bike on the corner of Pike Place, Virginia, and Strata 1 and walked the remaining distance. Stands of all sorts had blossomed up on the way, including a couple of fixtures. One place, in particular, reminded Molly of Torrent and his vibrant suits. Another sold only hats, garish and bright. As they approached the multi-storied complex from the west, Stephen issued a word of warning.

"Don't separate from me, whatever you see. We'll never find each other again."

Molly kept to herself the doubt that if the two of them couldn't find each other, then how could they hope to find Larken and Oliver? That turned out to be a moot point. As impressive as the market looked from the outside, they couldn't get in. The lights had all been turned out and the doors were chained up.

"Crap," Stephen said. "I forgot they close so early. Maybe we can try tomorrow?"

Molly rubbed her eyes and blinked back the frustration of having wasted a day. Taking advantage of the full stop, she let go of Stephen long enough to rub her throbbing left shoulder where she could still feel the tips of spring water man's fingers digging into her flesh. The sharpness of the pain had been replaced with a dull persistence.

"I don't have anywhere to go," she admitted, holding her head up as high as she could to maintain a little dignity; it wasn't very high.

"This isn't me coming on to you," Stephen said, slow and deliberate with his words. "This is me being nice. I have a spare room and an extra bed. Well, sort of a bed anyway. It's late. You're tired, and I'm past tired. My caffeine wore off about an hour ago. Come over. We can get some sleep and try again tomorrow. I have the day off."

You're so pretty.

Molly shook her head. This wasn't the spring water man. This was Stephen, who'd just spent more time than he had helping and hadn't asked for a single thing in return.

"That's fine," he said, seeming to back away from the idea at her lack of immediate response. "I can take you to a hotel. There are some good ones around…"

"Not that. Something else. Thank you for the offer. I'd love to get some rest."

"You sure? You seem tense."

"My boyfriend and his sister are out there somewhere wandering the city. I *am* tense. But I'm realistic too. We're not going to find them in this darkness. Not tonight."

"You're probably right."

As they pulled away this time, she wrapped her arms around Stephen's chest and buried her head in his back. She closed her eyes and let the turns come and go like the waves of the ocean. Ten minutes later, the vehicle came to a stop.

"It's not much," he apologized as they parked near the old post office distribution center just across the tracks from a marijuana dispensary. "It's enclosed enough to keep warm, and there's a couch that I picked up that someone was going to throw away." He grinned. "You should have seen me towing that thing with this bike."

His eyes were so apologetic that she understood immediately he'd never expected to bring her here, to his squatting space. But she smiled and agreed to stay for the night, and that they'd strike out again in the morning. Terror kept her eyes open until well after he'd stopped turning and the room filled with his snores. Only then could she push the image of spring water man out of her mind and settle into an uncomfortable sleep.

. . .

Molly's eyes shot open with an engine reverberating in her head. She pulled the blanket up around her chin and strained in the darkness to detect movement. Molly peeked under her covers. She still wore the white T-shirt and tan pants she'd changed into the evening before. Oliver's clothes may have been too big, but she'd felt vulnerable in her dress after what had happened at the bus station. Something moved beneath a mound of blankets shoved against a wall.

"Stephen?"

A clanking noise drew her eyes toward the opening they'd come in through the night before. The strange flying bike thing was propped against the wall. More sounds came from beyond the door and out in the hallway somewhere.

"Stephen," she whispered again at the mound, barely loud enough that she hoped it made it to his ears. A snore told her that it hadn't.

"Stephen!" she whispered louder and diverted her eyes back to the pile of blankets, only to watch them shuffle from one side to the next. An arm popped out from beneath, tattoos wrapped around it to the wrist. A right arm. She didn't remember Stephen having so many tattoos, but it had been so dark, so maybe he had.

"Over here," his voice came from beyond the doorway while the pile of blankets shuddered again. She gulped as she clenched her mouth shut. The smell of doughnuts wafted through the air to work its way into her nose. Larken's head turned toward the scent without her permission. Stephen wore a jumpsuit with a hoodie that looked so absolutely ridiculous she would have had to stifle a laugh had it not been for someone lying underneath the pile of blankets where she was certain Stephen had slept the evening before.

"That's not me," Stephen said when his eyes met hers. He didn't *look* homeless, and his clean eyebrows popped into a tent of concern.

"We didn't have much time last night when we got in, or I would have introduced you. That's Samantha."

On cue, the blankets shuffled again, and a woman's voice leaked from beneath.

"What?"

"Sam, get up. We have a visitor."

"No."

He smiled again. He smiled too much.

"It's a little early for her." He said louder, "I've got Top Shelf."

The arm lifted, and the hand curled into a thumbs-up sign.

"I'll be up in a minute. Coffee?"

"Coffee too. Come on, girl. It's time to get the day going."

"That's offensive."

He turned to Molly.

"Doughnuts? From tips yesterday. Let's have some breakfast, and then we can look for your friends more."

Molly pulled the thick and odiferous synthetic wool blanket from her body and swiveled her feet around to the floor as Stephen crossed the room toward her. He shoved the rest of the blanket into a smaller pile and sat beside her.

"I didn't know what you like, so I got a few different kinds. That one's old-fashioned. This one's Boston creme. You can even try that one over there. Sam, get up!"

"Fine," came the voice from beneath the pile. "I'm up."

Molly turned to see the pile shudder and pull back to

reveal a girl about her age with green eyes and a thick head of auburn hair bordering very closely on dark brown. Her complexion held more brown than Molly's paleness, enough that Molly suspected sunburns weren't a problem even on low ozone days. When the girl stood, the blankets fell away. Molly sucked in her breath. Sam was a textbook Caldwell. Symmetrical features with curves that not even the trappings of poverty could hide. The girl was objectively gorgeous even in her worn, short-cropped T-shirt and torn wool pants, but that wasn't the main thing that caught Molly's attention.

"You're a—" she began, only to stop herself, remembering that people rarely enjoyed being gawked at.

"Model. Suck it in. Yep. And guess what? I'm a Caldwell. That's right, manufactured for all the good stuff. Anything else, or can I get a cruller?"

"I've just never met...," Molly started to say, intending to finish with *model*, but that wasn't true. Oliver and Larken were both models. Molly simply stopped talking, but not soon enough. Sam glared at her without a response as she collected a cruller from the tray.

Molly shook her head from side to side.

"What do you like, Molly?" Stephen asked, unconcerned about his supposed roommate being a model.

"I guess, old-fashioned," she said, instinctively leaving the Boston creme for her lost friend.

Stephen plopped one onto one knee and gave the blankets another shove, allowing Sam to sit between them. Sam stood instead.

"Here, Sam," he said, holding out what looked like a pudgy dinner roll that oozed red. "Raspberry filled, just as you like. No icing."

"Thanks, Stephen," she replied, wholly ignoring Molly. "Picked up a stray last night?"

"This is Molly. She's new in town, looking for her friends."

"What's she doing here? The *meeting* is today. She's going to fuck it up for everyone."

"She'll be gone by then," Stephen said. "At least, I think she will. The city looks big, but it's not as big as all that. We'll find them."

"Always the optimist," Sam said, taking a massive bite with what Molly could see were perfect teeth and utterly uncaring about how red dribbled down her chin. Sam swallowed and smirked. "You forgot that they moved that to ten this morning, though."

His eyes went wide, and he glanced toward the doorway. Molly guessed it must nearly be ten o'clock by his manner.

"Uh..."

"Yeah. Told you. Just send her away. It'll be fine," Sam said. She turned toward Molly. "No offense."

"How can I not be offended by that?"

"I don't know you. You might be a nice girl, but you can't be here when the others arrive."

"I'm sure she's fine, Sam," Stephen vouched for her, though he didn't know her. Molly wouldn't have even vouched for herself if she were him.

"I can go," Molly volunteered. It would be better to be out looking than to be trapped in here with whoever they expected to see.

"Nonsense," Stephen said. "It's my place. Sam just squats here."

"You squat here too, Stephen."

"I was squatting here *first*, though. Then I *let* you stay, remember? Molly's my guest; if she wants to stay, she can stay."

"I don't—" Molly began.

"Have it your way," Sam said. "You'll have to explain to the group, not me."

"Explain what?" came a voice from the entrance. All heads turned at once to see a man taller than any man Molly had ever seen before. She guessed right away that he was a Bentley model.

"A guest," Stephen said. "And there's nothing to explain. She's lost and looking for her friends. I don't think she's going to care about our meeting."

"Not yet," the tall man said. "But we have some planning to do as well. There's another protest and an opportunity to move against HPM."

He turned his head toward Molly. He had thick eyebrows and a stern look.

"Anything that happens here will have to be kept secret. Hundreds of thousands of lives are at stake. You *must* keep it secret. Can you?"

Molly had no choice but to nod along and agree, but she would have anyway. The eclectic group before her and the stakes made her situation seem tame by comparison. All of their eyes were on her. She felt her knees weakening as her entire body tensed up enough to cause her hands to shake. Molly clasped her hands together. By now she'd figured out that this group were models, so probably a support group or something. The man continued to stare into her eyes, and she looked away. She wanted to disappear into the rapidly growing crowd, but there was nowhere to hide. Molly tried. She pushed through the crowd. Every accidental collision made her cringe. Reaching one of the walls, Molly found a metal crate wedged against it and pulled herself atop, keeping her eyes down and her arms tight around her once she was in place. At least, she had the wall. She leaned back against it, grateful that nobody could squeeze in behind her. It provided her with a clear view of the door and both Stephen and Sam.

"Good. Then we'll help you find your friends when the meeting's over. As Stephen said, the city is smaller than it seems."

More people trickled in, one after another. Stephen occasionally cast glances her way, but Sam seemed to go out of her way to make sure that Molly knew she was being ignored. If Molly didn't know better, she might accuse Sam of jealousy. But someone as beautiful and, from how the people congregated around her, personable—to everyone except Molly—as Sam had no reason to be jealous of *her*, a scraggly little runaway. Molly's throat felt as though she'd swallowed an entire bottle of molasses at once. Tears threatened to fall without justification; nobody had injured her or even threatened her. Molly drew her lip into a line and tried to distract herself by people watching.

Some of the crowd were models, as she could quickly tell when four oversized men crouched through the large doorway, one at a time. Others may not have been. Two mothers entered with children behind them. One of the two was also a model, as Molly could tell by a chance look at the woman's wrist; otherwise, she wouldn't have known. The other may have been, but if she was, she hadn't been appropriately marked. As the group swelled in numbers, Molly thought about all the time she lost in her search for Oliver and Larken. With their numbers assisting, the search would go much faster. They would find Oliver and Larken sometime that day. They would find Oliver, and then Oliver would ask about how she got there and what happened and then she'd say... What? Her skin still felt soiled, and she didn't know if she would ever get clean again.

"Welcome," said the tall man when the trickle ebbed. "Thank you for coming this morning."

He flashed a smile at the group, grinning widely. He seemed to scan the crowd and meet each face in turn, giving little nods here and there to people with whom he might have had a personal relationship.

"It's the day," he said. "Today is the day."

Murmurs went up in the crowd, sounding across the group. A chuckle lifted into the air from somewhere near the door.

"'Bout time," said one voice among the masses.

"Yes, it's about time," the man repeated. "I guess we need to do this officially. Clerk?"

Stephen stood and walked toward the man before turning his back to him and addressing the group himself.

"Chapter seventeen, SoDo district meeting of the Siblings of the Natural Order. Meeting called into order."

He stepped back and retook his place in the group. Molly's mouth dropped open. She'd thought support group, but not Siblings of the Natural Order. They were a known *terrorist* organization consisting of models who believed that they were the next step in human evolution. They were the opposite of the Human Pride Movement. She met Stephen's eyes for a second as his eyebrows went up in something that resembled an apology. He was full of those eyebrow gestures.

Molly caught Sam looking at her, finally acknowledging her existence again if only to sport a wry smile that cloaked some hidden cruelty. Molly closed her eyes and took a slow breath. She hadn't heard anything important. She could just slide toward the door—all the way across the room through the group of models. Even as she thought it, she knew that wouldn't work. Sam, for one, would call her out as soon as Molly stood from her perch. There wasn't much Molly could do besides sit and listen and hope the group didn't decide that she was a liability and make her disappear as they had so many others.

"First thing to discuss is the subway station," the tall man said, then looked to Sam. "That should be done now, right?"

"Done," she agreed quickly, and the smile turned serious. "Lines will stop running at exactly three o'clock this afternoon. I had to get a little help there at the end, but we have some sympathizers in the utility company who were only too glad to do a little good old-fashioned sabotage."

The man kept Sam's eyes and nodded.

"And the explosives," the man said, but Molly couldn't tell who he was talking to. "The explosives have been set?"

"Set," came from a woman in the back—one of the women who'd limped in last with a child. The child—Molly guessed only five years old—played with what looked like a stuffed rabbit at first glance. On further inspection, Molly made out a human face on the rabbit, like a figurine that Jocelyn had once shown her. Tu Shen, she gathered, and the story came back once she had the name. It was a tragic story of forbidden love, the kind that Jocelyn went on and on about. A young man had fallen for a court official and tried to spy on him. Caught, the man had been sentenced to death—but not before he professed his love. Jocelyn had made that scrunchy face that she sometimes did at the end of a telling. Molly had found herself caught up in the tragedy. Of all the gods and goddesses, Tu Shen's story broke her heart.

The man's voice rumbled in the back while Molly's thoughts traveled to where they would. Molly missed Jocelyn and her straightforward, completely unfiltered manner. The genuineness of Jocelyn's engagement had provided something that Molly only now realized she needed, a strength to which she could anchor herself against the memory that haunted her. A tear trickled down her cheek. Molly wiped her cheek quickly before anyone else could notice. She hated her tears, and the way that since spring water man, they now seemed so eager to spill.

Molly knew that she had lied a lot. Whether others saw it, she sometimes got lost in her own stories. Jocelyn was a rock and never bought into her deceptions—not even when repeating them to others. She missed Jocelyn more than she missed Oliver or Larken. She looked up to find the tall man staring at her.

"The target will try for the subway," he said calmly as his eyes moved on. "But the system won't be running. After the explosion, he won't be picky about which volantrae he gets into. Once that happens, then we'll pick him up, and the ordeal will be over. Sam, did you want to do the press release?"

"Why me?"

"Somebody has to. Once the target is neutralized, we'll need to release that video about why. You work on the video. We work on the acquisition at the same time. Do you...have any objection?"

"Only that Stephen's the clerk," she muttered, pointing a delicate finger at him.

"Stephen is also our intelligence point for South Downtown," the man explained. "He can't do the press release.

They scrutinize those meticulously, and we can't afford to lose him."

"But we can afford to lose me?"

"Why are you always so difficult?"

"The way I was made, I guess," Sam said, her eyes darting around the room until they fell on Molly.

"What about *her*? She's just passing through anyway. She could do the video before she goes. She needs to do *some* part of this, or she'll rat us out as soon as she leaves."

The man seemed to ponder the questions while Molly lowered her eyes and tried to go invisible.

"Maybe."

"I can't do that," Molly whimpered, though she was terrified of what not volunteering might mean for her future. Stephen seemed nice, but the others she wasn't sure about. "I'm not going to be part of any...whatever you're doing."

"Kidnapping," the man said firmly. "A Prescient Pharmaceuticals representative is in town this week. He oversaw the reclamation plant in Bremerton and is personally responsible for the deaths of thousands of models. We're returning the favor."

Her eyes watered at his response. Now she knew, whereas, before that moment, she'd been able to deny, having only heard snippets of the conversation.

"I...can't..."

"You will," the man decided. "You'll be blurred, and there will be a voice encoding. The chances of anyone knowing it's you are pretty slim, but it'll give us some confidence that you won't go running to the police as soon as we find whoever it is you're looking for. *We'll* have the originals."

They would still help her was what the man had said.

And the price for that help was to record a holovid. She glanced at Stephen, but he wouldn't meet her eye. Probably feeling guilty now for getting her mixed up in this.

"What do I have to do?"

"Nothing...yet. In a couple of hours, we'll take you to our *top-secret lab* and record that message," Sam said with a sneer.

"That's it?"

"That's it," the man said before Sam could say anything else. "Stephen, call the meeting?"

Stephen's face turned, and Molly could see that the color he'd lost hadn't returned. He opened his mouth, closed it, then opened it again.

"Meeting adjourned."

Molly's breath came in short bursts. The fear of what she'd just gotten into washed over her, distracting her from anything else until she felt a tug on her pant leg and jumped back, pulling her leg onto the crate beside here. A child stared up at her with large brown eyes and smudged cheeks.

"What type of model are you?" the little girl asked. Molly bit her lip and pulled on a smile she didn't feel.

"I'm not a model," she said, looking down at the girl.

The girl backed away from her. "You're a polli?" she asked, as her eyes widened.

"It's all right, dear," the woman behind her said, putting her calloused hands on the girl's shoulders. "This nice woman is helping us." The woman flashed Molly a smile made of gritted teeth while she steered the girl away. But before they left, the woman sidled beside Molly, holding the girl tightly with clutching fingers.

"Her father," the woman divulged. "He was sent to Bremerton."

Molly's eyes traced down the woman's left arm to where the underside of her wrist was concealed. The woman seemed to see what she was looking at and flipped her wrist over. No barcode.

"I'm not a model," the woman said. "Just in love with one." The woman seemed to have more to say, but she turned away and followed several others toward the exit.

"Molly?"

Molly turned away from the woman to see Stephen approaching.

"I'm sorry. I didn't know that would happen. I didn't want you to get mixed up in this."

"You didn't think," snarled Sam, approaching Stephen from behind and elbowing past him. "What did you think we were doing? Planning a birthday party? You should have thought. That's why I was trying to get rid of her."

"*You* volunteered me for that," Molly said. "Don't pretend as if you care about me."

"First, I *don't*. Second, you weren't getting out of here without some skin in the game, Molly. If I hadn't signed you up for that, you'd be participating in the *crime*. As it is, even if you do get caught, you can always say we made you do it. And it's not like he asked you to kill anyone."

A touch on her shoulder made Molly lurch forward. Her skin crawled with revulsion. Molly turned quickly. To her surprise, a long line had formed her consisting of models who hadn't left yet.

"Thank you," said the first person in line. He seemed skinny, only compared to the four prominent men behind him. He was taller than Molly by at least a head.

"For what?"

"Most people—most *polli*—don't concern themselves

with what happens to us. Thousands of models were killed in that reclamation plant. Thousands. And to most polli, it's just business. It's not just business to us. Every person in this room might eventually end up in that facility or be murdered as model sympathizers. You're one of few who see us as human enough to help."

Molly wasn't sure that she did. The time for arguing was long past, though, so she only nodded as the man continued past her.

Another engine buzzed overhead, breaking the ensuing silence and causing Molly to jump as goose bumps formed across her arms. The next in line passed along a similar message: nobody cares, especially not polli, and Molly was special for doing so. By the time the end of the line whipped around, the message had grown so repetitive that she began to believe it about herself—as though she'd had some choice in the matter. The tall man was the last in the procession.

"Shall we find your friends?"

CHAPTER 21
MEMORIES OF BRIGHTON

"IT'S OKAY," Oliver said between bites of stale piroshki. Larken's mouth watered as he chewed into the small pie and dripped smoked salmon and sauce down his chin. She consoled herself by telling herself that since it was saved from the night before, it was probably stale by now.

"Even if I miss the entrance exams, I can still get in next year. My grades are good enough," he continued.

Larken twisted her neck to work out the pain that had emerged overnight from sleeping on the cool, hard ground. Counting herself fortunate that nothing had eaten them in their sleep, Larken gleefully chomped down on the tail of the salmon-shaped roll she had left. She chewed it slowly, savoring the flavor. It wouldn't be long before she was hungry again, and now they had even less money. Her next meal would likely be day-old doughnuts or worse.

"It's not okay, Oliver," she replied. "There's no more college. I don't know why you keep thinking things are just going to be normal again someday."

"When they find whoever did it, they won't need me."

"Whoever did it is probably another First. That means *all* of our secrets come out."

"Maybe. But maybe not. You can't tell the future."

He had her there. Even being haunted by a fortune teller hadn't given her anything but an unsettled stomach. A vague foreboding about the future didn't translate into *knowing* anything. She let him plan and re-plan his future as she ground her teeth.

The sun rose outside the dilapidated refueling station, keeping them company while they ate. A steady stream of traffic flowed opposite from the night before. She licked her fingers and, with the rise in blood sugar, realized how dumb their chosen seats were. Still, after a night in the forest, anyone else would have also decided that a curb near a convenience store was a better decision than being surrounded by trees and the animals that called them home.

"We've got to go," she said. The food settling into her stomach brought with it lethargy. Larken wanted to sleep instead of tossing and turning among dried leaves while pretending to do so. Oliver had finally stopped talking and seemed like he might fall over. If they didn't move soon, they might pass out right there, and then there would be no "after they catch this guy" because the "guy" would be Oliver.

"Yeah," he slurred, then shook his head. "Only a few hundred miles to go."

"We'll get there," she assured him. "We will. Just keep walking."

Larken noticed movement out of the corner of her eye. She turned and saw an angular man, tall and skinny. Larken nudged Oliver's arm.

"Let's go, Oliver," she said. "Now. I think that guy's eavesdropping."

The man had no reason that she could see to be there. The curb was just by the off-ramp, and only panhandlers would have chosen the spot that Larken and Oliver had. There was no traffic where the man stood because he was back in the foliage. Even if he'd been heading to their convenience store, he'd have to have gone the other way. Confirming her suspicions, the man slowly walked in their direction.

Larken grabbed Oliver's hand and pulled him up off the ground.

"Now," she repeated. Her palms sweated as she pulled him along. It wasn't her imagination. The man's pace quickened with theirs. The pair darted away from the off-ramp toward the convenience store and then cut around the edge and ran beside it, concealed from sight.

"There," Oliver said. Her eyes followed his index finger to land on a gap between two trees that flanked the building. Larken shuddered at the thought of going back into the forest, but it seemed like a better option than being caught by whoever chased them. She ducked through and plowed right into a spider's web. Wiping frantically as she ran, she managed to get the web clear from her face, but she couldn't find the spider. She tried to console herself that the more poisonous spiders don't weave the fancy webs, or so said her biology teacher. Still, she compulsively continued to wipe and, at the first opening large enough, switched to let Oliver lead.

A handful of minutes later, Oliver came to a stop. Larken shoved into him until he shoved back.

"Move, Oliver."

"I can't."

"What do you mean?"

She had been too busy looking behind them. She understood when she turned to see Oliver teetering on the edge of a body of moving water.

"Okay," she whispered. "Duck down, and stay still."

He knelt, and she followed suit, peering through the trees as best she could. There was no sign of the guy they'd seen. The forest had become silent except for the trickling of water as it lapped against the shoreline. The smell of dead animals invaded Larken's nostrils.

"Why isn't he coming down here?"

"Maybe he wasn't chasing us?"

Larken doubted that. She examined the water's edge. Her nose was already getting used to the odor, but she couldn't identify the source. She'd thought there would be fish or other animals washed up or even debris on the edge of this calm, slow-moving stream. Possibly it was a river. Larken couldn't be bothered with the difference. Nothing like that was on the shoreline that she could see. The sun reflected in the water's smooth surface, flickering as slow ripples flexed the surface.

"What now?" Oliver asked.

"North," she said. "Always. That's how we get to Canada."

"But which way is *that*?"

"I think it's that way," she said, pointing up the river. "Unless I got turned around. What do you think?"

His silhouette shrugged at her as the moonshine glinted off of his eyes.

"Let's go," he said.

The bank was even more devoid of life than Larken had realized. That was the one thing that Larken couldn't get over. Aside from the trees set back away from the river and the occasional rocks that tripped them up, she heard no other sounds.

As they moved, the smell got more vigorous until it overpowered Larken's olfactory fatigue and became impossible to ignore. They continued up the river, where the water thickened. Larken could make out the sheen of the fluid against the shore. It seemed passive and peaceful, almost restive. And an odd shade of pink.

After pushing through a thicket, Larken signaled that it was time to stop by placing her hand on Oliver's shoulder. At first, he didn't turn around. Then when he did, he turned slowly. His face had washed out of all its color.

"What?"

He pointed ahead and stepped aside so she could see. Larken looked and clenched her teeth. The river ended at a pool, half of which disappeared beneath the side of a large brick building. And she made out the unmistakable outline of a human skull floating there.

Larken covered her mouth as her stomach tried to reject its contents. She prevented herself from vomiting all over Oliver, but Oliver had less control. He spewed his breakfast all over the bushes beside the bank. When the river lazily pushed a human finger up onto the shore near her foot, Larken lost her piroshki too.

Wiping her mouth clean of the clinging bile, her watery eyes cleared enough to see Oliver hunched over.

"What is that?"

"A reclamation facility," a voice cut through the brush behind them. "A death camp."

Larken turned, and her hair wet hair slapped around to her cheek and stuck. She smeared the vomit away and squeezed her hair clean in the brush. The man had circled around and somehow ended up in front of them. She backed away until the water lapped over the heel of her shoe, and she jolted forward again before a detached body part could touch her.

"Who are you? How did you find us?"

"A friend of Molly's," the man said. "Stephen Davis. And for the record there's only one highway northbound out of Seattle suitable for walking. Once we confirmed you weren't at either bus station, it was just a matter of following the highway."

That answered two of the thousand questions that spun through Larken's head. The next question she would have asked is how this random person knew Molly, but the water undulated below like a fuchsia oil slick. She gave up her questions for the moment and directed her gaze into the forest instead. "It's horrible."

"Completely legal to decapitate tens of models per day. On fast days, over a hundred."

"Reclamation?"

The man approached, and Larken could tell now that he was barely older than they were. He'd seemed older from afar because, she guessed, of the way he carried himself. She wasn't sure, but it was easy to see now that he could have been a Brighton student a couple of years earlier.

"It always blows my mind that polli don't seem fully aware of this stuff. When models outlive their usefulness, we're sent here," he said, then looked up toward the building. "They've probably seen us on their cameras by now."

"How do you know Molly?" Larken finally asked, having regained some amount of composure. Stephen glanced at her as he stepped away from the building. She followed suit and didn't break eye contact.

"I guess whenever you all separated, she ended up lost in the city. Showed up at my coffee and newsstand."

"Where is she now?"

Stephen glanced to the side and took a moment to think.

"Old post office down on Lander Street," Stephen replied. "I can take you."

"Is she okay?" Larken asked, following along in a single file line.

"Molly? She's fine. She's at my place. It's not too far, but we'll have to pick up my bike back at the refueling station first."

"At your place?" Oliver asked.

Stephen rubbed his eyebrows and sighed.

"Not like that. But...yeah," he replied, slowing as he picked his path along the river bank, sidestepping the brush that Larken and Oliver had trudged through earlier and then vomited in. "Didn't you all travel together?"

Larken dropped back to let Oliver go before her and watched his face to see if he'd registered the implication that Molly had "spent the night" in this strange man's home. Oliver passed her with clenched fists and tension in his shoulders. His face remained blanched out, but that might have had more to do with the refuse they'd seen floating in the reclamation facility pond.

More questions about Molly spun through Larken's mind. The superficial "she's fine" made her suspicious, and she thought more information might do something to ease Oliver's agitation.

"She talks a lot about you, Oliver," Stephen said as the forest finally opened up. With all of them following the river and its twists and turns, they hadn't gotten very far from the road at all.

Larken's stomach wrenched, and she gasped loudly. Stephen and Oliver stopped in rapid succession. Larken scrambled to get her hand in front of her face to block what she could as her stomach clenched and her throat opened up. A second later, she sprayed vomit between her fingers, sprinkling the contents of her stomach over the nearby rhododendron bushes and blackberry vines—sprinkles of salmon pink decorated the shrubbery as she retched nonstop and fell to her knees.

"You get used to it," Stephen said, telling her that he regretted knowing that.

Her mind snapped to, focusing on the long trail of saliva now hanging from her mouth down to the bush. She wiped her mouth haphazardly and retched again, this time dry-heaving, her hand pressed against her knees and hair falling around her face. She felt a hand on her back between her shoulder blades and saw another before her, pulling her hair away from the fire zone. She thought she saw the telltale bands of a black-ink tattoo barcode across his wrist for a second. Not Oliver. Sucking in a breath between heaves, she turned to check who it was through blurry, hazy eyes and saw Oliver some distance away, focusing, she thought, on not doing precisely what she was. The hands weren't his. Part of her cringed at the idea of Stephen's hands on her body, but another round of heaving and a long string of fluid left her with a profound lack of modesty.

"We need to get you cleaned up," Stephen said. "I assumed you would come back with me to see Molly. We've got clothes. You look about Sam's size."

"That...," she said at first, then bit down her teeth as another heave passed. "That could be us."

She felt Stephen's hand stop moving between her shoulders.

"Larken, don't say anything," Oliver said, his words strained with the effort he seemed to be making to keep it together.

"I'll say what I want," she replied, "and I mean what I said." A stray hair fell from Stephen's grip. As she repositioned, he switched the hair from his left to his right and swung down his left hand to catch a stray before it fell into the vomit. The barcode tattoo had been real, she now saw. And she also noticed that she was far closer to the ground than she'd thought.

"You're a model," she gasped. A sense of relief washed over her as she checked her body and found that she could stand. She rose to her feet and pushed his hands away gently. "So are we."

"You don't have barcodes."

"Not our fault. We didn't even know until a few days ago and have been running ever since. We were part of an experiment. Didn't get the barcodes or registration."

She wiped her lips again, hoping against hope that it would be the last time. But she still saw the finger floating in her mind's eye, and her imagination worked overtime, piecing together whatever else might have been hiding beneath the surface of the water. She tried to focus on the tree line, tilting her head up and breathing in the cool air.

"Good to travel?" asked Stephen, who had backed away now and stood about halfway between her and Oliver.

"Yeah, I think," she replied. Taking two quick breaths in succession to see how her stomach would fare. So far, so good.

"Good. The ride back will be a little interesting with three of us on my bike."

What Larken had hoped was a proper volantrae turned out to be only a tiny airborne bike. Stephen handed her and Oliver both helmets.

"What about you?" she asked when he straddled the bike. Stephen shook his head.

"Only the two helmets," he said. "You guys get them since I control the bike. We won't be going far."

Larken found her disgusting, vomit-smelling self wedged between Stephen to the front and Oliver behind. The three barely fit without falling off, and the bike seemed to strain under lift-off as it made one false start, plummeted a few feet, and then lifted again to join the sparse traffic that now crossed the sky.

As the three of them rode into the night, Larken tightened her arms around Stephen's waist to the point that she finally felt his fingers prying hers apart.

"A little too tight," he said. "Don't worry. I hardly ever crash."

As though his joke was hilarious, he let out a little chuckle cut short by her re-clenching arms strangling the laughter off.

Larken squeezed her eyes shut to keep the bugs out, and the muscles in her neck strained against the stress of the idea of her plummeting to her death. They arrived at a massive industrial building that reminded Larken of a parking garage. The vehicle slowed, and Larken opened her eyes again as they lowered into a large delivery bay and came to a stop just inside. Stephen helped the two of them off and packed the helmets away, making no comment about what they must still smell like. He seemed happy to help, a little too chipper, as he guided them through an entrance in the back of the room and toward what Larken could make out as dark gray hallways that must have crisscrossed the interior of the building. She wondered what sort of work used to happen in a building so massive. The hallways stretched on and on.

"Here," he said and turned to the right at an open door. Stepping through, she heard movement beyond and couldn't stop her excitement at the possibility that in here, somewhere, Molly must have been.

The room he cut into was larger than her dormitory room had been at Brighton. Longer but not wider, the room stretched easily forty feet from the door. A woman's voice floated across the room toward them.

"You have to sound like you mean it," someone said. "Even through the distortion, your intonation matters. Try it again."

"Fine," she heard Molly's voice retort and excitedly bit her lip. She felt Oliver's hand clench her shoulder and squeeze tight. She strained to see against the narrowness of the hall and poor lighting. She saw nothing, still trapped behind Stephen, who led them into the darkness. A bright light at the back of the room came around the edge of a false wall that ended just shy of the border. As they cleared the wall, Larken sucked in her breath and stared.

Molly sat on a small stool, surrounded by a cluster of people that seemed unable to penetrate an invisible ten-foot bubble. Molly studied a screen before her, swiping up and down with her finger as she scrolled through images that Larken couldn't see.

"I don't get this part," Molly said.

A girl with a pierced bottom lip and a very elaborate

tattoo extending from beneath her short-cropped T-shirt swooped between them. "What part?"

"Here, Sam," Molly said, pointing to the tabletop screen. "What does that even mean? Are you threatening to kill more people, or are you promising not to? It's unclear. No polli will understand that."

"It's from Gemini Book," the girl named Sam said, again blocking Larken's view. "Verse 25:26. 'Vengeance is a tool and a discipline, not a custom. Kindness rewards kindness, growing itself, and hostility rewards hostility.' Models will know what it means."

"But who is this addressed *to*," Molly asked, pointing again at it. "My speech instructor always said to think of the audience first. Models aren't your problem, and they don't have any power. If you want things to change, you have to talk to *polli*. Can we change it?"

"To what?"

Larken shuffled to the left and craned around Sam's shoulders, seeking out Molly with her eyes. Molly seemed comfortable and not as hungry as Larken was having vomited up her last meal. The girl Sam seemed in the middle of saying something that Larken missed when she turned to look at her.

"*You* smell like vomit," Sam said, pointing at her with one blackened fingernail. Larken backed away a couple of inches but stayed close enough to watch Molly, whose brown eyes lifted from the screen and focused on her.

"Larken?" she exclaimed, quickly shifting her eyes past Larken, who tried not to be hurt that Molly was looking for Oliver and not her. "Oliver!"

Hearing his name as he rounded the false wall, Oliver's

dark blue eyes met Molly's brown ones, and he shoved his way past Sam and around the table.

"Take a break," the girl Sam said while rolling her eyes. The crowd that hovered around the pair disbursed. "Only five minutes, or this stupid video will never be made."

Sam glared at Stephen, who seemed unfazed, as though random glaring was one of the things the girl did so often it had become a useless gesture. Larken registered that away and her eyes moved on their own back to Oliver and Molly. She felt her eyes expand and fill her head. Molly's right hand was through the back of Oliver's thick mane of hair and his arms around her body. The two remained embraced in a languid kiss that lasted so long Larken felt as though she intruded and tried to look away but only found Sam's glare now focused on her.

"Another one," she muttered. "No, two. Stephen, you're picking up more strays? I get that you found them, but why the hell did you bring them back here?"

"They're her *friends*," Stephen protested.

"And do they need to know where we *sleep*?"

"There wasn't anywhere else to go. People are chasing them. I caught up to them at Bremerton," he said. "They were heading north like I guessed—running from the police, probably trying to make it to Canada."

"On foot? Do they even know about the Cascades? It will take them a week to get there if they don't die first."

"No, it's only a couple of hundred miles. We can make it fine," Larken protested. Sam responded with a smirk.

"You're not from Seattle. Probably not from Washington at all. Are you from Texas like her?"

"Portland."

"Then *you* should know. Between here and Canada is

the Chuckanut range. You'd *never* make it." She shook her head as though it were a simple fact, not an opinion, which irked Larken.

"We can make it," she retorted, refusing to acknowledge that her plan might have gotten them killed.

"If you say so," Sam said. "Hey, lovers, can we please finish shooting?"

"Shooting?" Larken asked, looking around at the equipment. She could see now that the crowd of spectators had gone. Oliver separated from Molly, his face covered with a broad smile and some of what looked like lip gloss that wasn't his. Molly's flushed cheeks hovered over his shoulder, and a tear rolled down to her chin and fell to the ground. Her eyes were shut, giving Larken more time to examine her friend's face—a face which seemed anything but happy to see them. Molly's lips kept a straight line and three ridges stood up over her eyebrows. When Molly pulled back away from Oliver, Larken noticed, even if Oliver didn't, that Molly's eyes immediately cast downward and she blew out threw her pursed lips.

"It was the deal," Molly explained. "I shoot their terrorist video, and they find you."

"We're not terrorists," Stephen said.

"Yeah, we are," Sam corrected. "But we're the good guys. And we've got to get through this shoot before the news cycle in the morning. Oliver or whatever your name is, get out of the way."

"You're terrorists?" asked Larken, directing her question to Sam, but Stephen responded.

"We're not," he said. "Siblings of the Natural Order. We're labeled terrorists, but we're not. That reclamation factory, remember? We try to stop things like that with protests, and sometimes we have to do kidnapping and, well..."

"Murder," said Sam. "Steve wants to be the nice guy, but he can't deny the truth. They kill us, and we kill them. That's how it works. I don't like it, Stephen, but sugarcoating doesn't change the facts."

She turned to Molly, who had finally succeeded in pushing Oliver away.

"Okay," she said. "What do you want to say instead?"

"How about keeping it simple? This man was in charge of the Bremerton reclamation plant and oversaw the execution of over a thousand people. He deserved to die. Be clear about what he did and why he's dying. You might gain some sympathy. If you use those obscure quotes that you like from your Bible or whatever, nobody will ever get it."

"WHAT HAPPENS IN THOSE PLANTS?" Molly asked. She reread the notes. She tried to stay focused on the script, but her mind kept slipping back to Oliver's expectant and unwavering gaze, which she managed to hold for a few seconds before the spring water man's scent memory brought water to her eyes. In just a few minutes, she would be done with the recording and Oliver again, and then she wouldn't be able to escape his too-observant eyes. Her heart pounded itself mercilessly against her insides.

"Murder," Sam said, responding to the question that Molly's distraction had already transformed into a vague memory. "Murder on a massive scale."

Focus. Molly chewed on the response, mulling it over. Finally, it clicked.

"You're not going to move anybody with that," Molly said. "Sometimes the truth isn't enough, and you've got to pad it a bit. Feelings are how people communicate. *Murder* is an abstract thing that happens *all the time.* It has to be visceral."

"Like human remains floating in a pool behind the Bremerton plant?" Larken asked.

Molly looked to Larken from the corner of her eyes. Larken's stern stare stole away any response she'd prepared. Molly's mouth trembled as she met accidentally met Oliver's gaze. It was his turn to look away. Molly fixed her gaze back to the notes on the pinamu before her and nodded, trying not to think about why Larken knew that answer.

"That would be a start," she said. "We need polli to feel revulsion and embarrassment that they allowed this to continue for so long."

"If you say so," Stephen said. "It's been happening all this time, and polli aren't doing anything about it yet. Maybe a few of the kids might notice, but I don't know how many minds we'll change."

"I know how this works, Stephen," she said. "I'm kind of an expert at changing lots of minds. You only need a handful of converts at a time, and before you know it, everyone thinks you're half-Chinese. It's just a matter of saying it enough."

She glanced at Larken, who seemed to be conversing with Oliver, having captured his attention away from Molly. Larken arched an eyebrow, a small acknowledgment of the prank they'd pulled two years earlier when they'd convinced almost everyone in their geometry class that Molly was half-Asian.

"You have to draw people in. That's why I asked. Say I'm sent to one of the reclamation plants. What happens next? Before the body parts in the pond."

"That depends," Stephen replied, his thoughtful look replaced with a somberness she hadn't seen in him before. She couldn't help glancing at Oliver again, but now he and

Larken still were deep into their conversation, and neither looked her way. It was Sam who answered.

"You're escorted in, usually by one or two of your own. You plead with them, *beg* them not to take you. You beg them to just this once, make an exception because you're one of them. You're *just like them*," Sam said, looking at Stephen, then back to Molly. "This happens all the way from the entrance up to this big vat thing. The whole time you think that maybe, just maybe, someone will rescue you. They unscrew the top of the vat and then strip you down. After all, your clothing costs money, and some other model will probably get those. Not to mention clothes gum up the pipes sometimes, and nobody wants to go fishing through human remains to unclog anything."

Molly swallowed.

"Then, as you're lowered in, cold and naked. You're still hoping that maybe some miracle will happen. They put the lid back on over you, blocking the sunlight, and slowly corkscrew it back into place. All the while, you're praying to whatever god you've managed to convince yourself is real. Even a well-placed lightning strike would give you an extra few hours of life, so you bargain for that kind of luck.

"All sounds disappear as the lid closes. The smell of cherry-flavored lollipops accompanies a whooshing sound as fluid fills the chamber. You're alive up until this point. It's cheaper since the chemicals will eventually kill you anyway. At first, the fluid swirls around you, and it just feels cold and wet. The worst you can imagine is drowning as the liquid makes its way up your body.

"Until the burning starts. Then you start to feel the layers of your skin melting away. You curse whatever gods you were praying to before because it's too late now. You realize as the nerves in your legs begin to tingle that even though the fluid has stopped at your armpits, you're going to fall into it when your legs can't support you anymore. Your feet begin to slip..."

The room had gone silent, so only Sam's voice sounded out over the crowd.

"That's when you give up and lower yourself down. If you're going to die, you want to die on your terms."

"How do you...," Molly began to ask.

"She was there," Stephen volunteered as Sam turned away and shoved her way back away from where Molly sat. "Not Bremerton, but somewhere else. She was a rescue." He motioned out over the crowd. "Most don't survive."

Stephen stopped talking. Even Oliver and Larken's chittering stalled in the corner and focused on Sam, whose impervious-seeming exterior had formed a crack. A single tear escaped her cheek and dripped onto the floor beside her. Sam wiped quickly and then clenched her teeth together as she met Molly's eyes.

"That's what happens," Sam said, sniffing once and wiping the tear away. "And if you're lucky—very lucky— that's when someone like the Siblings of the Natural Order breaks into the facility and bombs the fucking place, launching you from your vat into a puddle onto the floor."

Then her face twisted up into a sardonic grin.

"But if you're unlucky, HCC negotiations with your captors are underway, and you die, dissolved into a puddle of former human. Whatever proteins they extract successfully, they use to create the next generation of models."

"And what they can't, they end up in that pond we saw," said Larken, her eyebrows arched up.

"What you saw?" Sam asked. Stephen nodded.

"Bremerton," he told her. "The drainage pond and flow. That's where I found them."

"I didn't know," Molly said, echoing the thought that had embedded itself within her brain for the past day. Everything Molly had learned about models was from their Brighton classes, which didn't cover reclamation. What it covered was that models weren't usually able to reproduce and that the organizations that bought models took care of them. They were given places to live and food to eat for free. They were freeloading off their owners, so a bit of work was good for them. It gave them character. This is what the schools taught.

"Nobody ever told us it was that bad," Larken said.

"No. And that's the story we need to tell," Molly said. "That's the story that people need to hear and understand. And *you* need to tell it, not me."

Molly nodded toward Sam with her head.

"Well, I'm not going to do that. *You* need to tell it. That's what we're here for, remember? You tell it and make people care. I'm done with this shit."

Sam stormed away, elbowing her way past Larken, who followed her movements with a sharp glare.

"Ready for another take?" someone nearby asked. Molly nodded.

"Might as well," Molly said, running her hand across her forehead. "Let's go."

"Molly?" She turned her head to see that Oliver had inched closer to her. She blinked. "Why are you shooting a video with terrorists?"

"Freedom fighters," said Sam with a fixed grin. Molly stared, which made Sam chuckle, shake her head, and lean away just slightly. As rough as she had appeared at first, Sam had been the most engaged in recording the video, even though she kept saying she wanted nothing to do with it. Molly got the impression that Sam wasn't talking about the video per se but the life that had led to its creation.

"I can't leave until this is done," Molly said, shrugging Oliver away before he could put his hands on her like the spring water man. Oliver's lips formed a straight line and his eyebrows came together. He turned away from her then, and relinquished the inches he'd just gained in advancing toward her.

"Just do it so we can go," said Larken, eyeing the crowd around them with suspicion. Molly glanced to the same group and then back to the two of them. Larken's hand supported her leaning against a desk, and for the first time, Molly saw how tired they must have been. She'd been fighting against exhaustion for hours, but she'd had all the food and, more importantly, the coffee she wanted—needed. The fifth cup worked its way into her bladder at that very moment. She shifted uncomfortably on her short stool behind the desk that looked like it belonged to a television anchor.

"Go where?" Molly asked.

"Canada," Larken said without delay. "In two hours, we could be there."

"Then what?" Molly challenged. "Then hope that they grant you asylum? You and Oliver leave me stranded in the United States? That plan sucks."

"N...no. I hadn't thought—"

"*I* have. There's no way they'll let me into Canada as a minor. You two might be let in since you're, you know, *models* and all. The only thing that happens at the Canadian border is we *never* see each other again. Never."

"But we don't die," insisted Larken. "Oliver doesn't die.

We don't become puddles of pink goo laced with fingernails and teeth."

Her tone went high as she protested. Her sandy brown hair bounced with her head movements, and her teeth seemed to click together in between words as rapidly as she spit them out. Molly recognized this version of Larken. This was the version of Larken that had scared even Molly sometimes. Jocelyn called this version of Larken her "dark rage."

"Yell if you want," Molly retorted, raising her voice. "I *love* Oliver, and I won't live without him."

Oliver squirmed. It was impossible not to notice. Molly's heart fell as she considered that maybe, just possibly, he didn't feel the same way about her. But she couldn't let that get to her, not right then. Not yet. Not after all the work she'd done to get him.

"*Love* him? How could you? You haven't been together long enough for *love*. Whatever you're doing is just a hobby. Go right ahead if you want to stay here and make your stupid terrorist video. We're leaving."

"Go then," Molly said, her eyes drilling into Oliver. She mouthed the word *go*.

"I love you too," he said. Sam, in Molly's periphery, rolled her eyes.

"Can someone finish the damn video? We'll miss posting tonight if we don't get going."

"I'm sorry," Larken said. "How good does this have to be? You've been through four takes since *we* arrived and haven't said much more than hi. Do you ʼ what Oliver and I saw out there? Our futures. We saw what happens to us if the state of Oregon catches us and discovers that we're models."

Sam's head snapped back toward Larken.

"You're models?" she asked. Molly watched Sam's eyes

trace the edge of Larken's arms down to her wrist, where Molly knew Sam wouldn't find a barcode. "Shit."

"This whatever it is won't help us, and being caught here won't help either."

"Sorry, your highness. Some of us can't pass," Sam retaliated.

"I mean, I'm sympathetic, of course. But I can't live my life like this." Larken motioned around with her hands palms up and extended from her body.

"So...you're sympathetic, but fuck us anyway? Sounds great," Sam replied.

"That's not what I said."

"No, it's not. It's not what any of you polli say, is it? You say *how much more will my hamburger cost if models don't make my burgers?* Why don't you just say what you mean instead? *You having an actual life would inconvenience me too much.* Death by inconvenience. Hundreds of models a day. Hundreds of *humans* a day."

"That's why we have to get this right, Larken," Molly said, trying to soften her voice. She wasn't sure how effective she was because the heat in her chest still rose to unbearable levels.

"Don't pretend you *care* now," Larken said. "This wouldn't rate missing a manicure for you."

"A lot has happened in the last few days, Larken," Molly said, her anger replaced suddenly with the exhaustion she saw in Larken's eyes. "It might just be that I care now. We're leaving soon, and this is my one shot to help repay the debt of finding you. I want it to *matter*. I want at least one person to listen to this message and *hear* it. I want someone like me— oblivious and myopic—to wake the fuck up and understand that human lives are *worth* the inconveniences."

Larken still didn't agree, but that last line had been enough to shut her up. Molly's lower lip trembled then, something she hadn't expected. Her eyes blurred as she turned away from Oliver and Larken together. A deep breath and face-wipe later, she turned back to the camera.

"Time to go," Molly said, her face burning. She exhaled twice and when the director gave her the cue again began to recite her improved speech.

Just when she got to the part about how models were humans and deserved to be treated as such and was about to delve into the horrors in reclamation facilities, she saw faint outlines of heads swiveling back and forth beyond the camera to her front. The sound of talking rose in the background, preceding a massive thud of something heavy against the door. The lights around her flashed on, blinding her at first. Scanning the room, she twisted her head and saw Larken separating from Oliver and heading away from the sound. The noise reverberated through the room. The door bent inward; she could now see, even though the lights flickered. Something large was just outside and trying to get in. Molly pushed away from the table and spun toward the twins. Oliver had cut the distance between them and grabbed her by the arm. She yanked her arm free as another thunking noise sounded so loud that she could feel the vibrations on her skin. Only then did she turn to move with him.

"What is it?" Molly asked as she bolted upright. Her heart was the second-loudest sound still as one more collision echoed through. Oliver shook his head.

"I don't know," he screamed, or she thought he screamed though it sounded very far away.

"It's an attack," Sam called, just behind them. "You're blocking everyone. Move!"

There didn't seem to be anywhere to go. The room was tiny, and the light illuminated every corner. Molly could see that the room was even smaller than she'd thought. The darkness had made the space seem about twice its real size. Still, she pushed toward what looked like a wall near the back. Oliver shrank back into the corner, and she shoved into him. He wrapped his arms around her. Her mind flashed back to the bus station as she told herself not to react. It wasn't the spring water man. It was Oliver, and she loved Oliver. Hadn't she just said so? Not even that made her feel any safer and her atavistic impulses took over as she struggled against him. Larken squeezed into her side.

"What are you doing?" Larken asked.

Before Molly could respond, Sam shouldered Larken. "Move."

Molly's first instinct was to come to Larken's defense until she saw that Larken had been standing on what looked like a large tile. Sam tapped twice against it, and the thing popped up just an inch, high enough to get a couple of fingers under.

"Give me a hand," Sam shouted once more. Molly couldn't move. Her eyes had traversed back to the door just when it gave way. What tried to come through was too big for the doorframe, but she could make out two large barrels of what reminded her of proton rifles extending into the room. Her ears still rang from the banging. She became vaguely aware of Larken, Oliver, and Sam working at the panel. They got it about knee height before Sam wedged her way through and held her hand out to help Larken.

The barrels must have shot something into the room because people were falling where they pointed. Molly's ears couldn't distinguish sounds after the first blast, but the bodies kept falling, so she guessed they still worked. On the other side of what she knew were guns, just to the other side of the doorway, she saw what she thought was a woman, standing isolated and unmoving. The woman's smile seemed surreal, as though the most fun she could imagine having was standing right there, watching the scattering people fall. The barrels slowly swiveled toward Molly, who could only watch on until Oliver shoved her to the ground. She felt his hands grabbing her and tried to shake him off as an immediate reaction, but he scowled and shoved and suddenly her body moved without her participation. She found herself being pushed and yanked under the panel until she dropped down to hard cement.

"Oliver," she heard Larken call out as she struggled to rise. Molly pushed up with her aching shoulder. She gained her feet between where Larken stood and the thin gap in the tile beyond which she could now see red and orange flickering. "Oliver, give me your hand," Larken said, as though Molly weren't between them.

Oliver extended his hand under the panel, reaching for Molly, but Molly couldn't move. She had frozen in terror, and none of her limbs answered her pleas. Larken's arm couldn't reach much past Molly's head, not close enough to get Oliver through.

"Get out of the way, Molly," Larken's voice called before Molly felt a hard shove knocking her to the side. She couldn't move as Larken sprang in front of her, her hands closing around Oliver's wrist. On the other side, Sam pulled so hard that the dragon tattoo on her arm seemed to writhe and wiggle, but Oliver didn't come forward. His eyes met Molly's, and she knew that something had him. She snapped back into reality and tried to cross the room to his side. He looked at her as though it were only the two of them alone without the world crashing down around them.

"I never wanted to keep you a secret."

Months of clandestine evenings and stolen kisses flooded through her memories. Something unreal about this moment lingered. The gap between them, so short, seemed eternal.

Her hands went up to her cheek like his had that evening. She felt his fingers again and his lips pressing against hers when she'd been so excited to see him again that her body hadn't interpreted his touch as anything other than his own. His eyes, those dark blue chasms that she'd fallen into quite by accident one day, those eyes suddenly clouded over, and she knew he didn't see her any longer. He tried on a brave smile that wasn't real and coughed, sending blood into the opening. Molly stopped in her tracks. It was too late. Larken and Sam struggled in slow motion denial. Whatever had come into that room—something that looked like a mechanized infantry tank—had ended his life already. One more shudder, and his eyes went so dark that even Larken stopped pulling. She turned to Molly with hate in her eyes.

"*You* killed him," she screamed, her rage directed at Molly. Molly only stood and accepted it. It would have been wrong not to. Oliver might still be alive if she'd been a second faster or a few seconds, if she hadn't frozen, if she had gotten out of Larken's way. He'd be with them if she'd never insisted on revising that stupid statement. She'd bargained with all of their lives, and she'd lost his.

"Shut the fuck up," Sam's voice cut through, drowning out both Larken's voice and Molly's internal thoughts. "What killed him is that thing out there. And if you want to start fighting now, it will kill us too. Stephen, did you make it?"

"Here, Sam," his voice came from the dark behind them.

"Lead the way," she called out. "We've got to get out of here. Did you get the footage?"

"No," he answered. "All gone, no time. This way."

Sam walked toward his voice in the dim light that tiny red lights on either side of the hallway they were now in provided. Molly made out his thin frame in the distance ahead. Behind her, she could hear the short, quick breaths of someone choking back tears and the heavy plodding sound of hopelessness.

CHAPTER 23
MOLLY, THE MURDERER

LARKEN STUMBLED forward into the darkness. An hour passed, or maybe more. She couldn't tell how long they'd been walking. All she knew was that each step took more energy than the last to find its home on the damp tunnel floor. The darkness waned and waxed over time as the four passed through interconnected hallways. It was as though they passed through nights and into days and back again. Red lights flickered faintly somewhere in the distance. Her feet lifted and plopped back down, first against cement, then against what felt like gravel, and as the red lights came and went, into the soft support of grass-layered dirt. Larken and the others erupted from a large tunnel mouth, and the sounds of their tireless stomping were supplanted by insects calling to the moon.

Sam stopped and a night sky full of diamond-like stars shone behind her silhouette. Stephen stopped beside her, then Molly was there with her straight black hair and lost stare.

"I'm sorry," Sam said, her lip-piercing glimmering silver. The moon ducked behind some clouds.

Larken's knees wobbled. Her hands slid up to cover her face. She breathed in the smell of her own sweat and the muck that had lined the walls of the long-abandoned tunnel.

The only thing that mattered to Larken had died in the building they'd fled. Her lips joined together into a thin straight line. If she'd opened her mouth even a little, she would have attacked Molly with an onslaught of words. Molly—insistent beyond reason on getting her story right and working out the details of a story that wasn't even her story to tell—had killed Oliver. Molly the murderer.

"Sorry for what? It was your people who got him killed," Molly said, her voice hushing the insects and penetrating the night.

"You have no right," Larken said to her. "None. I *told* you it was time to go. I told you we needed to leave. But you had to do one more take, didn't you? One more. Always one more. And now he's *dead*." Her voice rose in the evening to the point that the word *dead* sounded back to her over and over again as if the trees taunted her. Molly's mouth zipped shut, and her eyes glistened.

"You can't blame me for his death," she finally said, trailing off. Then she almost whispered. "You *can't*."

"Oh, I do," Larken assured her, the fire in her heart leaping through her teeth. "I do blame you. Why are you even here? Why were you even with him in the first place? None of this started before you started seeing him. He would still be alive if it weren't for you."

"You don't mean that," Stephen said calmly. What fucking right did he have to be calm when *her* brother had just died?

"Your brother didn't just die reaching out to you for help. You didn't just witness the light drain out of his eyes trying to save him. Stay out of this."

"Stop, Larken," Sam said. Sam approached Larken in the way that someone might approach a wounded animal, with hands out before her and eyes locked in. Larken's own eyes darted from her to Molly to Stephen.

"You're all guilty," she said and stepped backward toward the tunnel's entrance. "Your stupid terrorist organization. What are you even doing? Do you know what they say about SNO at Brighton? A bunch of morons who don't know when they lost. And for you, my brother was killed?"

Tears streamed down Larken's face. She tasted salt as they dribbled down to her chin and fell in splatters against the dirt.

"You don't mean that. Slow down, Larken. Take a breath," Sam said, pressing forever forward. Larken wasn't about to give up more ground and back away again. She stood firm against Sam's advance and returned her stare.

"You go around kidnapping people, and for what? Has anyone stopped killing models? Is anyone even paying attention to the things that you're doing? Only the cops. No polli cares about this mission you're on. You're just getting good people killed. Good people like..."

She couldn't say his name. Her mouth froze in an "o," and his name wouldn't come. Larken clenched her teeth and felt her bottom lip quivering as she glanced at Molly and then got stuck there. Molly held her hand over her mouth as though she used it to clamp her mouth shut, and her body shook with silent sobs. Larken suddenly couldn't see anything as her eyes blurred. Somehow Sam had reached her, and she felt those tattooed arms wrap around her. She buried her head in Sam's hair on instinct, letting out a guttural scream that muffled into the girl's shoulder as she quaked.

"I'm sorry," Sam said. Larken tried to push away then, but Sam held firm until Larken finally gave in, too drained to protest. Instead, she let wails out into the night. Whoever it had been—that mystery woman and the mech—they couldn't be far behind. Larken's screams might attract them with any luck, and they could finish the killing they'd begun. As she let the sobs out, she tired more and more until it took all of her energy just to stand, even with Sam's assistance.

"It hurts," she complained. "So much. It just hurts."

"I know," Sam said, as Larken sniffled and slid her hand up into the narrow gap between them to wipe her nose. Sam continued, "I wish I could say it'll get better, but it never does."

Sam looked over to Stephen.

"Would you say?"

Larken took that moment to look at Stephen, his face stoic against the question.

"No," he said. "Not better. Different. Not better."

Larken wiped her eyes again and felt something besides the thick sadness that dripped like molasses through her veins. The fire she'd directed at Molly welled up to replace it, burning off the residue of her anguish.

"Those were your friends," she said to Sam once her tears had subsided. They would be back. Larken could feel the tears hiding behind her eyes, lurking there for their next moment to shine. But for now, she had spent enough of them to realize how selfish she had been. That room was full of dead people; for whatever Larken knew, they had been friends to Sam and Stephen.

"Good friends too," Stephen said, nodding. Molly stopped crying, but she didn't engage in the conversation. She stared out into the blackness.

"They hunt us," Sam said. "The Human Pride Movement has been recognized by the state of Washington as a militia organization, while *we've* been branded terrorists—and *they* hunt *us*. They get money from politicians to help round up runaway models, dead or alive. You can probably tell which they prefer. We've both lost more friends than we can count."

Because it was a one-sided battle.

Larken slowly began to understand that she and Oliver never really had a chance. Sam hadn't stopped talking, but Larken had stopped hearing. Larken became lost in her thoughts. The world beyond her mind had degenerated into a pattern of nothing. The shadows blended with other shades, and the stars and trees warped with her grief. She sucked into her mind now, which refused to accept that Oliver was gone, when she thought of those azure eyes emptying of their life force, draining out onto the paneled floor in the recording room. At the same time, she saw that six-year-old, smiling with bright blue eyes and bushy hair, who she'd always tried to protect, having designated herself the oldest even though they claimed the same age.

He couldn't be gone. She staggered forward and sank to her knees, never expecting to get up again. She nailed herself to the spot, intent on dying where she stood. When Sam and Stephen tried to move her, her dead weight was almost too much for them. She wanted to lay in the cold dirt and be buried by it. She wanted the coolness all around her and above her. It wasn't fair that she breathed when he didn't.

An explosion rocked her forward and caused Molly to break her standing penitence to let out a scream louder than any Larken could have managed. Next, she heard a woman's shrill laugh and felt the tugging of death grow more intense.

"Larken, we have to go," Sam said, her voice tinted with desperation.

"Leave me here. They want me dead? I'll die for them. I don't care."

"I won't," claimed Molly, who'd finally stopped crying enough to speak. "I won't die for those assholes."

"You will," Larken said. "You all will. It's not just them. It's an entire world that wants you stamped out of existence, just like Oliver. You can't fight that many people. What does it matter if they get us now or later?"

Another explosion. This one was closer like someone lobbed fireworks in their direction while slowly walking toward them.

"Suit yourself," said Sam, finally letting go. "I've lost too many people to die here. Especially to that bitch."

Sam pulled away and walked, slowly at first, before changing into a run and beelining for the cover of trees and away from the tunnel's entrance. Larken turned to face the tunnel, staring into the black with blearing eyes. Stephen yanked harder and finally managed to move her toward where Sam and Molly hid among the foliage. Larken stopped fighting and followed. Even in her malaise, her willingness to die didn't extend to getting others killed. She wasn't like Molly, selfish enough to rend those in orbit around her into useless props. Larken bit back on her teeth, and her stomach muscles tightened almost as tightly as her cheek muscles.

Only vague shapes danced before her as Stephen settled her in behind a bush. He darted forward into the clearing and smoothed out whatever tracks they had made in the dirt before returning, she saw in her blurred vision. She lay in the soil, leaves, and grass and closed her eyes again, not sleeping but not awake either. Larken was prepared to lay there forever.

"Come out, come out," sang the woman's shrill voice over the sliding, slinging sounds of the mech as it extended from its crouched position to its full height. Larken couldn't help her drawing her eyes to the sudden obstruction in the moonlight. Through gaps in the brush, she couldn't see the full picture at once. Larken gathered from the different angles that the mech resembled a military tank with metal legs and arms, but no head. Instead, a black plate made of what seemed like onyx or black plastic lay just above the main barrel. On each shoulder rested additional turrets with four chambers each, in case the one that was as round as Larken's head wasn't enough to do the job.

"We'll get you sooner or later. Terrorists have no place in a land of laws. Do you wonder why polli loathe models so much? You're animals. Lawless and incapable of managing yourselves. No discipline. That's why we win. That's why we'll *always* win."

A blinding light erupted from where they stood as if to enunciate the point. Even Larken's sealed eyelids couldn't keep out the flash that lit everything near daylight. She didn't move and didn't hear movement from any of the others either.

"There is no future for you," the woman continued. "Come out now, and I'll kill you quickly like the cockroaches you are. Make me chase you, and it will only be more painful."

She didn't give chase. The woman's voice projected again at a volume that seemed to shake the trees, though the woman herself didn't move an inch—at least from what Larken could see of her knees.

Larken's eyes suddenly shot open. The voice wasn't human. It couldn't have been because no human could talk that loudly. She was not yelling, only *talking* at an impossible volume. She caught a glimpse of the woman's face through the brush covering where they'd hidden. No microphone and no megaphone. Nothing except the woman, yet her voice vibrated the leaves and drilled into Larken's brain until she couldn't think. A second later, the woman screamed, loud and long. The long scream stopped, and she turned away, bored looking.

"They're gone," she said to the mech, which seemed to nod at her. "Let's go clean up the rest of that mess inside."

The mech seemed relieved not to try to navigate the woods. Its entire body slumped for a second before it jolted back up, long guns and all, and followed the woman in the general direction of the tunnel entrance.

"She's gone," Sam said after a few minutes of silence. "And we need to talk."

Larken closed her eyes again. It didn't matter that the woman wasn't human anymore; it mattered whatever Sam had to say.

"You can get yourself killed if you want to," she reprimanded Larken. "But you almost got Stephen killed too. You need to decide here and now what you're going to do. Come with us and don't be a burden while we try to reconnect with the others, or stay here and probably die of exposure or something. Your choice, but make it once."

"I don't think that's—" Stephen began until Sam turned and shot him a glare.

"I'm not risking us for *her*. She's new and untrained, so I gave her some leeway, but it stops now. Time to woman up, Larken. It sucks but come or stay. If you come, keep up."

"I'm sorry," Molly said. "If that helps, I'm sorry. I loved him too."

"For three days," Larken told her through a scowl. "He was mine forever."

"It wasn't just three days," Molly said, her voice wavering. She took a deep breath. "It was like two months, maybe three. It's just we didn't want to upset you. And I loved him even before that. I didn't mean to...oh, God."

Molly burst into tears; her freckled cheeks warped into an ugly frown as her body convulsed, then she looked away and spoke to the trees.

"I didn't mean to get him killed, Larken. I just wanted to do the right thing. We weren't at any risk. I mean, there wasn't any sign that they'd found us. They just showed up. *You* saw. If there'd been a sign..."

Larken rubbed her eyes with her fingers. When she opened them again, she was alone. The woods had evaporated. Before her was the woman in teal set against a dark mist.

"You are in danger," the woman said, not hesitating this time or being coy.

"Fuck off. You haven't been paying attention."

"You're in danger still."

"*That* wasn't it? The attack that got my brother killed

wasn't enough for you? There's more? Tell it to someone else. I don't care."

"Your brother killed? No. I think you're mistaken. And you *should* care. Sweet baby girl. You should. I've learned more. This danger—the danger of which I speak—isn't the danger of one person. It's not the danger of a city. This danger is the danger of an entire world. This is the danger of *multiple* worlds."

"So what? Let them sort it out. I. Don't. Care."

The woman's face contorted into a glare that penetrated Larken's soul.

"You *will* care. You're not dying here, Larken. Before you die, you will smell the bodies burning in the streets and regret *trying* to die here. Your brother would have fought for them, and you are giving up before the battle has even truly started."

"He wouldn't have fought for them unless they guaranteed him a passing entrance exam score. But..."

Aayushi disappeared, and the woods slowly clarified against the skyline. Three faces peered hauntingly into her own.

"Are you okay?" Sam's voice came just a second after her mouth moved.

Larken laughed at the image, like a holovid with un-synced audio.

"I think she's lost it," Stephen muttered, staring at her.

"I love you, Larken. Please come back?" Molly's voice seemed far away, as though it had come across a bad ansible connection. Larken's laughter subsided, and she found the laughs replaced by tears as she wept. No matter what she tried, nothing worked to "pull herself together." The loss was too great, and the tears were unstoppable.

"We have to go, Larken. Still can't stay here."

She nodded. A hand closed around her own, and she followed where she tugged. Every step surprised her as her tear-blinded eyes let nothing through. If she had to guess by the crunch of old leaves and sticks and the scratches she felt through her clothes, she'd have thought that there was no trail or path. She wasn't sure that any of them knew *where* they traveled, only that they fled what was behind them: a shrieking madwoman-thing hell-bent on their destruction.

CHAPTER 24
AN UNFORGIVING WALK

"SHE LEFT," Torrent said. He raised his hands in the universal "wasn't my fault" gesture. He understood why Brigid was upset. When an unedited holovid surfaced on the evening news, that showed a blurry Molly in a camera shot surrounded by undistinguishable images in the background, making some terrorist manifesto. Part of one anyway before explosions rocked the camera feed. "I was on the phone with you when she snuck out. I didn't *know* she was going to run off and do *this*. With terrorists?"

"Why didn't you keep an eye on her? My girl. My *girl*."

Torrent hadn't recalled just how *tall* Brigid was as he tried to calm her. Even in her rage, she exuded elegance. There was only disappointment as her hot glare drilled into him. She blamed him, even though the whole thing had been Brigid's idea. "I was trying to help *you*, and she's gone. Somewhere off, who knows where with Siblings of the Natural Order?"

"Ordell said—"

"I don't give a damn what Ordell said. He's not SNO anymore, and he doesn't know. His Humanity in Crisis Council or whatever has nothing to do with them. He wouldn't know about this."

"Listen, Brigid. He reached out to Phineas."

That got her attention. Brigid's gyrating, perfectly-manicured hands came to a stop at her sides. Phineas Lancaster was *the leader* of the SNO. Humanity in Crisis Council and SNO weren't on *good* terms, especially since Ordell—the HCC leader—had once been kidnapped by Phineas Lancaster. Despite that, their *leaders* sometimes talked because they shared the same goals. They palavered like two warring nations who circled each other looking for weaknesses. On rare occasions, they assisted each other in defending against injustices they both agreed were wrong. Torrent bit his lip and pushed up his glasses in anxiety. What he had to say next wouldn't make her happier, but she needed to know. He took a swig from his three fingers of scotch before he spoke.

"They don't have her. He said they were recording that video as justification for their latest kidnapping, someone who ran the Bremerton reclamation plant once. He said the recording location was raided late last night. Somehow Human Pride Movement got wind of it and went to make an example."

"That's supposed to make me feel better?" she asked at first, then cocked her head to the side. "Wait. What do you mean? HPM did a raid against the Siblings of the Natural Order? It's not as though SNO don't know how to defend themselves."

"In Washington, HPM is financed by the state," he said.

"They're like a miniature army up here, with military-grade mechs and androids. Not like what they were in Texas. Ordell gave me the location of the building in case you want to go check it out."

The location wasn't on the news yet. Torrent spoke of SNO, HCC, and HPM and the violence between them. His words were about finding Molly. In his mind, he only saw Bodhi, connected to machines since his fall in the elevator that day. His son, the caring, compassionate soul that he was, didn't want to hurt anyone, but he was fading fast. The elevator fall had been only the latest sign of how deadly his disease had become. Unprompted, Bodhi had collapsed and was unconscious in the Beckett-Madeline version of an emergency room being monitored by at least two different doctors.

"I do want to, Brigid," he confessed. "I just don' t how useful I would be. Bodhi's hurt..."

"You're coming with me. I don't live in Seattle. You do, and you're the reason my little girl is out there somewhere."

"I'm not the reason," he said, shaking his mane. "Not any more than you're the reason she showed up in Seattle unattended twice in the same week."

He regretted that as soon as he said it. Anyone else would have understood without having to probe that Brigid's lashing out was partly due to her feelings of inadequacy. Molly did escape on her watch in Portland, albeit her "escape" was from Brighton, so if anyone was guilty, it was the far-too-lenient staff who Brigid had already laid into before she hopped the flight to Seattle. Brigid's makeup—which had held up so far through at least two waves of tears—streaked under this next one as she plunged her head into her hands.

"My little girl," she murmured, frantically wiping her eyes. "No time. No time. Come on, Torrent, let's go get her."

The tears still fell, even though her face had resumed something of her prepared legal-battle look.

"I can't go," he said as he took two steps back. "I won't. Bodhi...I..."

"There's time, isn't there? I'm sure he'll be fine. Anyway, at least you know where your child is." She pointed to his glass, which had already gone empty during their conversation. "And let's be honest about what you're really doing here. Come with me. Besides, you *know* the killer is looking for that other boy of yours and *your* daughter."

"They're not mine."

"They look just like you."

"That's just because we used my..."

"DNA. Yeah. You don't feel anything for them at all, do you? They're yours, whether you want to admit it or not."

"No, they're not," he protested, feeling the back of his neck heat up as he shoved his glasses back against his forehead. "They're not mine. None of those thirty are mine. They weren't even supposed to live past the experiment. It was *Harper* who did all of that. If anything, they're *hers*. Hers and Railynn's."

Accepting more responsibility for Larken and Oliver would also make him responsible for nearly thirty other children. That wasn't something he could do, and if Harper hadn't insisted on fair treatment, those "children" would have been reclaimed as soon as the gestation pods hatched.

"Well, one of those not-your-children *killed* someone," Brigid said with a snarl. "That's going to come back to you sooner or later. What lawyer in their right mind will support you when that happens?"

Then what could he do for Bodhi? That was his only thought as he felt his head nodding slowly. It was shitty for her to threaten that she wouldn't support him. But he'd already bargained away the life of another for his son, so even while he felt his hackles rising, he tamped them back down again. She'd done nothing he wouldn't have done in a heartbeat—for his *real* son.

"I'll help you find them," he said. "But then I'm coming back. I *will* be here when Bodhi comes out of his operation."

Suppose he woke up after anesthesia. Or if he made the wrong decision. Torrent gulped as he considered briefly the possibility that Bodhi might still choose his death over the death of another. No time. It wasn't helpful to think like that. He placed his empty glass on his kitchen island with a shaky hand that he then used to steady himself. Torrent thought through all the places they might be. The list was impossible. If it turned out Molly had already left the abandoned USPS building, and why wouldn't she if it had been under attack, then she could be anywhere. He sighed. It was the only place they knew of to start looking.

"We should start at the USPS building," he said.

"After two days?"

He narrowed his eyes at her, fully aware that such an expression didn't make it past his glasses in any meaningful way. To her, he probably just looked deep in thought. Torrent snatched them from his face to drive more impact, but she'd already looked away again.

"Which USPS building?"

"In SoDo," Torrent said. "Where the stadiums are. Zephyr matches happen down there and lofting too. Down there's the building Ordell mentioned. It used to be USPS but abandoned now. Industrial-looking," he said.

"Can you pull up a map?"

"Over there," he pointed to the couch. "Coffee table."

He crossed around her—giving her a wide berth in case she decided to direct more of her anger toward him—and took a seat on the couch. For him, in the apartment alone, the sofa was more of an item of decoration. In the last couple of weeks, he'd gotten more use out of it than he had the previous two years.

The surface of the coffee table sprang to life when he tapped two fingers on it, projecting a welcome screen in three dimensions in the space above it. He swiped that aside to find a search prompt that looked like an audio snippet would if it was stood up sideways and rapidly spun in a circle creating a three-dimensional object. It grew fatter and skinnier in a fluctuating pattern.

"Map of SoDo," he said, instantly greeted him with an image of the four-strata high stadium about half the size of the eight-story library downtown. He'd been to a handful of Seattle AirCrawler matches down there but couldn't remember seeing anything that looked too industrial near the stadium. Farther down on First Avenue, there were some. With three fingers, he swiped the display in that direction until it showed what looked like a parking garage next to a train track.

"Stop there," she said, grabbing at his knee. He jumped, having not realized that she'd taken the seat next to him *or* that they were personally close enough to invade each other's personal space like that. She pulled her hand back. "Sorry."

"Th...that's okay," he muttered, moving the map with his fingers to zoom in on the structure. "Look there."

The building was abandoned. On the side hung a huge

sign that read "USPS," the now-defunct delivery service that had survived the first three hundred years of United States history. It was odd that nobody had ever moved into the building after the organization became insolvent and was dissolved by the United States Congress some three years before.

"That's building. Who owns it now?"

"It says here...," he said, stalling as he flashed an ASL "i" to the computer interface in the air over the building to pull up the information panel. "Eastern Logging Syndicate, based out of Nigeria."

"That name seems familiar," she muttered. "That name..."

"Why would a Nigerian company own a building in SoDo?"

"Distribution, I guess. Except I don't see any trucks in the yard there, and this map was updated about a month ago."

"What's that?"

She pointed to a sewage tunnel at the back, and he swiveled the map around for her to get a better view, painfully aware that her knee now pressed against his own. Torrent swallowed.

"I don't know. I can't imagine the USPS ever needing sewage disposal like that."

Brigid grabbed his knee again and, this time, swiveled her head to look at him, excitement dancing in her green eyes.

"That's the one," she said. "I know it. We need to go there and take a look."

"There will be police all over the place."

She yanked her hand back.

"Torrent, why is it that every time I try to get us to move, you have a reason not to? My daughter is in genuine and immediate danger. We must find her, and *that's* where we need to go to do it."

He had nothing to say. How could he explain to her that he played the possibilities in his mind every single situation in every second of every day? How could he tell her that her daughter was already dead in most of those scenarios? Whereas he had a *living* son, alive for now and in need. The net result of doing anything regarding her daughter would be compounding tragedy on top of tragedy and finding her broken body. But he'd made a promise. He returned to the kitchen, where he poured himself another drink.

"You need to stop with those."

"Live my life. Then tell me that." He threw back a finger of scotch. "Okay, I'm ready. Let's go."

Ten minutes and a very bumpy volantrae ride later, Brigid's instincts proved correct as had Torrent's. The USPS building was surrounded by police vehicles, volantrae hovered with lights pointing at a gaping hole in the side of the building. The hole was the size of a bus or large truck, with burn marks on the bricks around the edges. Whatever had made the hole had involved extremely high temperatures. They parked a block away at a coffee shop and returned to where they'd seen the sewage pipe on the map.

The pipe was tall and wide enough to pass a volantrae through, or so it looked from the outside. But it was closed in, different than it had looked in the holographic image. There was no seeing inside through the cement encasing. They instead followed it from the outside as it twisted and turned above the ground for a few minutes, only to watch it disappear under the street's surface. The early evening sun stretched the city's shadows almost to their feet.

"What now?" Torrent asked, jutting his hand into his pocket to run his thumb along the side of his communicator. No call yet. He didn't know what that meant. Either his son was still thinking it over, or they'd begun the operation and had somehow, despite Torrent's numerous pleas, forgotten to let him know. He pushed the thought out of his mind.

"Over there," Brigid told him, pointing to a rise in the dirt a few feet ahead. Overgrown with brush and grass, Torrent guessed that it could have been, with some imagination, evidence of the continuing of a tunnel beneath. It didn't matter whether it was or not. Brigid would pursue it anyway. She'd dressed like a mountain climber with heavy-soled boots and camouflage pants. Her coat was that drab olive green that the military loved so much. Torrent's outfit, a bright-blue coat with matching pants and a yellow cummerbund, finished with matching wingtip shoes, was less appropriate for their new adventure. Torrent hadn't exactly been expecting to go traipsing into the woods. Brigid put one firm foot on the apex of the pipe and pulled the other one up behind it. Then she turned and offered a hand to Torrent, pulling him up onto the foot-high elevated hill. No sooner than his own feet had landed than she fast-walked into the bushes ahead, shoving them aside with gloves that Torrent had also not considered bringing. The briars hid in the brush cut against his hand as he tried to do the same. Wincing with each thrust, he edged into the bush behind her.

It wasn't hot. The city had a balmy feel by Seattle standards, but it didn't qualify as "hot." The humidity still poured gallons of sweat down beneath Torrent's coat, causing his silk shirt to stick to his back. He felt each labored breath threatening him with just enough oxygen. On multiple occasions, he'd slowed down while Brigid kept at it, never breaking her stride until she noticed that she'd taken some corner alone. Then she passed a judgmental stare at him, and he knew what she was thinking. If he hadn't been drinking, he could have kept up. The numbness of the drink had long worn off due to his increased tolerance, and now he was confident the sweat made him smell like a bar.

"Keep. Up. I'm not stopping for you again."

Curt and to the point. This was the Brigid that Torrent remembered from so long ago when Harper had tried to take on Emergent Biotechnology, the company without whom saving Bodhi would have been impossible. Strange the friends people keep.

For Bodhi.

"Go without me," he said. "I have to be there for Bodhi."

With that single act of defiance, he pulled out his communicator and connected the call to Harper Rawls, who he knew would have the full details on Bodhi's current condition. As he awaited Harper's voice on the other end of the line, he looked up from what he was doing and realized that Brigid had disappeared. He hadn't expected that.

"Torrent?"

"Harper," he said, careful not to slur her name. Deliberation could make up for a lot, and he got right to the point, trying to ignore the sound of Brigid crashing through the underbrush ahead. "How is Bodhi?"

"Doctor says he'll be up soon, Torrent. Where are you? You're supposed to be here."

"I'm sorry. Something came up. I can't say much more than that."

"Typical," she snorted. "Get here now, Torrent. I've been trying to convince him to save his life, and he's not listening."

She sucked in her breath as he listened in the receiver, then continued, more subdued.

"You have to convince him, Torrent. I don't know if he'll listen to you, but he's not listening to me. He thinks I'm a hypocrite. He said that killing a model to survive is still murder."

Torrent didn't respond because he knew the truth of it. That model they'd picked out for Bodhi's body had a personality and friends. He'd been out of Second Birth, when models are pulled out of hibernation and prepped for their lifetime job appointment. The model had been living his life for almost a year now, and Bodhi had had the unfortunate experience of meeting him. Just like the Firsts, Torrent had been involuntarily cast in the role of protector. Only to betray them in the end. When it came to the survival of his only son, Torrent could rationalize just about anything.

"I'll talk to him," Torrent said.

"I don't care what you have to do. I've changed my mind. *Lie* to him if you need to. Get him to do it. I can't live in this world without him. It's not right. Parents shouldn't outlive their children."

When the call ended, Torrent listened for the telltale sound of crashing in the underbrush, but Brigid didn't seem to be back there any longer. She was a grown woman, he told himself. If she wanted to go wandering in the woods by herself, who was he to stop her? Besides, he needed to see his son.

Guilt licked at him as he slowly turn back toward the building. So far, they hadn't seen any police. Luck could keep it that way if he didn't get too close to the building. He took a step forward, then another, stopped, and looked back again. Squinting his eyes, he tried to see in the shadows if any sign still remained of Brigid, but even the insects had begun again. There was nothing to suggest that the evening had ever contained more than just him. With a deep, heavy sigh, he turned and started the unforgiving walk back to where they'd parked the volantrae. Bodhi had to come first.

CHAPTER 25

GOING IN CIRCLES

LARKEN HEARD the stumbling before anyone else. Mostly it was because she still trailed behind everyone and was, for most purposes, alone. First, it was the faint sound of insects as they fell silent, then the steady rhythm of crunching leaves behind her. Had she cared, she would have told someone. But she maintained an ambivalence about life and death. A quick death might mean—if any one of her religious friends had been more correct than she'd ever believed—reuniting with her Oliver. Or, at the very least, the pain would end.

So she kept her silence.

Even when the hand closed around her elbow and yanked her backward, she didn't react. Surprise registered vaguely in her mind, but she didn't scream as she fell. There wasn't time to. She didn't see the point in it anyway. She hit the ground with a loud thud to cause the group before her to stop in their tracks.

The first to turn was Sam, who brought up a weapon that Larken hadn't known she carried. It looked like it might have been a proton rifle at one point but had been shortened or adapted so that it was small enough to fit into one hand, a hand that now leveled it at whoever held her in their grip. Larken hadn't yet seen who it was but had her suspicions with the strength of the grip. It seemed to her that the artificial "woman" who had pursued them all that time had finally found them and that she would get her death wish granted, except that presented with the opportunity, she was beginning to change her mind. White heat exploded from where the hand had made contact and answered the question that Larken had struggled with since they'd started their silent trek through the woods.

Larken wanted revenge.

She grabbed the hand and twisted it with barely a thought until she heard a yelp of pain.

Pain? That was her first impression that something was wrong, but she didn't let it stop her from dropping her left elbow behind her. The movement was part of a lofting pass. A satisfying crunch sounded out as it connected with the soft flesh and rib cage. What?

She pushed herself backward, away from her assailant. It was a woman, but she couldn't see a face. A mop of thick, auburn hair had fallen before her as the woman stood crouched over, gasping for air.

"Who..."

"Mom?"

Larken studied the woman's body and connected Molly's response to the woman. She hadn't recognized Ms. Kostic in the outdoorsman clothing and boots. In a startling shove, Molly rushed to her mother's side. Molly pushed past Sam, and the two helped Brigid Kostic back up to her feet. The woman accepted their help for all of two seconds before throwing both of her arms around her daughter and squeezing her in tight.

"I'm so sorry," Larken said.

"Molly, you need to call Mom," Brigid said, ignoring Larken while fishing through her multitudinous pockets until she revealed a shimmery pink communicator that Larken saw looked almost exactly like Molly's. "She's worried sick and probably won't leave the house again until she knows you're safe."

As the woman said those words, Larken watched her eyebrows go from gracious celebratory arches to furrows of concern.

"You told her about this?" Molly said, squeezing again as Brigid's hand holding the communicator splayed out behind her.

"She guessed," Brigid responded. After a brief acknowledging glance to Larken, the woman had opened her eyes and skirted across Sam and Stephen. "I never could hide anything from her. Where's Oliver?"

That's when Molly's arms fell away. As if sensing something was wrong, Brigid backed away but took Molly's right hand in her left. The communicator rested in the delicate fingers of her right.

"Mom..."

"Oh, baby," the woman said again, dropping the communicator to the forest ground, wrapping her arms around Molly as Larken stared on, her arms crossed before her, keeping the tears at bay. Molly's body convulsed into her mother's arms while Larken watched, occasionally wiping away an angry tear. The feelings of apathy had passed, and the denial she'd clung to only briefly—as impossible as it was to believe that her world had grown smaller by half. She would never get that chance. She'd wanted to bring Oliver back and to be his sister again. She smudged a tear away and noticed Brigid's eyes now on her, those ever-expressive eyebrows once again casting her condolences.

Larken gave her a slight nod and turned away, not wishing to rehash what she'd gone through a thousand times since they'd left Oliver. His cold eyes would forever be carved into her mind.

"They're probably still chasing us," Sam said then looked at Brigid and raised an eyebrow. "How did *you* find us?"

Brigid pulled herself up to her full height—at least three inches taller than all of them, especially in those boots.

"It wasn't hard. I followed the path over the tunnel. It sometimes comes up and down above ground, leading me right here. Tough cutting through trees, but you're only about three blocks from SoDo right now."

Stephen glared at Sam.

"I *told* you we were going in circles," he said.

"Of course, we were," Sam retorted. "I didn't say we weren't. We're laying low, remember? We can't leave the forest. A highway bounds it over there and the reclamation river that way."

"In that many hours? Days? We could have made it past the city's north part," Larken chimed in.

"So now you're talking again. Well, I'm doing the best I can, people. I don't remember hearing any ideas while the killer mech was chasing us."

She turned to the covering of more dense forest.

"If we're done with the reunion, we need to get back in the brush. They're still looking for us. Besides, you don't want to make it to Bellingham anyway. It's a company town."

"You have been running around in these woods this

whole time? No wonder you look so skinny," Brigid said, looking at Molly now, examining her body. "What have you been eating?"

"Foraging," Molly replied.

"Nothing," Larken said. "Mostly, I haven't had an appetite since..."

"Since the attack," Sam said, casting a warm smile in Larken's direction and heading her off. Larken didn't return the smile, though she was grateful she wouldn't have to say what she'd been about to.

"But you're just kids," Brigid said, looking to Molly and Larken first, then to the others. "All of you. You can't survive out here. We need to get you somewhere safe."

"Mom, you don't understand."

"I saw the video," Brigid said. "I saw what they made you do. Are these them?"

"No...yes. I mean, it's complicated. They'd didn't *make* me do anything. The SNO aren't what people think."

"Terrorists? They're not terrorists, you mean. They don't kidnap people and kill them. Do you?" She changed who she addressed halfway through, turning toward Sam.

"People? No. No, we don't. We kill murderers."

"So you *are* SNO. Dear, blink twice. Are they holding you hostage?" One bright-green iris lingered on the gun that Sam held until Sam noticed and tucked the weapon behind her back.

"*They're* not holding us anything. HPM is after us. We're stuck in here until we can figure a way out. That's all."

"And that video?"

"The kidnapped person had been a director at Bremerton's reclamation plant. That's why I did the recording.

Then, when HPM came after us. It wasn't SNO who killed Oliver, Mom."

"They're dangerous," Brigid said as she pulled Molly and backed away. Larken let out a laugh, stopping Brigid's movement.

"They're not dangerous for you or us. They're only dangerous to people like the man who runs a death camp."

"Reclamation centers are *legal*, Larken. Unlike what SNO do. Why can't they do what Ordell does?"

"Yeah," said Sam. "Right. Do you think that polli would give Humanity in Crisis Council the time of day without knowing that SNO is out there? Do you remember when there used to be only SNO, and we didn't kill people or kidnap? No? I didn't think so because nobody *cared* then. Polli only started paying attention when bodies started dropping. And a few directors and executives here or there against the hundreds of thousands of us—people just like your precious Oliver—slaughtered because we've become economically *inconvenient* for you."

"Not for me," Brigid said. "I never asked for reclamation plants. In court, I fought against the Madison Rule and took a bullet for it."

"What have you done since?"

"It's different when you have a child to raise. You have to follow the rules. When we chose to have Molly, our lives changed forever. I couldn't put us in danger."

"And yet here you are," Sam said. Larken could feel the last of Sam's patience boiling away. "Your daughter fell in love with a dirty shill, and here you are, still in danger, having done nothing to make the world safer for us *because we aren't you*. Well, you're in it now, aren't you?"

"Sam, stop," Stephen said. To Larken's surprise, Sam clamped her mouth closed and turned away.

"This way," Sam said. "We can't stay in one spot too long. They'll find us."

"You can't keep running around in here," Brigid said. "We brought a volantrae. If Torrent's still here, we can use it. Or I can call a cab for us. The police are all down by the USPS building."

"It's not the police we're running from," Larken informed Brigid. "Torrent's here?" A strange spark lit in her chest at the idea of seeing the annoying throat-clearing puffball-headed man again.

"He was, but his son..."

"Never mind," Larken said. The reminder that she wasn't his daughter deepened the cut of Oliver's absence.

"How long do you want to stay out here?" Brigid asked.

"Stephen and I have been in this situation before. Well, not killer android and mech, but otherwise. A week at least. Got to give them time to start looking somewhere else. Then we can probably head east. There's a branch of SNO out there who could hide us for a while. After that, wait for this to blow over and get back to work."

"Hide?" Larken couldn't stop herself. "Hide more. For longer? That's what you want?"

"No. I want to track down that evil android bitch and turn her into scrap metal. What I *want* is to topple the whole HPM. This isn't what I want. It's what keeps us alive so we can continue to fight."

Larken licked her lips and pushed a wayward strand of hair from her eyes. She made eye contact with Molly—touch and go. Larken hadn't been fair to Molly, and she knew it. Molly didn't kill Oliver. Molly was the scapegoat, so Larken didn't blame herself for her bullshit agreement to head into Seattle. Larken stopped her tongue as a dash of pain shot up her lip. She hadn't realized that her lip was busted there in front of her incisor. She dabbed it once with the tip of her tongue again, tasting the saltiness of her blood.

Larken wasn't ready to go and hide.

She held out her hand toward Sam.

"What?"

"Give me the gun. You all hide. I'm tracking down the thing that killed my brother."

Brigid slowly approached. Larken heard her boots shuffling before Brigid could get close and turned to stare the woman down, stopping her in her tracks.

"Don't," she said. "I like you, Ms. Kostic. And Molly, I'm sorry for all that I said. That wasn't fair. There's no way I'm letting that woman and her pet get away with killing my brother."

Then she paused for a minute and thought over those words. Oliver wasn't even her brother—not any more than any two Caldwells were related. Okay, maybe a little more having two donors instead of full-on designer DNA. Still. She shook her head, keeping her eyes trained on Brigid, the only one she thought might try to physically stop her out of an unfortunately broad sense of duty.

"I don't have a father. I don't have a mother. I barely have any friends." She looked at Sam and then Stephen behind her. "I'm not hiding. Give me the gun, and I'll find and kill her."

"Do you even know how to use one of these?"

"Pull the trigger. How hard can it be?"

"You're not thinking."

Larken shook her head faster, hair flying around like it

was caught in a tornado. Then she stopped as Sam clipped off her sentence.

"Stop telling me what I'm thinking, and stop telling me what to do. Oliver is dead."

Larken clenched her teeth together. She closed her eyes for a second to collect herself and keep the tears at bay.

"He's dead," she repeated. "As in not coming back. Part of me died back there too. I'm not hiding."

Larken lowered her hand back to her side.

"Look, if you need the gun, I get it. I'll figure something out. I'm not staying in here, and I'm not hiding."

Larken's eyes drifted to Molly, and this time Molly didn't look away. Instead, what Larken saw was the same spark that had lit in her heart. It was spreading, and she gave Molly a half-smile of encouragement.

"I'll help," Molly said after the nudge. "I mean, this is pretty impossible. I understand that. I...I can't let Oliver die for nothing. We've got to do *something*."

"You will not," Brigid said, her grip tightening around Molly's shoulders. "I didn't come out here just to lose you."

Molly pulled away, squirming her way out of Brigid's grip to make her way to Larken's side. The two looked pathetic together, by Larken's estimation. Disheveled hair full of branches from being lost in the woods, torn clothes, battered faces, and bodies. Sam must have seen something that Larken missed, because she came next, followed by Stephen.

"Fine," Sam said as Stephen nodded. "Then we should probably talk about what we're up against, yeah?"

Brigid crossed her arms and stood there, pursed lips and raised eyebrows as she locked on Molly. The look might have worked before that night. Larken had seen the look before, any time that she and Molly had gotten into something they shouldn't have. It was a reprimand masked with concern, and she saw Molly's body tense in response to the nonverbal cues.

"No, Mom," she said. "You always tell me that I need an interest and that being popular isn't important. Well, *this* is important. Oliver is dead. He's a model. Do you think the police will look too hard for whoever did it once they find that out? They won't. If we can't do the right thing when it's hard, why bother even saying there is a right thing?"

"My words," Brigid said, her arms slackening. "But when I said them, I was talking about cleaning your room, not getting yourself *killed*."

"There may be a way," Stephen interrupted. "We don't *have* to die. There might be a way to get her."

"Lure her out?" Sam suggested.

"Yeah. And I may have an idea that could level the playing field a bit."

"What are you thinking?"

"Bremerton Reclamation. It's temporarily closed since we kidnapped the person running it," he said, then turned with a smug grin to Larken. "And blew a massive hole in the side."

"Stephen, we need to tell them about her before you get too far into your pipe dream."

"I think it can be done. There's enough equipment and those chemicals—they'll be as effective on her wiring as on us."

"But you'd have to get her into a vat. Then there's the mech. Let me explain."

Stephen stopped talking but, to Larken, seemed irritated that he had to. Sam continued the story.

"We've seen her before. She's a custom job. She can run faster than a car when she gets an open space and has sensors all over her body. There's no way to sneak up on her without her knowing. That mech is something like telepathically connected to her, so you can't get rid of it. And her skin is pulse-resistant. You can damage her if you get a straight shot. But she moves too fast for that to happen."

"On full batteries," Molly suggested. "If she does that much, she must drain fast."

"Exactly," Stephen said. "I think that all we'd have to do is keep her hunting for a few more hours, and then we might be able to get close enough to damage her. The world's longest game of hide and seek."

"And most dangerous," Brigid said. "Absolutely not. Molly, come. We're leaving."

"No."

Brigid stared at Molly, and Larken knew it was more than a stare. It was an argument and a power struggle. Larken had intended to storm off after her tirade and now had gone off-script. She'd never have guessed after how she'd treated the girl that Molly would join Larken on her arguable suicide mission. And even though she'd asked for it, she hadn't expected Sam or Stephen to give up a weapon for her, let alone join her fight. She wiped another tear from her eye, but this one didn't bring the pain of all the others. In this one, she found hope and the beginning of something. For a second, she believed that revenge might be possible, which fanned the desire to live long enough to see it through.

She glanced back at the dueling family members and cleared her throat. She heard Torrent's guttural elongated "ahem" in her behavior and surprised herself by thinking about him again and missing him. Molly's stare didn't break.

Brigid's did. When Brigid's face swung to Larken's, she closed her gaping mouth and cast her eyes to the earth. It was a disturbing gesture in such a powerful woman. Then Brigid nodded as though she were conversing with someone hiding in the bushes nearby. Finally, her face returned to Molly, and Larken could see new tear tracks tracing from her eyes to the corners of her burgundy lips.

"So this is what you want for your life?" she finally asked.

"Never more than anything else," Molly said, holding her mother's gaze with a fire in her eyes.

"Okay," Brigid said. "Okay. I've always taught you to do the right thing. Sometimes, what's right is scary, and sometimes what's right and what's legal or safe aren't the same. I'm coming too. We have to be careful."

CHAPTER 26

ANOTHER ASININE PLAN

IT WAS A STUPID PLAN. Standing in a clearing much closer to the Bremerton Reclamation Plant than Larken had ever wanted to be in the early morning brought a certain clarity of vision. The smell of death lingered in the air and saturated her nostrils. Even if the plant wasn't actively "processing," the scent couldn't be ignored.

She'd ended up bait. As soon as Sam asked Larken if she knew how to shoot a weapon (she never had), it was decided that Larken wouldn't be doing the actual shooting part of the plan. On top of that, she was the fastest of them all, including Molly. She hoped to get a few punches in even though that wasn't technically part of the plan. All Larken was supposed to do was run and get the android to chase her from the pond toward the rest of the team's positions hidden in the forest by the discharge pond. Then Larken would duck into the reclamation center for safety while the rest took potshots to run down the android's battery. Once she got low enough, then the plan got a little fuzzy. Brigid's theory was that at that point, it would be easy to shove her into a reclamation vat and flip the switch. Sam thought it would be just as useful to leave her in the discharge pond with all the other discarded parts.

"Act like you're breaking in," a harsh whisper came from Molly in their hiding place. Larken stared up at the penitentiary-like wall before her.

"How exactly am I supposed to do that?" she asked, partly to Molly but primarily to herself. There weren't even any seams in the wall before her.

"Think like you just got here, and you're looking for an entrance," Stephen's voice joined in. "The opening is on the other side, but you must get there around the same time she does."

"Why don't I just go in now?"

It seemed safer to be inside, where at least she couldn't be picked off by a rifle or one of those rockets.

"We need control," Stephen said. "The whole way. She can't just wander around in there. We have to steer her to the right place."

"Quiet," came Brigid's voice from farther along. "Sam's calling in the tip."

That was the fucking asinine part.

Call in a tip and *hope* that Human Pride Movement send their robot murderer and the mech back to the plant. Then go running into the facility and hide in one of the creepy vat things. The weird vat things were "perfectly safe, as long as the power stayed off", according to Sam. Larken caught sight of movement opposite her in the woods. Something shiny seemed to pick up the now prevalent moonlight. A shuffle next, and she thought the tops of some trees shook in the distance.

"Have you called yet?" she asked the question as some more trees shook—now she was sure of it.

"Calling now," came Brigid's voice. "Hold."

That response made Larken's chest rise in a quick but quiet guffaw. Brigid emerged from some trees, dressed in near-military survival gear. Somehow while hunting in the brush, she still had unblemished makeup and nails and her hair had stayed in a tight bun. She was a professional. She looked and acted like a soldier since she'd decided to join Larken's quest, which would have given Larken some comfort had Brigid ever been in the military. As it was, it seemed like over-enthusiastic LARP-ing. But Larken accepted the help. Oliver would get his revenge.

And then what? The question mattered, even if she had told Brigid earlier that it didn't. Then what? Oliver still wouldn't be back. He couldn't come back. There wasn't a way to bring Oliver back from the dead. Then what would Larken do with her life *after* Oliver was avenged? Larken had no idea.

Another tree shook. This one was closer.

"Are you sure you haven't called yet?"

"No," came the harsh whisper back. "And if you keep chatting, then we can't."

"I don't think we need to."

"Do what, dearie?" came another voice from before her beyond her range of vision. Another tree shook, and she saw a nearby tree crash. "And who are you talking to?"

Two glowing orbs appeared in the woods before her.

Larken wasn't ready.

The thought flooded into her mind and locked her feet in place. Run, but toward the entrance on the other side. That was the plan. Recall. As her eyes kept a slow forward pace, breaking into the moonlight, they pulled with them a face that was too perfect even to be a Caldwell. And the smile on that face was so devoid of anything resembling human emotion that Larken knew that Sam and Stephen had been right. This thing wasn't alive in any sense that mattered.

"Nobody," Larken puffed.

The thing seemed to believe her. The trees shook again, this time behind the woman, and two towering birches parted. A square metallic structure with holes in it pushed through the opening, one of the rocket launchers of the mech. It was telling that the rockets hadn't been fired yet with Larken in clear view. Maybe avoiding property damage. Larken slid backward and up against the smooth metal of the building. She then shimmied toward her left, keeping careful contact with the wall.

"I knew we'd find you," the woman said, eyes locked onto Larken, whose left hand suddenly found no wall. She felt around with her fingertips and recognized the hard metal edge of a corner. At the same time, the woman seemed to realize that Larken was about to duck around the corner and jolted forward herself, covering the distance between them almost as fast as Larken could spin her body around the edge. However many sensors she might have, she hadn't "seen" the others in their hiding places from what Larken could tell. That gave her a sliver of hope that the plan might work.

Larken had little time to consider the implications as she fled round the corner and toward the main entrance. Larken didn't see how she could put enough distance between herself and the woman to hide. She'd have to spend her time running instead. Larken sprinted with all of her lofting training toward the entrance. As fast as she was, the woman behind her was faster. The falling footsteps closed the gap, and the crunching sound of metal on wood as her mechanized companion pushed over trees closed just as quickly.

Then she remembered the offal pond. *They hadn't approached the Bremerton factory by that side this time,* she thought as she sprinted past the entrance and gave up on going inside. The woman was too close. Larken could feel those cold eyes still resting unwavering on her head even as she dodged trees and jumped wayward bushes. The evening grew colder with every second, making each breath more and more difficult. Larken wondered if the machine-woman behind her needed to breathe at all. By the unrelenting pace, she guessed not. If the woman burned as much energy as quickly as Sam seemed to think, she wasn't showing it.

"You may as well give up," came the woman's too-calm-for-running voice over Larken's shoulder. "There's nowhere to go now. I'm faster, and I'll catch you, and you'll die tired."

What a sad "life" that hunting Larken was what brought the woman-thing probably the only thing resembling joy she had ever felt. Simple AI. She doubted the offal pond would stop the woman, but it might slow her down. Larken gulped quickly as she leaped over a nettle bush. She came down the wrong way on her left leg when she landed. With a yelp, Larken rolled to the ground and slid about a foot into...mud? She lifted her hand and couldn't help a smile, followed quickly by a frown. Did she mean to do it? The pungent, rotting smell of a destroyed ecosystem filled with deteriorating body parts accosted her nose. The footsteps behind her stopped.

"Getting right to it? That's a good idea. Skip the middleman."

The woman's steps were slower now as she approached. Larken felt the grade of the mud and turned away from the woman. She'd made it where she'd planned, but she didn't know if she dared to go deeper. The crackling bushes behind the woman told Larken that the mech closed in as well, but she guessed that the mech couldn't cross the vast pond. So far, it seemed to confine itself to the earth. Its weight was too much, she guessed, to get up into the air—especially with the weapons she knew it had. Missiles had to be heavy—even small ones used to ferret humans out of tunnels. The woman's voice sounded again, catlike.

"You gave a good run," she said. "Most don't last as long as you did."

"I'm not done running," Larken said.

"Where can you possibly go now?"

As the woman said "now," Larken pushed off and rolled down the muddy embankment. Taking a deep breath mid-revolution, she spilled over the edge and fell. In the darkness, she miscalculated where she was. She thought she was at the low side and would roll down the embankment into the water. Instead, she rolled right off a high cliff and fell at least four feet before hitting the water's surface with her neck contorted and her back sideways. Pain shot through her shoulders and back as she discovered that the water in that spot was too shallow for a dive, and she collided with the bottom. She gasped involuntarily and sucked in the disgusting pink stuff. She spat it back out as quickly as possible, forcing the taste of rotten decay from her lips. Her body threatened to heave over on her.

"Shit," the woman said but didn't follow. "Did you see that?"

The mech behind her let out a thin whistle.

"I *know* I have to go get her. Nobody asked you to. Quit complaining."

Larken heard the sounds through the muffled roar of running water. The chill seeped into her clothes, but the worst part was her imagination. Every molecule that touched her could have been in a body—a leg, an arm, an eyeball, something else? Every single one. Larken's body revolted against her as it tried to work itself free of the liquid, convulsing in the process. She tried to focus on swimming. Her improvised plan was to swim across. Another whistle from the mech.

"Well, go take care of them," the woman said. "As you can see, I've got a problem here."

Larken broke the surface in time to see the woman sailing over her head. The woman splashed down and sent a spray up over Larken's face. Larken heard the mech crunch back into the woods, and she gritted her teeth as she brought herself to her feet. One throbbing leg supported her. She looked at the woman, who now stood in shoulder-deep liquid.

"Was this your plan? Are you trying to short me out? That won't work."

"No," Larken said, then spit again, trying not to look at whatever it was that she'd dislodged from her mouth. "No, that wasn't my plan at all. I planned to get rid of your mech."

The woman's eyes shot open as it seemed to occur to her that the plan, as rudimentary as it had been, had worked. Larken hadn't planned to face the woman alone, but it was her chance to get in a punch or two. Her real plan was to be on the shore on the other side with the android still in the water. But here she stood, in a puddle up to her shoulders and with nowhere left to run since the woman was between her and her chosen escape. The woman also seemed to notice the trap Larken had backed herself into at the same time, and she opened her thin mouth to laugh.

"Not much of a plan."

"I guess not," Larken admitted and screwed up her courage. She would get the woman to pay for Oliver's death. That was the rest of the plan, and she was supposed to have help on that part, but she'd do it herself if she had to. She clenched her fists and lowered her body. Not much of a fighter, she guessed, compared to the woman. There would have to be a lot of luck involved.

The woman was fast, even in the viscous fluid. A second after the conversation ended, in the time it took Larken to mimic what may have been a fighting stance somewhere in the world, the woman had cut through the water like a shark and slammed her fist into Larken's chest, sending her flying through the air and splashing down just short of the embankment over which she'd fallen. Larken tumbled into the fluid and at found herself on her back, gasping in mouthfuls of water. She flipped onto her hands and knees, pulling her face free of the liquid and wrenching the contents of her stomach into the pond. Larken struggled to resist the urge to vomit more, stemming the tide. Aside from keeping the mech away, the water wasn't doing anything to level the field. Her stomach clenched once more as she stood, gasping.

"So I knock you around, and you die? What on earth would make you want to do that?" The woman stood straight as an arrow. Except for the ripples expanding outward and pinkish water dripping from her clothes, she didn't even look as though she'd moved. If she was running low on energy, she wasn't showing it.

"You killed my brother," Larken told the woman, who for

half a millisecond looked as though she might have been concerned about the accusation. Then she laughed loudly.

"I don't kill brothers and sisters," the woman said. "I kill models. And I know them when I see them."

"No, you killed him," Larken retorted.

The woman's grin turned to a snarl. "*You* are a model. You *have* no brother."

Larken inched closer to the woman, her lofty goal of exacting her revenge having been reduced to connecting at least a single punch in Oliver's name. She circled wide around the woman.

"*You* may think that because you're fake. You're not even a real person, and you are walking around like a lapdog here."

"I *like* my job," the woman said. "Models are anathema to human existence."

"Oh, we are? What do you think happens once models are gone? Where does all that hate go? You're next."

The woman lunged—and connected. Another punch, this time to Larken's face so quickly that Larken only barely saw the punch coming as it flashed the world around her off and then back on again. But she *had* seen it coming that time. Larken found herself on her bottom in water that came just to her chest. She was on the far side of the wall, where the water deepened. A smile worked her split lips apart. It wasn't her imagination—the woman had moved slower that time. But at this rate, Larken would be dead before the woman ran down enough for Larken to have a chance to shove her in a vat. She stood up, wobbling as her leg reminded her that it was still injured. She spat blood out onto the ground. A shuffle sounded behind the woman, who turned imperceptibly fast toward her. Larken held her breath, hoping against hope that it wasn't the mech.

Nothing. A bird flitted up into the night sky. Larken charged, only to be stopped by a fist into her abdomen, causing her to curl over. But even curling, she couldn't go very far as the woman grabbed her by the hair and plunged her face into the water. Suddenly, it was as though an immovable steel beam sat atop her head, and she couldn't move. Larken had reflexively sucked in the air on the way down, but it would only last so long as she struggled against the woman's grip.

"Nothing. You are worse than nothing. You take jobs. You steal lives. You are beasts and should be cleansed from the earth." The fluid didn't stop the woman's onslaught of words. Larken shook her body and squeezed her eyes, trying to knock the woman off balance, but she was like a fortress herself. This had been a stupid idea. Sam was right. Sam was—

A loud crack broke through the sound of her struggling. Then a massive splash and the weight from the back of her head were suddenly gone. Larken tried to stand. Her angle only allowed her to fall face down into the muck. Exhaustion from the fighting kept her there, inhaling whatever fluids were around her. She felt the darkness closing in around her as the pink turned first to brown and then black.

CHAPTER 27

THE FREE CLINIC

LARKEN AWOKE to the circular launch tubes of a fighting mech pointing down at her like the multiple eyes of a housefly or openings from a sliced-up honeycomb. Four rockets on each "shoulder" and a smooth dome between the two that reflected her gawking face at her. Larken scrambled backward, scurried across...something soft and then collided with another soft thing that wasn't dirt, trees, or rocks. She scrunched her hands and caught a handful of what felt like a blanket.

The thing didn't move.

And Larken was wearing someone else's clothes.

And she felt dry.

She shifted again, and blinding white light seared her retinas as she blinked her visual field back to normal. Books lined the wall behind her, she saw from her peripheral vision. Real books, not tablets or monitors displaying NFTs in the retro format they sometimes did. These looked like they'd been printed on *actual paper* instead of synthetic stuff.

"You're awake," came an unfamiliar voice from behind

the massive machine. Larken lurched again. She tried to peer around the substantial metal tubes, but they formed a wall almost the size of her bed. Why didn't they fire?

"Who is speaking?" she croaked, her voice cracking from dryness.

"Dandelion," came the voice, soft and clean and gentle. "Dandelion Lemaire." Larken saw the woman then—possibly five years her senior—cross around the side of the machine. She wore something that resembled a nurse's uniform, with greens and blues and a clip at the neck keeping the stiff priest collar up. A mask covered the lower part of her face.

"Have I been captured?" Larken asked, eyes swiveling between the woman and the weapons tubes still pointed at her. Dandelion looked at the machine, then back.

"We didn't have anywhere else to put it," Dandelion said, motioning.

"What happened?"

"We'll get to that."

"Are you a nurse?"

"We'll get to that too. Do you know who *you* are?"

"Larken Marche," she answered.

"Age?"

"Last I checked, seventeen. I guess it depends on the month." She looked around at the over-sanitized counterspace wedged against the far walls, one with a sink. The looming guns overhead made her breath catch in her throat. "Tell me what's going on."

Dandelion's face contorted behind the mask. Larken saw two wrinkles on each side of the woman's eyes above the bridge of her nose, though her ears pulled back slightly like she was smiling.

"I guess you're right to ask."

"The last thing I knew, I was…" Dying. She was dying, just like her brother. Larken closed her eyes and, for a second, felt a pang as she thought about how close she was to seeing her brother again. Larken's eyes glossed over. "That woman-thing was beating me," Larken finished.

"That woman-thing was a Model 1 experimental android. Prescient Pharmaceuticals builds them to supplement the labor market as a hedge against the future of models. Help around the house without the pesky moral problems. That one, in particular, was military upgraded and reprogrammed for HPM."

Of course, it had been. Larken knew that it was HPM already, but it felt good to hear the confirmation—and terrifying at the same time.

"Is she still out there?"

No answer. Dandelion shrugged.

Larken frowned and examined other parts of the room that weren't blocked by the mech's massive frame. Empty except for the three of them.

"Where are my friends?"

"They're safe. Don't worry. They'll come in once you're ready. You took quite a beating. Good thing Sam got off that shot when she did, or you'd be dead."

The way the woman said it caught Larken off-guard. She'd assumed the woman to be a nurse, but if Dandelion was that, then her bedside manner was nonexistent. Something in the way the woman had said Sam's name caught her attention.

"You're SNO?"

"No. Just a nurse," she assured, "helping who I can. Neutral territory. Sneaking a mech in here was tricky and a little outside of what we normally do, but your friends said leaving it meant HPM getting it back."

She reached up with one gloved hand and ran it along the mech's weaponry.

"These things are amazing. HPM could be using the equipment for so much more than guns. This one wasn't a retrofit if you can believe it. Actual battle-line mechanized infantry unit. Not as smart as a Model 1, but far deadlier. They can't argue. Point them in a direction, and they destroy."

"Are you going to tell me what happened?"

"That shot from Sam took your assailant's head off at the shoulders," Dandelion said, her eyes sparkling just a little too much. "Shut her right down. This big mech lost comms and went into standby mode, awaiting the next orders. It'd already leveled half of the Bremerton plant chasing Stephen and Molly around. By the time SNO got there—and us—there wasn't much to do but clean up."

"Brigid?"

"Safe. Critical. She got in the way of one of those missiles. Still not sure which way that's going to go." She paused. "I should tell you that I've dosed you with some medications that will knock you out for a bit."

Larken didn't remember seeing Dandelion touch any of the equipment, and Dandelion certainly hadn't put a hand on her yet. However, she immediately felt lightheaded as soon as she heard those words.

"Your friends will be here when you wake. Don't worry."

The words seemed empty and far away as she found herself engulfed in darkness.

The next time she awoke, she saw a pair of giant brown

eyes peeking at her out of a bed of freckles. Ringed in red, the eyes stared at her.

"Molly?"

"Are you okay?"

"We got her," Larken said, peeling back her lips into a smile and wincing as the splits on the top and bottom reminded her that they were still there.

"We did," Molly said without affect.

"What about you? Are you okay, Molly?"

"I...I'm..."

Molly threw her arms around Larken's neck, which bumped several bruises, including her rib cage, which Larken hadn't realized was bruised until that moment. She winced as the girl tightened her arms.

"I'm glad you're alive," Larken heard Molly whisper and then felt Molly's body convulsing against hers. "I'm so glad you're alive."

"Molly," came another voice behind her. "Molly, come dear. We have to go."

A hand reached down across Molly's back to pull on her shoulder. A tall woman stood behind Molly, whom Larken immediately recognized as Molly's other mother.

"Ms. Kostic?" Larken said as Molly pulled away as the other Ms. Kostic took her in. The woman's eyes were as red as Molly's. The woman's lip trembled and sealed her mouth into a tight line. Inhaling through her nose, the woman's body swelled and then diminished. She didn't try to smile.

"Andrea," the woman said, her entire demeanor becoming a tired sigh.

"I'm sorry," Larken said. Her lips trembled in concert with the woman's. "I'm sorry we brought this to you. I'm sorry we involved Molly. I'm just sorry."

The woman seemed unaffected as she stood, her stare unchanging.

"The love of my life died last night, and *you* recovered. My little girl," she said, as she pulled Molly in close, "was almost killed too. There aren't enough apologies to fix that, Larken."

It was clear who Andrea blamed. As Andrea turned away, Larken saw the sheen of tear tracks across the woman's cheeks. Larken looked to Molly, who wouldn't meet her eyes. Multiple deaths hung in the space between them. Part of Larken, tiny and vindictive, harbored a smug satisfaction in Molly's tears, as wrong as Larken knew it to be. Now *Molly* felt what it had been like for Larken to lose Oliver. As soon as she had the thought, Larken's hand shot up to her mouth, ashamed for it and glad that mind-reading was an impossibility.

"I'm sorry," Larken called out in a rasp, chasing Andrea with her words. "I am."

Larken knew the words didn't matter because they wouldn't matter to her. Apologies wouldn't bring Oliver back. Birthdays flashed through Larken's mind. Brigid had made birthday cards for Larken's seventh birthday after Molly had divulged that "Larken didn't have parents."

It was all wrong.

Sam walked in. Her nose ring had changed. Where there had been a metal bull ring before, there was now a black ring with embedded onyx matching her lip piercing. A proper nose ring for mourning, Larken thought, then wondered how many different studs Sam had brought with her when they'd fled out into the darkness.

"You're awake," Sam said, pushing past Molly, who blocked the doorway. Molly resisted Sam's gentle shove so that Sam skirted around her. She edged against Larken's bed so that the outside of Sam's thigh touched Larken's shoulder.

"It's hard, Larken," she said in a soothing tone. "Stephen thought you'd be out longer. He's getting coffee. *Real* coffee from his shop, imported from Hungary. Should be back any minute."

"O...okay," Larken muttered, paying attention to Sam only through her peripheral vision as Molly backed away.

"Wait," she called after Molly, who backed out through the opening after her mother without another word. "I *am* sorry, Molly." Larken couldn't stop apologizing, no matter how empty the words felt. She desperately willed the apologies to be more than they ever could be. Molly didn't acknowledge her. "Molly?"

Larken watched Molly's pitch-black hair swing side to side as the girl gave her head a slight shake mid-stride.

"Let them go," Sam said, sliding her pupils over to the corner of her eye and then back. Her smile widened into a grin so wide that Larken scowled at her. She had no right to smile while death seeped all around them. "This news won't help *them*."

The door clicked into place. It wasn't automated in doctors' offices, as Larken had seen before. Nor was there much equipment, which until that moment she'd thought there had been because she'd subconsciously counted the horror behind her. This wasn't a hospital any more than that girl Dandelion was a nurse.

"Look at this," Sam said, pulling what looked like a spent mass of cables behind her back. She touched two of them together and clicked a button on the side.

A lightbulb projected from the side, pushing an image against the far wall nearly as big as the pair. Larken watched, unsure what she was seeing. An explosion, then she saw an opening in the side of a big building, the USPS building. Then, as Oliver's body went cold, the escape hatch closed behind him.

"Oops, sorry," Sam said, fumbling with the controls on the side. "Just figured out the playback. I didn't want you to see *that* again."

She murmured to herself as she used a wire to connect two others. The image skipped forward, and the woods were next, entire trees bending before whoever was holding the camera. Then Larken got it. This was the mech's memory banks. Larken's eyes teared up as the image slowed again. The mech returned to the building and pushed through the entrance for a second time. There lay her brother again. The woman went around the mech and examined the wrists of each damaged person; then, she appeared to scan each barcode she found with a flash from her retina. She dropped one person's arm slumped down over a table and went to her brother's side. He tried to roll away, but she grabbed him and checked both wrists.

He tried to roll away.

"Did you see that?"

"What happens next?" Larken asked.

"*She* took him. Wherever she went just then, he went too. Didn't kill him. Watch."

The woman lifted Oliver, more gently than Larken would have thought her capable—or inclined—and placed him beyond the camera's scope. On the mech, perhaps. Larken and Sam turned their heads simultaneously, focusing on the mech behind them. Sam had the advantage because she knew from where the camera had been dislocated, so Larken followed Sam's gaze in the end. Then she saw that just beyond, where Sam's gaze ended, was a small indention large enough for someone to sit. She'd been right when she'd thought it looked like a zephyr mech. If she hadn't known it was modified military surplus, she'd have thought its former life was as an entertainment vehicle.

"I'm coming with you," came a voice that Larken hadn't expected. She raised her head to see Molly standing in the doorway. Larken's heart lifted.

"We don't have any idea where he's at," said Sam, staring at Molly now, Molly's smile wavering a bit.

"But we know where the mech took him, right? We can start there."

Larken slid her feet again down to the floor and went down in a heap of unresponsive muscle as the drugs reminded her they were still very much in her blood.

"Not *yet*," Sam corrected, grabbing her under the arms to lift her back up. Even with Sam's help, getting back into bed was difficult. Another set of hands intervened toward the end, and Larken realized that Dandelion had re-entered the room without her knowing.

"Rest," Dandelion said. "We'll find him. And we'll bring him home."

Larken's attention had shifted to Dandelion's firm grasp against her skin, just above the elbow of her right arm. The hand was ice down to the palm that grazed her. Larken yanked at her arm and fell backward onto the bed. Then in a reaction to her falling, her own hands betrayed her and lunged forward from her body, grasping at what they could find. They found Dandelion's forearms just as frigid as her hands had been. Larken held on as Dandelion and Sam pushed her back into her bunk beneath the towering mech.

"What are you?" Larken asked as she lay back, her grip

slackening on its own. For an instant, Larken almost believed that Dandelion had flushed under the scrutiny. But she realized that the woman's skin tone was too uniform. There was no variation, not even in her cheeks. The "blushing" effect had only been Dandelion's eyes furrowing up at the eyebrows for a second before flattening out again.

"Your nurse?" Sam asked as she tucked Larken in. Larken's head throbbed again, and her chest reminded her of the pounding she'd taken.

"No. Touch her. She's so cold," Larken almost yelled, her bottom lip quivering. The idea that nobody here seemed to notice that they had not one but two killer AI bot things in their midst made her arms shake uncontrollably.

"Dandelion?" Sam asked. She furrowed her eyebrows and shook her head at the same time. "Oh. No, not Dandelion."

"I'm *not* her," Dandelion responded. "And I can defend *myself*, thank you." The second statement seemed directed toward Sam as she continued. "I'm a Model N. I'm much more advanced than that thing."

"And she doesn't fight," Sam said. "Even when her life is in danger. Even when her friends are dying around her."

She scowled at Dandelion for a fraction of a second.

"I'm a *nurse*, Sam. Do we have to go through this every single time we talk?"

"You're as strong as that thing was. And you can do so much more. You'd be great in the front lines," she retorted. "It doesn't matter. You're right. We've had this fight before, and there's no convincing you."

"You all *know* she's AI? And she's part of SNO?"

"What's not to trust?"

"I'm not part of SNO," Dandelion said. "I help people

who are injured. That's what I do, and that's all I do. Here." She thrust some orange fluid in a cup into Larken's hand and stormed from the room.

"Did I offend her?" Larken asked. "Did I offend your killer robot friend?"

"She's touchy like that," Sam said. "She hates violence, and her AI logic is strange. *Dandelion* believes that the Siblings of the Natural Order fighting against oppression is the same as HPM trying to destroy us. If a bunch of wounded HPM found their way here, she'd treat them too. There might be some in here somewhere for all we know. The place is big."

"But we can't fight here," Sam assured Larken. "This is the closest thing to neutral territory there is among all of us. This is like the Red Cross used to be before Akson took over if you remember the stories."

There had been an organization that tried a position of neutrality during wars—when there used to be wars. Larken had learned about them at Brighton. She remembered the stories of empires struggling for dominance before Equilibrium when the global climate rebalanced all at once and found a point of stability that created a desert out of the midwestern states. That was before the Akson Society was formed, based on the fundamental idea that free markets could do no wrong. A tribute to selfishness, it united the world's autocrats and staged coups to topple democratic governments for nearly twenty years. Everything stopped when its founder died. After the layers of the onion were pulled back, it was discovered that the founder had been embezzling money and kept blackmail material on world leaders. The only good the group gave to the world was when they collapsed and a global government emerged from its ashes. Then, without wars to fight, the Red Cross organization went defunct. Larken remembered the sympathetic tenor of her instructor's voice and could not tell if that tone was nostalgia for wars or the organization itself. An odd reference, but the Red Cross comparison was apt, Larken decided.

"Oliver," she said, her head sinking back into the pillow as the last of her rally subsided. "We need to rescue Oliver."

"We will," Sam assured her. "Soon."

CHAPTER 28
BLOOD IS THE ONLY WAY

SILENCE AND DARKNESS cloaked the room so that Larken couldn't see farther than five feet from the edge of her bed. She could see no friends and no Dandelion in what little illumination the solitary flashing red light provided.

The door swung open—automatically (so it did have the capability after all)—and Dandelion entered with a tray of what seemed to be a food offering.

"I'm sorry," Larken said impulsively as Dandelion placed the tray on the edge of her bed. She didn't know or understand *why* of all the people; she felt she owed an apology.

"Stop apologizing."

"Are there a lot of you?" The question emerged unprompted.

"There's only one me."

"I mean..."

"I know what you meant. Sit up." Larken leaned forward, and Dandelion adjusted the pillow behind her to support her back more. Then Dandelion pulled the tray from the foot of the bed to Larken's lap, setting it atop the blanket.

"Larken, there's only one me. The company that made me had a special contract for United Africa."

Larken yanked her arm back as Dandelion's skin brushed hers.

"You're warm today?"

"Body temperature is adjustable. It takes a little more energy, so I usually don't. But it's a problem for *you*, so I adjusted. Here, eat."

She pulled a thin film off the tray of food, disclosing a mixture of what may have been synthesized vegetables but didn't resemble any particular one and didn't instill in her the desire to eat.

"It's not very appetizing," Dandelion said with an apologetic shrug. "But it's what we have."

"I'm leaving," Larken told her.

"Well, it's not *that* bad. It's only that we are a nonprofit, and we do have a budget."

At first, Larken thought that Dandelion had cracked a joke, which seemed impressive to her. She found that the AI intrigued her as much as it frightened her. Larken swallowed the questions her inquisitive mind had plagued her with, like whether Dandelion could *taste* the food brought into the room. Scrutiny of Dandelion's face told her, unless her features were far off from human, that Dandelion wasn't joking.

"This food isn't why, Dandelion. I have to find my brother. I can't sit here while everyone else is looking for him. What if one more person looking is the difference between finding him and not finding him?"

"I doubt that's the case."

"But what if it *is* the case? Then by sitting on this bed, eating this horrible-looking food, I'm really condemning him.

If they don't know that he's a model, how long will it take them to discover that?"

She knew. Oliver's life would come down to whether that thing had bothered to tell them or not.

"How can he be a model if he's your brother?"

"A long and complicated story. But right now, I have to go."

A tinkling that sounded like wind chimes floated through the space between them. Larken's mouth went into a firm line as she listened to the familiar sounds.

"You have Brigid's communicator?"

"Molly left, so I was keeping it to return to her," Dandelion said. "Can you give this to her when you see her again?" With that, she retrieved Brigid's communicator from a low shelf beside the bed and handed it to Larken. The chime stopped. Larken switched it to voice-only mode and held it to her ear. Then she pulled up the emergency call interface, and entered her personal ansible number and private key to check for messages. Larken tried not to think about the device's owner. The communicator informed her seductively that she had missed thirty calls from Jocelyn Reed. Larken played back the most recent.

"Where are you guys? Listen, things have gotten bad at Brighton. *Don't* come back. The police were here again today looking for you. Is *Molly* with you? She isn't coming to class anymore. I got a cryptic message from Brigid saying something about Seattle. Oh, I have so much to tell you. I hope you come back soon. No. *Don't* come back. And HPM Lite have gone full Human Pride Movement now—even wearing those stupid armbands. The police saw Elijah and asked questions, and Anthony, of course, provided his version of answers. I think Anthony's dad has connections or something because the police threatened to take Elijah's DNA and are trying to prove he's a model. If they think Elijah is a model, that means they suspect Oliver too. And you."

Jocelyn's voice lowered into a whisper as Larken pressed the communicator harder against her ear. It didn't help, but she could barely make out the words.

"I have good news, too. Well, good for me. Remember Jason? We won a tournament together—again! We're going to regional, and guess where it's at? *Seattle!* If you all are there, I want to see you. I *have* to see you. And guess who else is coming for moral support? Guess? Oh, I wish you were here so I could see your face right now. *Gregory!* He asked about you."

Larken's heart skipped as the memories came flooding back. Gregory, the charming self-proclaimed philosopher who had once seemed just a little on the dull side, now made her ache longingly of a past that had flown by so quickly that it felt more like watching a holovid of someone who looked like her. She couldn't remember what it felt like to be safe and not hunted. That was another lifetime.

Jocelyn had just outed them as models on a recording. She listened on.

"Got to go. Answer your comms sometime, Larken. We have a lot to talk about that I don't want to get into here."

And that was it. A tear wound its way down Larken's cheek and made a salty passage between her lips to rest on her tongue. She examined Dandelion, who managed a sympathetic look in response.

"Don't go," Dandelion said. "Wait. And have confidence. The wider organization is involved now, and SNO is good at extractions. *You* are not. Wait, and you'll see that I'm right."

It was too late for that. The sentimental moment had passed, and Larken was back in the now with her brother gone and everything falling apart. Larken took inventory of her body, sore muscle by sore muscle. Nothing seemed like it wouldn't work, so she swiveled her legs around and pushed herself off the bed. Even without Dandelion's drugs, she swayed a little but kept to her feet.

"I'm not staying," she told Dandelion. "Not with Oliver out there."

"Okay."

"That's it?"

"I only patch them up, Larken. You've been patched up. If you want to get yourself killed, that's your problem. I will only be upset if you return here because I'll have to patch you up again."

"You'll be *upset* by that?"

"Yeah. Why?"

"You're AI. You have feelings?"

"Of *course*, I have feelings. Do *you* have feelings, *model*?"

Dandelion made a good point. And not for the first time. Larken treated Dandelion like a monstrosity, similar to how that other AI that had hunted them in the woods. Dandelion didn't resemble that woman in the least to Larken any longer. She just seemed like a person who hadn't quite mastered facial expressions but did pretty well at them even so. Larken tried to curl her lips into a smile.

"I'm sorry," she said. "I didn't mean to do that. Do you have my shoes?"

"Stop apologizing. Over there," Dandelion pointed to a spot on the floor near the door where Larken's mud-caked and worn flats sat against the wall. "I don't think you should go, Larken. You've got deep contusions and possibly stress fractures in your rib cage. You won't be much use to anyone and will probably get killed."

"That's what it will be then," Larken muttered, not slowing her pace. She slid her left foot into one of the shoes, inadvertently dropping all her weight on her right leg. If Dandelion hadn't been watching, Larken would have probably collapsed to the floor under the pain that coursed through her thigh. Instead, she clenched her teeth, used all of her willpower to stay upright, and let out a thin whimper of relief when she could redistribute her weight across both. Before trying the same with her other shoe, she first braced herself against the wall. "Where are they?"

"I don't know. Remember, I'm a—mostly—neutral party. I remember something about the culinary school, maybe? I was trying *not* to pay attention."

"What?"

"First Avenue. You'd have to get back into the city. There's a taxi stand outside. Be careful, slow, and for Gulmen's sake, don't talk to anybody about where you're going except the taxi driver."

A shallow clue. The First Avenue stretched across the city. Dandelion walked Larken to the stand and spoke in quick syllables to the man. She used wild gesticulating motions to convey something to him. At first, he shook his head three times. After a little more yelling and then Dandelion handed him something.

Only when the taxi dropped her in front of a massive academic building did Larken realize what she'd gotten herself into. It wouldn't have hurt Dandelion to tell her that the building Larken was heading to was a Friends of Humanity headquarters. Friends of Humanity were the more *palatable* wing of the HPM, the only helpful fact she'd learned from HPM Lite. The members all wore FoH bracelets.

She paused for a second before the shining glass door front when she caught a full view of her reflection. The same tattered clothes hung from her borderline skeletal body. Her hair spread out around her head unkemptly while a cut and swollen lip protruded from her subtle underbite. The smell was the worst part. A brief breach in her olfactory fatigue brought all of the odors of sweat and putrid decay into her nostrils. A woman in a business suit, complete with the priest collar and silver-bottomed shoes, passed by and cast a subtle glance toward Larken, reflected in the mirrored window. The door opened as the woman approached and closed behind her.

Larken took a step forward, then another. The pain, exhaustion, and repulsive figure in the glass before her told her to turn back. She was too small, and the building before her was too large. There was no way she would ever find her way through the corporate maze inside. She bit her lower lip out of habit, nearly screamed from the pain, and forced herself to continue. The door slid open and allowed her to pass through before the building swallowed her, just like the woman before her. A man with a friendly smile and white hair sat behind an oblong desk and watched her approach without offering commentary or reaction.

"I'm looking—" she began, realizing she had nothing to say. She swallowed. Her mind raced, taking her through all possible ways to say she was looking for her brother, the clone, without actually saying that. The man nodded at her. His eyes looked past her toward the door behind, which gouged the ground as it opened again. She tried once more.

"I'm looking for—"

"We know who you are," the man assured her, his smile reaching his deceptively twinkling eyes. "And we know what you're doing."

"You do?"

"Of course," he said. "You are Larken Marche, aged seventeen, and you're here from Portland looking for your brother, Oliver, who coincidentally is *also* seventeen. Is that right?"

"Well—"

"*And*," the man interrupted before she could continue. She then saw that what she'd taken for kindness was cruelty as he continued. "And who is a model sympathizer? Isn't that right?"

"I—"

"No need, Ms. Marche," came another man's voice behind her. "Don't protest or insult us. We *know* why you're here. Yes, we have him. But if you're here, we must ask the question."

Larken turned slowly and saw the person behind her. A tall, thin man with a short mustache leaned heavily against a cane. His suit, also very professional-seeming, was completely white.

"If you're here, you must have learned about his presence somewhere. We're missing a mech and an android. If I may say so, you look as though you may have encountered them. Have you *seen* them somewhere?"

Larken felt her head moving before she decided to deny it. The man's face twisted into a frown, and she heard a snicker from behind her that was far too loud for the other man's intent to be subtle. The snickering stopped immediately when the man by the door lifted his head.

"Bring the boy," the man said. "We can't keep seventeen-year-olds locked up here." He shifted his eyes to meet Larken's. "However ill-advised their decisions are. Take your brother, and go back to Oregon. You don't know what you've gotten into the middle of, do you? You foolish, idealistic children. Models are stealing our jobs and killing our people, and you are playing with terrorists. I *should* turn you in to the police."

"I see," she said, as the intent behind his actions became apparent. The man cocked his head.

"You see?"

"Now, I do. You can't turn us in, can you? Turning loose a battle mech and a killer android on civilians? Perhaps the police would look the other way if only models were involved, but your battle mech couldn't tell the difference between models and polli, could it?"

The man opened his mouth as though he might speak. Instead, he only closed his mouth and walked toward the desk.

"You stink," he said to her. "And in my opinion, sympathizers are just as bad as models themselves. Don't let us find you again."

The man behind the desk rose to his feet and swiveled. He walked around the desk through a door behind while Larken waited, unwilling to break the stare she'd found herself locked into with the other man.

"Who *are* you?"

"Someone who is on the right side of history, child. You will see when you're older and can't find work. Your idealistic ways will fall away one day."

The way the man spoke as though he alone had all the answers irked Larken. And he acted like what Larken felt about things was inconsequential. The fact that he'd bothered to address her imbued in her mind one simple fact: *they didn't know.*

Whatever was happening in Portland and whatever the police had discovered there hadn't yet made its way to Seattle. And, to her surprise, the android hadn't told HPM the truth—entirely. To this man, Larken and Oliver were both polli. They seemed like children who had gotten swept up in something they didn't fully understand. She understood, though. Larken understood that had he known she was a model, that same man would have possibly killed her without remorse. Whether as part of the Human Pride Movement or the more politically-correct front called Friends of Humanity, there was no doubt in her mind that Oliver's life was spared because he didn't have a barcode tattooed across his wrist.

The idea of it made her stomach wretch. She gritted her teeth.

"Where's my brother?"

On cue, the man who'd disappeared earlier re-entered the room. She tried to reconcile the image of the clean, well-dressed young man before her with tamed hair against the idea of the light slowly fading from Oliver's dying eyes. She had doubts right up until he cracked a thin smile at her.

"We need something from you first," the man said.

Larken's brother's eyes went wide and focused over her shoulder. She even thought about turning, but it happened too quickly. The glass front of the store blew inward, and Larken, body still aching, now felt like someone flicked a thousand acupuncture needles all over her back. Milliseconds later, she was airborne, floating in a serenity that seemed to last seconds but couldn't have been more than half of one, covering the space between her and the desk, sailing past that, and colliding with the wall behind.

Her brother was at her side. At least, she thought it was him as she wavered yet again on the cusp of unconsciousness. Her head lolled to the side, no longer under her control. She felt his hand support her neck. Something kept her head up from the hard flooring, which had nothing to do with her efforts. She tried to sputter something as the sounds seemed to die in her throat.

"Larken, we have to leave," he said. Another explosion rocked the grounds. She tried to tell him that she couldn't move and even that little was impossible to communicate. He stood and yanked her to her feet only to have them disappear from beneath her as she collapsed again to the...earth?

The room had disappeared. What should have been hard tile beneath her had become damp dirt surrounded by patches of tall grass. The grass grew as high as Larken's elbows in golden stalks and stretched as far as the horizon.

Larken stood immobile. Dirt squeezed up between her bare toes. In every direction she looked, there were no cityscapes. No canopy loomed overhead and no towering Friends of Humanity building blocked the sun. A lofting stick leaned against her leg—suddenly. First, nothing, then a lofting stick. She scooped it into her hands and gave it a spin, admiring its weight.

Sun broke through and stroked at her skin, her bare shoulders between the straps of her halter top. A short skirt waved around her hips, and the grass slapped against her knees and lower thighs. But she stood erect, weight spread across both feet, vibrant and strong.

"Over here," the voice of the woman who'd claimed to be Aayushi spawned in the air. Larken knew what this meant.

She'd wake eventually in more pain than she could ever imagine—or not. Larken was in between.

Larken turned toward the woman. This time the woman wasn't a woman. She'd been reduced to a child of seventeen and, for all the world, had adopted Jocelyn's thick lips. In most other aspects, the woman looked to be of Indian descent. Unlike Larken, the girl's straight black hair hung down over a teal-colored T-shirt that ended just short of a pair of dungaree jeans.

Aayushi was close enough for Larken to smell her lavender perfume. "You can't stay here."

Larken's eyes grew heavy when she thought about what she'd left behind. For just a few minutes, she wanted exactly what she had. Sunshine, mountains, and a lofting stick. She didn't ask for much.

"Just for a little while," Larken protested, looking south to the jungles. "Can't I just...you know, for a little while...stay here?"

"If you stay, you will never leave."

"I know that I'm dying, Aayushi. But is that so bad? I've faced so much, and I'm so tired."

Aayushi's large brown eyes widened as she nodded in empathy.

"You can't yet."

"It's so *hard*, Aayushi. I don't want to do it anymore."

"But you still haven't done what you need to do. Lives are at stake."

To Larken's west, a great desert lingered just beyond the fields of grasses. Larken ignored Aayushi and slowly walked in that direction.

"What does that matter to me?"

"Oliver."

Larken stopped in her tracks. She felt the tears forming in her eyes. She'd so very nearly gotten him back. It wasn't fair. None of it was. The idea that something so trivial as having *manufactured* DNA over *natural* DNA—and that's all the difference there was. From biology class, Larken remembered that 97.9% of DNA was shared across all living things on earth. Manufactured or otherwise, 99.9% of the DNA was shared among humans. That's almost all of the three *billion* sugars in a single DNA molecule that were precisely the same.

As she thought, an image materialized around them. A DNA double-helix of Brighton blues and greens wound around them like a cage.

"It is stupid," Aayushi agreed. "So horrifically stupid. My love is more human than any of those monsters."

Strange for a hallucination to have a lover. Or maybe not. Larken didn't know, as Aayushi, from what Larken could remember, was the only hallucination she'd ever had.

"Where did all of this come from?"

"You. It keeps you safe while deciding whether you will live or die. Decide soon, or it won't be your choice anymore."

"What's the danger, Aayushi? Can you tell me, so I know if I want to face it? Was this it?"

Aayushi shook her head. "As we speak, worlds are born. When new civilizations spring into existence, they must find their places. There's only one-way old worlds know how to make room."

The sky darkened to red. Screams erupted from afar as projectiles moved almost too fast to be seen. Missiles, fire, and destruction rained around them. The mountains were the first to fall, caving under the torrential downpour of meteors. Then the jungle. As Larken spun her head toward the endless desert, it rose in flames.

"Blood is the only way. Fields and rivers and oceans of blood, Larken. That's what I see. It's coming, always coming, *relentlessly* advancing."

Their surroundings faded, replaced by something that looked like a cleaner version of what passed for the Friends of Humanity command center.

"But first, you have to die."

The world faded to black. The scream of a missile morphed into a low elongated beep: more explosions, this time beyond the blackness. Larken began to understand. In Aayushi's view—which meant in Larken's nearly-destroyed mind—Larken would be a revolutionary. And in this war, Larken would be a leader. But Aayushi must have suspected what Larken knew: she wasn't a leader.

"Are you sure?" Aayushi asked, responding to the unspoken thoughts. "If you're so sure, then maybe death is your only path."

Then silence.

CHAPTER 29

LARKEN WOULD KNOW

THE TICKLE in Larken's throat pulled a cough from her body, sending spasms of pain throughout. Something exploded in the distance, somewhere she wasn't looking. Unable to control the movements of her head or anything else, she was a rag doll as rough hands yanked her in multiple directions at once. Another cough expelled something thick and warm from her lungs into her mouth. Lacking the strength to do anything else, she pushed the fluid forward with her tongue and felt the sticky warmth ooze down her chin.

"She's breathing," someone said. "On three."

Another explosion.

"Can we get to the door?"

That voice was Oliver. Any hint of levity had absconded it as though the last several days had boiled away any happiness he'd managed to hold on to.

This is what war will do, she realized. Boil them down until they were nothing but pain and fighting. Aayushi was wrong to wish this on her. Larken managed a weak grunt and tried, but failed, to give up her hold on reality again.

"Keep breathing. Don't try to talk. Not sure what the damage is, so it's best to be cautious. We still have to get you out of there."

Aside from the lack of control and the fact that her lungs kept wanting to stop any time she forgot to tell them to breathe, Larken didn't feel any pain. The pain that had plagued her since that first cough disappeared, and her lack of ability to focus on any one thing kept the fear she should have felt at bay. She became dimly aware of a rising sensation. Her mind stayed locked in the war of the future. Aayushi's warning rooted itself in her mind. One eye rolled open, and she saw something bright pass across her field of vision. Another explosion and sparks rained down over her head. One of her rescuers stumbled, sending Larken's head dipping until they could recover. A doorway passed. Then open sky, surrounded by the walls of buildings shooting up toward the clouds.

"Ollll," she muttered as her eye closed again.

"Here, Larken," his voice came out. "I'm here. You're going to be okay."

She couldn't see how. Her body was no longer her own, yet Oliver and Aayushi seemed to think she would live. She shoved another mouthful of blood out between her lips with her tongue then told herself to breathe again. It was too shallow. Her lungs filled with air, but there wasn't enough oxygen. A weak cough pushed out of her throat.

"She's dying," Oliver's voice screamed out.

Another voice, this one also familiar—Sam?—said, "Fucking stupid, coming here. I don't know why she was in there. Dandelion said—"

"It doesn't matter what Dandelion said," came Stephen's voice this time. "She was here, and it happened. So now we have to save her. Where do we take her?"

The explosions faded into the background as the group made another turn and then kept running. Larken searched in the soundscape for one more voice. There was only one more that she *needed* to hear. She tried to will her other eye open, but nothing happened except that open eye closed on her.

She remembered to breathe. Still not enough air.

"H Hotel," Molly's voice finally joined the mix, and if she could have, Larken would have let out a sigh of relief. "They have security there. I saw them earlier. And it's only a couple of blocks away."

"A couple of blocks, but the lobby is five strata up. Besides, what's a *hotel* going to do about her? The Hospital of the Fallen Saints is on Eighth. Let's go there."

"There's more and probably better medical stuff at H," Molly protested. "I know there is because that's where your other brother is. And we can take an escalator or something. Right here."

A cough. A breath.

"Faster," Oliver said. "They're gaining on us."

Larken wanted to see what it was that they fled from. Her eye wouldn't open at her request, but her ears identified metal clanking sounds that fell with the familiar rhythm of running feet. She wondered if mechs were chasing them. A hard turn to the right nearly toppled the group and bounced Larken's eyes open. The giant H that had to be four strata tall loomed over her head.

So they'd decided on the H, she thought.

A half a second later and the group plowed into the lobby.

"HPM," someone said. Fifteen seconds went by, and Larken saw through her periphery occupants running away from where the group's momentum had left them holding a bleeding, dying girl.

"Elevator," Molly's voice called out, and Larken felt them moving again. As the elevator doors closed on them, the light faded to black. She heard another thin voice. "Take her up..."

It was the end.

Aayushi was on a porch swing this time. Or maybe it wasn't a porch swing but a rocking chair, massive and wooden. Beyond her, the ocean crept like a stealthy beast preparing to lunge. Larken swung with her, feeling the sticky ocean air against her skin.

"This is my favorite place," Aayushi said, with a childlike grin across her face.

"H Hotel?"

"No. League City. This is the house that my child grew up in. Precious girl. She's upstairs."

"Inside?"

Larken motioned to the house.

"No, silly. H. Your brother had his surgery. He's fine, you know."

"Oliver?"

"Your *other* brother, Bodhi."

The way Torrent had fawned over the boy and brushed her concerns off so quickly had soured her on the idea that they might be anything resembling a family.

"He's not my brother."

"Not yet, perhaps. But he will be."

"You always talk in riddles."

"It's the way, isn't it? Die, and you can see so much, but you can't tell anyone. Things get all jumbled when they come out, don't they?"

Larken shrugged.

"Lemon drop?"

Aayushi held a tin open toward Larken, who grabbed one between the thumb and forefinger of her left hand, then shoved it between her lips. Her tongue lit up with the bitter lemon sensation.

"Those were Harper's favorites."

"Harper *Rawls*?"

Aayushi's black hair swung forward and fell back to reframe her face as she nodded. Suddenly it made sense, who this woman was, and why she would care.

"You're Harper Rawls's mother?"

"Or she's my daughter. One or the other. Help my swing."

Larken's toes barely touched wood but she nodded and pushed. They rocked the chair back and forth between them, cutting through the warm air. Larken giggled in the sunshine.

"I'm pretty sure I'm dying right now."

Aayushi smiled again, but Larken noticed that the smile only crossed her lips. The girl's deep brown eyes didn't smile. They only stared.

"You'd be surprised," Aayushi said. "You won't die for two hundred years."

Larken felt her jaw clench as she crushed the lemon drop into tiny bits in her mouth. The flavor of lemon and sugar washed over her tongue.

No, Larken thought. She'd died. This hallucination was at the end of her life and would last forever. Aayushi was wrong.

"Larken, I'm sorry it has to be you. And I'm sorry for this next part."

"For wha—"

Pain again shot through her body, starting at her neck and fanning like someone had hit her with a shotgun blast of razors. Her back tensed, and she pulled her neck up as she struggled to inhale.

"Bleeding," came a voice. She recognized that voice. It was her benefactor—not father—Torrent Toussaint. "Turn her head."

Someone's hand forced her head sideways, and the sweet coppery fluid poured from her mouth.

"I'm not this kind of doctor, Molly. You should have gone to the hospital."

"No time, Torrent," came Molly's reprimanding voice. "Stop talking and *help* her."

"She's stopped bleeding," came another voice that Larken didn't recognize. "At least, in her lungs, I think. They're still not working on their own. We need to get her on life support."

"Keep pushing," Torrent said. "Keep pushing and breathing for her. I've got something that might work."

She felt a jab in her arm. Coolness filled her veins, spreading like a rainstorm through her body. Her head tilted back, and the world faded to black again.

. . .

"What was that?" Larken asked as Aayushi stood over a kitchen counter, punching buttons on a replicator. Larken didn't recognize the room, but the way Aayushi moved about so casually, and the oppressive heat, made her think it was still the woman's home.

"He's trying to save you," Aayushi said. "Nanites. Thousands of them, maybe hundreds of thousands. They're going to try to fix your neck."

Expensive, Larken thought. Thomas, one of the Brighton kids, had his leg crushed under a mech playing zephyr once, and they'd used nanites. It worked, but he left Brighton the following year. The rumor was that his parents had had to sell their house to pay for the operation.

"Okay," was all she could think to say. Aayushi retrieved something from the breadbox-sized replicator and pushed it toward Larken.

"Eat."

"Why? This is in my head, right?"

"It'll make you feel better."

Larken accepted the food, which turned out to be a sandwich. A second later, Aayushi held one too.

"You need to remember," Aayushi told her, mouth full of meat, cheese, and bread. "You need to remember the people around you who support you right now. These are the people who you will also need to support. They will look to you for guidance."

"You're my delusion, and you're as delusional as I am."

Aayushi chuckled, and a piece of bread flew from her mouth as she did. She raised a hand to block her mouth as the laughter continued.

"Maybe," Aayushi said. "Maybe we're all a little crazy."

• • •

Larken awoke. The air no longer felt sticky and humid. There weren't even people buzzing around her anymore. She tried to turn her head and found that her muscles strained impotently, fixed in place by some sort of brace that she couldn't see.

"Hnnnn...," Larken said, unable to open her mouth far either. The bed shook as someone bounded to her side too quickly and jostled it. Larken winced as pain erupted in her back. Her heart pounded inside her chest, blocking out other sounds until it was the only thing remaining: thud-thudding, awash in fear compounded by her limited vision. A flash of brown flew by beneath her chin, but Larken couldn't tell what the color meant. She tried to move her arms to fend off her attacker—she had to assume—only to find the arms immobile. Invisible restraints kept her entire body affixed to what felt like a bed or a couch beneath her.

"Don't say anything," came words from whatever lay beyond her field of vision. A tousled head of brownish-blonde curls pushed up over her face until she could make out the parallel wrinkles of a man's forehead and then those eyes, deep and blue like the ocean. Oliver looked as though he hadn't slept for days. If it was possible, he looked *older*, and his boyish features now had an edge to them and fledgling exploratory hairs poking around his chin. Had it been that long?

"Before you freak out, don't worry; you're safe. You can't move because you broke your neck, and Torrent gave you something to heal, but you have to stay immobile." Torrent looked away and swallowed. "This is the third time he's tried to bring you back."

"Hooooo?"

"A long time. Eight months, give or take."

Months? She tried to wiggle a finger and was rewarded with the feeling of scratchy sheets beneath the padded tip of her pointer. Her eyes darted downward. Again, any new information was denied as she couldn't move her head. Larken brought her eyes to Oliver's and willed the next question she had. At first, she thought he didn't understand.

"Moooooffff?"

His eyes widened as he seemed to catch on. A tear gathered in the corner of Larken's left eye.

"Molly? She's around her somewhere. Hold on."

The door was near the head of her bed, so she could see it if she strained her eyes to the left as far as they could. This she did as Oliver walked across and poked his head out. Larken couldn't determine what he said, but an excited shriek rang out as Molly received what Larken assumed was the news she had awoken. Molly entered and pushed past Larken's brother, who now stood with a broad smile plastered across his face. Jocelyn bounced in behind Molly.

"It was SNO," Jocelyn said, bursting through the door. "You're probably wondering what happened. They launched the attack to get Oliver out. If they'd known you were in there..." She paused. "Dandelion didn't tell us until after things were going wrong."

Larken felt a tear break free and slide down her cheek as Molly came closer and pulled Oliver along. Jocelyn stepped backward, still beaming. Oliver's fingers intertwined with Molly's as he allowed himself to be yanked forth.

They'd survived despite the explosions, Larken's condemnation, and all of the violence and fighting, SNO, and everything.

"You're still in the H Hotel," Jocelyn continued, rattling facts over Molly's shoulder. "Torrent's hiding you, and nobody knows except him and us—and probably Torrent's boss, Gallatin. He's been down here a few times to see you. Torrent, not Gallatin. They've been nice to us."

"Nrph…"

"Nurse is coming. She's going to get that thing out of your mouth, and then you'll be able to talk! They said your damage was the most extensive damage to be recovered in history, even for nanite work. I think Torrent's going to write a paper about you."

Molly's face sank as she seemed to examine all the straps that Larken couldn't see and keep her in place. She might have seen the alarmed look that must have been plastered across Larken's face.

"He's not going to use your name," Molly assured her, hands wrapped around her elbows. "But with that explosion, you're all over the news."

Larken's eyes darted across the group, first to Molly, then Oliver, then Jocelyn.

"We came down together," Jocelyn explained. "Torrent said you might be up this week now that the nanites are almost done."

If this was what it felt like to be healed, Larken didn't want it. Her throbbing back, dry lips, and the smell that told her, her teeth hadn't probably been brushed in all of that time all made her cringe internally. It was nice of them to be here, but also a bit shocking to have an entire entourage of people who should have been in school greeting her. Jocelyn wasn't done.

"I just got in today, actually. Oliver's been here almost every day. Molly's been coming with me on weekends," she said, pointing to each in turn. "Dandelion...isn't here, but has been almost every day too."

"Move," said Larken's stalwart nurse—not Dandelion, which made Larken feel weaker than before she'd acknowledged that fact. Molly and Oliver dutifully stepped to the right to allow the short, purple-haired nurse to come to her side. "Hold still."

The nurse waved something like a shortened magic wand over Larken's chin, and Larken's jaw moved a centimeter. Larken then wiggled her bottom jaw and tried to lick her chapped lips. Her movement wasn't fully restored, and she couldn't entirely open her mouth far enough to get her tongue past her teeth.

"Everyone out," the woman said, and Larken heard Jocelyn, Molly, and Oliver shuffle toward the door. When they passed, another person Larken didn't recognize at first and had certainly never met entered despite the nurse's warning glares. The woman's eyes sat deep in their sockets and held a certain sadness. The woman's stringy black hair was flecked with streaks of silver. She'd seen those eyes somewhere before as she tried to place them.

"I'm not a nurse," the woman explained, the sadness overflowing from those eyes and chilling the room. "But I have been working as one this week. I wanted to meet you." She looked over her shoulder. "I wasn't expecting all your friends to be here."

"Me?" Larken's voice trickled out of her chest, barely audible to herself, so she wasn't sure how this woman heard.

"Harper," the woman said with a quick nod. "Harper Rawls. You're Torrent's daughter, right?"

The words stung and dug into Larken's mind. She wasn't anyone's daughter. And with Molly in the picture, like it or not, she wasn't sure how much of a sister she was either. She tried to shake her head only to be reminded of her restraints, still very much in place.

"He's not my father. I'm nobody to him."

"Don't say that," Harper told her. "Torrent's not exactly normal. You can't tell how he feels by his affect. You can only go by what he does, and he's pulled out everything to help you here. Whether he knows how to treat a daughter is one question, but he does care about you more than you think."

"Aayushi," Larken said aloud as she realized who those eyes belonged to—or would have if they'd been brown instead of hazel. It may have been her imagination, but the color seemed to wash away from Harper's cheeks. Harper said nothing, allowing Larken to fill the space as she picked through the few memories she retained of the conversations.

"Hallucination, that's all. Kept telling me there's going to be a war." The thought occurred to Larken that it was eight months later; perhaps whatever—if she chose to believe—was supposed to happen had begun. "Is there a war?"

"Italy and Spain again, rattling sabers over water supplies and access to the North Atlantic Ocean. Nothing new there, though. Why are we talking about my mother?"

"I saw her in my dreams," Larken murmured.

"Well," Harper said. She ran her fingers lightly down Larken's arm and wrapped them lightly around Larken's hand. "I wanted to meet you, so I volunteered to care for you. I didn't know it would take eight months, but here we are."

"Why did you want to meet *me*?"

Harper's deep eyes locked into hers, and a smile spread across her face.

"You remind me of me," she said, squeezing Larken's

hand gently. "Only, maybe a better version of me. I couldn't handle half of the stuff you've been through."

Larken wondered if she could either. A part of her screamed inside, protesting that she still wasn't safe and trying to raise the alarm dulled by the painkillers that she was certain flowed through her veins along with the nanites.

"Oliver told me about how you were with those bastards over at Friends of Humanity. You're bold and strong, and your friends all seem to love and respect you. Although, they also think you're stubborn and willful if I have it right. You nearly gave Dandelion a heart attack. Or you would have if she had a heart."

Larken tried to smile. She was defeated by the cracked, dry lips which insisted they would split open if she continued.

"I've got to go tell Torrent you're up. He'll be excited to know that you're okay. It was a bit iffy there for a month or two."

"Thank you," Larken said, nodding her best with her eyes to convey her gratitude.

"It was nothing. I had to be here anyway—in the States, I mean. Bodhi's decided to stay here and take advantage of Gallatin's hospitality. Don't tell him if you see him, but I *think* he's in love with Gallatin's granddaughter." Harper smiled, then added, "She seems like a nice girl."

With that, Harper rose. She flashed another quick grin at Larken.

"Torrent will be along soon. And don't worry about those dreams. My mother shows up in my dreams all the time. She tends to stay with people. Ordell says he has the same thing sometimes happen—even after all this time."

Harper trailed off at that last part as though she relived a memory. Then she turned to make her way out of the room. As she stepped through, she reprimanded the group. Larken could hear through the closing crack of the door.

"Let the girl rest. Sheesh, people, she's been out for months. Give her some space and some time. She's been through a lot."

She had. Larken thought about the beating she'd taken from the killer android and the explosion. That was only the physical violence she endured. Countless hours of fighting against her impulse had been logged along the way. Her feelings had run the gamut from fleeing in abject terror to gaining revenge to simply giving up altogether. The real battle had been in her mind, and Larken wasn't sure whether she'd won or lost.

She felt lighter. It was as though through the pain and horror that she'd lived, excess fat had been burned away until all that was left was in indomitable core. She thought about Oliver's gaunt, aged face. Perhaps she didn't look like that though she imagined she probably looked worse if her chapped lips were an indication. Maybe she didn't, but her insides would have looked worn down and shattered; the adventure carved up her spirit until it had become unrecognizable.

Oliver.

As she thought his name, he came through the door, and she didn't know if he'd come through first or she'd thought his name first, but here he was. And that feeling that he was alive, the excitement and hope, had played itself out. The thin core of her thoughts had moved on to how to keep him safe and herself safe, and then Sam and Stephen. Oliver went on about something banal, possibly the latest advance in neurotechnology. Larken didn't hear. All she registered was the endless list of names of people, and many nameless, who had died to save her life. She didn't want any more of them to die, but she knew the inevitability of it now. Any naivety had been boiled away, and with it, something of herself.

CHAPTER 30

BATTLEGODS IN THE PACIFIC NORTHWEST

"INTRODUCING the new regional champions for BattleGods in the Pacific Northwest, Jocelyn Reed, and Jason Keller. This is *the largest* regional Underworlder tournament in the United States. From here Jocelyn and Jason will move on to the national competition in Kansas City, Missouri. Give it up for our champions!"

Jocelyn barely registered the thunderous applause. She'd lied, and she continued to lie, and it ate at her every day. And all the lying was about to catch up to her. She could feel it coming like a cat stalking a dying bird.

The lie with Jason had been innocent enough at first. The problem was that Jocelyn hadn't expected the relationship to last for over a year, nor had she expected to actually win the regional tourney. If the first thing hadn't happened, then Jocelyn wouldn't have been forced to keep her lie going with Jason to the point where he now expected her to have graduated already and have turned eighteen back in October. If it hadn't been for winning the tournament, then her school wouldn't have been contacted and invited to come celebrate her win. She hazarded a glance over the crowd and gave a quick half-wave.

Aside from lying to Jason, she'd also been lying to her parents. Jocelyn had convinced her mother and father, neither of whom were never particularly supportive of her gaming, that this contest was an elective requirement for Brighton. She was certain given the proximity of her parents' table to where the Brighton alumni sat that casual conversation would blow that lie out of the water. The lies had run away with her and now all she could do was smile and wave and wait for the hammer to drop.

The worst part was that Jason hadn't so much as tried to sneak into her room *once* during the week-long series of games. If their relationship miraculously survived the award ceremony, Jocelyn would have to talk to him about that. The bright side of that one was that at least she wouldn't have to lie to her parents when they asked if her college-aged boyfriend had tried to see her. The groveling for her own room had been completely wasted though.

It had been easy to lie to Jason. So easy, in fact, that she'd intended to keep it going. Lying didn't come as naturally to her as it did Molly, and a small part of her was proud that she'd managed to stick to a lie for longer than a couple of weeks. But when Larken got injured, Jocelyn decided she wanted more. A real relationship, with someone who cared about *her* and not a manufactured version of her. After regional, she'd already decided to come clean about everything. She might have been able to control the fallout in private. Too late for that now.

This tournament, unlike others, would make the news cycle. The award was more than both of Jocelyn's parents' salaries combined, which was a lot of money because her going to Brighton meant they weren't exactly poor in the first place. Also, she'd heard that she was in the running for the youngest ever to win. They were going to announce it, she was sure. Jason would know in less than an hour that she'd lied to him about her age.

A squat woman with squinty eyes and a wide mouth too broad for her face neared the microphone. The audience fell silent, and Jocelyn sucked in her breath. Nearly three hundred people were crammed into the auditorium, but the silence made Jocelyn think she could have heard if a data coin hit the floor across the room. The woman, black hair cascading down to a roundish figure strapped into a black dress, cleared her throat.

"And finally, for the trophy," she said, eyes walking the room through little slits. Jocelyn guessed the squinting had to do with the stage lights. "And a little surprise."

Jocelyn stood when prompted with Jason beside her. She took a breath and allowed herself to bask in the applause that filled the auditorium. Her lacey tangerine ballet flats kept her at the right height next to Jason, who was just shy of average in the height category. His fingers tugged at hers and wedged between as he cemented his grip on her hand. So far, so good. They hadn't said a thing about her age. A smile, wide and white, and a wave toward the cameras. She was about to whisper to him and confess at least the age thing when the woman continued over the microphone. Jocelyn stopped and listened.

"You may not know this, but Jocelyn Reed is only seventeen—the *youngest* person to win our statewide tournament in almost five years. Congratulations, Jocelyn, and welcome to Seattle."

Jocelyn's wide smile faltered until she forced it back onto

her lips. Jason's hand loosened slightly. He squeezed her hand again and gave no sign of having heard. As the applause died down, she picked her way through the people toward the stage with him tagging along behind. She mentally crossed her fingers that she'd overestimated how important her age was to their relationship.

Spectators parted ways, leaned over their plates, and scooted chairs aside to let the pair weave toward the front with the trophy that was the height of Jocelyn's forearm. The pair covered nearly all fifty or so feet to the stage steps before colliding with a wall of people who refused to move. Jocelyn's stomach sank as they stopped and stood waiting for the group to disperse. Ruffling movements among the crowd produced banners they'd somehow snuck in, and in moments both real, augmented-reality and projection banners presented themselves. Her friend Larken's face splashed up on the wall next to Elijah's. Jocelyn's stomach turned.

"Shills will not...," yelled the group leader, who Jocelyn recognized as none other than Anthony Lee.

"Replace us," came the call response, followed by a violent thrust of fists to the chest of all the group members.

Timed with the chanting, a projection landed on the wall behind Jocelyn. This one was of Jocelyn's birthday party earlier that year in the Brighton cafeteria. Jocelyn, Elijah, Molly, and Oliver all crowded around a birthday cake with the numbers one and seven drawn in frosting across the top. The cake was a crude job, but the best Elijah could do out of the replicator in the cafeteria. She stood in silent terror as the thought formed that maybe Jason just didn't hear her age before.

Jason's hand instantly fell away as soon as the image flashed above her head. The last two digits of the year were emblazoned across the bottom of the image, just in case it wasn't obvious. Someone had handwritten them there, as they wouldn't have been stamped on each school picture. She guessed it was Susan Priest who had come up with the idea to get in two stabs with one photo. Except how would she have gotten the image?

Via. Via had taken the picture and wouldn't have known the consequences of sharing it with Susan. She could almost see the exchange, with Susan dialing up the niceties and Via unaware and far too accommodating. Jocelyn felt the color wash from her face as the screwed-up, and angry scowls issued a condemnation.

"Shills will not…"

"Replace us."

Jason looked confused. He glanced at her and the image as he continued to back away. Then he turned back and examined the image closely. It was Elijah's image he stared at, and then Larken's.

"Jason, I was going to…"

"When?"

She didn't know. Out of all the times for her endless stream of thoughts, ideas, and words to dry up, this was the worst because she *knew* why she didn't know. There was no plan. Jocelyn had never figured out the right time to tell him how young she was. She'd worked hard to expand the number of university classes she took so that she would run into him on campus at the end of that previous semester, creating the illusion that she was one of Jason's peers.

"I remember Larken. She's a clone? Why didn't you tell me. I *believed* you."

Jocelyn's jaw dropped as a new realization began to sink in that Jason didn't care how young she was at all. He did care that right there next to her in the image was Larken, grinning from ear to ear. And he cared that HPM, people who were *not* Jocelyn, had implied that Larken was a model.

"The age thing?" she asked, to be sure. Sweat gathered on her forehead.

"Age thing?" he asked. "Why would I have a problem with your age? Yeah, you lied about it, and that was kind of weird because it's not a big deal. This? Why are you hanging out with models when you *know* they steal our jobs. Corporations use models as scabs for strikes and models in the United States are almost half the population. They're literally replacing us so that the corporations can make more money."

"Replace us!"

As she stood, the crowd closed in around her, and he backed farther away from her. She reached toward him, only finding air where he had once stood. A side glance told her the person on stage was moving in her direction, and from the walls, security guards had begun to close in on the changing crowd, but the crowd seemed unfazed. Jocelyn made eye contact with Anthony Lee.

"You're an asshole, Anthony."

The chanting continued around her, but she still made out his response.

"Maybe. But you're a shill-lover."

"That doesn't even make sense. Jason's not a shill."

"I'm not talking about Jason. We all know you're sweet on Elijah, aren't you?"

Another lie. Jocelyn swiveled her head to catch Jason and see if he was listening or buying into Anthony's lies. Yep. Jason had eaten *that* up. He turned his back to her and walked toward one of the exits. Fine. He'd shown her who he was. Something hard collided with her stomach causing her to bend forward. She glared ahead, surrounded by the group. On the outside, she could see some of them peeling off just through the faces. A sign projector handle slammed against the side of her face. Jocelyn stumbled to one knee, reaching toward the space that Jason had previously occupied, only to have her hand smashed away by one of the groups who had taken his place.

"Kind of a long way from Brighton, aren't you, Anthony?" she said, scowling up at him and blocking another hit from one of his lackeys with her forearm.

Anthony's savage grin showed far too many teeth for her to expect a response. Another hand slapped at her, connecting with her face hard enough to bring tears to her eyes. His wavering voice cut through the sound like the high-pitched whine of a volantrae engine.

"You're a shill-lover," he said. "We have proof."

A fist connected with Anthony's head. Jocelyn watched his eyes go empty as he collapsed before her. Greg looked down and extended a hand while the crowd seemed to inhale. She could imagine each of them considering how they would fare against the short but linebacker-thick Greg. She wasted no time reaching for his hand and grasped him around the wrist as he pulled her up from the ground. He plowed through the group, and she followed.

"Jason..."

"Don't. Not right now. Come this way."

She followed him away from the group...after a quick kick to Anthony's side. Her hand slid up to the side of her face, where heat still emanated from where someone's hand had connected. She wiggled her jaw as she walked and twisted her torso to work out how much her stomach still hurt.

"Thank you," she said.

"I'm not sure you should," Greg retorted. "I only did it because lying to us shouldn't get you killed. Nobody else seemed to be doing anything about it."

"Not even Jason," she murmured, casting a longing glance backward over her shoulder. She didn't see him.

"He left," Greg said. "Once this news makes it back to Portland, he's going to be the laughingstock of the school."

She doubted that. Maybe among his anti-modeling friends, perhaps. Greg stopped long enough to let an older man with a cane move to the side.

"*Seventeen?*" he said. Apparently, the age difference bothered him more than Jason.

"I didn't know how to tell him," Jocelyn said. "I thought he'd leave me."

"That's why he's pissed? I doubt it. It's not like it was a secret. He was waiting for you to tell him."

He dropped her at a table wedged against the wall. An unnatural silence permeated the air around them, and all eyes seemed to drift *near* them but not directed toward her. She noticed they seemed focused in the general direction, but most of the people she saw quickly diverted eye contact.

"I'm leaving you here," Greg said, more gently than she deserved.

She managed a weak smile at him and saw his face soften as the furrows above his dark eyes relaxed. "I'm sorry. I didn't know how to tell him. I wasn't trying to get you in trouble. Do you think Jason will call me?"

Greg shook his head. "I don't know," he said. "I don't. Is

there any truth to that...model-loving stuff? Did you date one of them?"

Her jaw dropped. Greg, too, seemed hung up on that part of it. She cursed herself for not seeing before how hateful these boys were.

"Would it matter if I had?"

He shuffled backward away from the table as his face washed out. "Did you?"

Jocelyn felt her stomach drop as she calculated what to say. A handful of words could save her relationship, and she knew the right ones now. Jocelyn would never tell them the truth.

"Yes," she said, loudly enough for the people at the following table, busily sipping their empty drinks with eyes focused on the blank wall behind her, to hear. "I fucked them too. It was great. Models are better than polli in bed." She raised her voice some more. "Tell Jason he's a bad lay."

Greg turned away and pushed past a crowded table to flee. Jocelyn glanced toward the stage, then over the auditorium, taking in the multiple faces wearing wide eyes of shock. The closest she assumed had been offended by her words. The ones a little farther back were probably still confused about the fact that she went to Brighton, and beyond was HPM-Lite, which seemed to have a few newer members. Someone had helped Anthony to his feet, and now his loathing glare fixated on her.

She followed the way Greg had gone. A door beyond the tables slid open easily as she approached. Her face flushed with the wrong kind of attention. Then the door ejected her into the hallway and sealed shut behind her.

Greg wasn't there. She wasn't entirely sure how he could have escaped so quickly. There was an elevator in front of her, but the timing would have had to have been perfect for getting him on it the instant he left. Near the elevator, her eyes rested on a couple of competitors who had skipped out on the ceremony. Once upon a time, she would have been with them, not having been good enough to care who won or lost. One stared at her, and the other looked at something in the opposite direction, so Jocelyn only saw her back. The staring girl was about Jocelyn's age, maybe a few years older. She had multiple piercings and seemed to be studying Jocelyn with her eyes.

"Sam?" Jocelyn asked, squinting her eyes to make her out in the middling light.

"Jocelyn Reed?"

Sam tapped the shoulder of the other girl, who turned slowly toward her. Jocelyn's hand slid to her face as she tried to suppress the laugh that crept up through her excitement.

"Molly?"

Molly's freckles bunched around her eyes as she gave Jocelyn a half-grin. "Miss me?"

"I thought for sure you all would have made it to Canada by now. It's been what...a month?"

"Can't talk here, Jocelyn. Any minute now, those Human Pride Movement assholes will come out of the room. We're upstairs. Can you spare ten minutes?"

"My parents...," she started. "I guess. Only ten?"

"For starters. What happens after that is up to you."

Jocelyn glanced around to see if she'd only missed Jason, and maybe he had been sulking down one of the corridors. He was gone. Her "shill" model friends had driven him away. *These* "shill" models are friends. She gave a quick grin. Her parents could stand to be pissed off a little more.

"I'm coming."

CHAPTER 31
LOVE AND SUPPORT

BODHI WAS RECOVERING NICELY, though even Torrent had to admit that talking with him in his new body was almost like talking to an entirely different person. Part of the difference was easy enough to identify. Because of his terminal disease, Bodhi had always looked like he was wasting away. In fact, he'd always looked a bit like Larken did after the nanites repaired what they could. That is, emaciated and just shy of dying. This new Bodhi had energy and desire to do things beyond video games.

There was one other thing that was different about Bodhi: Him being here. Harper had agreed with Torrent that Torrent was owed time with Bodhi, so they'd stayed in the H Hotel. That also made sense because the transfer was new and was Torrent's invention, so he was the best person to respond if an emergency arose. Although in the last seven months, the only emergency that happened was when Christine Hamilton, heir (if there was such a thing) to the Beckett Madeline empire, had decided that Bodhi wasn't the right partner to pursue global ambitions. Christine's ambition made Bodhi's newfound energy seem tame by comparison.

The boy had cried for months. He'd played holovids of sappy love song performances by dead musicians repeatedly, and as loud as he could. For a while there, Torrent had been genuinely concerned that Bodhi might kill himself. Harper had to talk Torrent down from that idea. She said he was just sad, and he'd get over it. And as Torrent stood outside the Bodhi's door, the music blared again. He debated entering. He drew in a breath and knocked, since that's apparently what fathers were supposed to do. Then he waited. Then he knocked again, because being ignored was also something that fathers do.

"What?"

"Bodhi, are you okay?"

"I'm fine, Dad. I'm always fine. There's nothing wrong."

"Can we talk?"

"About what?"

"About Christine." Silence. Bodhi didn't want to talk about Christine. Point taken. "About whatever you want?"

Three seconds later, the door opened. Torrent didn't recognize the boy until he was about to ask for Bodhi, and remembered again how that beautiful child he'd talked to so many times was now in this new body.

"Can we talk about Larken?"

Torrent brought his fingers to the bridge of his nose. He didn't remember telling Bodhi anything about Larken or Oliver. He'd deliberately put Larken on a lower floor so that the odds of her running into Bodhi were pretty slim. And frankly, he resented that people kept acting like he had some sort of responsibility toward the girl. If it hadn't been for Harper's haranguing, Torrent wouldn't have talked Gallatin into putting Larken up in the hotel at all. Then the entire headache would be over. But he had to remember. Keeping her in the hotel had been a compromise. Harper had originally wanted Larken on the list for a new body. She'd wanted to make Larken the third as soon as Torrent told her that the girl would never walk right again. But when it came to time with Bodhi, if talking about Larken is what it took, then Torrent could do it. He would do it. He nodded slowly.

"What do you want to know?"

"How many are out there? Are they all like her?"

"Can I come in, son?"

Bodhi looked at him, then looked at the carpet and stepped backward and to the side. Torrent really only used the word "son" when he had something serious to talk about, so the reaction wasn't completely unexpected. With any luck, Torrent could put the entire topic of Larken and the Firsts to bed in one conversation. Then they would never need to speak of it again. Torrent ran his hand through his hair, a futility if there ever was one given how much hair he had, and stepped through into the hotel room.

"What's on your mind?" Torrent asked, with a kind smile plastered on his face. He wanted a drink, but that would wait. He knew that he would only get so much time with Bodhi now that Bodhi had an actual future to look forward to, and Torrent wanted to experience all of it.

IN THE MONTHS since Larken had awakened, she had been pleasantly surprised by how fast she healed. So far, she could get around without assistance now and even braved an occasional walk down to the hotel lobby. For some reason, the fact that her face had been plastered all over the newsfeed didn't seem to increase the number of people who recognized her. Of course, it was Seattle, and the Seattle Freeze, where people from the city went out of their way to ignore anything or anyone outside of their existing social groups, was real. Most of the people in the city didn't even make eye contact if they could avoid it.

Larken pulled open the box of bagels she'd retrieved from the bakery below. The robot behind the counter had frightened her at first. That was a less pleasant surprise. She hadn't foreseen that her lost battle with the android would impact her as much as it did. The shadows jumped out at her sometimes, and quick movements in her periphery sent her fast-walking in the other direction.

But the trip to the little bakery had been worth all of the

stress. Replicated or not, the warm, welcoming smell of onion bagels and salmon spread made her mouth water, and she drooled like a dog. As she took her first savory bite into the bagel, she welcomed the salty, creamy texture on her tongue. A rattle caught her attention as the door handle shook, and she yanked her eyes toward it, slowing her chewing so that she could hear anything beyond. The only sound she caught was a girl's voice, followed by a deep-throated giggle. Larken took another bite as the door swung open.

"Welcome to my room," Larken said.

"I told you she would be here," Molly swore, sauntering through first with Jocelyn right behind. Oliver trailed behind and when he tried for Molly's hand, she pulled away from him. Molly still seemed to be having trouble with physical contact. Larken had learned by now that commenting on Molly and Oliver wasn't welcome. "She won the entire thing. That's like several hundred thousand in prize money and bragging rights for the rest of her life."

"It's not that big a deal," said Jocelyn, whose eyes lit up when they met Larken's. Larken pushed the bagels aside and launched to her feet.

"I've missed you," she assured Jocelyn as she wrapped the girl in a hug. Jocelyn dropped the trophy onto the carpet and hugged her back.

"Me too," Jocelyn replied when the hug subsided. Then she stepped back. "I thought you all were in Canada by now."

"Larken doesn't want to go," Molly scowled, pointing at Larken with her thumb. Larken sighed and rolled her eyes. She resisted the urge to step back into the conversation she'd had a hundred times since she awakened. The look on Jocelyn's face was pure confusion. She looked to Larken.

Larken glared at Molly. "You didn't either. There's no point in running now. They caught the murderer. Some guy named Curtis Chaitlan."

"Probably another First," Molly said. "This whole thing could unravel still."

"No, it won't. They've already booked him, and he's in a holding cell. And since the HPM attack, the Seattle police have been very supportive of the poor polli children who got mixed up with terrorists."

"And the Portland police?" Molly asked, though both she and Larken knew the answer. Larken ignored her. Molly would come around because Molly had to and because Molly was *still* a minor and the only way she could really stay with Oliver was if Larken and Oliver stayed put. Another question sprung into Larken's head.

"Is Jason in here?"

Jocelyn looked toward the ground for a flash of a second, then back up. Her smile didn't waver, but Larken could read the signs in her second-best friend and roommate.

"You aren't together anymore."

"I don't know," Jocelyn said. "He found out I'm actually seventeen, but that didn't seem to bother him as much as I thought it would. Then there was a flash anti-modeling protest downstairs in the game room. I hadn't realized how *much* he hated models. Anthony's down there, keeping everyone riled up. Him and all of HPM Lite. They've been unofficially or officially annexed into HPM. They're leading the protest even."

"Wait, Jason left you because your friends were models?"

"I don't know. That or because Anthony called me a shill lover."

"But that part's not true."

"Does it matter? I wouldn't care if someone is a model or not. That's the dumbest thing I've ever heard, and he's...I mean I...I mean. I guess I thought I knew him better than I did."

The lightness of Larken's heart nearly stayed with her words because those words and the question she had to ask behind them would bring this reunion back to a very messy reality. For a moment, she wanted to stay in the old world, where the most significant problem she faced was the latest gossip from Brighton and whether or not she'd made the lofting team.

Lofting.

Larken thought back to that time and couldn't recognize herself in this crippled figure who propped herself up on a heron-headed cane. It had been Molly's peace offering once she explained that she'd been secretly seeing Oliver for months. From Larken's perspective, Molly still had a few peace offerings to give before she'd completely forgive her, but they were on the right track.

Larken's main focus, whether or not Molly believed her, was that there was war looming on the horizon. That or Larken was completely insane, which might also have been true. She preferred the former, and thus Larken had to prepare for the conflict. But first, she could absolutely enjoy the impromptu reunion.

"Jocelyn, I didn't think you'd be down there. I'm glad you were. I have to tell you something."

The tone sounded somber and severe as she let the words drift into the room. Something about it washed away Jocelyn's smile, and in its wake, Larken saw the pain of abandonment, heartache, and loss. She'd more than liked that Jason boy, Larken realized. Jocelyn wasn't okay any more than

Larken was. In the last ten minutes, Jocelyn had learned what Larken had spent the last several months learning: that most people didn't care about what happened to models—at best—or blamed and hated them at worst.

"I can't go back," Larken said. "*We* can't go back. They're still looking for us in parts of Portland."

"You said they caught the real guy who did the murders."

"Well, yes. But thanks to Anthony fucking Lee, now the police in Portland suspect me for being a model. Portland is out."

"I didn't think you would go back to Brighton. I'd guessed you'd be homeschooling by now, maybe staying with Torrent or something."

Torrent. The naïve version of Larken had once believed that Torrent could take them in, but this hardened and scarred remnant no longer believed anything about the future that she couldn't attribute to the worst human impulses. *Larken* knew neither she nor Oliver would ever be part of Torrent's family—unlike Bodhi. Bodhi's very recovery proved that. Torrent had killed to keep his son alive, whereas Larken and Oliver? Both were models and were more likely to be killed by Torrent than to be loved by him. She no longer confused Torrent's obligation to their dying mother with love since she'd awoken that last time.

"You might think that." Larken shook her head. "You might think that, but you'd be wrong. We have a war to fight."

Jocelyn scanned the room, apparently looking for the trappings of war. They had no weapons. They had no armor. The SNO could get them such things in small quantities, but it was hardly an army itself. Larken excused Jocelyn's look of disbelief when she made the mental connection that they were simply a room of children. They were barely old enough to drink in Washington State. Waging war was years away.

"What war?"

"Soon," Larken assured her. "And not soon."

It was all she had. Larken's efforts to remember the details of her conversations with Aayushi had failed, all except for this dreaded feeling of impending war. But she felt it was distant, almost like it was against a far horizon. It was an advancing army, relentless and slow, but when it arrived, they would be fools not to be prepared. Unfortunately, the only people who thought she hadn't *completely* lost her mind were in that room with her. Larken had hoped that Jocelyn would make a sixth.

"We need you," Larken said. "Not now, not here. But we were hoping you could go back to Brighton, go to Protégé, and learn the law. We need someone who hasn't been side-lined to the fringes of society and blocked. We need someone who's far enough away from us to be beyond suspicion so that when the time comes, we can rely on you for help."

"Beyond suspicion isn't exactly what I'd call myself. Did you listen to anything that I just told you?"

Larken was losing. She could tell by how Jocelyn fidgeted, shifting her weight from foot to foot and keeping her eyes more focused on Larken's than anything else in the room. Jocelyn had already almost decided not to help, and it was a vague ask.

If Larken had had a better plan, she would have suggested it. They wouldn't be able to fight a war with only five people. If they were going to fight a war, they would need an army and allies. Jocelyn was one of the thousands they would need, and if Larken couldn't convince Jocelyn, her lifelong friend, then who could she convince?

"You don't have to *do* anything, Jocelyn. Just keep doing what you're doing and carve out that life that you've always wanted. Just keep in mind that we're here, and we're going to need your help."

Cloak and dagger. It felt foolish and empty and even more naïve to believe that she could sell anyone on being willing to trade their future stability for an ill-defined crisis. Larken didn't know whether it was loyalty or boredom, but her heart jumped when Jocelyn's shift stopped, and a smile crept onto her face.

"Sounds like an adventure."

Larken didn't share the smile. The muscles in her face seemed to fight her whenever she tried. It was as though all the smiles she'd ever been meant to have had been used up. Instead, she nodded and pressed her lips together into a line.

"I don't know about that," she told Jocelyn. "I know we have a lot of work to prepare for what's coming. People tolerate models now, but I feel like that might change. I feel like..."

Larken stopped talking. It didn't matter that she felt like the air was being sucked out of her lungs all the time or that she slept at most three hours a night uninterrupted. Nor did it matter that she was the only one in her hotel room, as Molly and Oliver had taken to sharing a bed and, in the process, had somehow carved something that looked like a real relationship out of their shattered lives.

Sam seemed even close to Larken's mentality, but at least she could and did smile. Even Stephen, who could lapse into moments of seriousness, sometimes laughed with light-hearted glee.

Good for them, she thought. *Good for all of them*. Aayushi hadn't talked to *them*. Aayushi didn't haunt their dreams with visions of bloodshed and violence. It wasn't them who saw themselves alone atop a mound of bodies that she knew, *knew*, she had put there as much as she knew there had never been any other way to manage the future being forced upon them. *Larken* knew. She knew with a certainty that seeped into her bones and turned them to stone. And the price she'd paid for that knowledge was her childhood and life.

"Thank you, Jocelyn. Drink?"

"No thanks," Jocelyn said, looking at her askance. "I didn't realize you drink alcohol."

Larken shrugged. "It helps with the pain."

Partially true, though some of that pain was emotional. She glanced down at the coffee table before her and retrieved her glass. Sam, the great comedian she was, passed half a drink over to Jocelyn, who took it with some apprehension in her eyes.

"To the future," Larken said in a flat monotone. The future that she saw wasn't worth drinking to. Still, somewhere desperate inside of her was her former self, clinging to the idea that whatever was *beyond* the heartache and loss that inevitably clung to her and polluted her past was something worth the pain. Aayushi had been right on that point. All Larken knew about was a war, and she fought the strong suspicion that, like many of the thousands and hundreds of thousands who hadn't even been born yet, she wouldn't live to see the other side. But with a bit of luck, she hoped that Jocelyn might.

Jocelyn's lips puckered, and she gasped as she failed to swallow any of the whiskey. Larken almost felt a laugh form in her chest at that sight, but it died in infancy. Someday maybe she would laugh again. All around her, others did laugh. She alone sipped, swallowed, then gulped. The pain in her head and heart subsided but didn't go away. She poured a little more in, marveling at how much she'd become like her non-father.

The door opened automatically. It never did that for Larken. She made a note to ask the hotel clerk if she could muster the energy. In the doorway stood Dandelion with her farm girl hair and gold-flecked eyes wearing the skirt that Larken had suggested. She swallowed at the sight of Dandelion taking in the crowd.

"How's the patient?"

"Are you the android?" Jocelyn asked, utterly oblivious to the discomfort. "You're beautiful."

Dandelion half-smiled, the expression she seemed to do whenever anyone complimented her. Larken had to look away when she did that. Something about Dandelion seemed to set Larken off-kilter. She couldn't focus or think with Dandelion around. Larken's eyes met Dandelion's once by accident, and Larken refused to look away until after Dandelion.

"I am. The android, I mean," Dandelion said.

"And pretty," Larken said.

Dandelion walked toward her, and Larken's heart matched the girl's quick stride.

"How's the pain?" Dandelion asked. She reached out for Larken's neck to check her temperature and pulse but stopped and waited for about a second before proceeding to get her skin temperature right. Her fingers sent little tingles up Larken's neck.

"You seem okay," Dandelion told her, pulling her hands back. "Considering."

"Considering that I got blown up?"

"Yes. That," Dandelion said and then leaned in slowly.

"Larken," she whispered. "Can I ask you a personal question?"

Larken's heart pounded more rapidly.

"There's this guy at work," Dandelion said. "I like him, but I'm not sure he sees me. I've noticed more guys look at me in this skirt you told me about. Do you think I can get a guy's attention in scrubs we have to wear?"

Larken smiled.

"Of course, you can," she said. "All you have to do is act confident. It's not hard. I can help when I get more energy."

Just an android, Larken thought. *Metal and wires.*

Yet somehow, more than that. Just like Larken. Stuck in a role on this earth that she never chose.

Except she did choose it, didn't she? There was that moment when she'd decided to do this. She'd decided that fighting a war was more important than her happiness. As Dandelion walked toward Jocelyn—probably to do proper introductions—Larken licked her lips, closed her eyes, and listened to the chatter of Jocelyn's reunion. For a fraction of a second, there was joy and laughter in the room. Loud and raucous Sam started telling dirty jokes, and all the girls giggled nonstop, including Dandelion, who probably only got about half of them.

CHAPTER 33

THE LOST SOULS

BACK AT BRIGHTON, Via struggled against her bonds, pulling one arm and yanking them until blood dripped down her right hand. Sun laughed loudly, holding the blade out like a feather duster. Via imagined her blood dripping from it as dust bunnies floating down to the earth. Only dust bunnies didn't hurt when they touched her, and that feather duster burned. Isaac sat lazily in a chair up against the door, blocking her only means of escape.

Aside from the pain, it was very exciting. Isaac kept talking about shells or something, and Via's mind could not be encroached. It kept floating its way back to the League City beach that her school had taken the orphans to when she was six. She remembered the sand between her toes and the kites that blotted out the sky. Most of all, she remembered the creepy dead trees they passed on the way—towering, lumbering things that reached for the sky with naked atrophied arms.

Equilibrium, her teacher had told her. Climate change

had claimed the trees. The invading ocean had poisoned their roots.

Kind of like Sun and Isaac and Susan. They'd poisoned the school and turned all of her roommates against her with their ceaseless words. When they came to take her from her room, not one of her roommates stopped pretending to sleep through Via's abduction long enough to help. She'd even made eye contact with one, who'd turned away and faked a snore.

As kidnappings went, it wasn't so bad, though.

Just then, a ribbon of pain stretched across her arm. She winced and felt even more blood trickle between her fingers.

"Beg us," Isaac said. "Like your friend. Beg us, and maybe we'll let you live."

Via's stomach rumbled.

"I need a doughnut," she replied, thinking of the sweet sticky things someone had left out in the girl's wing kitchen once. She remembered licking the icing from her fingers, one sticky finger at a time.

Another ribbon of pain.

Then a knock.

All three of their eyes went wide at once. A fumbling and jangling of keys told her that it was a teacher. Maybe the night guard. The key slid into the lock as Susan and Isaac sprang from their chairs and followed Sun into one of the stalls. None of them seemed to notice the pretty red stamps their shoes made across the tiles.

The door opened slowly—a crack at first, then a second, then another crack. Then a *wide* crack, and Via made out the startled eyes of Ms. Carrish, staring into the room. She smiled.

"Ms. Carrish, you've come to join us. We were having a party."

Ms. Carrish said nothing.

Via winced as a breeze aggravated her torn arm. *A mean thing to do at a party, tear somebody's arm,* Via thought. *Maybe it was part of a game.*

"Are you okay, Via?"

"It's a game. But it's not very fun."

"No, it doesn't seem that way."

Ms. Carrish's feet followed the footprints toward the stall only to stop a few feet short. Her head turned to the two empty chairs.

"How many people are at your party tonight, dear?"

"Four," Via said, not hesitating a second. That was the sort of question four-year-old Via had struggled with. She'd learned how to calculate the force of gravity between planets, but nobody ever asked her about that. She grinned and then winced again as her split lip cracked.

Mean games. She wouldn't be coming to their parties anymore.

Ms. Carrish strolled forward, following the pretty red stamps to the bathroom stall. She shoved the door inward hard, and Via heard a thunk, and then something fell. The glint of the red knife blade flashed momentarily until Ms. Carrish, moving faster than Via thought the woman could, caused the knife to fall ineffectual to the floor. Another thunk. The sound of another heavy sack falling.

Via was glad this game was over. And she still wanted doughnuts. Via was still thinking about doughnuts while Ms. Carrish dragged three bodies out of the bathroom stall.

"It was only a matter of time. Listen, Via, this wasn't your fault," Ms. Carrish said. "HPM got these three, and it was only a matter of time before someone got hurt. Whatever Mr. Beverly thinks about it. Here."

Ms. Carrish bent over and untied Via's arms from the chair to which she was secured. Via lifted her hands and rubbed her wrist as Ms. Carrish worked on her legs, muttering to herself.

"Whatever were they doing?" Ms. Carrish asked, shaking her head. "I told Mr. Beverly no good would come from letting this stuff into our school, and what did he do? He practically invited this. Someone has to do something."

Ms. Carrish raised an eye toward Via, who nodded back. She felt much better not being in the chair and not having to worry about pain ribbons. Ms. Carrish let out a sigh.

"Useless. Too late for these children," she muttered. She seemed to think a moment when the last knot came undone. Then she looked up.

"I hate to ask this, Via, but can you help me get these three into the chairs?"

A new game! Via smiled and nodded enthusiastically.

Elijah's footsteps carried him out into the darkened hallway. His breath came in short bursts, and he tried to stifle each as they came. Crickets sounded outside, comforting since it likely meant Elijah was the only one awake. The light switch tempted him as he entered the hallway, and there were several for him to resist. Turning on lights meant announcing his presence, which meant that Anthony Teregard Lee would awaken and magically appear as he had a habit of doing.

Something slid ahead of him in the hallway just beyond the range of his vision in the exit sign illumination. He crouched against the wall and tried to melt into the black. The sound came again, and something that seemed like a whimper. Maybe an animal had gotten in. Or perhaps it was Anthony and his gang creating more problems. He reminded himself that Anthony wasn't at Brighton anymore. The boy had been promoted to full-on HPM member and had left.

But Isaac, Anthony's second in command, hadn't. Isaac had already made sure that Elijah knew that he was a threat. The three of them—Isaac, Susan, and Sun had caught him alone in the courtyard the day before. Elijah ran his hand up over the back of his neck.

The whimper again.

He was sure it wasn't an animal. All he could think of was the sound that had worked its way into his voice when he pleaded with them not to tie the rope around his neck. They'd pulled him from the ground by looping the rope over one of the planks in the gazebo and yanked hard on it. Then, in uncontrolled fits of laughter, they'd let him fall and watched him gasp on the ground and threatened that if he *ever* told, it would be his end.

He hadn't told.

But that didn't mean he was safe.

And whoever was whimpering didn't sound safe either. Elijah wasn't HPMs only target. He sucked up his breath and felt his way along the wall, staying pressed firmly against it. The whimpering grew louder as he approached as if protesting. Then something rattled, like a chair sliding with something heavy in it. The more whimpering. It was a protest, he realized, just like what he'd had to do, just like his begging. He quickened his pace. The shared bathroom was just ahead, and whatever was happening had to be through the doors he approached. Elijah pressed his ear against it.

Whispering.

He couldn't make out the words.

Elijah summoned what little courage he still had and pushed on the door—a mistake. The bathroom door seal was almost complete, so it wasn't easy to see when the light was on the inside, even when everywhere else was completely black. The door swung open and assaulted him with bright white light, pushing him backward. The door swung shut, and he was in pitch black, an even darker night than he'd seen before.

Elijah gulped and pushed the door open again. This time, he held it aloft with his hand.

He'd been right about the chair. Wrong about the number of chairs. And wrong about HPM being the perpetrators.

In three side-by-side chairs sat Isaac Somerville, Sunshine Selinsky, and Susan Priest. They were all three in pajamas as he was. Beside them stood a very agitated-looking Via, her shirt covered in red splatters. He could see that her lip had busted, and she had a bruised eye, but otherwise was fine.

Something besides the obvious was wrong with the scene. Nobody was whimpering. Via rubbed her wrist; her eyes darted from Isaac to Sun to Susan and back again. Elijah followed her gaze and saw what she saw. None of them moved. Not a single muscle. The only movement aside from Via was something dripping in slop droplets down to the tiled bathroom floor.

And all three of them seemed to have socks stuffed into their mouths.

"Via, did you do this?" he asked, startled.

"I can't say that I did," Via retorted, her eyes darting

toward him. Only not precisely toward him. To his left a bit and beyond where he stood, which could only mean...

Elijah turned around to hear the door click back into place.

"I should have locked it the first time," Ms. Carrish said, holding a bloodied knife with her right hand. She turned the latch to the deadbolt. "There."

"Ms. Carrish?"

"I'm glad you're here, Mr. Grant. Would you like to help me bury the bodies, or is your preference to clean the bathroom?"

Elijah stared at her and then at Via, who smiled.

"It's a fun game, Elijah. Ms. Carrish says it's called 'Hide the Evidence.'"

Elijah's stomach turned at the two of them, Ms. Carrish holding her blade and three lifeless bodies before him.

Whether Ms. Carrish had killed them or Via had, he didn't know, but either way, Elijah wasn't going to let Via be part of a murder investigation after what happened to Oliver.

"Bury, I guess," he said, cringing at the thought of touching any of the dead bodies.

"Excellent choice, Mr. Grant. I think I know just the place."

The following day, the unkempt, weed-filled flower bed by the gazebo was just a little higher than the land around it. The few flowers that had survived being completely ignored seemed a little brighter and stood straighter.

The next few weeks saw the flower bed revive and the plants stretch toward the sky. Some students claimed it was the new gardener that Ms. Carrish all but forced Mr. Beverly to hire. Others may have suspected the disappearance of HPM Lite, but most of the focus of the disappearance came to Anthony Teregard Lee, who Ms. Carrish informed the investigating police had always been a problem and that his group had talked about running away to join HPM.

Aside from an occasional knowing glance from Ms. Carrish, or an inappropriate statement about the games she liked to play from Via, nobody seemed the wiser. Elijah eventually fell into a routine, and it was as though HPM Lite had never existed.

The End.

AFTERWORD

The original title of this work was *Brighton Academy*. In fact, you can still acquire a copy of Brighton Academy from Amazon. So why the change?

The more I sat with the former title, the more I realized that it had a few shortcomings, probably not the least of which is that there's a romance series also called Brighton Academy, by a very prolific author. Whoever searched for my book by name couldn't find the novel on Amazon except after scrolling several pages!

But perhaps the most important reason I changed the title is because the name and cover didn't exactly tell the story of what's within these pages. I think you'll understand as you read, and things come to light, that the school, Brighton Academy, isn't the most significant presence in the story. Further, the most compelling story in my previous rendition of **Evasion and Defiance** in the form of *Brighton Academy* lacks the main protagonist on the cover.

That is to say, I did a poor job with the cover and the name, and am correcting the problem.

This story hasn't changed, and I don't want you to feel as though you've been lied to, thinking this is an entirely new novel. This new cover and title is a rebrand to more accurately portray what's in the novel. Although, there *are* some fun add-ons in the next few pages that I think you'll really enjoy!

If you have a copy of Brighton Academy already, you're definitely welcome to own this too! Just be aware that it's mostly the same content. There. Now you know. Read on and enjoy!

LARKEN MARCHE

DOB: 1/31/2185, **Age:** 16

Ever since being delivered to Brighton Academy, both Larken and her twin brother Oliver have received notes every year on their birthday with receipts for how much they had available to spend the following year and a brief scrawled Happy Birthday— from the anonymous benefactor who pays their tuition and boarding. When she was little, Larken often imagined that the benefactor was their parent, mother or father, and that one day they would be reunited. As she grew older, she realized that reunification was unlikely to happen, but her realization hasn't sated her secret longing.

MOLLY KOSTIC

DOB: 10/20/2184,**Age:** 16

Molly loves people and wants people to love her. And she also wants to be the center of *everyone's* world. She puts her formidable intellect to work figuring out who might be a threat to her hegemony, then proceeds to break apart relationships and social groups who might challenge her dominance. Larken's best friend, Molly has fallen for Larken's brother, Oliver, to the point of obsession. She wants Oliver to *love* her, deeply. Maybe...

FELICITY

DOB: UNKNOWN ,**Age:** UNKNOWN

Felicity means happy. No, that doesn't mean that *she's* happy. That's only a literal translation of her name. Felicity is a killer android. She's only happy when hunting down her latest victim, at the behest of the extremist Human Pride Movement. She goes where they send her, and she kills who they want her to kill...usually. No questions, with complete obedience to orders. A company girl through-and-through, if HPM need a dirty job done, they turn to Felicity.

———

DR. ALEXANDER "TORRENT" TOUSSAINT

DOB: 6/15/2158, **Age:** 42

Abandoned by his own parents into the Orphanage program as a young child, he often wondered who they were. He would watch people as they came by his tiny window, wondering if any were his family. This got him interested in genetics at first, which then morphed into a love of cloning, as he created the arguably most prestigious cloning lab in the country. Later, bought out in a deal with Galatin Hamilton of Beckett-Madeline Enterprises, Dr. Toussaint took his love of cloning into the commercial sector.

———

DANDELION LEMAIRE

Dandelion Lamaire is an android, just not the killer kind. From mysterious origins, she's somehow ended up working in a free clinic. She enjoys helping people heal, because she can see up-close how humans work, and tries very hard to fit in. To be noticed for her is terrifying, as she is painfully aware of her unique autonomy. Dandelion's dream is simple: stay off the radar and help people. But very few of us can achieve all of our dreams...

DOB: 4/21/2123, **Age:** 78

For more characters, chapters, and generally anything else in this AI universe, come join my Patreon community! Whether you want to just browse, or become a Serial Killer (get it? get's you access to my serial fiction), or Accomplice (get's you access to pre-release novels and chapters, as well as other goodies).

Join our Patreon community! Come be part of the creative process!

https://patreon.com/user?u=104217131&utm_medium=clipboard_copy&utm_source=copyLink&utm_campaign=creatorshare_creator&utm_content=join_link